Good News from the

Bullpen Café

To Judith
A fellow Wanaminoite!
Thank you for your
interest in the book
Hope you like it

To Candace Marie

The Story

Charlie Finstune is a recent college graduate who comes from a long line of attorneys and is planning on attending Harvard Law School in the fall. But upon the unexpected death of his Uncle Roy—a little known member of the family and the owner of a small town café in Bullpen, Minnesota—Charlie decides to take a year off to run his uncle's café and blog about his experiences.

So who was his Uncle? And why had he chosen to give up a promising law career of his own to run a small town café?

Charlie Finstune, whether he knows it or not, is about to find out...

Good News from the

Bullpen Café

A Novel by Robert Ringham

www.goodnewsfromthebullpencafe.com

TABLE OF CONTENTS

June 5 . . .
"Houston? We have a problem."

As I reached for the keys to the door of my uncle's café, I suddenly sensed that I was not alone. Instinctively, I turned around to see if someone was behind me, but no one was. The rain had stopped, and Bullpen's main street now glistened under the solitary street light, looking as lost and forgotten as any other small town that was not even found on most state maps. As a warm breeze blew across my face, I looked up at the endless array of summer stars that lay just beyond the clearing in the clouds, and for a moment—for one brief moment—it was as if someone, somewhere, was looking down through the hole in the sky and trying to communicate with me, the way that Houston's command center would communicate with a spacecraft orbiting the earth or lost in space.

"Houston?" I found myself saying out loud, "Do you copy?"

My name is Charles Robert Finstune. I come from a long line of attorneys, and next year I will be among them, hitting the law books at Harvard like my older brother Karl and my mother and my father and my father's father before him. Law is in the Finstune bloodline like racing in a thoroughbred's genes. I can't remember a family reunion where there were not discussions on law: statutory law, common law, tort law, and everything-else-under-the-sun law. Discussions on law inevitably led to discussions on religion and the Lawgiver, and then that, of course, led to politics—and legislation and philosophy and finally the weather. If sports were ever discussed, it was usually in the context of law. The O.J. Simpson trial was a major event for us Finstunes, because it was the first case in fairly recent history that married the two venues together in an odd, interdisciplinary study. The only other case that came close to that was the case Grandpa Finstune recalled years ago that involved Shoe Less Joe Jackson and his alleged betting scandal with the Chicago White Socks—did I mention Johnny Bench?

11

So with law deeply enveloped in the Finstune bloodline, what Finstune in his or her right mind would ever consider taking a sabbatical from law?

I, for one.

I had actually started thinking about taking a break from law or a "hiatus" (a legal term used to describe a breach or a break—and one of those sophisticated words you can say when you want to validate the cost of your college education). And when I told my parents that I wanted to take a year off before entering Harvard Law School, where I had recently been accepted, I was telling only half the story. What I really wanted was to experience life from the other side of the tracks and take a break from the mold in which I was cast at birth. I wanted something more than law and corporate America.

Enter my Uncle Roy and the Bullpen Café.

Now Uncle Roy was the black sheep of the Finstune family, and I knew very little about him other than what my mother had told me in between family reunions, which he rarely attended. According to my mother, Uncle Roy had no ambition and was the by-product of his own lethargic nature. He had attended Harvard Law School for two years, but then he suddenly dropped out and moved to "Small Town, USA" where he was content to live the rest of his life. His only claim to fame was that he owned a small cafe in Bullpen, Minnesota, which was creatively named the Bullpen Café.

Bullpen?

That's what I said the first time I heard the name.

The town was legally named Bullpen in 1894. Up until that time it was named Pink Prairie by Hans Running—a bachelor farmer desperate for a wife. Hans was Norwegian and owned most of the pastureland east of what is now called County Road 30. In an attempt to woo his mail order bride, Gladys—a large and stubborn woman with a fiery tongue—he told her that he lived in a country filled with pink, which was only partially true considering that there was only one cherry blossom tree that bloomed (in pink) every April for three weeks in Hans' back (very back) pasture. It was apparently the month of April when he last wrote to Gladys, who fell in love—not so much with Hans but with the Pink Prairie she had envisioned in her mind. She arrived in January of 1876—the coldest day on record. Hans met her with his wagon team, and she fought with him all the way to the log cabin Hans had built with his bare hands. By spring, she realized the truth of the matter, but by that time it was too late. She was already married. Rumor has it that she drove Hans, a relatively quiet man, to drinking and he died of an overdose of homemade whiskey in 1891. Gladys, who never took a liking to Pink Prairie—or to Hans for that matter—left on the boat back to Norway in the summer of 1891.

Two years after Gladys left, the community wanted and demanded a new name. Two factions were divided as to which name was appropriate. One camp was made up of the local crop farmers, led by Sven Nordstrom. They wanted to name it Green Leaf—after Leif Erickson. The other camp was made up of livestock farmers—led by the notorious Ole (pronounced Oh Lee) Gunderson. They wanted to name it Lily—after a nightclub singer Ole had met a year earlier in Chicago (the fact that Ole had brought back some indiscriminate pictures of Lily may have clouded their better judgment). Now even though both camps were church-going Norwegians, they sat in separate pews on Sunday, lived in separate areas of Pink Prairie, and even walked on separate sides of the streets—often eyeing one another contemptuously. They disagreed about everything from politics to farming to religion to family to everything else under the sun—including the weather. The one thing they could all agree on, however, was baseball.

Now back in 1893, baseball was a novelty and was just coming into its own. And how it came to Pink Prairie is still a mystery, but it came nonetheless. After three days of gridlock between the two camps, it was agreed that a game of baseball would decide the matter. The game was held in a field just south of County Road 14 and lasted well into the evening with neither team very adept at hitting a small ball with a wooden stick. When Pap Farkas, the only Hungarian farmer in the group, hit a foul ball that went into Ole Gunderson's bull pen, the game was called on account that no one—not even Ole—wanted to risk being gored to death by his prized bull while looking for a lost baseball—especially at dusk. After church on Sunday, the game was to be resumed. But after securing the prized bull and searching all afternoon, neither side found the lost baseball. Ironically, during all that time looking for it, the two camps got to talking to each other—on friendly terms—about farming and politics and religion and family and, finally, the weather. Each side had the opportunity to hear the other side's views and had come to realize that, after all these years, they had more things in common than not. What started out as a feud ended in handshakes—a miracle by anyone's standard. And when the Pastor mentioned the incident from the pulpit the next Sunday, it was all agreed that losing the baseball in Ole Gunderson's bull pen was no accident. So the name Bullpen, as if ordained from heaven above, had stuck.

Now, how it was that Uncle Roy had decided to settle in Bullpen was a mystery to the Finstunes. He was, after all, born and bred in Minneapolis—a good and reputable town. He had even attended two years of Harvard Law School. So, how could a good man with a clear and logical mind (as my dad would often say) be so careless as to settle into a little bitty town not even mentioned on most state maps? The question seemed to plague me growing up. I remember asking my dad why he simply didn't ask his own brother why he moved to Bullpen. His response?

The Finstune family glare.

Yes, I remember it vividly. I was standing at the kitchen sink, drinking a root beer float, when I flippantly popped the question. I was a young lad at the tender and impressionable age of 13, and I had not yet been fully introduced to the full fury incurred by the Finstune family glare, but I would remember it forever. It was that disapproving smirk that said in essence: "Don't ask stupid questions and mind your own business, as others mind theirs." I vowed to never challenge my father again on such hallowed ground.

So why had Uncle Roy settled in Bullpen? What had possessed him to do so after he had two years of law school—Harvard Law School, mind you—under his belt? Depression? Drugs? Alcohol? Did he suffer from dementia or some other fatal disease? What was he thinking? Apparently, he wasn't thinking when he bought the restaurant over 25 years ago. And that was the problem: he simply wasn't thinking—the sin of all Finstune sins.

It was a question that I had pondered from my youth, lying in bed at night, looking up at the ceiling and trying to get my mind off the Minnesota Vikings and the lost opportunities that plagued them in the playoffs all those years. A kid can do a lot of thinking at night, and Uncle Roy was often at the top of my list. Why had he bought the restaurant and disgraced the Finstunes? It was probably that question, more than any other, that intrigued me.

When my uncle died last year, I remember I could not attend the funeral due to a sudden illness at school. When I found out he had left the restaurant to my dad, I laughed. Since Uncle Roy never married, he had no children of his own to inherit the café, so my father—being the only "real" family he had left—defaulted into possessing my uncle's humble estate. Yes, my dad was now the proud owner of the Bullpen Café. I could see him behind the cash register, counting pennies and giving change back to smiling customers. I could see my mother flying in from London and then racing down to the cafe to don the greasy-spoon apron and flip burgers. It would be a regular Finstune family affair! Then Karl would come from Harvard Law School to try out a new college recipe: Soup de jour. A regular Julia Childs my brother would have been. "Never apologize." Yes, never apologize, Julia would say, and so would the Finstunes.

My dad had tried to sell the restaurant for the last several months, but to no avail. After all, who in his right mind would want to buy the Bullpen Café?

So after graduating last May and coming back home to live for a few months—and having some time on my hands, and staring up at the ceiling in my old room at night, and thinking about the Vikings and other things as young men sometimes do—I got to thinking about running the Bullpen Café. I dismissed it as indigestion at first, like eating pizza at midnight—but it kept coming back night after night like a bad habit. Then a few weeks into home life, I was drinking a root beer float by the kitchen sink when I decided to face the Finstune family glare head on. I put on my big boy pants and asked my dad if I could give the restaurant a shot.

That's when all hell broke loose.

As I stood there with the keys to the dilapidated restaurant in Bullpen, Minnesota, I found myself suddenly asking the same question—again. It was the same question to which I thought I had all the answers while being grilled at the family board of review—my mother smirking, my father perplexed. It was a mystery to them as it had been to me, but I had to defend my position. I had to take the affirmative in the great debate: my mother shrewd and sharp, my father articulate, calculating, and foreboding. Why in the world would I want to take time out of my predisposition in life to run a café—something I knew nothing about? Hey, it was not a Starbucks or McDonalds. It was an entry-level position—oops—wrong word (too permanent). It was an entry-level *experience*. Yes, that was the right word. If I had learned anything at school, it was that it was hard to argue against someone's personal experience. Experience had no time frame attached to it. As far as my parents were concerned, that experience might only last for a few months or, better yet, a few weeks if I grew tired of the matter. The discussion went on night after night with objections and out-of-orders and overrulings. Recesses were brief, and the witness stand was hot, swelteringly hot, as I sat before the bench. It's funny, but as the interrogations heightened, I found myself defending my position, not so much because I believed in it, but because I could not stand the thought of losing. I dug in; they pressed on. In the end, they simply tired and resigned themselves to that fact that it was going to be just that—an entry-level experience.

I had tried my first case and won.

So, what was the reason I had decided to take over the restaurant for a year, again? Standing outside the doorway, it suddenly hit me, as if I were asking myself the question for the first time, even though I had defended it vigorously only two weeks before. Was it for the challenge of restoration—taking that which is dead and bringing it back to life? There was always a certain satisfaction of restoring that which was lost or broken or forgotten.

Was it the autonomy of having something of my own and, therefore, I could make my own decisions? With the help of the Small Business Administration, I had developed a detailed 40-page business plan with visions of grandeur. The Retro Café I'd call it. It would feature various espresso coffees—vanilla, apple cinnamon, Chi Tea, mochas, and lattes—with WIFI Internet access where you could come and surf the Internet and Google anything under the sun. I would have a gas fireplace to warm you on a cold winter day like Caribou Coffee or Starbucks. I would offer scones, homemade blueberry, cherry, and pumpkin pies, homemade pastries, strawberry smoothies, and pineapple upside-down cakes—or at the very least, right-side-up cakes. And I would franchise the business model after only a year, make millions, impress women as Donald Trump's new Apprentice, and pay my way through Harvard Law School. I had actually gotten excited about the endless possibilities and envisioned the success of my own establishment like reruns of *Cheers* in Boston. Yes, everyone would know your name. I could see Frazier coming in after a hard day at the office and asking me for my advice about this client or that client and, of course, I would give it to him at no extra charge, because that's what friends are for.

Or . . . was it adventure that drew me here, like the adventure that had called Ferdinand Magellan or Thor Heyerdahl? I felt the sudden twinge of excitement as I had weeks ago—and then utter fear. It was as if I was the only astronaut on board Apollo 13. And just like the movie, everything had suddenly gone awry.

As the warm summer breeze continued to blow across my face, I wondered how many explorers, astronauts and pilots, like Amelia Earhart, had ventured out but had never returned.

Houston, this is Apollo.

What was I thinking taking over a forgotten restaurant in a ghost of a town—with no nightlife or any signs of life at all? What *was* I thinking? Those condemning words rang out as if spoken by my mother herself. What was *I* thinking? Or was I *thinking* at all? Or was there something else drawing me to my uncle's restaurant, like a planet's gravitational pull that trumps all other means of escape? I had a free choice in the matter. No one had put a gun to my head and told me to do it. So why on God's green earth was I suddenly jingling the keys to the Bullpen Café with cold feet? I thought I had all those questions covered only a week ago at a local bank in Zumbrota, Minnesota, that was to give me a $10,000 line of credit.

Why all of a sudden was there doubt, that nauseating, doom-like feeling that I was making a terrible mistake and that I was going to pay for it the rest of my life? Yes, the rest of my life I would regret having done this thing,   this . . . un . . . un . . . unthinkable thing.

Up to this point, my life had been dictated for me. They told me what to think in 1st grade and how to color within the lines and then how and what to think in 2nd grade—on up through high school and then college. They told me what to do and how to do it; and now suddenly I was faced with my own thoughts and my own choices—a real life-changing choice with no teacher to guide me or parent to instruct me. I was suddenly free to boldly go where no man (at least in his right mind) had gone before. Was it any wonder that most of my classmates had fallen victim to this all-too-apparent predisposition and had failed to grasp (or wanted to grasp) the awesome responsibility of real freedom—and had instead defaulted to a safe and comfortable track upon which to run the rest of their lives? Up until this point, my life had been no different. It was a life dictated by others with licenses and degrees and whims of their own. Study hard and you, too, can be like us. I suddenly saw it all as one big, predictable security blanket, and I wanted it.

Houston?

I felt a sudden comfort in knowing that I had only committed myself to a year. That wasn't so bad, was it? Yes, I could always go back to the familiar if I had to. The familiar had become a psychological backstop that provided a boundary to keep my life in play, unlike the lost baseball that had fallen prey to Ole Gunderson's bullpen, back in 1893. The familiar was what I was wanting, and changing my course was like stopping a freight train that had been gathering momentum for over 21 years. Suddenly, I could now feel the full weight of its significance bearing down upon me. There was a fork in the road, and I was careening carelessly out of control by going in another direction.

Houston? We have a problem.

And what would I tell Karen? What would she say about my sudden decision to run my uncle's café?

I met Karen during my sophomore year at the university. I was an English major, and she was a political science major. It was a cold and rainy autumn day—one of Minnesota's ugliest—and she was coming out of the political science building with a boatload of books. I had seen her at a frat party a few weeks before, and when I saw her carrying all those books, I asked if I could help—and I did, hauling all five hundred pounds of books (or so it felt) all the way to her dormitory. I don't remember what we talked about, but I remember her laughing a lot. The day before, a young man she had never seen had stalked her. I told her not to worry, because I knew karate. When I said that, her eyes lit up with an admiring flair. I also told her I knew judo, tae kwon do, and thirteen other Oriental words. She laughed, a soft and tender kind of laugh that was comforting against the rain. And suddenly, all I wanted to do was to make her laugh. I remember her eyes that afternoon. They were clear and bright and alive—and looking into them was like taking a peek behind a curtain into her very soul, without apology or embarrassment. And as we continued to walk across the campus that cold autumn afternoon, I found myself falling in love with Karen and making a point to be there every day thereafter, to fend off any other would-be stalkers with my thirteen other Oriental words.

There was nothing pretentious about Karen. She did not carry a presumptuous air as some women on campus did, nor did she carry a callous sophistication, even though she could have easily done so, knowing how wealthy her father was. What you saw was what you got, and what you got was good. She cooed around little babies and tenderly caressed cats that deserved to be strangled. She loved and cared for squirrels and chipmunks and robins and wrens and tomcats and top cats and top dogs and underdogs. She loved them all, but especially the underdog. That was the dog that always touched her heart and got the preferential treatment. I loved her for that. I loved her for many things, and I suddenly missed her more than words could say. I suddenly wanted to thank her for her first and only attempt at making me a flannel shirt for my 21st birthday. I wanted to thank her for making birthdays special.

So what are you doing now, Karen?

She had gone to Italy with her family for the summer, as she had done since she was five years old. Italy was a good seven hours ahead of me—and so far away. Perhaps she was eating breakfast with her grandmother or grandfather near the vineyards where they lived. She talked fondly of them and of her great grandparents. Her great grandfather had fought in World War II and had seen the famous Field Marshal Erwin Rommel and his African Corps first hand—and before he died, he had more stories to tell than most should or would want to hear.

And what are you thinking, Karen?

And what would she think when she got back from Italy and discovered what I had done? "I am so proud of you, Charlie, for bucking your predisposition to save that defunct café you had told me about. My hero—how noble a cause, how forthright your mission!" Yes, I was her knight in shining armor, and now I was going boldly where no man in his right mind had gone before. Yes, the man from La Mancha was proudly going where no man had gone before.

As I stood there outside the door of the café, the reality of what I had done was beginning to sink in. My God, what *have* I done? I had never told her what I was doing in my text messages. We had both planned to go to law school in the fall, but I had a sudden—very sudden—change of plans. Should I have told her? Would she have understood? Did I understand?

Houston, do you read me? Over.

As I unlocked the door to the Bullpen Café, a faint, musty smell came out to greet me. I flipped on the light switch and looked about.

One side of the café looked like a 1950s time capsule, where a soda fountain and a severely dented malt maker sat behind a long counter. The other side of the room looked like a classic, small-town restaurant with vinyl-backed chairs, chipped Formica tabletops, and a few booths with bright orange seat covers that looked as if they had been taken from the seat of an old truck. A toy train track ran completely around the room on a shelf above the exit sign. So where was the train? On a wall opposite the soda fountain hung no less than fifty stained coffee cups. Each one was uniquely different, bearing its owner's name: Slater, George, Lenny, Mavis, Millie, Homer, and others. They were stacked in neat rows of nine or ten, reminding me of the cheap, plastic trophies I had displayed so proudly on my dresser as a kid. To the left of the coffee-cup-hall-of-fame, sat an old upright piano that proudly displayed its missing ivory keys, like a little kid who displays his missing teeth.

Above the cash register hung a large mounted moose with a Christmas scarf draped around its neck. On its face one could see what appeared to be the slight resemblance of a smile. How much could a guy get for a smiling moose with a Christmas scarf on eBay?

I wondered.

Opposite the moose hung a large mounted muskie with a tiny spinning lure that dangled from its mouth. The wide-mouthed muskie looked mean and menacing, while the little lure looked gaudy and flirtatious, as if bragging about the size of her date. When her spinner sparkled off the incandescent light bulbs, the two looked like an odd couple dancing to a strobe light.

Then there were shelves upon shelves of more knick knacks and paddy whacks than I could count. There were bobble heads representing famous players from the Minnesota Twins and, yes, the Minnesota Vikings. There were John Deere and International Harvester toy tractors and toy trucks of all sizes and shapes and designs—all looking used and beaten and old. There was a faded yellow golf ball with the words "hole in one" that sat on a slightly elevated "trophy" stand made from an aerosol can and duct tape. There was a wooden croquet mallet—yes, a croquet mallet—and one battered blue ball that sat quietly beside it. There was an old glass pop bottle and a bottle opener and a minnow scooper and an ice pick. Individually, there may have been a few items that some would have considered to be antiques; but cumulatively, it was all junk. And then beyond that was a large community billboard made up of crayon drawings, newspaper clippings, and a collage of recent and not-so-recent photographs. And beyond that lay the kitchen—the final frontier—and I could only imagine what lay beyond that.

So this was the Bullpen Café—a self-portrait of my uncle's insignificant life.

As I stood in the entryway, I surveyed the wreckage where real people had sat for over twenty-five years, holding conversations longer than I had been alive. If I had appreciated anything about college, it was the late night discussions and arguments about religion and politics and philosophy that would carry on into the wee hours of the morning—conversations that would have been completely foreign to such a meager clientele that had frequented the café. It was great to pontificate from the comfort of your own loft. You could argue philosophy with Kierkegaard and Nietzsche and Young till you were blue in the face. You could discuss art with Rembrandt and Picasso. You could think great thoughts and believe great things, whether they were true or real or not, because you had no accountability to anyone or anything other than your syllabus. You were free to think and do as you damn well pleased-- and argue with anyone who told you not to.

But then came responsibility—real, life-threatening responsibility—the gravitational pull that sucked you back into reality.

"Earth to Charles—this is Houston. Do you copy?"

"Yes, yes, come in Houston; this is Charlie."

"Are there any signs of intelligent life in Bullpen? . . . Charles, do you copy? . . . Are there any signs of intelligent life in Bullpen?"

"No, Houston, there are no signs of intelligent life in Bullpen."

Later That Evening . . . News from the Bullpen Café

I could not fall asleep, so I decided to drive up to the top of Thomforde Hill and text Karen to see how she was doing in Italy and then blog some of my thoughts about the day's events. The town of Bullpen lies in a sleepy little valley between two steep hills along County Road 30: Thomforde Hill and Paulie's Peak. Since I could not get any cell phone reception down in Bullpen, I went to Paulie's Peak and then Thomforde Hill. But after driving up and down and experimenting between the two points, I found out that I had a better cell phone reception from Thomforde Hill. So that is where I parked—along the side of the road—listening to the crickets and staring down into the quiet little town that is not even found on most state maps.

As an English major at the University with an interest in film and writing, I had thought about keeping an ongoing diary by blogging about my experiences in Bullpen. I decided to call it *News from the Bullpen Café*. It would be a story that would be comprised of comments from fellow bloggers as well as my own thoughts and observations about my life in Bullpen and life in general. All blogs would be posted for everyone to see; and like an interactive diary or interactive video game, each blog would have the capability of influencing the story's outcome, but only those observations, events, or blogs (or parts of those blogs) that would best drive the story forward—whatever that story might be —would be included in the story itself. In essence, *News from the Bullpen Café* would be a story within a blog, a hybrid of both a narrative and a direct discourse with my fellow bloggers. I would then broadcast it to the world at night or, as time permitted, from the top of Thomforde Hill, using my cell phone as a point of connectivity. I decided that I would blog in both past and present tenses and use whatever tense I felt was best to describe any particular observation or narrative that day or that moment; and if there were any grammatical or spelling mistakes, I hoped my readers—or in this case my fellow bloggers—would be kind enough to point them out. I also realized that some of my own philosophies or perspectives about life would inevitably change during the course of my story, and that such changes would require an acknowledgement.

The big question, however, was whether or not my experiences, narratives, observations, and stories from Bullpen would be interesting enough for people to follow. In other words, would there be a story here that was worth telling?

I wondered.

I wondered what lay before me and what obstacles I would face in the weeks and months ahead. As an English major, I had read many books and had seen many movies and had heard many stories, but this one was my own—good, bad, or indifferent. It would be my life in Bullpen--as open and candid and transparent as I could describe it. It would be what it would be, and at the end of the day or the week or—finally—at the end of the year—maybe, just maybe, I would stumble upon something significant that would make a difference in the life of someone else, someone out there in cyberspace—someone beyond the scope of small-town America.

After I had sent Karen a text, I was eager to see if I had connectivity between my phone and my laptop, and when I saw that I did, I envisioned my computer as an old cartoon tower bleeping radio signals throughout the world. I then registered my site on *WordPress*, and then sent out my first narrative, my first blog about Bullpen. After hitting the send button, I smiled.

News from the Bullpen Café is officially online, fellow bloggers.

June 6 . . . Missing Karen

I awakened early this morning around 3:30 a.m. to the strangest of dreams. Karen and I were paddling effortlessly in the pristine Boundary Waters of northern Minnesota in a birch bark canoe, when suddenly the canoe started taking on water and began to sink. As we swam to shore, two moose came swimming up to meet us. She mounted the first moose, and I mounted the second. We rode them like cowboys, steering them by their antlers. Cool, huh? I remember thinking in the dream that I was actually riding a moose in the middle of the lake. We began laughing, but then her moose began to swim faster than mine and, sure enough, when I looked down, I saw the Christmas scarf around the neck of the moose that I was riding. "Doggone it," I yelled in my best Texas accent. I had been riding the smiling moose, of all possible moose, and it was the slower of the two. As I lagged further and further behind, I began to kick its sides like a jockey. "Giddy up you old dog," I yelled as loudly as I could and then I began to whack its backside . . . but to no avail. It continued to plod along no faster than a rented mule. I yelled for Karen to slow down, but her moose continued to gather speed, leaving me and the smiling moose further and further behind. When her moose finally reached shore, it galloped out of sight—and I never saw it, or her, again.

What do you do with a dream like that? You go downstairs and rip the head of the smiling moose clear off the wall—that's what you do. That's right—take that smile right off its smiling face. I remember getting up to settle the matter, when I found myself wondering what I was doing at 3:30 in the morning. Had I gone mad? I could just see the locals spreading gossip about the new owner who was found frothing at the mouth like a rabid dog while ripping apart the smiling moose with his bare hands or, at the very least, trying to strangle it with its own scarf in the wee hours of the morning. That would be good for business, wouldn't it?

No . . . It was, after all, just a dream.

I suddenly found myself missing Karen. I missed the way she would hold her coffee cup in her long afghan sleeves that extended beyond her fingers that

23

wrapped around her coffee cup like a tea cozy. I missed her giddy, high-pitched laugh that was a cross between a guinea pig and a hamster. I missed the way she would rest her head on my shoulder while sitting next to me at the tavern near Dinky Town, as we conversed about everything under the sun and stars and moon with my fraternity buddies sitting across the table. I missed walking across campus while we held hands. I missed the smell of her hair and listening to "Fields of Gold" by Sting. It was her favorite song, and soon it was mine, as we played it over and over and over again on short-lived autumn afternoons while driving past amber waves of grain on long-forgotten country roads.

Even though cell phone reception was not an option down in the valley of Bullpen, I just wanted to hear her voice in the stillness of the night.

What are you doing this morning, Karen? What fills your day? And what are you thinking or feeling . . . so far away . . . so far, far away . . .

Later That Morning . . . A Clean, Well-lit Place

I had gone back to sleep after my dream about Karen, and I had awakened late Saturday morning. I scoured the apartment for any signs of intelligent life: namely coffee. And in doing so, I began to notice how different my uncle's apartment looked in the light of day. It was bigger than what I had first imagined. It was a simple apartment above the Café, with an efficiency kitchen that stretched out into the dining room, where a beautiful cherry-wood pool table stood in the middle of the floor. It was covered with an ornate, handcrafted, cherry-wood top that rested on the pool table, giving it a grandiose look like that of a Steinway piano centered on the stage in a famous concert hall. Six matching chairs stood at attention surrounding the pool table, like guards at the Buckingham Palace, giving the apartment's simple, common demeanor a sense of elegance and royalty. On the wall behind the table hung the pool cues, as if they too were standing at attention.

The dining room spilled into the living room without any boundaries—giving it a larger sense of openness to the already open room. It was furnished with a simple leather sofa, two wingback chairs, and a few bar stools that were pushed back against the wall, as if making room for an imaginary maple-wood dance floor.

Beyond the living room were three doors.

The door to the left led to my uncle's office. It was a room filled with clutter: old newspapers, letters, magazines and other debris that spilled out and over the vintage roll-top desk like a papier-mâché volcano. The walls were covered with numerous pictures and posters, but only the framed scores above the desk caught my eye. One was the song "Take Me with You in Your Dreams," by John Everett Fay and James Oliver. The other was the score to the song "Fire and Rain," made famous by James Taylor.

The door to the right led to my uncle's bedroom. The bedroom was a stark contrast to his office. It was neat and clean. There was a clothes closet that had more closet than clothes, and each garment was neatly aligned on hangers, as if awaiting inspection from their commanding officer. A simple wooden dresser, nightstand, and queen- sized bed filled the rest of the room. On the nightstand beside the bed was a digital clock and a small framed photograph of my uncle and my father at what appeared to be a YMCA summer camp years ago. They are both dressed in Indian apparel with leather vests that spell "Kickapoo" across their chests. I guess that my uncle is about ten or eleven years old at the time—two years older then my father. A mischievous smile is written across my uncle's face as he holds up two fingers above and behind my father's head. My father appears to be clueless about my uncle's little prank behind him because he simply stares into the camera without any expression. Across the top of the frame is written: Indian Guides Forever.

It's funny, but had not noticed the picture last night because I had decided to sleep on the sofa. I had felt uncomfortable about sleeping in his bed, knowing he might have died there. But this morning it occurred to me that he could have died anywhere. Now why the thought of death suddenly felt so uncomfortable, I don't know. Growing up, we used to laugh about death. "Croaked" is the word Grant Ferguson used to describe the "departed."

Grant grew up in Alabama and had moved to Minneapolis and had the distinct accent of a country gentleman, complete with "yes, sir" and "no, sir" and "yes, ma'am" and "no, ma'am." I was, in fact, dumbfounded at the politeness of his speech and the gentle nature of his presence. He was the first to say "please" and the first to say "thank you." Our nanny, Gertrude, would always encourage me to spend more time with Grant, hoping that someday his demeanor would rub off on me. Whatever the word "demeanor" meant, it must have done just that, because one day I found myself saying "please" and "thank you" about as much as Grant. I even started to talk like him—in a Southern dialect. We were inseparable buddies until he moved away when I was in fourth grade.

But Grant liked to use the word "croaked" when it came to death—"this croaked" or "that croaked" or "my grandpa croaked" or "my grandma croaked." I even started using the word in Miss Bartlett's third grade class. I don't remember much about third grade, but I remember Miss Bartlet. She was a battle-ax of a woman who would not take no for an answer. When they dismissed her from the military, she found her true calling as a third-grade teacher at Creek Valley Elementary School. Push-ups, sit-ups, and strict adherence to rules and regulations were the norm and not the exception. What Miss Bartlet demanded, Miss Bartlet got; and the day I used the word "croaked" in front of her was the day she got in my face and pointed that stubby, crooked finger at me, demanding that I never use that word again. Needless to say, that was the day I stopped using it altogether. It was almost miraculous how the word "croaked" vanished from my vocabulary after that. "Croaked" was too cavalier a word she told me, and death was not a subject to take lightly. I knew not what *cavalier* meant at the time, but I got the message. I told Grant the same thing that Miss Bartlet had told me, and as far as I remember, he stopped using it as well.

Yes, death was a serious thing, even to a third grader. It was a mystery—a subject I knew nothing about. The only thing I did know–even then—was the finality of its separation. Why it was treated so flippantly in westerns and countless movies and television shows, I don't know, but it was. There was even a braggadocio's air about death from teen idols and famous rock bands, including such bands as the Grateful Dead. How could you be grateful for death if you knew not what lay beyond it? Was there anything beyond it? The great writer Hemmingway didn't think so, nor did the great philosopher Camus. I read Hemmingway in college, and in his short story "A Clean Well-Lighted Place," he describes a late-night café with two waiters waiting for a deaf-but-dignified old drunk to finish drinking so the two of them can go home. "Go home to what?" is the question. The younger waiter has a wife in bed, but not the old man. He has *nada*, nothing but a lonely existence. To him, the well-lit café is a sanctuary from the darkness and death that lies beyond it. After the old man departs, the older waiter expounds on his existential view of life through his mockery of the Lord's Prayer: "Our *nada*, who art in *nada* . . .*nada* be thy name. Thy kingdom *nada*, thy will be *nada*, in *nada* as it is in *nada* . . ." *Nada* is Spanish for "nothing." During my freshman year, my literature professor required us to memorize those lines from Hemmingway's short story for our final exam, as if he too believed in nothing beyond the darkness and beyond the grave. But that was Hemmingway's philosophy of life. The very nothingness he believed in was the very nothingness that caused him to take his own life in his latter years. Was he correct in his assumption? Was there nothing beyond death, as other philosophers and writers and professors had believed? And how was anyone to know the truth, apart from dying?

Growing up in the Lutheran Church, we were taught during confirmation about heaven and hell and life thereafter, but to me that had always been a "theory" that could never be tested, apart from dying. And once you were dead, it would then be too late to change your "theory."

To me, church was nothing more than a ritualistic affair, complete with acolytes, candles, wicks, offerings, a sermon, and some songs—and then out the door once you have done your "duty." As acolytes, we would often smash the wicks on the candles above the altar and sit back with giddy amusement as our former buddies struggled to light the smashed wicks prior to the end of the introductory song, which always ended with some kind of rising crescendo, played by our tiny 80-year-old organist, Mrs. Jensen. God help anyone who might have dared to suggest that she was too old to play. And God help the tone-sensitive and musically minded church members who had to suffer through her missed cues and inadvertent keys, as her ailing hands often spiraled out of control, trying as best they could to keep pace with the hard, driving beat of her foot, which could barely reach the pedals. And God help you when you were the lone acolyte who didn't succeed in lighting all the smashed wicks before the crescendo ended. It was a fate worse than death, standing there in utter silence, trying to light the last candle, knowing full well that all eyes were upon you and that nothing, nothing could begin, until all the candles were lit. If there was ever urgency for prayer, it was then. And it was amazing what kind of confessions and pleas an acolyte can make when desperately trying to light the last remaining wicks in the deadpan silence of the Sanctuary, in front of God and everybody: "Yes, God, I will never smash these wicks again for my fellow acolytes. I will never put gum under the pews, and I will pray at least ten times a day, if necessary, and I will never, ever light farts during the church all-night lock-ins."

Yes, lighting farts during the all-night church lock-in. It was all coming back to me now. The memory was suddenly clear and vivid: the memory of Chris Ortis. Chris Ortis was a big boy, one year older than the rest of us, who liked to eat—especially tacos. And on the night of our first all-night, church-youth-group lock-in, he had downed a record eleven—repeat eleven—tacos, pushing the last one into his mouth like Paul Newman in the movie *Cool Hand Luke.* Paul Newman Chris was not, but he did have a creative flair for the dramatic. After taking time to digest all eleven tacos, he gathered the acolytes together near the back entryway of the church. Next he sat down on his haunches, beaming like a blinking idiot. And then, with a braggadocio's air that trumped anything he had ever done in church before, he told us to watch him. Curious, we all did. He started to bounce up and down on his haunches, and then, as if on cue, he rolled over on his back, reached down, lit a match next to his butt, and farted. An orange flame shot up at least six inches without so much as burning his big-boy jeans.

We were amazed.

Brighter flames and bigger sounds. Yes, boys—to the men's room before Chris could lose his urge to fart again. And off we went, scurrying into the cramped quarters of the bathroom where we waited with wild anticipation to hear the new acoustics that would amplify Chris's performance. We all sat on the bathroom tile while he did his ritualistic dance until he felt the "big one" coming. "Quick!" he cried, "The—the match!"

The lights were cut, and eight pairs of eyes peered into the dark, anticipating the flaming outburst. Jeff Kisrud was the pyro-technician and struck the match that sizzled in the dark, as those eight pairs of beady little eyes followed the flame towards Chris's haunches. And then it happened. Chris jettisoned back and forth, milking his new found fame and ephemeral glory. "Now, Jeff, now!" He screamed and then he rolled over on his back. But as we watched the flickering flame descending towards Chris' big boy jeans, the lights suddenly came on. And there—horror of horrors—standing the in the doorway, was Pastor Olson, asking us what was going on.

That night, after being sent home by Pastor Olson, I found it hard to explain to my parents exactly what had happened. It's amazing what kind of political spin you can put on any event if you have to. Even as a kid, I intuitively knew how to spin a message in my favor—and how I suddenly found myself in the middle of a bathroom was beyond me . . . . I had no idea how I got there. All I knew was that I had been minding my own business, when a bathroom full of acolytes with matches came upon me and left me no choice but to join them.

But none of that fancy footwork fazed my dad. He called the lock-in incident for what it was: foolishness. Now my dad was not the spanking kind, but that night I must have disgraced the Finstune name beyond recognition, because he was angry, preposterously angry, and waived the paddle high in the air as if brandishing a sword. All I remember before he spanked me was that I was terrified as I stood there, bent over at the waist, with my own big-boy jeans on the floor, awaiting my fate. I remember thinking this is what it must be like to be strapped to an electric chair, waiting for the switch to be turned on, only that "switch" was not one that flooded a bathroom with light, as Pastor Olson had done, but was rather a switch that would send a man into utter darkness—forever.

Yes, death had always been a mystery to me. And what if I *was* wrong about death? Could a wrong belief send me to hell? Where was Hemmingway? Where was Camus? Where was my uncle? Could a person have a second chance in hell? "Sorry, I made a mistake, but I will do better next time." The Hindus believed in reincarnation. Why didn't the Lutherans?

No.

Like a game that ended at the buzzer, death was not the doorway to a second chance. There were no humans like the Hindus or Houdinis that had ever come back from the grave to play the game again—and that permanence suddenly scared me. If there was a God, I reasoned, then he would have to be just and would first have to warn or tell or teach us mortal human beings about the reality of hell before holding us accountable to it. After all, wouldn't a just teacher have to tell his students about a certain subject matter before they were held accountable for it? Would it be fair to test students on a subject they knew nothing about?

No, I reasoned. There had to be clues about God and there had to be clues about the afterlife.

Looking about the rest of the apartment, I saw the last door. It was the middle door, and I opened it. It was a quaint and smaller room that led to a balcony outside with a sliding glass door. When I stepped onto the balcony, I looked down onto the street below and the lifeless little town. It was 9:40 Saturday morning, and there were still no signs of intelligent life. I stepped back inside and noticed a comfortable reading chair, a lamp stand, and a fiddle that stood beside a wall of books, as if just waiting to be discovered. It was as though my eyes were suddenly opened for the first time, and I saw what looked like a secret library. There were paperback and hardcover books of all sizes and shapes and subjects: bird watching, history of flight, old encyclopedias, and books on science and history and travel and gardening. There was the *Time Life* series on World War II and books upon books about the Vietnam War and the Korean War and the Civil War and the Revolutionary War. There were biographies of Lincoln and Jefferson and Franklin and John Adams. There was a whole row of books dedicated to the Constitution and common law. There were no fewer than five Bibles and two concordances. There were books on Edison and books by Steinbeck and Sinclair Lewis. There was a copy of Chaucer's *Canterbury Tales* and books upon books of short stories and poems by Robert Frost.

As I looked at the library, it suddenly occurred to me that there was a conspicuous absence of any electronics in the room, much less the whole apartment, apart from the digital clock beside the bed. Why? Was it an issue of adequate reception? Bullpen lay lost between two valleys, and like the back eddy along a forgotten stream, it had miraculously, or not so miraculously, escaped the clutches of modern technology. It was as if the people in Bullpen had yet to receive the company memo regarding such change. Yes, there were a few that had reception from cable or Dish, and there were those homes who had partial cell phone and Internet reception near the top of Thomforde Hill, but for the rest of us along Main Street, the only way we could connect with the real world was to drive to the top of Thomforde Hill.

Was there something else that had kept the modern necessities of electronics at bay in my uncle's apartment?

I wondered.

When I looked at the clock, I felt the need to keep moving. I would explore the rest of the apartment later, but today my goal was to find my uncle's truck and see if it was still operational after months in storage.

Later That Afternoon . . . My Uncle's Truck

My uncle's truck had been kept in Lenny Jorgensen's barn, about five miles outside of Bullpen. I called his home number and got a hold of his wife, LuAnn. I then got directions to his farm.

She met me at the entrance to their long driveway, grinning from ear to ear, while holding her cell phone that had guided me to their farm like a human GPS. Her smile resembled that of the smiling moose, and she kept smiling while we talked, as if she knew something I didn't. Then she kept thanking me for "taking on" the Bullpen Café. Apparently, I had been the first to show any kind of interest in such an "undertaking."

Was that a good sign?

She then directed me down the same gravel road to anther barn where her husband, Lenny, was to meet me. As I drove off in my old Toyota Camry, I continued to watch her out of the rear view mirror—smiling.

I had waited a good fifteen minutes in front of the barn before seeing a big John Deere eight-wheeled tractor coming down the road in a cloud of dust. When the tractor came to a halt, LuAnn's husband Lenny, stepped out of the cab and shook my hand.

He was a big, middle-aged man with strong hands and a hearty laugh. In spite of his middle-aged wrinkles, he possessed what struck me as a baby face that was clean-shaven and—like his wife—it could not stop smiling.

"So, you are Roy's nephew, huh?"

I guess news had gotten around fast in town.

"Yep," I replied in my best country accent, as if trying to blend in.

"We liked Roy a lot," he said. "And we're sure glad to have you here—and we're sure glad you're taking over the cafe."

"*Well don't get your hopes up,*" I thought to myself sarcastically, but I didn't say it out loud. Thank God I didn't say it out loud, as I had often said stupid things in moments like that—sarcastic things that I had regretted later. Sarcasm was a way of life at the university. It was the fuel that fueled late night TV and *Saturday Night Live* broadcasts. But there was no life in *sarcasm*. There was humor and there was insight, but there was no life at the expense of someone else, as much as that person might deserve it. It was a pecking order, and those to whom it belonged were the ones who could peck the most. It was like laughing with Karl about our aunt's big feet and feeling bad afterward that she had heard every word. But, like my aunt, I too had been the scapegoat of sarcasm and knew all too well its sting. Upon repeated use, it would harden your heart like calluses on your hands from hard work. And in that brief moment, I had the sudden realization of how much of my college life had been devoted to sarcasm and how hard my own heart had become. Suddenly, looking at Lenny was like looking into innocence that was void of scars from the dog-eat-dog world around him. I sensed intuitively that there was something unique about this man, something tender and genuine and huggable, like a teddy bear.

So I simply nodded.

Then he opened the service door and escorted me into the barn. When he pulled back the sliding doors, shafts of daylight broke through the darkness and rushed upon my uncle's truck.

"It's a beauty," Lenny announced, referring to the shapely form draped in light. Then he pulled back the custom cover like an artist pulling back the canvas of a great masterpiece . . . and there it was—my uncle's deep blue 1953 Chevy pickup, in all of its splendor and glory.

It was as if time itself had broken from its daily routine, slowed down to a complete stop and then stood still. And I was in the middle of it all, looking down at myself like an out of body experience that was taking me back in time to a road less traveled and long forgotten.

I am sitting on my uncle's lap, driving down a long stretch of a grassy knoll, feeling the wonder of movement as the truck responds to my every command with the slightest turn of the steering wheel. It is the feeling of power and grace. I can barely touch the floor as I see the quick-grass before us getting sucked up under the rounded hood that moves effortlessly across the open field. It is the pure joy of driving all over again with no particular destination as my hand turns right and then left. As we gather speed, the wind from the open window is now whipping across my face and hands—and I am feeling safe on top of my uncle's lap and guiding hands.

Suddenly conscious of the silence between us, I glanced over at Lenny. He, too, was staring at the truck, but tears were streaming down the sides of his face. When his eyes met mine, he grimaced, as if embarrassed by his own deep feelings. His big body began to shake, and then he wiped his eyes with the back of his dirty sleeve.

Struggling to regain his composure, he stammered: "Your uncle was a good man."

Early That Night . . .
Landing in the Sea of Tranquility

The trip back to town was a historic event in Bullpen. Lenny drove my Toyota, and I drove the truck. Since I was not familiar with the stick shift, Lenny gave me a quick lesson around the barn. It took some getting used to as I jerked back and forth, trying to find the right gears. Lenny just smiled as he watched me wrestle with the stick shift. "The mad shifter" he would call me later. Even the cows had stopped grazing, staring with bewilderment as this rookie struggled to maintain his speed. When I rounded the barn for the tenth time without stalling, I gave Lenny the thumbs up, and I roared off to Bullpen, jerking and sputtering down the gravel road.

Miles later, I could still see Lenny smiling out my rear view mirror as he followed close behind. We must have looked like a carnival with the Toyota's flashing lights announcing the new circus act. When the truck stalled coming down Thomforde Hill, I simply popped the clutch and coasted into town. And to my surprise, I saw what looked like an audience waiting for our arrival. Parting like the Red Sea, the host of onlookers gave way to the truck until it had come to a complete stop in front of the Café. Suddenly, as if on cue, they all began to clap, as though I had successfully splashed down in the Sea of Tranquility.

Houston? Do you copy?

Later That Night . . . The Revised Business Plan

I was greeted like a conquering hero that afternoon, with people of all ages patting me on the back and shaking my hand. Yes, the town had suddenly come alive with excitement over the new café owner. And when I unlocked the door to the café, they all came inside. Before I knew it, each family had taken a portion of the café to clean, like an "adopt a highway" program. They came with vacuum cleaners and shop vacs and handy wipes and spray bottles and dishrags and pails and mops and paper towels—and who was I to tell them otherwise?

It was as if all 187 citizens of Bullpen had come to resurrect the old café. There were young hands and old hands and feeble hands and strong hands and tiny hands and large hands—but each of them with a common purpose. I had heard about Amish barn raisings, but had never seen one, until now. I stood amazed at their interdependence and their sense of community. In my world, we farmed out our community to corporations and paid them a premium to do so. We paid health insurance premiums to corporations that would take care of us when we got sick. We paid life insurance premiums to corporations to help out with an untimely death in the family. We paid mortgage payments to corporations that knew us more by our social security number than by our name. In my world, everything revolved around the dollar. The dollar was king and dictated the extent of your community and the size of your barn. But here, I sensed that if I was to offer them money, I would offend them.

Then break time came.

Women brought in pies and homemade breads and cookies and hot dishes and warm dishes and goulash—lots of goulash—and when the coffee finally arrived, there was mass exodus to the coffee cup hall of fame, where each person laid claim on his or her own special coffee cup. Each cup owner would first dust it off or rinse it out and gaze at it longingly, as if having been reacquainted with an old friend. We all ate standing up with a plate of food in one hand and a fork in the other, carrying on with all kinds of gestures above the conversations that resonated throughout the old café, like the buzz of bees in a field of clover.

According to Oscar Nordby, a dairy farmer who lived just inside the Bullpen Township, this was the best thing to happen to Bullpen since the local farmers had gotten together to appeal to their state representative to petition the Air Force to stop "buzzing" their cows over Bullpen. Years ago, Bullpen was located directly along the flight path of the F-15s that flew out of the Air Force base at Grand Forks, North Dakota. And as trigger-happy pilots sometimes would do to break the monotony of their daily flight paths, they would swoop down over the grazing cows and "buzz" them. It was all fun and games, until the milk production had dropped a good 23 percent, according to Oscar. A good 23 percent, he emphasized, along with all of the other farmers, who would bob their heads up and down in agreement. Yep, a good 23 percent—maybe a good 24 percent if you had counted Felix Westby's cows, just east of town. And then it took another five months after the "buzzing" had stopped before milk production had gotten back to normal, since the cows still weren't convinced that the F-15s were not predatory birds.

As I listened and watched all of the activity around me, an out-of-body experience suddenly came upon me, and I was outside of myself talking to this old man or that middle-aged woman or this toddler or that young kid. I felt like a queen bee with an army of workers before me, as I saw yet more people come through the front door and greet the crowded mass, pushing their way toward the coffee cup hall of fame, like treasure hunters looking for buried treasure, stopping in between to carefully examine the various artifacts along the shelves, then gaze upon the smiling moose that beamed with what looked like an even bigger smile.

There was so much activity that I could barely hear myself think, as conversations whirled around me from baseball to Bret Favre to those damn Yankees to Pioneer seeds to Monsanto seeds to fertilizers to John Deere tractors. There were little kids pulling down the old toy tractors and trucks from the shelves and running them along the table. "Help yourself," I found myself saying more than once, twice, three times to these little guys, and then I stopped saying it all together. Why bother when it was as if they thought these were their own toys and the café was merely the storage facility for them. I overheard that Agnes Larson was going to get a hysterectomy in February—more information than I needed or cared to know—and that Homer Robertson had befriended yet another elderly lady in town and that Slater Gray had won yet another trophy for his chocolate chip banana bread recipe, and Mavis Rinehart's arthritis was acting up again—but Bayer aspirin seemed to offer the most relief. It was as if hundreds of little conversations were suddenly sprouting up like seedlings from a long and dormant winter. I thought of the movie *The Lion, the Witch and the Wardrobe* and how the land of Narnia had suddenly come alive when spring triumphed over winter and the curse of the wicked witch.

"So what do you plan to do with the—"

Someone was asking me a question, and I was suddenly pulled back to earth from my out-of-body experience.

"What was that?" I yelled over the clamor.

It was a middle-aged man with bib overalls and a John Deere baseball cap.

"So what do plan to do with all of the—"

I still couldn't hear him. He smiled, then redoubled his effort and shouted above the crowd noise.

"What do you plan on doing with the café?"

I nodded to let him know that I was in reception of his message and would now give him my one sentence business proposal for the Bullpen Café—the 40-page business plan that I had carefully crafted with the help of the Small Business Administration, the business plan that some people had taken years to write in order to obtain the necessary funding to launch their new venture.

"Oh!" I shouted out loud. "After I get rid of all this junk—"

Suddenly silence filled the room.

It was, as if on cue, every conversation had come to a screeching halt. Even the kids had stopped playing with their toy tractors and trucks and simply looked up at me. I could hear a pin drop as every other eye was drawn to me and my reply. I had said the "Junk" word, the "J" word, and was now reeling backwards from an all-too-apparent catastrophe that I had created by demeaning what they considered valuable. I glanced about the room, nervously eyeing the sea of people—my would-be paying customers—who were now hanging on my every word.

My business plan was suddenly in need of revision, and I had to think quickly or I could send Narnia back into a frozen wasteland.

It's funny what you can recall in a split second of time. It was as if the tumblers in my brain had kicked into overdrive and I was desperately searching my mental archives for that something—that one thing that was relative to this urgent and delicate situation that could send everything spiraling out of control. It's funny, but the only thing that came to mind in that fraction of a moment was a joke I had heard, years ago, about a grocery clerk—a young whippersnapper of a youth—who got himself in trouble by spouting off his mouth. When a lady in the store had asked him for a half a head of lettuce, the clerk approached the manager in his back office and told him that some *stupid* lady wanted to buy a half a head of lettuce. Unbeknown to the young clerk, the lady had followed him back to the manager's office and was listening to his every word. With his job on the line, the quick-thinking young clerk turned to the lady and without so much as a moment of hesitation, said to the manager that "this *nice* lady wants to buy the other half." Yes . . . I had found the diversion that I had been looking for.

"After I get rid of all this junk *sitting by the dumpster. . .*" I replied. There was a corporate sigh of relief, but the expressions of concern still hovered in the air. They were still waiting for my business plan.

"I plan on ah . . . ah . . ."

They all began to nod as if trying to help me along, like offensive linemen who try to push their own running back into the end zone. What was it I was going to do with the café again? Somewhere out there was my business plan—the one I had imagined when I had first thought of the idea of taking over the café. Oh, yes—the quaint coffee shop with Internet access, where people could come and plop down and converse about anything under the sun or finish their assignments on the internet. Yes, Internet access and smoothies and lattes like Caribou or Starbucks. Retro Café—that was it.

But as I caught site of the bib overalls and John Deere caps, the hope of such a plan began to fade like the fin of a fish sinking back into deep and dark waters. No, suddenly I couldn't see that concept working in Bullpen. Maybe a family type restaurant? Yes, a family restaurant: the Bullpen Buffet. But where was I to put all the pre-assembled food? On the long counter in front of the soda fountain? And where would I put the severely dented malt maker? No, I couldn't see that working either.

As the crowd pressed in to hear my reply, I continued to grope for words, for an idea, for anything to pacify the would-be mob. Suddenly the long-awaited business plan surfaced from the deep waters below like a latent bobber.

"I plan on ah . . . ah . . . just restoring what we already have here and making a go of it."

A deep sigh of relief swept across their earnest faces. Smiles broke out and then laughter broke out and then conversations started up again with a new level of excitement and people patting me on the back again.

Suddenly I was a hero—through no fault of my own.

When they finished cleaning that night, they all lined up, shook my hand and told me how much my uncle had meant to them and how much he was missed. It was only later that I began to realize that cleaning the café was their way of paying tribute to a man I hardly knew, but who had apparently meant more to them than words could describe.

Still Later That Night . . .
Apollo 13 and a Gravitational Pull

It was late tonight, but I wanted to broadcast the day's events and then text Karen and tell her my decision about Bullpen. So I drove my uncle's truck to the top of Thomforde Hill and hopped in the back. As I looked skyward, I saw the brightness of the stars as if I was seeing them for the first time. They were bright and clear and stunning as they have always been, but I had never perceived them as such before. Where I had grown up, there were too many distractions and diffusions of light that kept me from seeing things clearly. But here—here—there was nothing but an unadulterated backdrop that illuminated even the faintest of stars. I suddenly thought of Moses tending his father-in-law's sheep on the backside of a forgotten mountain, looking up at the same stars. I thought about how the once-great Prince of Egypt had been humbled to the status of a mere shepherd. Could pride cloud a man's perception of reality like the diffusion of city lights could cloud the night sky?

I wondered.

I wondered what would have become of Moses had he not killed a man and then fled for his life to the backside of a mountain. I wondered how long it had taken him to come to the realization that he could not save himself from his own shame, having tasted royalty from the most prominent table on earth. Yes, Moses had been taken out of Egypt, but how long was it before Egypt had been taken out of Moses? How long before Moses would clearly see the stars before him and understand the magnitude of his own destiny? What had he thought about all those years as a shepherd looking up at the night sky? What devils of regret and what "could-have-beens" did he wrestle with on that lonely mountain during all those silent years?

"Let's see now. It states here on your resume, Moses, that you were Prince of Egypt from 2009 BC to 1998 BC and then a shepherd from 1889 BC to 1859 BC. Why the sudden demotion? Oh . . . I see. . . . So you killed an Egyptian. Hmmmm. And how long did you serve for that? I see. So let me get this straight: you killed this Egyptian and then fled to this mountain and tended your father-in-law's sheep for over 40 years. Hmmmm. Did you do anything else while attending those sheep? Anything at all? Any kind of middle management job or experience? I see . . . . .Oh, that 's too bad. Well, my suggestion would be to go back to Egypt and serve under one of Pharaoh's assistants for a few years, and then come back and we can review your resume at that time and see if there are any openings for leaders given your qualifications."

Perhaps distance was a good thing. Perhaps the further removed you were from a situation, the better perspective you had of it. Perhaps the backside of a far-away mountain gave Moses the clarity he needed to become a great ruler that he would not have been without it. When he arrived back in Egypt to appeal to Pharaoh to let his people go, he had come full circle, but with an entirely different perspective.

His journey, and the journeys of those like him, was a paradox of sorts—a seeming contradiction that defied intuition. Life was full of paradoxes. The circle itself was a paradox. The very arc that took you away from the point of origin was the very arc that brought you back. And life seemed to be like that— the very thing that took you away was often the very thing that brought you back, but with a new perspective—a life-changing perspective.

As I looked up at the moon, I thought about how the Apollo space missions were like that. I had always wanted to be an astronaut and travel to the moon and back—full circle like Apollo missions. But as I continued to stare, I could not help but think of Apollo 13 and the nearly catastrophic event that had taken place in 1970. Apollo 13 had never accomplished what it had intended to do. The astronauts never landed on the moon. They never reached their destination, and yet they had accomplished more than any other mission in the history of space. Why? Because Apollo 13 was not about gathering moon rocks or moon dust or moon temperatures or moon beams. It was not about exploring the Fra Maura region where the geology and topography was different from the other landing sites, nor was it about any other kind of discovery. It was about something far greater: it was about life—it was about bringing three astronauts home alive.

I began to recall the events that surrounded Apollo 13 from my first assignment for freshmen English class at the University. Three days into their journey towards the moon, astronaut Jack Swigert stirred the cryogenic oxygen tanks when, suddenly, an explosion erupted in the Command Module. Thirteen minutes later, commander Jim Lovell looked out the window and saw the final evidence pointing to a potential catastrophe: they were venting oxygen into space.

"Houston, we have a problem!"

Throw out the flight plan. Yes, throw out the 40-page SBA business plan, because we now have a different mission to accomplish with different rules of engagement that featured a whole new set of problems, which Houston had never considered. Answers had to be found and found quickly. No one had ever calculated that the survival of three men would depend on the preservation of electrical energy and the precise method of powering up the command module

(Odyssey) as it approached the earth's atmosphere. No one had ever considered how to jettison the craft around the gravitational pull of the moon and send it back towards earth like a slingshot. And no one had ever considered the CO_2 buildup in Aquarius, the lunar module that housed the three astronauts for four days but was only designed to support two men for two days. There were enough lithium hydroxide canisters in the Odyssey to remove carbon dioxide, but the square canisters from the Odyssey were not compatible with the round openings in the Aquarius. And after a day and a half in the Aquarius, a warning light showed that the carbon dioxide had built up to a life-threatening level. Mission Control had to devise a way to make a new CO_2 filter, using the square Odyssey CO_2 canisters to fit the round Aquarius CO_2 system, or the men would asphyxiate themselves. Yes, there were other things that had to go right, including their precise 23-degree angle of re-entry into the earth's atmosphere—less than 23 degrees meant they would burn up in the earth's atmosphere, and more than 23 degrees meant they would ricochet off into space—forever. And yes, the heat shield had to hold. And yes, the parachute had to open. But all that would be a moot point if the astronauts could not filter their own carbon dioxide. For now, Aquarius needed a simple CO_2 filter or the astronauts would die.

I suddenly recalled the scene from the movie *Apollo 13* where, back in Houston, one of the chief technicians gathers his colleagues together and throws onto the table the same materials they had on board Apollo 13, including plastic bags, cardboard, and duct tape, telling his team to build a filter. They do so and relay the information to Lovell and his crew so that they could do the same on board the Aquarius. And they do so—just in time.

In the end, the mission of saving their lives came down to plastic bags, cardboard, and duct tape. Ironically, Apollo 13's four-billion-dollar mission had come down to the creative assembly of these simple, common household items that astounded even the wisest of technicians. When they splashed down in the Pacific Ocean six days later, they had come full circle, but with an entirely different perspective. And what would have been one of America's greatest catastrophes had become one of her finest hours.

As I continued to stare into space, I saw to the right of the big dipper what appeared to be a satellite, drifting ever so slowly across the skyline like a tiny firefly crawling across a big black ceiling. Then I was suddenly brought back and became conscious of earth and the windless but not-so-silent night. The sound of crickets and other night bugs provided a little symphony of their own as I began to recall the day's events: from Lenny to my first stick shift lesson, to coasting into town, to the communal cleaning of the Bullpen Café.

I recalled one little old man by the name of Harold who had invited me to church tomorrow morning. Not being a churchgoer myself, I politely declined his offer. I usually sleep in on Sundays. I like sleeping in on Sundays. Why did the Sabbath have to be on Sunday? Why not Saturday or Friday or Thursday? Why not get all that church stuff done during the week so a person could enjoy his Sundays?

I seemed proud of myself for declining his offer, until the mayor himself asked me again. Now you don't get an invitation from the mayor every day, so as a proprietor of my own café, I thought it would be a good business decision to accept the invitation: nine am sharp. Yes, I'll remember. Yes, I can be there. A little coffee and I can do nine am. The only problem was I had forgotten to get coffee before I arrived—and where was I to get coffee at midnight in Bullpen?

Houston, do you copy?

Then there was the issue of help. I had no fewer than seven people asking me if I needed a waitress or a dishwasher, but no cook. Apparently, Ernie Sloan was the last cook at the café, and he died last year at the age of 88. But a Mavis somebody had a friend, who had a relative, who knew this guy, who was a friend of someone else, who knew of a good cook and, miracle of miracles, this cook happened to be looking for a job. Great. A cook looking for a job. Is that an oxymoron? I thought all the good cooks were employed and all the bad cooks were, well, looking for work because they were, after all, bad cooks. No, I was not going to settle for just any cook. The Bullpen Café was to be different. I had standards. So I wrote down his name and thought I'd give him a call.

Then there was the proverbial question of how many waitresses I needed to help run the café. One, two at most—one to man the till and the other to wait on people? How many people would be there in the morning for breakfast? But what if everyone who had his or her coffee cup on the coffee cup hall of fame came at once? We could have trouble on our hands. Yes, impatient coffee lovers clamoring for coffee like adamant, obnoxious school children clamoring for lunch. One of the waitresses would have to be a big woman to enforce the crowd control. Crowd control in Bullpen? Maybe not.

And then there was the whole issue about menus and what to serve. Hush Puppy Pancakes seemed to be a big favorite for the Bullpen Café. Yes, more than 15 people told me that the Bullpen Café was known for its Hush Puppy Pancakes. "Oh, really . . . ?" I asked. "Yes," came the answer, "—with real maple syrup." Real maple syrup? Whoever eats real maple syrup? And where would I find a recipe for Hush Puppy Pancakes? God help me if I don't.

"And are we going to serve lutefisk at the Friday night fish fry?"

Who said anything about a Friday night fish fry? And lutefisk?

It suddenly became clear. I had done the unthinkable. I had forgotten to calculate the profits from lutefisk dinners in my SBA business plan and it had skewed all of my financial projections.

But who in their right mind eats lutefisk?

And that was just it—they weren't in their right minds. They were delirious. It all began—according to tradition—when ancient Scandinavian men and women—once good, ordinary, God-fearing people—had gone stark raving mad with Lutefisk disease—a contagious, infectious disorder that came by simply staring at cabin walls, day after day and night after night, during the long and bitter Minnesota winters. Over time the monotony of it all would take its toll until our once proud ancestors finally cracked under duress. In a desperate attempt to end it all, they stuffed themselves with lye-soaked codfish with their bare hands, hoping to put an end to their misery with the poisonous brine. But as fate would have it—and to their own amazement—they lived. Elated after having had a brush with death, they encouraged others to do the same. And so a tradition was born that would be passed down from generation to generation, the last of which would at least have the decency to use silverware.

I often wondered about the concentration levels of the poisonous brine made from lye. Had there ever been any deaths that had come from a disproportionate ratio of lye to water? I wondered how many Oles and how many Svens or Lenas had lost their lives, or had become seriously maimed, trying to figure out the right ratio between water and cod and lye. Three parts cod and one part lye to four parts water? You be the judge. No, you be the judge. No, seriously, you be the judge . . .

As I looked into space I noticed that the satellite I had seen earlier was now nowhere to be seen. I suddenly felt alone, as if my broadcast was falling on deaf ears or was lost, like the communications from Apollo 13 when it circled the far side of the moon.

As I looked at the moon, I suddenly remembered the last event of the day. It was an old man who took all night to dust the toy train tracks that ran around the café. It was a man named Homer. He moved gingerly among the swarming bodies with his small stepladder, and miraculously avoided every possible mishap. By midnight, he had dusted all of the train tracks and seemed pleased with himself. He was the last one to leave, and when he did, he bowed politely and thanked me for coming. Then he grabbed his stepladder and shuffled away. As I stood in the doorway, I watched his humble, hunched, silhouetted body for what seemed like an eternity, until it turned at the first available corner and faded out of sight.

I don't know why that touched me, but it did. In an odd sort of way, in a small sort of way, I was beginning to feel as if I was being drawn to this place, as if its gravitational pull was tugging on my soul.

Dear Karen,

I am missing you more than you can imagine, and I wish that you were here with me tonight, looking at the stars. I am sitting in the back of a pickup truck just outside of Bullpen, Minnesota. It is the only place that has cell phone or Internet reception, so if I don't respond right away from now on, you will understand.

You, however, must be sound asleep on the far side of the moon— In Italy—so very far away.

There is something I need to tell you. I have decided not to go to law school next year. I have decided to take a sabbatical. I have decided to take over my uncle's café in Bullpen, Minnesota, for a little while. I know how strange it must sound after all the plans we made on attending law school together, but there is something here that compels me to stay—at least for now. I hope that you will understand.

XOXO,
Charlie

June 7 . . . Ole's Closet

Nine o'clock can be a regular train wreck for a guy without coffee. I had done the unthinkable. I had overslept and had rushed to church the way I had rushed to my morning classes throughout my college career, jumping into the back of the classroom, undetected in the midst of a sea of students. Fortunately, I had laid out my pants the night before, but where I had laid the shirt I had planned to wear is still a mystery. In my feeble attempt to wear something clean, I had inadvertently grabbed my "PARTY HEARTY" fraternity shirt from Phi Kappa Kegga. Yes, a white T-shirt with the big black and bold letters that read, "PARTY HEARTY," which was silk-screened on both sides of my shirt, along with not one, but two kegs of beer. If I had had some coffee this morning, I might have caught it.

I was only a block from the church when I realized what I had done. By then I had already violated the "Thou shalt not be late" commandment and was now destined to violate another by the very shirt I wore. As I pulled up to the parking lot, I thought about turning the T-shirt inside out, but that would look even more conspicuous. No, I needed to fly under the radar, hoping that I could sneak in the back during one of those all encompassing hymns, with the spiraling crescendo, that I had come to appreciate in my childhood church.

I parked my car with all of the others in the grassy parking lot around back and then opened what I thought was the back door. But when I stepped inside, I suddenly found myself staring at the congregation head on.

So what do you do facing a congregation of ghastly faces while wearing your PARTY HEARTY T-shirt? You thank God that you didn't wear your Daytona Beach T-shirt—that's what you do. Like a knee jerk reaction, I instantly jumped into the next available door.

It was a closet.

Houston. We have a problem.

Who on God's green earth would ever design a sanctuary with a closet up front?!

44

I was to find out later that it was Ole Gunderson's doing back in the 1899. Yes, the notorious Ole Gunderson had designed it because he couldn't bring himself to see the cemetery at the back of the property where his 5th (and supposedly his last) wife had been buried—God rest her soul. And being one of the biggest and perhaps the only tithing member of the church, Ole persuaded the deacons and elders to build a closet up front so he could relieve himself of his big bearskin coat in the winter. Rumor had it he shot the bear in self-defense in northern Wisconsin after he and the bear had been taunting each other for over an hour.

So what do you do when you are trapped in a closet in front of the congregation that knows you are in there, and you know that they know you are in there, and they know that you know that they know?

You do the only noble thing you can do. You stay there and hide like an ostrich. But as I hid my head in shame, something began to rise up in me that morning. It started from my feet and rose like rolling thunder. It was like the Grinch's heart that grew three sizes that day while looking down on Whoville. It was a new confidence I had never felt before, a confidence that rendered me able to stand before my accusers and face them without shame and without apology. "Never apologize." The words of Julia Child seem to ring out in her distinctly formal accent, as if calling down from heaven like an angel, a godsend to help encourage this wayward soul. Yes, never apologize. I had decided to face my destiny head on. I had decided to make a stand. It was in that fraction of a moment that I felt a sudden rush of adrenalin. Yes, liquid courage had come upon me, and feeling like Braveheart, I reached for the handle . . .

. . . But there was none.

Doggone that Ole Gunderson—that cheapskate Ole Gunderson who had decided that an inside handle was too expensive.

When the pastor finally opened the door, he told me that he was glad that I could join them for church.

Blinking like an idiot, I found myself saying, "No problem."

Later That Afternoon . . . The Church Picnic

I had changed my shirt before coming to the church picnic at Miss Maddie's farm. Miss Maddie's farm was not so much a farm as it was a southern plantation.

The neatly manicured yard was clothed with flowers of all colors and sizes and shapes: begonias, daisies, marigolds, and lots and lots of heather that all led up to its jewel: a huge Victorian home with a wrap-around porch that offered a pristine view of the valley in all directions, but one. Her late husband's great-great-grandfather had built it. He was a soldier in the civil war and had met and later married a Southern belle from Atlanta. The young lady's father fiercely opposed the engagement, but when Miss Maddie's ancestor offered to take her whole family back to Minnesota after the war and build them a Victorian home like the one that had been burned by Sherman's march to the sea, it was more than her father could resist. The home was updated at the turn of the century and then again in the 1930s and 1950s and again recently, with each update putting its own stamp of approval on the timeless treasure. There were mahogany floors and two oak spiraling staircases in the great room off the main entrance that also featured beveled glass windows and two chandeliers. The study was clothed in cherry wood, as were the built-in-shelves that housed the extensive display of leather-bound books. The large, spacious kitchen had recently been remodeled with marble countertops, stainless steel appliances, and soft, indirect lighting that integrated the past and present into a seamless ensemble of old and new architecture that was all tastefully arranged, like the very tapestry upon which tiny feet had run and older feet now stood.

The kitchen itself was the grand central station—the hubbub of activity where all the food had been gathered. And there was a smorgasbord of foods on that Sunday afternoon that came in a smorgasbord of plastic bowels and Tupperware tubs. There were hot dishes. Lots of hot dishes and noodle dishes and meatball dishes and lasagna dishes and salads and breads and every imaginable desert, strategically placed at the end of the long kitchen table where watchful parents stood to supervise the distribution of proper nutrition. One little guy had tried to abscond with four pieces of cake, three cookies and two big scoops of chocolate pudding, but was apprehended just short of the goal line—just short of the screen door—by his father.

As the newcomer, I was the center of attention and found myself saying hello more times than I can remember, and then trying as best I could to keep track of people's names and faces. The name of the old man that had spent all night clearing the train tracks at the café was Homer Robertson, a bachelor farmer who had lived outside of town until his bachelor brother had died and left him the entire homestead. Unable to manage the farm alone, he sold it and moved to town and was now—at the tender age of 91—beginning to enjoy city life, as he put it. He smiled wryly and told me in confidence that he was a hot commodity among the widowed ladies in town and dared not date any one of them lest he offend any of the others and tarnish his reputation as a playboy.

I agreed.

When I went back for a second helping of food, I saw that two mothers were now nursing their babies at the far end of the table, and one had zeroed in on me and began to ascertain my background. When she found out I was a graduate from the university, she smiled and told me that she had graduated from the university five years ago. I was tempted to ask her what an educated woman like herself was doing in Bullpen, but I didn't. And she must have sensed the question because she proceeded to tell me about the uniqueness of the town, but I couldn't hear a word she said above the noise of the breast-feeding baby. And me? I had, ah . . .Well, you know, I had ah . . . ah . . . I had actually never tried to carry on a conversation with a breast-feeding mother with a ravenously hungry baby before—not that I was embarrassed or had the words "feeling a little uneasy" written all across my forehead or anything. I had always thought of breastfeeding as—you know—a kind of private moment—but not here, not with her.

Was I the only one feeling a little warm?

Her baby suddenly gasped for breath, and in a nervous frenzy I blurted out, "He's drowning!"

Instantly, the kitchen became quiet and then laughter broke out. I felt like an idiot. The mother smiled at me and then cajoled the baby boy as if to cover my embarrassment. It was in fact a covering, like the little blanket that covered her and her baby—and I knew it. The irony was that she was the one who was supposed to be embarrassed; she was the one feeding the little guy, not me. And yet, I sensed that she was the one trying to make me feel welcome, in spite of myself.

When a friend of hers approached and asked her a question, I thanked her and departed to the front porch where bluegrass music had been playing. As I sat there listening to the music, my head and heart began to settle. I never really understood bluegrass music. I had grown up under rock and roll and the hard pounding in-your-face rhythms that often pulled you into an artificial passion and carnal knowledge. But bluegrass music was different. There was innocence about its style that offered an almost medicinal effect to the listener. As I sat on the porch, I stared at the musicians' skilled fingers as they moved effortlessly across the various stringed instruments they were playing. An older man played the guitar, a younger man played the mandolin, a young teenage boy played the banjo, and an elderly woman played the penny whistle as if it was a natural extension of her own voice. I found myself tapping my foot to the music, and as I did, I looked out over the valley that reminded me—in a small way—of the Ozark Mountains near Branson, Missouri.

When the music ended, the musicians praised each other, and then mingled into the body at large, leaving their instruments on the porch. Curious, I went up to look at the banjo, and it was then I heard a voice behind me.

It was Miss Maddie. Her real name was Madelyn, but she preferred Miss Maddie. She was an elderly woman in her 80s who had a stately appearance and a milk-white aura about her. Her face was kind, and her eyes were soft and understanding, as if crafted by years of silent pain.

She was carrying a glass of lemonade and offered it to me. I don't know why, but I hesitated in taking it, and sensing my reservation, she told me it was made from real lemons—nothing artificial. So I took it and thanked her.

She then sat down next to me and asked if I played the fiddle. "No," I replied. She nodded and told me the group could use a good fiddle player. "Your uncle played the fiddle," she said. I then told her that I had seen it in his apartment above the café. She nodded and began to ask me a series of polite, conversational questions, but I had the feeling that she was probing for something beyond words. And as we talked about small, peripheral things of the day, I had the feeling that she was looking for something deeper in me, something that desired to be apprenticed by the teacher in her. And suddenly I felt like a little schoolboy who didn't know what he needed to know.

"Your uncle was great man," she said. The statement seemed to come out of the blue, and it took me by surprise.

"I never really knew him," I said.

She smiled, and taking the liberty that only old people can do, she patted my knee and replied, "Someday you will."

Later That Night. . . A Rendezvous with Karen

It was late that night when I reached the top of Thomforde Hill. I set up my broadcast booth from the back of the pickup truck and began to recall the day's events. It was then I saw that I had a text message from Karen:

Got your news about Bullpen. Wow. I am not sure what to think. All I know is that I miss you too. Reception is bad here in Italy and, like you, I can only get a signal when I am outside of town. Dad left for home, and it is just mom and I with family. I have so many cousins! They speak faster than I can communicate in my broken Italian. Having a great time. Tomorrow my cousin Vinnie is taking us to Rome to see the Coliseum. I am soooo excited. Mom and I plan on staying in Italy another three weeks. Can we catch up tomorrow by phone? I need to hear your voice. I will call you at 10 pm your time and I will be in a place where we can talk.

XOXO,
Karen

Don't you just love the way she signs her name?! Don't you just love the Xs and the Os and the way they kind of intertwine above her name?

Isn't life good?

10 pm my time tomorrow. Got it… can't wait to talk to you then. Signing off.

XOXO,
Charlie

June 8 . . . In Search of a Cook

Monday morning came early, and I staggered out of bed, purposing in my heart to find coffee. That was my number one mission of the day, and so I said it out loud, and I wrote it down on the palm of my hand in bold black ink: COFFEE. I found in college that messages written on the palm of my hand were never lost. It was, after all, my own palm pilot—no pun intended. I also wrote down 10 pm. Yes, I would rendezvous with Karen at 10 pm from the top of Thomforde Hill. Life is good.

So what do I do on my first real day as the proud owner of the Bullpen Café? Thanks to the loyal patrons, the place had been cleaned. But where was I to begin?

A cook. I needed a cook who, if nothing else, could teach me how to cook, and maybe that individual could teach me how to order stuff like—food.

"Food" is a great word, isn't it? I mean, just say it a few times. It's a funny word, really. Food. Who thought of the word food for food anyway? I suddenly thought of the musical *Oliver*, and I could see Oliver and his cohorts singing "Food Glorious Food" in their stately attire.

I would go to Zumbrota, the nearest big town, and buy some coffee and more food and then find this cook that I had been told about. I felt like a detective in search of a cook that I knew nothing about. Was he an ex-con? An ax murderer? When I got beyond the Bullpen valley, I would call the number that was given to me, and if I could get a hold of him, and if in fact he was a cook, and if in fact he did know how to order food and was not an ax murderer, then at least I could hire him for the interim—until I learned the ropes. That was my plan, anyway.

Later That Afternoon . . . Jerome Boatman

I found the cook that I had been looking for, and he was everything that I had hoped he wasn't. Yes, he was an ex-con, but not an ax murderer, to my knowledge, anyway. His name was Jerome Boatman, or so he told me. Jerome was a big Black man in his mid thirties—the kind of man that could play both offensive tackle and fullback at the same time. The man had no neck. His head just seemed to kind of rest on top of his massive shoulders that had swallowed up his neck and refused to return it. When he turned his head, his whole body seemed to move with it, as if the vertebrae had been soldered into one single chassis.

When I had finally gotten a hold of him on the phone, we had planned to meet at a local café, but he was late. Very late. Not knowing if he was going to show up or not, I began to peruse the restaurant for ideas. As proprietor of my own café, I began to look at things differently now. I was reminded of Sam Walton from Wal–Mart. I was told he would always go into his competitors' stores, along with his colleagues, and ask them to find one good thing about the store that made it successful. It was good business practice, and I was now taking his advice. You can always learn something from your competition. On my table was a disposable placemat with advertisements from the local businesses in town. Not pretty, but effective. I couldn't think of too many businesses in Bullpen, but maybe I could offer pictures of local activities or local celebrities. Yes, Ole Gunderson for starters. I could have fun facts or weekly readers that featured poetry from British literature. Yes, Chaucer and *Canterbury Tales* right next to the won/lost record of the Twins or the Vikings or the Timberwolves or the Wild. I could have little quizzes about the history of Bullpen. Yes, multiple choice questions or fill in the blank questions with riddles. Yes, lots of riddles, and free pie to the ones who got it right. My placemat would take the place of Bullpen's nonexistent newspaper—and much to the chagrin of any librarian, it would be the most read item in Bullpen. It would be the talk of the town and beyond. Yes, people would flock to Bullpen just to read the latest placemat with all of the latest gossip and who's who in Bullpen—and birthdays and anniversaries and whatnots. Yes, lots of whatnots and recipe contests and bake offs . . . ESPN bake offs—live from Bullpen, Minnesota, on Super Bowl Sunday—yes, finally a taste of the NFL.

I glanced at my watch and noticed that I had spent over 25 minutes contemplating the disposable placemat and free pie. I had ordered only coffee and thought that my cook was a no-show. I was about ready to leave when I saw him walk in. I knew it was he the minute I saw him. He had that dogged "I hope I'm not in trouble" look about him, and he began to look about the restaurant, searching for someone who was looking for him. And then our eyes met.

51

He nodded sheepishly, and his big frame lumbered towards me as he carried what looked like a tennis ball. His big hand reached out and shook mine,

"I'm Jerome Boatman," he said. "You must be Charlie."

"That's me," I replied.

"Sorry I'm late," he said. "I had me some car trouble."

He suddenly started squeezing the tennis ball. Curious, I asked him why he was squeezing a tennis ball. He told me that he was trying to quit swearing and that by squeezing the ball, it would remind him of what not to do. Great—a swearing chef that would fly off the handle and tell our clientele what he really thought of them.

We talked small talk for a few minutes, and then I reached out and handed him an application that I had gotten off the Internet. It was a simple application, really, nothing too revealing or too difficult, but as I started to ask him more questions, he began to squeeze the fuzz off the ball. Do you know how hard it is to squeeze the fuzz off a tennis ball?

When I asked him about his previous experiences in the "previous experience" part of the application, he mentioned that he had served as a food assistant.

"Where?" I asked.

"The state prison," he replied sheepishly.

That's great. An ex-con. Why had I not seen it from the beginning? Did I have the words "naive white boy" written all across my forehead? What did he take me for, anyway? Yes . . . a white honky. But he didn't say it, and I was suddenly sensing that we were racially profiling each other: me, a yuppie, privileged white boy; and him, an underprivileged black man with an application in his hand.

A food assistant. Yup, looks good on a resume doesn't it? Food assistant in the state penitentiary—a regular gourmet cooking school where a whole platoon of ex-cons stood waiting in the wings with their clean white aprons, ladles and spatulas, serving only the finest, industrial, government surplus food money can buy.

"So, where do you live?" I asked.

"In a car," he replied.

"A car? What kind of car?" I asked—not that it really mattered. Not that it would affect the property values of the local neighborhood—as long as he could move it.

"A Chevrolet Impala," he said. "But it just broke down."

A Chevrolet Impala? Who lives in a Chevrolet Impala these days? Maybe a Buick Electra 225 in an upscale neighborhood—but an Impala?

"So, what makes you think you are qualified to do the job?" I asked him. His response was that he was a quick learner.

"Oh," I found myself saying out loud. "Oh" is a great response, isn't it? I mean, when you are at a loss for words, default to the "Oh" word. "Oh" covers a lot of ground without saying anything else. It implies that you understand, but its real meaning is found in your inflection. Apparently, I had said "Oh" with too much vibrato, because he seemed to shirk back. As I sat and drank my coffee, I saw him glance about nervously. I don't know why, but I suddenly asked when he had eaten last.

"Two days ago," he replied.

I told him to order something off the menu, and he did—three hamburgers and fries and a Coke. After the waitress had taken his order, we sat in silence for a brief moment. What else do you ask an ex-con? The interview was over, and he knew it. The rest of the conversation was merely academic and "politically correct" politeness so he wouldn't get mad and slash my tires or come looking for me in Bullpen on a cold and stormy night.

I told him that I had another interview to attend, but we both knew I was lying. The look on his face suddenly recoiled. He politely thanked me, and then I left the table and paid the cashier.

I don't know why I looked back, but I did. The waitress had brought his order, but he didn't touch it. He simply stared at me—not with pity, not with anger, but with a certain self-preserved dignity, as if he had met defeat and refused to play the victim—that nauseating victimization that came with guys like Donavan McNabb, when he blamed prejudice as the reason for his mistakes as the Philadelphia Eagles' Quarterback, while Eli Manning of the Giants had endured an even more brutal press in New York, but without complaint. You could always blame the color of your skin as your fate in life. You could always blame your background, or your parents, or your brother, or your mother, or your age, or your degree or lack of degree, as to why things didn't turn out. It was the blame game, and it provided the fuel for the scapegoat of failure. Yes, blame others for your own mistakes or lack of responsibility. Blame others for your lot in life. Blame others for the way the world treats you, because it is always someone else's fault. It was the flame that fueled Jesse Jackson's "poor

53

Black man" campaign and kept him pinned under an invisible glass ceiling that told him that he could rise no higher than the color of his skin. It was the lie that immobilized even the fittest of men. And if you believed it, if you focused your energies on what you couldn't become, then you would never be able to see what you might become. How could you if you refused to take responsibility for your own life because it was always someone else's fault? No, your only recourse, then, was to place your destiny in the hands of a self-appointed champion who would argue on your behalf, because, as a victim, you were entirely incapable of doing so yourself. Ironically, I saw black men on campus from foreign countries succeed because the Jesse Jacksons of the world hadn't told them that they were victims yet.

But victimization was not there in Jerome's face, and when I reached the truck and opened the door, there was something inside that would not let me go. I suddenly knew that I had to go back. When I did, I found him still staring at his food—untouched. As I approached his table, I told him that I had come back to hire him.

"You come to give me a job? I can get any cookin' job I want."

He was lying.

"Bullpen is a predominantly white community," I said.

This time I was lying. It was an *all* white community.

"But if you want it," I continued, "there are conditions: hard work, honesty, no lying, no drugs, no swearing, and no BULLSHI—"

I had almost said it—like a check swing in baseball.

He seemed to debate the offer like a premier athlete waiting to consult his agent for a better offer, but then a smile broke across his face, as if he had just gotten word from the front office.

"I'll take the job," he declared at last.

I had found myself a cook—I think.

Later That Night . . . The Right to Remain Silent

It was around six o'clock when we had finished buying supplies for the café at one of the local grocery stores. It probably wasn't the best way to order food, but it was a start. I bought foods to make an assortment of recipes that I had found on Rachel Ray's and other websites. The Internet is great. It gives you a whole assortment of experts to draw from at the click of a button. Yes, I was the proud proprietor and would subscribe to such magazines as *Bon Appetite*. We could be having ratatouille and escargot next week, if I played my cards right. I still couldn't find a recipe for hush puppy pancakes, but I thought I could wing it until I scoured my uncle's apartment. I had also bought strawberry jam and eggs and meat—plenty of hamburgers and French fries and chicken cacciatore with mandarin orange sauce and one-hundred dollars worth of small ducklings for wild game night, with wild rice soup and mixed vegetables. I bought lemons for lemon chicken—for our Monday night Chinese night. And for our Tuesday night Mexican night, I bought refried beans and flour tortillas for fajitas, along with lots of corn chips and salsa. Wednesday night would be German night with wiener schnitzel and sauerkraut. Thursday night would be Irish night with fish and chips, and Friday—yes, Friday—would be the coup d'état of all nights—Norwegian night, with all of the bland foods you could think of: white potatoes and white breads and white lutefisk with a tad of yellow butter to spice things up and give it some color. Yes, lutefisk night. The grocery store didn't carry it, and the young clerk wasn't sure what it was, but I had all week to find it on the Internet. Saturday would be the all-American night, with burgers and "cholesterol free" beer-battered onion rings and French fries and malts—strawberry and vanilla and chocolate malts—just like Dairy Queen.

When I asked Jerome what kinds of food he liked to make, he said smoked catfish and carp. Yes, mercury-free carp.

I nodded and drove on in silence as Jerome continued to squeeze his tennis ball. Suddenly I was beginning to regret my decision about Jerome. What was I thinking, anyway? Who in their right mind hires an ex-con out of the state penitentiary with little, if any, cooking experience? Was I that desperate?

I had decided to give him a couple of days and then lay him off—that was the more politically correct thing to do. "Sorry, but I can't afford to keep you—not enough revenue." In the interim, he would stay in the empty apartment across the street that was owned by the mayor. I had told the mayor earlier that I needed the apartment for my cook—whoever that might be. He was more than obliging and offered to paint it at no extra cost. "Deal," I told him. I had already paid him the damage deposit and wondered how many other things Jerome would squeeze or crush while there.

I glanced at my watch. It was now 6:30, and I was getting hungry and wanted to hurry home before the frozen foods began to thaw in the truck bed—especially the ice cream.

I stepped on the pedal and began to accelerate. When we went around the first bend in the road, I saw him in the gravel intersection between two adjacent cornfields. It was the sheriff, and it was as if he was waiting for me. He pulled out and followed me for the next two miles as if toying with his prey. Jerome looked back and began to swear and then began to squeeze his tennis ball in rapid succession. By this time we were going 45 MPH on a 55 MPH highway, and just when I thought the sheriff was going to turn off, he turned on his flashers.

I pulled over.

It's funny what you remember about all the times you have been stopped by the police, but it seemed like only yesterday when eight of my fraternity buddies and I were pulled over after a hockey game in St. Paul. Jeff—alias "Lead Foot Gordon"—was driving, and when the officer knocked on the window, Jeff decided to impress us all with his braggadocio's air. When the officer pulled out his pad and asked to see his driver's license, Jeff pretended he was going to take our order and told the officer that he would take 16 quarter pounders with cheese and the same number of onion rings. Jeff laughed. We laughed. Everyone laughed—even the officer, but he just kept writing. And we kept laughing, and he kept on writing and writing and inspecting the car and making more notes. Suddenly, things got quiet when he asked how many of us were wearing seatbelts. Seatbelts? Who said anything about seatbelts? The officer then handed Jeff a ticket totaling over 875 dollars worth of violations. It's funny how fast a state patrol officer can rain on a guy's parade.

As Jerome continued to squeeze the fuzz off the tennis ball, I tried to reassure him that we had done nothing wrong, and I was going to be extra polite. "No sir." "Yes sir." Because I knew he had more tickets than I had 20-dollar bills.

As he approached our truck, I could see that the officer was a kind man, a grandfatherly man, who was nearing retirement. That's a good thing, and whatever it was we had done, he would simply give us a warning. He asked for my license, and I gave it to him. He asked me if I knew why I was being pulled over, but I had been there before. The game was called "self-incriminating quiz bowl." The law enforcement agent would ask you what you had done wrong, trying to get you to confess to some violation, and then it would be easier to give you a ticket, since you had already confessed.

I acted stupid and said, "No sir, I don't." I thought I had been speeding, but I wasn't sure. I don't know if he took it the wrong way or not, but he started to get irritated, as if everyone should just naturally confess to a crime, whether guilty or not. "Don't play smart with me. I pulled you over because you have expired tabs on your license plate. Is this your truck," he asked?

"Well no, it is my uncle's truck and . . ."

It was as if Jerome couldn't hold it any longer. Mount Vesuvius suddenly erupted into a blaze of expletives that would make a sailor blush.

"His name is Jerome!" I quickly yelled trying to cover for Jerome. "He is trying to quit swearing like some people are trying to quit smoking. That is why he squeezes the tennis ball!"

The sheriff's mouth suddenly dropped. He, too, stood amazed at the variety and vulgarity of the English language. When Jerome was finished, the sheriff just stood there in amazement, blinking.

"Why, Son," he finally said, "that was the greatest display of vulgar language I have ever heard—and I am an old Navy man."

Jerome suddenly seemed pleased with himself, until the sheriff asked him to step out of the truck. Still squeezing his tennis ball, Jerome stepped out. The sheriff then asked him for some identification, of which he had none.

More expletives.

"He is my cook and we are going to Bullpen with some groceries for the café," I pleaded.

"Right!" he said, "And I am your fairy godmother."

The next thing I knew is that we were both up against the truck and he was frisking us. Jerome dropped his ball and began another flurry of expletives.

"You have a right to remain silent!" the sheriff yelled above Jerome's screaming voice. Then he put the handcuffs on us and pushed us into his car. Five minutes from the county jail, Jerome must have found another tennis ball in his pocket, because the swearing had stopped.

Still Later That Night . . . The Phone Call from Italy

It's hard to think behind bars. I was still not exactly sure why we were in the slammer. Slammer is a great word isn't it? I mean, who named it the slammer? It was like the name of a hamburger or something. Yes, I will have two slammers and an order of fries please.

After the sheriff had taken all of my possessions, including my phone, I suddenly thought of the time. Karen was going to call me at 10 pm. Doggone it. I glanced about at the clock. It was only 9:45. I had fifteen minutes to reach my phone.

As I began to converse with the sheriff, I found out that he had thought we were stealing the truck since the tags were expired and it was not registered in my name. The fact that Jerome couldn't keep quiet and had no identification and was the only black man in a region of almost all white men (did someone say racial profiling?), all contributed to the final conclusion: guilty as charged. I argued my case, gripping the bars with white knuckles, but he pretended he couldn't hear me as he finished his left-over spaghetti in the white Styrofoam box.

"My girlfriend in Italy is going to call me at ten o'clock," I pleaded. "I need my phone!"

He ignored my plea and continued to slurp up the last of noodles. Suddenly, I realized I didn't have an Italian night scheduled during the week for the Bullpen Café. I had left out Italy!

"I need an Italian night!" I suddenly blurted out loud.

He looked at me as if I was going crazy. I continued to cry out for justice.

"Am I not even allowed to make at least one phone call? Where's is my attorney. My father is an attorney. Hey! My father is an attorney!"

"And I'm your fairy godmother," he replied.

As I sat at the bottom of my cell staring up at the ceiling, I heard it ring. Yes, it was ringing. My phone was ringing to the familiar tune of "Fields of Gold" by Sting.

"That's my phone," I yelled. "It is Karen, my girlfriend, calling me from Italy . . . I need to talk to her!"

I could almost reach the phone on the edge of the table. One ring, two rings—just a little closer—three rings . . .

"Hold on, Karen!" I blurted out.

Four rings . . . five rings . . . six rings . . . seven rings . . . then, like a drowning man, the phone fell silent and slipped below the surface of the water, never to ring again.

Now I found myself swearing up a blue streak, while Jerome simply stared at me, apparently amazed that I could swear like him. When I was through, he handed me his tennis ball.

"Sometimes," he said, "it helps to squeeze it really hard."

June 9 . . . My Attorney

I have never actually spent a night in jail, and no, I didn't sleep at all. Jerome snored the whole night, and when he wasn't snoring, he was talking in his dreams. To my own amazement, however, he had not said a single swear word in his sleep. Screaming, yes. Swearing, no. If that wasn't enough to keep you awake, try sleeping without a sheet or a blanket or a pillowcase. The sheriff had taken both, including our belts. Perhaps he thought we would have hung ourselves, having been caught driving without tags. He even took off the toilet seat, thinking that we might hit ourselves over the head and drown. Then he took three 8-by-10 colored, glossy pictures, with circles and arrows and a paragraph on the back to identify us, in case we were found trying to cross the state line. Can anyone say *Alice's Restaurant*? Yes, we were hardened criminals. God help us if we had been caught littering.

He came in at eight am sharp, just as he had told us he would before he left last night. When I asked him what the holdup was, he told me he was waiting for my attorney.

"My attorney? I don't have an attorney."

"Your dad," he said.

"My dad? You talked to my dad?! My dad is coming to get me out of jail?!"

He nodded. "You were right. Your father is an attorney."

"So my dad is taking time out of his heavy workload to come and get his son and his cook out of jail?" I asked. "You are kidding, right?"

He wasn't.

"Do I look like a minor?" I yelled. "I don't need my dad to get me out of this. This is a big misunderstanding about the tabs. The truck belonged to my Uncle Roy Finstune and my name is Charlie Finstune. Do you see the resemblance in the last name?! Tell me you see the resemblance in the last name!"

I was getting ready to let go another volley of swear words when Jerome threw me the tennis ball.

My dad showed up two hours later—visibly upset. He signed the necessary paper work and, without so much as a word, pointed to the door. Jerome and I exited and stepped into my father's black Lexus. I suddenly felt as though I had stepped back in time and was riding in his Lexus toward home, after having been caught throwing snowballs at cars on Antrim Avenue.

"So where's the truck?" he asked.

I had no idea where it was or how to get there. Thank God Jerome did and told my dad what directions to take. Thank God Jerome didn't swear on the way to the truck—and thank God for tennis balls.

As we traveled in air-conditioned comfort, I tried to downplay the whole ordeal by making small talk, but it was as hard as trying to find your fraternity buddies at the State Fair without a cell phone. Then I blurted out that I had just hired Jerome as my cook and waited for his reaction.

He continued to drive as if he never heard me.

I, then, like a good attorney, tried to plead my case about the expired tabs, but he just sat there driving, so I shut up and watched the yellow meridian stripes come and go along the long-forgotten highway.

When we finally pulled up beside the truck, I saw that every imaginable animal had ransacked it. Jerome started to swear out loud, calling them blankety-blank varmints, but then he caught himself and simply fussed in low tones, while squeezing his tennis ball. All was lost. Not a single head of lettuce, not a single duckling, not an ounce of hamburger, not one corn chip had gone untouched. All of the ice cream had thawed, making one big, soupy pool of strawberry, vanilla and chocolate that swirled about like a contorted concoction of Neapolitan ice cream. And doggone it, if there weren't little tiny coons feet that had left their paw prints all across the hood of the truck, like the signature of a starving artist or a hapless vagabond. One little raccoon was still brave enough to stand his ground as we approached, defending his plunder to the last corn chip. He looked like a little pirate kid with one black furry eye patch and red lips that were smeared with strawberry jam. He suddenly screamed at us in raccoon language, as if we were the ones intruding on his booty. Jerome screamed back in what sounded like the same critter language and the little varmint abandoned ship.

Amazed, I was about to ask if he spoke raccoon, but my dad's voice suddenly interrupted my train of thought.

"You have your work cut out for you, Charlie," he said. He then handed me the license plate tabs and drove away.

I wasn't sure exactly what my dad was thinking that morning. As he did when he caught me throwing snowballs on Antrim Avenue years ago, I'm sure he thought of me as a disappointment, an embarrassment, and an inconvenience from his 375-dollar-an-hour job—and I was mad.

Then it occurred to me why there were people my own age who continually wore black— either on the inside or on the outside. They had tried to adhere to someone else's expectation or standard in life, but had continually fallen short. And the distance between what was expected of them and their failure to obtain it, was in direct proportion to their frustration. With no one to believe in them or accept because they had fallen short of that expectation, they wore black and began to embrace a culture of death, rejecting the very people who reminded them of their apparent lack of ambition to pursue that standard or their failure to obtain it. Ostracized, they formed their own culture and became proud of it, thinking that if the society in which they lived wouldn't accept them for who they were, then they would rebel against it, and define their own.

It suddenly occurred to me that I would never measure up to my parents' standard or expectation, nor did I want to. The irony was that that standard was, in and of itself, a standard of death, because it defined others not by who they were, but by what they did or the car they drove or the money they made, never taking into consideration other more prominent and important elements of life. And to chase that standard was like running a never-ending rat race that continually pitted a person's self-worth against that of his neighbor. Do I measure up, or do I measure down? It was a cancerous perspective that envied those who were more successful than you and frowned upon those who were not.

As I looked at Jerome, I suddenly began to realize that perhaps—perhaps— we had more in common than not.

Later That Night . . . Suppertime

I am getting to be a regular up here on Thomforde Hill and have started to recognize a few of the locals. One of them is a middle-aged man by the name of Gary Brogan. He is a handyman who fixes things. I am guessing that he comes here to get reception like me. He was one of the bluegrass players that I had seen at Miss Maddie's home last Sunday. He waved at me as I passed him on the road. Then I did a U-turn at the top of the hill and pulled up behind him. Finished with his conversation on his phone, he got out of his old pickup truck and walked back to greet me. We shook hands and talked about the café and how good it is that it is going to open. I told him that our grand opening would be this Saturday with a lutefisk dinner starting at five pm for only five dollars per person—and kids five and under eat free. Then next week we plan to open Monday morning at seven with a great big menu. He smiled and said that he will be one of the first ones there. I asked him about his bluegrass music band, and he told me that my uncle was a major part of the group before he died. He misses my uncle and told me that I have the same smile. Heredity, I told him. He smiled and asked me if I play an instrument, and I told him that my mother made me play the violin in fourth grade—but that's about as far as it got. He told me I ought to take it up again. I told him it would be a cold day in July before that happened. He smiled and then told me that we can only hope. He shook my hand again and told me was suppertime, and then he hopped in his truck and headed on down into town.

Suppertime always had a warm and fuzzy feeling about it for me, even if we didn't have many meals together as a family. During my freshman year at the university, I often walked past a simple box home along Elm Street that had a large living room window through which one could peer directly into the kitchen. Late in the fall, when the days grew shorter and the nights grew longer, the kitchen would be lit up in a soft incandescent light. And gathered around the table was a family of four, eating supper together: a father, a mother, and a baby boy in a high chair and his older sister who sat beside him. I would often stop there on the way to the library and would simply stare through the window, watching them eat while wondering what it was they were talking about: simple things, daily things—suppertime things. And I would hope that they would see me standing there and invite me in, but they never did. They never saw me standing out in the cold November wind that whipped across the Twin City skyline. It wasn't so much the food I wanted, but the company. I was a lonely freshman, longing for a place to call home.

I hopped in the back of the truck bed and began texting Karen. There was a text from her from the day before that was asking me where I had been when she called. I then began telling her about yesterday's events as fast as my texting fingers could type. I told her about Jerome, the sheriff, the jail, the raccoons, the groceries, and my dad coming to get me.

Missing you more than you know.

XOXO,

Charlie

Then I started blogging about the day's events and getting hungry thinking of the café and all the different types of menus. "Fellow Bloggers, we are going to have a grand opening this Saturday," I typed, "featuring a lutefisk dinner with Swedish meatballs, lefsa, and the works" (whatever that would be). "And then, starting next week, we will be open for breakfast, featuring French toast with real whipped cream, scones, blueberry pancakes, eggs, sausage, bacon, and gourmet coffee. And for lunch we will have different kinds of sandwiches. For supper, we will have international nights that feature foods from different countries," just like I had envisioned.

Suddenly, I noticed that I had my first blogger on the line. I felt like a fisherman gone mad with the first catch of the day. She was from Anchorage, Alaska, by the name of Queen Crab, and was asking if I had any good recipes for smoked elk meat. No, I replied, but I would look into it. "Do you have any good recipes for lutefisk?" I asked in return. "Wrap it in aluminum foil, bake it at 350 for 40 minutes, serve it with melted butter, and then air out the house for two weeks to get the stink out," she stated. "Funny lady," I replied. "No," she responded back, "I'm serious."

We continued to dialog for another 30 minutes or so, and when we were done, the sun was beginning to set over the top of the adjacent hill, casting a deep shadow across the tall pines, oaks, maples and elm trees that rolled down into the valley below. It was majestic, beautiful, and serene. It was suppertime, and I was missing Karen.

June 11 . . . D-Day Minus Two Days—Preparations for Liftoff

I hired a waitress on Wednesday who said she had some previous experience at the Bullpen Café. Her name was Mildred, but most people in town called her Millie. She was a character with a sense of humor, and I liked that. She was a grandmother with twelve grandchildren and had a knack with words. She was peppy and vivacious, and I got the impression that she could dish it out faster than she could take it. She had been a waitress at the Bullpen three years before, but when her daughter had been diagnosed with breast cancer in Pennsylvania and needed help with her own children, Millie left to help out. She returned when her daughter was cancer-free.

I had no fewer than nine applications for the waitressing job, and I told the rest of the applicants that I would keep them in mind, should we need more help. I did hire a local high school kid as a part-time dishwasher, and he seemed responsible enough. His name was Jared Hildebrandt, and he reminded me of a kid that wasn't quite sure of himself—a little sheepish under the collar. He lived with his mom on the outskirts of town, and I wondered at first if his mother had put him up to the job or if he applied on his own initiative. He was the only high school kid to apply, and I thought I would give him a chance. I told him the same rules I had told Jerome, and he seemed to understand that I was serious. I also mentioned that if I ever caught him texting or talking on his cell phone during work that would be the end of his employment. I had had enough people tell me about us Y-generation's techies and how soft we were when it came to work and how we all believed in entitlements. I told him that—and that he and I were going to prove our critics wrong. It's funny, even though there was only a few years' difference between us, I felt like a dad and a drill sergeant all mixed into one.

These past days had been busy, and I found Jerome to be a hard worker. There were times when he would reach his limit, however, and then shut

64

down, get grumpy and start squeezing his tennis ball. I just needed to find that threshold and keep him from reaching it. The apartment that I put him up in seemed to fit him just fine. The mayor had found us some used furniture and had brought them up himself. Nice man.

We went back to Zumbrota to take care of Jerome's stalled car, but it was nowhere to be seen. When we inquired about it at the police station, they told us it had been impounded for expired license plate tabs. What is it with expired license tabs in Minnesota? Do they have an annual convention with state troopers, county sheriffs, and city police—all getting the mandate from the governor that this month they will be checking for expired tabs?

I wondered.

We had to pay a fine to get it out of the impound lot, and thinking that it was a drug dealer's car, the police had broken into it and torn it apart, looking for secret contraband. In the end, they had found nothing but Jerome's personal belongings: toothbrush, electric shaver, dental floss, and other such weapons of mass destruction. They did, however, leave behind at least one change of clothes and the shirt on his back. The fine, however, was more than the retail value of all his belongings combined.

Now that Jerome's 1983 Chevy Impala had been officially removed and the property values returned to normal in the neighborhood in which it had been parked, we got him settled across the street in the apartment that the mayor had helped furnish. Jerome is up on the second floor, overlooking the main street. He has his own balcony and sits up there in a rocking chair, looking at who knows what. I see him in the early morning hours and late at night, when I get back from texting Karen on top of Thomforde Hill. At night I tell him to get his butt in bed so he can get his beauty rest. He tells me that he ain't gonna get any better looking than what he is right now. In the morning I tell him to get his butt in the café, but he tells me he ain't on the clock yet. It must look funny to the local townspeople having us converse with each other across the street like that. When he asks me about Karen, as I stand in the middle of Main Street, I see Mrs. Ferguson's curtains part just a little from her apartment downstairs. It was as if she had nothing better to do all day than to listen in on our open-air conversation. I had thought yesterday about feeding her a line that Karen was a secret agent in Italy, but knowing how fast rumors can start in Bullpen, I thought it might come back to bite me—and it would be bad for business if they found out later that I was just kidding.

In private, however, I asked Jerome about his own family, to which he told me that he hopes to see them at Christmas. I didn't know he had a family, much less a wife. I guess that was not on the application. Four kids, he told me. One just enlisted in the Navy and the other three are living with their mother's uncle in Memphis. It's funny, but I never really thought of Jerome as a family man. He came to Minnesota to find work after Hurricane Katrina and then got in a fight at a local bar in Redwing. I didn't ask what the fight was about, nor was it any of my business. Apparently, the man he hit was the son of an attorney. Not good. Didn't any one explain that you were not supposed to hit an attorney's son, daughter, wife or distant relative? Didn't he get the company memo? Being an attorney's son myself, I told him he better not hit me or my dad would lock him up for good.

"Yeah . . . ," he said. "I met your old man and saw how he bailed you outta them expired license tabs." He laughed.

When he asked about Karen, I told him about our texting situation. He laughed again and told me, "That ain't no way to love a woman."

"Texting!" he continued. "You and your generation texting . . . whatcha gonna do when you see each other? Text? You gonna text each other in the car and in the store and only god knows where else you gonna text her? . . . Texting . . . that ain't no way to love a woman. Your generation is all messed up with electronic mumbo jumbo."

We argued.

I told him that I am thinking about marrying her.

He laughed again. "You're too young to get married."

"And how old were you when you got married?" I asked him.

"Nineteen," he said, "but we were in love."

"So you were younger than I am when you got married," I replied, resting my case.

"Yeah, but that was different," he said. "We knew each other in grade school. Nowadays kids don't know jack 'bout life. They got all that electronic mumbo jumbo and can't even talk to each other face to face. They sit on them cell phones and text and play video games all day. They don't know what it means to work. . . . All they know is how to be entertained, and the reality of it is, they has got to learn how to work early in life or they'll expect somebody's to do it for them later on. . . . I seen it. . . . Oh yeah, I's seen it . . . Oh yeah .

. . I sees it time and time again. I told my oldest son, 'You better get your butt out there in the real world and stop playing these make-believe games. . . . That ain't doing nothing to prepare you for the real world.'"

We argued some more. Then he asked me when she is coming home. I told him at the end of the month. He smiled as if he knew something I didn't.

"What is it?" I asked him.

"You had better watch your Ps and Qs," he replied. "A woman like that with all that time in Italy? Hmmmm. Sounds to me like she'll be wantin' the world when she comes back . . . You ready for that? You ready to give her the world? And what's her daddy like?"

"Wealthy," I reluctantly tell him. "Actually, he's very, very wealthy."

"Hmmmm. Yeah, I'd keep a short leash on that woman if I was you. But, hey, that's just me."

"What do you mean, 'short leash'?"

He smiled and headed back up to his apartment. "You'll figure it out," he said. "You're one of them bright college graduates—you'll figure it out."

I texted Karen later that night. She had been waiting to hear from me to find out about our preparations for the grand opening on Saturday. She sounded as excited as I was about it. For some reason, the audio reception is bad between us, but texting is clear as a bell, and we had found a way to text each other in real time.

"Went to see the vineyard near Sicily today and thought of you and your homemade wine."

I laughed and texted back, "Moonshine."

I had made some homemade wine in high school, but unlike my friend, Tim Belcher, I had never filtered or processed it. It simply sat in the basement for over two years as the sediment settled to the bottom. The alcohol content was still intact, however, when I brought it to the frat house. It was there that one of my fraternity brothers, Jeff "Lead Foot" Gordon had an idea. Jeff Gordon was the one who asked the nice officer if he could take his food order while being asked to show his driver's license after speeding. Things happened when Jeff had an idea, and the consequences were always interesting, if not always legal. This time he had the brilliant idea of distilling my old apple wine into Everclear—198 proof Everclear. After having obtained the necessary equipment, we went to building the still. The only real problem we had was bending the copper tubing into a coil that would fit inside the Folgers coffee can. We were to heat the wine in the Erlenmeyer flask to the appropriate 78.4 degree temperature, distilling the alcohol vapors through the copper tubing that would circulate up and then through the copper coil that was placed inside the Folgers coffee can, full of ice to help the condensation process. With one hole in the cork top for the copper tubing, the other hole would be for the thermometer to keep it at the proper temperature. Anything less than 78.4 would produce methyl alcohol—a poisonous substance, which was how most moonshiners died during the Prohibition days of the 1930s.

But that would not happen to us. Our thermometer and copper piping (as opposed to lead piping, which results in lead poisoning) kept us—at least in theory—safe. The problem to the whole still, however, was getting the copper tubing to bend into a spring coil shape without kinking it. One of the frat brothers, Tony Wilson, had been a trumpet player in high school and had seen how trumpets were made years ago by filling the brass tubing with sand and then bending it. Sounded good to us. So we filled the copper tube with sand and then sought out the one cylindrical object that we could wrap it around to get the coiled affect. Whatever it was that we wrapped it around, it had to be smaller than the Folgers coffee can, and finding such an object created a challenge. It was then that we discovered that in the woods, not too far from our frat house, stood an elm tree that was the perfect diameter for our copper coil. After wrapping the tube around the coil without any kinks, we looked at each other, wondering how we were going to remove it from the tree.

It was reasoned and then agreed upon that we would have to cut down the tree to obtain our copper tubing. We did so, vowing among ourselves to replant at least two trees next year in memory of the fallen tree that had given its life for our moonshining cause. The fraternity vote was unanimous, and we budgeted two elm trees into our next year's budget and performed a brief but solemn ceremony honoring the dead tree. To our amazement, when we found the tree the next year, it was not dead as we had thought it would be, but was very much alive and had sprouted two more branches from the very trunk that we had cut the prior year. Knowing that, we revisited our budget plans and agreed that the two new branches, in fact, represented two new trees. It was unanimously agreed that no further funds were needed for another two trees.

Now, having our copper coil, we filled the coffee can with ice, fired up the burner, and to our amazement, the gurgling sound of distilled apple Everclear resounded in the kitchen of the frat house—it was almost like the smell of a hot apple pie coming right out of the oven. The sweet aroma permeated every room, and we were anxiously awaiting the results—198 proof Everclear. When Jeff spilled some on the kitchen floor, we quickly noticed that it had peeled the varnish off the dirty linoleum tile, after which some were skeptical to try it. But when Tony lit a spoonful of it and we all saw the baby blue flame illuminating the kitchen, we realized we were on to something special. We then bottled the "recipe" in an old Listerine bottle and would use it only on special frat occasions, signifying the importance of such an event. The motion was seconded, sustained, and passed (Hear, Hear!), then recorded in the annals of the frat book, where it was now authorized and agreed upon by the committee: *E Pluribus Unum*—*humorous sicondum*—to use such a substance only on special occasions—like weekends.

But why stop there, we reasoned. Having mastered the art of distilling apple wine into Everclear, we then proceeded to expand our distilling horizons by making our own mash. Yes, our own mash: bigger and better. Mixing sugar with the starch in potatoes and adding yeast would produce the appropriate results for creating our very own alcohol. The fraternity authorized the purchase of a bag of potatoes and sugar. We then mashed the potatoes while mixing in the sugar. What was missing was the malt that was to help break down the sugar into starch for the yeast to convert into alcohol. Malt was easy enough to find—or so we thought. We then bottled the "potato mash" in two one-gallon glass Mogen David (Mad Dog 20/20) jugs and secured them with their aluminum caps. Two months later, however, after we had forgotten to purchase and then add the malt and yeast, the "new recipe" was now decomposing and creating a CO_2 buildup that had bent and bowed the top of the aluminum caps. A decision had to be made. In an emergency session, we decided to draw straws as to who was to remove the now bulging cap and dispose of the recipe. I found myself on the short end. Not thinking clearly, I went into the bathroom, and as I began to unscrew the aluminum cap, the pressure from the rotten potatoes broke through the last remaining threads on the aluminum cap, and—BOOM!—rotten potato mesh shot out of the glass bottle in NASA proportions.

Houston . . . we have a problem!

The rotten smell took two weeks to dissipate, and of course, I was blamed for it all. Not only did the frat house stink for two weeks, but I was the one who stood there like an idiot, taking the majority of blows to the face. And adding insult to injury, Karen would not come near me for two weeks.

"I am laughing," I texted. "Does the word 'recipe' mean anything to you?"

"Yep," she replied.

I love it when she says "yep" . . . . I just love the way she spells that word. I can almost hear her say it—long and drawn out. It was then I realized that I was going to find an engagement ring and present it to her when she got back from Italy.

"Tomorrow Jerome and I go to New Ulm to pick up the lutefisk for the grand opening on Saturday," I wrote. "Wish us well . . . Missing you more than you know."

XOXO

Charlie

June 12…..Picking up the Lutefisk

We drove around New Ulm and finally found the lutefisk supplier. It somehow reminded me of a clandestine business, located in a secret cavity of society and somewhat inconspicuous of its presence. It's not like you see lutefisk being advertised right next to McDonald's or Arby's or Wendy's . . . . You see Mexican foods, Chinese foods and Italian foods, but why is it that Scandinavians are ashamed to admit they too have foods? Could it be that lutefisk has anything to do with it?

I wondered.

When I called in the order, I was trying to calculate how much to buy. It's not like people are clamoring over leftover lutefisk or anything, so I didn't want to fall short—yet I didn't want to be left with too much. I had tried to order it right in order to make the economies of scale work on my behalf. It was like those long-distance plans with Sprint or Verizon. You had so many minutes in your plan each month, and if you went over your minutes, you were charged more, and if you were under your monthly minutes, you didn't get your money's worth. You had to hit your usage of minutes right on or it was a win-win situation for the long distance providers and a lose-lose for you as a customer. It was smart marketing on their part.

So not knowing how many people would be there for the grand opening, I decided on the nice round number of 268, hoping that it would be enough servings. Who would know? I had run ads in the local papers surrounding Bullpen and hoped to get a decent crowd. One publisher was going to send out his food editor. That's right, food editor. Yes, I could see us filming the *Today* show with guinea pigs—literally guinea pigs—to sample the main dishes. My concern was would the people come? Getting the kitchen ready and having the health department out to inspect it was another story. Thank God my uncle had had it upgraded with stainless steel appliances, modern coolers and freezers, and everything else I needed to be street legal.

Jerome was grumpy all afternoon and complained about this and that the whole time we were loading the lutefisk. He even covered his nose with the top of his shirt, looking like an outlaw. It was an obvious exaggeration, and I let it slide, until he started to verbally abuse my Scandinavian heritage.

"I aint gonna cook this sh__! Whose gonna eat this sh__?! You mean to tell me that them Scandahoovians is really gonna eat this sh__?!"

It was like every other word had the sh___ word in it, and I had had enough. I told him he had better shut up or find himself another job. We were having lutefisk and that was that.

Jerome then grew quiet and began murmuring what sounded like swear words under this shirt.

On the way out of town, I stopped at the local hardware store and bought him another tennis ball.

Later That Night . . . T minus 22 Hours

We were scrambling when we got back. I wasn't really sure how this lutefisk thing was going to pan out. You cook things wrong, and things can go bad in a hurry. Your reputation can be tarnished for life. You don't get a second chance at a first impression.

I had asked Millie how my Uncle Roy used to cook lutefisk. She told me he used a large kettle and boiled it. Why hadn't I thought about that earlier? The only problem was I couldn't find it.

To my surprise, Jerome had found an old tool shed in the back of the lot, next to the alley. He suggested smoking the fish on racks with aluminum foil. Thinking that maybe the blogger from Anchorage, Alaska, was right, that we might not be able to get the stink out for at least two weeks, I made the first executive decision of my café career and defaulted to Jerome's idea of a smokehouse out back. That way we could keep the kitchen focused on the accessorial foods like Swedish meatballs and mashed potatoes. We had forgotten to buy the precooked meatballs, but Millie said that they were no good anyway. Handmade was best and she had a great recipe. I told her to go for it.

T minus 21 hours and counting . . .

Jerome was busy jerry-rigging the tool shed for the smoker. He had removed most of the tools and was now in search of a smoker.

T minus 20 hours and counting . . .

I'm helping Millie with forming meatballs, I called in reinforcements and texted Jared to come help. He did. It's funny how many little meatballs you can make in a minute—like one—if you are good. There has to be a faster way.

T minus 18 hours and counting . . .

Millie and Jared set up tables and chairs, and Jared checked to make sure the dishwasher worked—good thinking, Jared.

T minus 17 hours and counting . . .

Did I forget to mention the radio ad? We heard it on the local station and Millie shouted excitedly, "That's us!" I guess that is the first time Bullpen has been mentioned outside of Bullpen . . .

T minus 16 hours and counting . . .

Those little bugger meatballs. You try to roll them just right in the palm of your hand, and after a while it seems like all your hand does is spin around and around and around and around . . .

T minus 14 hours and counting . . .

Jerome found a smoker. It is a pot-belly stove from Alfred Morgan's ice fishing house. Jerome says it will do. It ain't the kind he uses in the Bayous of Louisiana to smoke shrimp, but it will do.

T minus 13 hours and counting . . .

It's four am. Millie went home at midnight and will be back in a few hours. Jerome fell asleep on the counter of the smokehouse while duct taping the PVC shelves.

T minus 12 hours and counting . . .

It was rumored earlier that Jerome was a French chef from Paris. When asked about his cooking background, I simply told people that he liked to experiment with a lot of different kinds of foods—including lutefisk. That seemed to appease them, and being an English major with an interest in marketing, I left it at that.

June 13..... The Grand Opening

It was 12:37 pm, and I didn't really know what I was doing. I found myself doing things for the sake of doing things, often doing the same thing that I had been doing only moments before. So what was there to be nervous about in Bullpen? Carnegie Hall maybe, but Bullpen? Who was there to impress? Could it have to do with the food editor from one of the local papers? It was like opening night, and if the reviews soured, so could my franchising opportunities. After all, there must be thousands, if not millions, of restaurant goers that are tired of the same old fast food every day. Who wants to eat hamburger when you can eat lutefisk?

I was now in constant motion trying to take care of the last remaining details. I had just hung our banner outside, announcing our "All you can eat lutefisk dinner from five to eight pm for $6.50 per person and free to children five and under."

Jerome's job was to man the smokehouse and make sure that the serving trays on the buffet counter were kept constantly filled. He was proud of his job and his makeshift, jerry-rigged, new-and-improved smokehouse out back. Quite honestly, I am surprised at how well it turned out. He had removed all of the two-cycle engines, cleaned out the place, and put up left over PVC pipe as shelves. He secured it all with duct tape that even Red Green would have been proud of. For the smoker, he simply turned the vent pipe of the pot belly stove back into the shed, then cut out a few exhaust holes on the side of the shed. As far as his obvious displeasure of the smell of cooking lutefisk, he wore a scarf around his nose, looking like a small kid whose mother had bundled him up to protect him from the arctic throes of a Minnesota winter. He then carried about a stoker he called a prod to tend the fire and maintain the proper temperature—whatever that was.

I gave Jared the job of potatoes: peeling, boiling, mashing and serving—in addition to his dishwashing responsibilities. Millie took care of the Swedish meatballs and the accessorial dishes like the lefse. Yes, lefse—that Scandinavian flat bread made from potatoes. We had picked it up the same day we brought home the lutefisk. Some people like theirs with butter and brown sugar. Others simply like it with butter. One fellow in town, Slater Gray, told me he likes his with sour cream, so I bought an extra bin of sour cream for Slater, if for no one else. I figured if this café is going to make it outside of the community, then I would have to please even the least common denominator—even Slater Gray.

Thirty minutes before takeoff, Millie discovered that the cash register drawer was not opening. She ran home and woke up her husband, Maynard, who had been minding his own business and taking an afternoon nap and enjoying his early retirement from the post office.

"This ain't no time to be nappin', Maynard!" she told him in no uncertain terms, pulling him off the sofa. She then dragged him all the way to the café.

She stood him up in front of the cash register while he was still waking up, and when he tipped over, his left elbow hit the dollar tab on the cash register. Lo and behold, the drawer popped open and caught him just below the belt. He worked the cash register the rest of the night and was still wincing from pain a few hours later. God bless him.

In need of more help, Millie grabbed one of her friends, Melissa Magnuson. Like Millie, Melissa was a grandmother and just as feisty. Watching the two of them working together, however, was like watching trapeze artists as they swirled in and out and around each other, laying down plates and cups and silverware with the greatest of ease.

As the clock approached 4:58, I took a look outside. To my amazement, there was a line a block long.

"Stations, everybody. Man your stations!"

Jared brought in the potatoes, Jerome brought in a platter full of fish, and Millie laid out the Swedish meatballs, lefse, and desert. I stood behind the counter ready to serve.

When the clock struck five, Millie let out a yell: "Now, Maynard—now! Open the front door!"

Bent over at the waist and still wincing from pain, Maynard shuffled over to the door, turned the latch, and the floodgate opened.

Houston, we have liftoff.

Later That Night . . . Very Smoked Lutefisk

When the fire trucks from the surrounding areas finally left, it was after midnight. The smokehouse had gotten a little too hot and had burned to the ground. I can still see Jerome's valiant effort to save it from total ruin as he ran back and forth with buckets of water. Those who had already eaten volunteered as a bucket brigade, until Slater Gray brought over his garden hose. Unfortunately, the water pressure was not enough to fight a fire that had already gone mad with flames. By the time the local fire department arrived, all they could do was spray the adjacent homes to keep them from catching on fire.

Not all was lost, however. Before the smoke house had completely burned to the ground, Jerome had managed to save the rest of the lutefisk by making mad dashes to the kitchen with the scarf still wrapped around his face while his dirty, outstretched hands cradled large globs of smoked fish. It was a noble cause by anyone's standards. He had risked his life (foolishly I might add) to save the very food he detested. In the midst of all the commotion, however, the food editor arrived. With nothing to do but eat, and not knowing at the time that she was eating lutefisk from the now defunct smoker, she declared that she had never tasted anything so delicious, and asked me for the recipe.

What do you say in a moment like that? The recipe . . . yes, the recipe: you first heat up the pot-belly stove in an old tool shed, stained with 40-year-old oil spills, until it is good and smoky. You then smoke the lutefisk, pulling it out with your dirty, bare hands just moments before the shed burns down. Could there be any easier recipe to follow?

As the fire trucks continued to pour water on the smoldering smokehouse, Homer Robertson, one of the first to arrive, told me he had paid for six of his lady friends and had not had such a good time in years.

"Quite an event," he said.

I agreed.

Then he winked at me.

"Thanks for coming to Bullpen," he said at last and then shuffled on down the street as he had done days before while the red flashing lights of the fire trucks danced across the silhouette of his fragile frame—on again, off again, marking time like a beating heart.

June 14 . . . Cajun Country

I never intended to attend church today. I had intended to sleep in after a red-letter night at the café. I was going to find a Sunday newspaper, make myself a big cup of coffee, and chill out on the balcony—until I heard someone pounding on my door.

It was Jerome.

"You in there, Charlie? You sleepin'? Cause if you is, you better get your sorry butt movin' boy. It's Sunday and you is gonna be late for church. Don't make me come and get you. Don't make me come and drag your sorry butt out of bed—you hear me, Charlie? You hear me?"

That was the problem. I heard him. We all heard him. Half the town of Bullpen could hear him. .

Mad and grumpy, I staggered out of bed and got dressed. We arrived 10 minutes late. This time I wore something respectable—my Minnesota Twins shirt. As we swung into the parking lot, I advised him not to enter what I had thought was the back door. "Why not?" he asked.

I then told him about my grand entrance last week, and he laughed.

"I ain't never seen no one lock themselves in a closet up front and all. Man you must a been embarrassed. Too bad I wasn't there to see it."

"Yeah, too bad," I told him, giving him my best imitation of the Finstune family glare.

We walked around to the back of the church where Ole Gunderson's fifth wife had been buried and entered as quietly as possible during the opening hymn. And doggone it, we would have gone undetected had it not been for the fact that Jerome had to sing his heart out—just a half note off key in his monotone voice, just enough to make you want to get out a tuner, go down his throat and tweak his vocal chords. And when the song came to an abrupt end, Jerome kept on singing.

Startled, he stopped and then stared at the congregation as if wondering what happened—as if someone had forgotten to give him the church memo about only singing verses one, two, and three.

He smiled apologetically and mumbled, "Well, ain't we gonna sing verse four?"

The congregation laughed, and the pastor nodded politely; then he told the organist to play verse four. And we did. We had done the unthinkable. We had sung all four verses out of the Lutheran hymnal. In all my church going days we had never sung all four verses of any song in any hymnal. It went against the teaching of Martin Luther and was specifically mentioned in the 96th thesis, an addendum to the 95 theses that he had originally nailed to the door of the All Saints Church in Wittenberg, Germany, in 1517. Every good Lutheran knew that. Seminary students were taught it from the classroom and preached it from the pulpit, knowing full well that it could be grounds for excommunication should the news ever reach the ELCA, the LCA, or the Missouri Synod headquarters.

"So why on God's green earth do they print all four verses if you ain't suppose' to sing them?" he whispered to me during the announcements that soon followed.

"Because no Lutheran service is supposed to last more than 45 minutes or go beyond the opening kickoff on NFL Sunday," I whispered back.

He nodded as if he understood.

The service continued, and the pastor's sermon was on the topic of forgiveness and the consequences of sin. But not having been adequately primed with coffee, I found myself dozing off. Jerome, however, had fallen completely asleep and was now in zozo land, snoring as loudly as he had done in jail. I poked him with a jab, and he woke up mumbling. It suddenly occurred to me that he had not sworn at all that morning, nor did he bring his tennis ball. He shot up apologetically and then, blinking profusely, he began listening intently to the rest of the sermon. The only other person that I could see that had dozed off was Homer, and you could hear him snoring above the faint noise of the ceiling fans.

Just when I thought Jerome was going to nod off again, the pastor made mention of sin and its consequences of hell. Like a knee jerk reaction, Jerome shot up and was the first (and only) one to cry out: "Amen! Oh yeah, you preachin' now, Pastor—you preachin' now."

I sat there a little embarrassed, as were others around me. When he interrupted the pastor for the third time with his amening and "preach-it-now" accolades, the pastor stopped midsentence. You could hear a pin drop. Even

Homer had stopped snoring. It was as if time itself had stopped in Bullpen. We all sat there in the awkward silence, awaiting the pastor's reaction. It was like NFL fans that waited for the official ruling from the instant replay booth after a questionable call. Would he allow such spontaneous outbursts in his congregation like that again? We wondered.

When a smile broke across the pastor's face, a sigh of relief swept across the congregation. It was as if a salty ray of acceptance had just been handed to the church on a silver platter. Even Homer was smiling, and the starch-infested atmosphere suddenly erupted into laughter.

Jerome suddenly seemed proud of himself, beaming with delight—as if he had single handedly pulled the emotions out of an emotionally constipated congregation. He began to affirm his new found place within the community by amening this and amening that. His enthusiasm was like a contagious sea, and the little children were the first to jump in.

When the last hymn was sung, it was Jerome—tennis ball squeezing Jerome—that was leading the charge by clapping his hands and singing at the top of his monotone voice. He had brought a new sense of joy to Bullpen that day. He brought Cajun spices to the plain bread, butter, and potatoes that it had been accustomed to. Although his enthusiasm was a little spicy for some, I sensed that all of us had at least come to respect its flavor.

When the service ended, the people flocked to the back of the church to shake his hand. Beaming like a rock star, he started in on the future of the café.

"Oh yeah, you ain't seen nothin' yet. We's gonna have gumbo shrimp and Creole with dirty rice and boudin balls, and Cajun deep fried turkey with dirty rice, and chicken okra gumbo with dirty rice ..."

Dirty rice? Who said anything about dirty rice? I suddenly had visions of the health department closing us down on account of "dirty rice." I was about to interject my own thoughts on the matter, but stopped. Jerome was on a roll. Mount Vesuvius had erupted—and instead of expletives, he was spewing out Cajun recipes as fast as his Louisiana tongue could talk.

"... and crock pot jambalaya with dirty rice, and bouillabaisse with rouille, and Popeye's biscuit twin, and ..."

Although he was speaking a foreign language and the folks around him looked like deer caught in the headlight of a fast-moving freight train, and although I wasn't sure about featuring all this Cajun cooking stuff at the café, I decided to let the freight train roll.

After all, who was I to stop it?

Later That Afternoon . . . Tea with Miss Maddie

I had received my first letter in the mail—snail mail as we call it—from Miss Maddie earlier in the week. I had never read it until I opened it after church. It was an invitation to join her for lunch, written on a small three-by-five-inch envelope with a formal invitation card inside. It was a most interesting card with a large Monarch butterfly on the outside, resting on what looked like a marigold flower. It almost reminded me of her garden. On the inside of the card was written a personal note inviting me to tea this afternoon at two o'clock on her veranda.

"I would love to have you join me if you can."

Signed, Miss Maddie

Tea, I thought to myself. It sounded so formal, so English, and so southern. It was then I remembered a book I had read years ago called *A Cup of Christmas Tea*, and in spite of all the things I had to do to prepare for tomorrow's unofficial first day at the café, I decided to go.

I arrived a little after two o'clock and found Miss Maddie on her knees, working in the garden. I didn't recognize her at first in her wide-brimmed straw hat, bib overalls, work boots, oversized gardening gloves and pruning shears. In an odd kind of way, she reminded me of Katharine Hepburn in her performance with Henry Fonda in the movie *On Golden Pond*. Only a few hours before, I had seen her in church looking so dignified, but she had made no mention of her invitation to me then. Perhaps she thought that I had declined her offer. I must have startled her when I came up behind her, because she took a good long look at me from behind her bifocals.

"Charles!" she suddenly cried enthusiastically. "I didn't recognize you at first. So good of you to come."

Before I could say a word, she handed me a pruning shear and told me that she needed help pruning some dead rose bushes.

"No problem," I replied.

She then took my hand, as only old people can do, and walked me over to a thicket of blooming rose bushes.

"It's time to get rid of these dead heads," she stated, peering down upon the roses above her bifocals.

She then gave me brief instructions on how to "summer prune" rose bushes by cutting out the dead branches and the dead blooms in order to make way for the new growth. She called it "dead heading" with an uncanny vigor that startled me coming from such an old lady.

"Got to get rid of all these old dead heads to make room for the new growth," she said like a military drill sergeant.

I nodded like a bobblehead as she showed me what to do with the pruning shears. Then it was my turn, and I was in the thick of it—literally—until I pricked myself.

As I turned to ask her if she had any gloves for me, she was already pulling them out of a five-gallon pail and throwing them to me.

"Thanks," I replied.

They were new gloves, soft and leathery. And they fit—well, like a glove. I found it odd that she would buy a larger pair of gloves that just happened to fit me. Perhaps she knew I would come despite the fact that I had not sent her an RSVP. Whatever the reason, they were a welcome addition to my work among the thorns.

When I finished, I stood back to admire my work, but the rose bushes all looked as if I had just given them their first haircut.

"What do you think?' I asked her.

She got up off her knees, approached the bushes, and without so much as a word, she peered over her bifocals and began to laugh.

"They'll grow back," she said reassuringly. "They'll grow back."

When we did finally get around to "Tea" it was after four o'clock, and the hot summer sun had begun its descent. I was sweating profusely as she sat me down on the porch and departed. She returned moments later with lunch: chicken salad sandwiches, pickled cucumbers, glorified rice (as opposed to dirty rice), pecan pie, and freshly squeezed lemonade.

"Miss Maddie, you can come and cook at the café any time you want," I told her. She smiled and told me that I had a lot of work ahead at the cafe.

I agreed and then I told her about my ideas.

"Instead of offering three meals a day, why don't you offer two to get your feet wet?" she suggested.

I nodded and told her that might be a good idea.

"Oh, it's a great idea. You will run yourself ragged. You need some time to yourself, Charles, and you can't get it making three square meals a day and doing all that Cajun cooking."

She winked at me. "Oh, that Cajun food is good. I've been praying we get some of that around here."

I smiled and suddenly felt at home. She took her glass of lemonade and held it out for me to toast. I took mine and we clinked glasses.

"To the Bullpen Café!" she toasted.

"To the Bullpen Café," I replied.

Suddenly she stopped, as if listening to something through an imaginary headset. She tilted her head and began to smile.

"And may the Lord bless you and keep you, and may the good Lord make his face to shine upon you and be gracious unto you and give you peace."

She paused as if she still had unfinished business. Then she reached out, grabbed my hand, and continued in what sounded like an earnest prayer request.

"Lord, guide this man's steps. You have brought him here for your purpose and your calling. Let his voice be heard from the north and the south and the east and the west. Oh God of humble beginnings, make your name known in all the earth and bring about revival in his heart and in the heart of his family and the nation. Oh Lord, we repent for our nation and how we have forgotten you. Bring about revival, oh Lord . . . Bring about revival."

She started to shake, and as quickly as she had started, she stopped and became suddenly quiet and still.

"Yes, Lord," she said aloud. "Yes, Lord . . . strengthen him for the work ahead. Oh God of Abraham and Isaac and Jacob, strengthen him for the work ahead. In Jesus mighty name I pray . . . amen."

She wiped the tears from her eyes and smiled at me. My hand was still held tightly in hers. She slowly let it go.

"That word was from the Lord, Charles. That was from the Lord," she said excitedly.

What do you do with something like that? My mind was racing. Was she a nut case? I suddenly felt awkward and wanted to leave, but something held me there. It was a velvety feeling that bypassed my better judgment. I felt like a drunk in a stupor, but I was cognizant of all that was going on around me. It was as if I had just come out of the operating room and wanted nothing more than to take a long, long nap.

Houston? Do you copy?

82

Later That Night . . . The Beauty of Blogging

I took a nap when I got home—a long nap—and then went over to Jerome's apartment to tell him the plans about only two meals a day as Miss Maddie had suggested—breakfast and lunch—until we get our feet on the ground. He seemed reluctant—as if I had taken the wind out of his Cajun sails—but then he agreed. His dirty rice recipes would have to wait. We then planned out breakfast. All of the scones and hush puppy pancakes and hash browns would have to wait for now. We would keep things simple. For breakfast we would have oatmeal, fried eggs, regular pancakes (until we found the recipe for Roy's famous hush puppy pancakes, which was, hopefully, in the archives of the office), ham, juice, and coffee. For lunch we would have three types of sandwiches—ham, turkey, and roast beef—with potato chips and coffee or a fountain drink. We would make it known tomorrow that we would be charging $2.50 for a cup of coffee. Jerome felt it was too high, but I felt we needed to fire a shot across the bow and see what the reaction would be. I wasn't going to serve just ordinary coffee. I was going to serve a special blend that we had obtained from a supplier in Montgomery, Minnesota. If for nothing else, the Bullpen Café would be known for the best coffee around. That, I hoped, would be worth the drive.

We were to open at seven am and close at three o'clock in the afternoon. Depending on help, our profits, and the interest in the community, we would forgo the supper menu until we could justify adding it. It was a business decision, and Jerome seemed to agree.

I had everything else we needed for the first unofficial day. Millie was to come in at 6:30. Jerome and I would be there at 5:30, just to make sure everything was prepared as it should be. I had place mats made up at a local print shop in Rochester, Minnesota. They featured a "Quiz of the Week" and "Bullpen Remembered" with a special article about the notorious Ole Gunderson. There were also local business ads highlighting the Bullpen Elevator, Baker's Garage, Eddie's Gas and Go, the Grandview Laundry Mat, Annie's Car Wash (and Wax), the Watkins Curiosity Shoppe, Jake's Welding, local insurance agent Terrell Paulson (AKA the Mayor). There was no grocery store in Bullpen or hardware store. The only thing that came close to a convenience store was

Eddie's Gas and Go. With the advent of the credit card swiping machine, it was open 24-7 for gas and eight to five for such necessities as milk, bread, eggs, candy bars, and, of course, dental floss.

Being the new owner in town, I had received an invitation from the local business owners to their monthly Rotary meeting next Wednesday at seven pm. The agenda? Beats me. I just felt it a privilege and honor to be part of such a prestigious society.

It had been two days since I had texted Karen and wondered how she was doing in Italy. I drove to the top of Thomforde Hill and parked in my usual spot alongside the road. Putting on some bug spray, I hopped in the truck bed. It is argued that the mosquito is better suited to be the Minnesota state bird than the loon. I tend to agree. It is a feisty little bugger, to put it nicely. I wondered why God had created such a despicable thing. Could it be that it provides itself as food for bats and other birds? Regardless of how it tastes to others, it is a pesky little thing that swarms, buzzes and bites. Tonight it was better up on the hill than down below, but after only a few minutes, word gets out on the mosquito community billboard or the company memo that there is fresh blood to be had—and they all come buzzing—grandpa, grandma, dad, mom, and their children with their blood sucking needles. It is as if they all suddenly appear after 9:30. I am guessing that is when their curfew ends. Needless to say, I came prepared with repellant. I could text and type in the cab, but on such a nice night as this, I preferred to be outside.

Karen had left a few messages, and I could tell she was not her usual self—not as perky as at other times. She said she was fighting a cold and it was wearing on her. I was reminded of the time I made chicken soup and brought it to her dorm in a thermos bottle. It was Campbell's chicken soup out of a can that I had heated up, but she thought it was wonderful—or at least she said so. She was so doggone cute in her extra-long PJs and her fuzzy moccasins and her stuffed-up Rudolph-the-Red-Nose-Reindeer nose. And seeing her smile at me as she grasped the thermos with both hands and sipped the soup like coffee did something to my insides. It's funny, but that was the first time I had thought about marrying her.

I left a few more texts describing the events of the Grand Opening. It suddenly all seemed so far way. I just wanted to hear her voice. I looked at the calendar on my cell phone. She would be returning in 10 days and I would be there to meet her at the airport and give her the engagement ring—well, maybe I would wait a *few* minutes until she found her bags. Wouldn't that be romantic, getting on my knees and proposing to her in front of the United baggage claim carousel? How many women had been proposed to like that with all of the baggage going on around them, huh? Not many. And the old security officer who would validate your baggage ticket would be crying, wishing he too had proposed to his wife at the United baggage carousel. And people everywhere would perk up, knowing that there is love in the air. Displaced flyers and disgruntled customers that had their luggage shipped to a different city by mistake would suddenly forget their desperate situation, knowing that the one, and now only, pair of underwear that they wore was nothing compared to the future bliss of two people who were in love. And we would hold hands and run through the airport in slow motion.

I would get her ring tomorrow, if time permitted. I would Google jewelry stores within a 40-mile radius and see what came up.

I then opened my laptop and began to blog about the past events from Bullpen. I told Queen Crab from Anchorage that I am still working on finding her a recipe for smoked elk meat, but that I do have a great recipe for smoked lutefisk.

She blogged back with a smiley face.

I now had four bloggers beginning to follow my life in Bullpen: Anchorage, Dallas, New York, and Oregon. Wow! I thought about four people whom I have never met who are out there in cyber space reading my stuff. I thought it must be a lot like a disc jockey at a radio station, late at night, not really knowing who is out there or who is listening.

Houston?

There was a sliver of moon tonight, and I thought again about Apollo 13, as the three astronauts rounded the far side of the moon, not knowing if they would ever regain communications with earth. What were they thinking during those silent minutes—those agonizing minutes—on the far side of the moon?

I looked at the stars in the sky and sat amazed at the notion of technology. It has brought us all together yet, at the same time, taken us farther apart. It is an irony. Are we really closer to each other than we were 15 years ago? Or 22 years ago? Yes, we can have more relationships, but are they any deeper than what people had before? Can you really befriend a blogger out there in space? I started thinking about relationships and commitment. You could have a circle of blogging friends that have a common interest, like cars or food or gardening, but that might be all the farther the relationship went. Was that any different than the traditional brick and mortar, face-to-face relationships between people? And what about my frat buddies? Were we any closer to each other than a blogger that you have never met outside of the Internet? Was our generation defying the normal definition of the word "relationship" by the tools we used and the number of Internet acquaintances we had?

I wondered.

The acid test seemed to be if they would make an appearance in the flesh—face to face—if they had to? Would they be there for you in the clutch or tight moments? Would you be there for them? Would there be any commitment apart from mere words?

I then had a blogger from Georgia tell me I am a prejudiced, white bast___. He had issues with what I said about Jesse Jackson. I replied to him that, since I am not running for office, I tell the truth. I call them as I see them. I assured him that I am not prejudiced and that my heroes are Denzel Washington and Bill Cosby—and not necessarily in that order. I also told him I love Chris Rock and Ray Charles, and if that doesn't make me colorblind, then what will?

He fired back with more expletives.

I told him that, since he is from Georgia, he should look up George Washington Carver and see how he, more than any other man, had saved the South from total economic ruin by his discovery of the many uses for the peanut. Until that time, the South had relied heavily on cotton as their primary source of income, but after the Civil War and the devastation caused by the boll weevil, cotton was anything but king. Think about that, I told him. The reason he made all those discoveries is because Jesse Jackson wasn't born yet to tell him he was too oppressed to do it.

I hit a nerve—more expletives.

Then I told him to think about not trying to think about a pink elephant with blue polka dots. Then I challenged him not to think about a red dump truck or a yellow pony. It is impossible not to do so. You cannot *not* think about what you have been told *not* to think about. And the irony is, in the process of trying *not* to think about it, you become the very thing you are trying *not* to become. Irony of ironies. If you try to think about not becoming a failure, then you will become one, because that is where your focus and attention lies. When you are constantly thinking about how bad you have it, you cannot possibly think about what you might do to succeed. You have an invisible, psychological glass ceiling over your head that prohibits you from doing so because your mind tells you that you can't—you are too oppressed. And it's not your fault—it never is. There is always someone else to blame for your problems, while you are simply the victim or the martyr. It is an ugly mindset, and I told him so.

More expletives and name-calling.

I told him that that mindset has no color boundaries. The same mental constraints can affect any one—especially athletes. The athletes that are trying so hard *not* to make mistakes are the ones more prone to do so. Look at old NFL films of Jim Kelly from the Buffalo Bills, I told him. During their fourth visit to the Super Bowl, you could see him ranting and raving on the sidelines when they were losing. Why? Because they *had* to win the game. Why was he so vehement? Because Buffalo had already lost three other Super Bowls and the pressure to break that "curse" was exponential. The problem was just that. They weren't focused so much on winning the game as they were on not losing it. And that was the problem. Their focus was on "not failing" rather than playing the game for the game's sake and allowing their own physical abilities to take over, which would free them from the shackles of a premeditated constraint that preoccupied their entire thought process. "We cannot lose this game" is a completely different focus from what it should have been. "We can win this game" should have been their focus—and they could have won, they *should* have won—but they didn't. They were thinking about pink elephants with blue polka dots.

"Well, what about racial profiling?" he suddenly interjected. "You said yourself that you had racially profiled Jerome the first time you met him, and that is why you almost didn't hire him—and then the sheriff was racially profiling him, too. You don't call that prejudice?!!"

Wow…so this guy *has* been reading my stuff! I am impressed. I suddenly feel like a real, full-fledged writer that has something people are interested in reading, whether they agree with me or not . . . I am honored and amazed. I am feeling like a talk show host, and we are now starting to engage in a real argument, with real points of discussion, rather than resorting to name-calling and swear words. It is like a good tennis match, and he has returned my serve. I suddenly feel those ancient, argumentative Finstune family genetics kicking in—the same genetics that were there at the Diet of Worms and the pre-battle plans of Waterloo and at campfires, generations ago, when great-great- great-great-great grandpa Flintstone—I mean Finstune—decided to fight with words instead of clubs.

"I am impressed," I told him. "You have been reading my stuff. Good point. But the sheriff and I were not the only ones racially profiling that day. We all racially profile—even Jerome. It becomes our point of reference to make sense of the world. Of course, we are going to see differences. We can't help but see differences and make judgments. But racial profiling goes beyond just race. We profile based on age, sex, economic status, body size, clothes, language and culture. It is part of our makeup. When 911 happened, do you think Americans were not "racially" profiling people who looked like the terrorists? Everyone did—especially those who were flying. Yes, black people and white people and yellow people and red people and green people and blue people were all profiling after 911. We all profile—it is a way of making sense of the world. Look at the Dewey Decimal system in the library. It archives books based on topics and authors and fiction and non-fiction. Do you call that racial profiling?"

He told me that I never had to sit in the back of the bus.

I asked him if he has ever had to sit at the back of the bus.

"No," he replied, "but that attitude is still there after all these years."

How can you argue with that? You can't. It is one man's opinion on how he sees his world.

"If a black man in a sharp-looking business suit walked into Macys (which they do), how would you profile him?" I asked.

"Yeah, but that's different," he replied.

"How?" I asked.

"You don't know what he had to go through to beat out a white man."

We were not going anywhere, so I decided to end the tennis match.

"If you are looking for excuses not to succeed or blame others for your own failures, then you will find them. It's called 'playing the victim,'" I told him. "I rest my case."

He called me a bigot. I called him blind. We ended by calling each other names. Isn't blogging great?

I finished the night thinking, "Wow! . . . I just had a deep, psychological interlude with someone out there I don't even know—through technology. I have never had a discussion like that before with any of my frat buddies—and four of them are black.

You copy that, Houston?

June 15 . . . The "Official" Opening

Things went relatively smooth at first for the first official opening day of the café. There were a few minor glitches, like finding the oatmeal and the toaster that had been misplaced Saturday night. But other than that, things went well. I believe that hearing news about the grand opening had a great deal to do with its success. It's funny, but word spreads like wildfire—literally—in a small community. We had a few "guests" from the surrounding towns, and there was actually a line at the door (only five, but hey, it was still a line) when we opened at seven. No, Maynard did not open the door again. Millie did, and she looked as proud as a peacock in her checkered black-and-white apron that resembled the starting flag for the Daytona 500. We were now officially open for business, and Slater Gray—the one who had lent us his garden hose to put out the fire Saturday night—was first in line with a bouquet of flowers from his garden. Nice.

Slater was a retired schoolteacher who taught botany, and he prided himself on knowing every kind of herb and plant this side of the Mississippi River—and beyond. He liked our placemats and had a few riddles of his own he wanted to suggest.

"Great," I told him.

It appeared that Slater was taking mental ownership of the café. This was good. He read the article about Ole Gunderson and told me I had made a few grammatical mistakes. What? I am an English major, and I told him so.

"I proofread everything." I told him.

"Well, not this time," he told me proudly and pointed out that *weather* and *whether* are commonly confused, as are the words *then* and *than*.

"Well *than* . . . er . . . *then*," I told him, admitting my mistake, "I guess I had better let you proofread my articles before I send them to press."

He seemed delighted to help out. Than . . . I mean, *then* . . . he told me that the article about Ole Gunderson was not entirely true. Ole Gunderson never went to the Chicago World's Fair of 1893 and never met a nightclub singer there by the name of Elvira.

What?! The Bullpen annals of history have been distorted?

"Yes," he said. "Quite so. Harold Flom was Ole's second cousin and had invited Ole to Chicago to see the World's Fair and all the vaudeville acts that accompanied it, but Ole's fourth wife, Agnes, would not let him go. She knew the inherent dangers of the World's Fair mania and all that could lurk there. She told Ole, in no uncertain terms, that if he went, they were through—caput." Slater then ran a finger across his throat like a knife blade.

"Caput? That serious?" I asked.

"Worse," he replied. "She would go back to Norway and spread vicious rumors about Ole to his kinfolk."

"Wow!" I found myself saying out loud. "This is like tabloid news stuff."

"It gets worse," replied Slater. "To prove he wore the pants of the family, Ole took off for the Chicago World's Fair of 1893 in spite of her warnings. Halfway to Chicago, however, his conscience got the better of him—and not willing to part with his beloved wife, Agnes (or be talked about back in Norway), he stopped in Racine, Wisconsin, for the night, planning to turn back the next day, but found himself in a nightclub with Sven Osgaard—his traveling buddy—and that's where he met Lily."

"Lily?"

Slater nodded profusely. "Precisely."

"Well, did he—you know—did anything ever come of that night between— you know—Lily and Ole?"

"A good Lutheran like Ole . . . ? Banish the thought! Banish the very thought."

"Well, what about the . . .you know . . .the . . . indiscriminate pictures of Lily that clouded the better judgment of his livestock farming buddies when they were looking to name the town. How did they get in the hands of Ole?"

"They weren't actually pictures of Lily. They were of another showgirl named Elvira! Sven was a real practical jokester and put them in Ole's traveling bag. When Ole got home, who do you suppose found them?"

"Agnes?" I replied.

"Precisely—but it was all Sven's fault! Ole pleaded innocent, and Sven even came to confess the truth about the matter, but Agnes had made up her mind and sailed on the next boat back to Norway."

"No…why it sounds like a reoccurring theme of a lot of disgruntled women heading back to Norway"

"Oh it was. It was a real problem back then," Slater assured me.

"But why did Ole let on like those were pictures of Lily to all his livestock-farming buddies, when they were actually pictures of Elvira?" I asked him.

Slater grimaced and then continued.

"Oh…oh…oh…oh how he tried to set the record straight, but you know those livestock-farming buddies of his. They thought for sure he was lying; and knowing what a blowhard Sven can be; they thought Ole had paid Sven to lie to Agnes about the pictures. But it wasn't true. Ole had done nothing of the sort. But I am getting ahead of myself. When Agnes started missing Ole, her better judgment got the better of her, and she made plans to return to America, but she died before she reached the shores. Ole then wrote to Lily, and fate of all fates, she wrote back. When Lily arrived in Bullpen in 1895, Ole gathered together all of his livestock-farming buddies, and then—one by one—they passed in front of Lily as Ole held the indiscriminant picture of Elvira next to Lily. In the end, all of Ole's livestock farming buddies agreed: Elvira was not Lily, and Ole had been right all along. Even though some inquired about where they might find Elvira, the doubts concerning Ole's good name and reputation were finally put to rest."

"So they got married?" I asked.

"Precisely," replied Slater. "Now you know the truth."

"Why, Slater," I told him, "Thank you for setting the record straight."

Slater nodded as if pleased with himself, and then ordered oatmeal.

"But I thought Ole had more than two wives. What about the others?" I asked.

A few of Slater's coffee-drinking buddies suddenly entered and greeted Slater, then begin to search for their coffee cup along the wall, and I realized that conversation was for another day. Millie was the first one to take the cups down and pass them around. The coffee buddies balked at the $2.50 coffee, but in the end, they found it better than what they had had before.

"Free refills?" one asked Millie.

"Yep, free refills," she replied.

I was beside myself knowing that she told them so without asking my permission.

"Hey! Who is the owner around here anyway? That's a lot of coffee," I reminded her, in private. "All these old timers do is sit around and drink it like there is no tomorrow."

"Oh, quit your fretting," she told me. "They will make you more money than they will take. Believe me."

I had no choice but to believe her now that she had given away the farm.

To my amazement, more customers entered and started to order oatmeal and eggs and pancakes. I took their orders and went back to the kitchen, only to find it a complete mess with Jerome reading directions on the back of the Quaker oatmeal box.

"Don't you know how to make oatmeal?" I asked him.

"No, I don't. I don't eat oatmeal. I eat grits, but ain't nobody ordering grits around here. All they is ordering is oatmeal, and this stuff is nasty."

"Well, you had better figure out fast how to make it, because we got guests."

"Guests?" he asked.

"Customers." I told him firmly.

He muddled about, still reading the directions, and I asked him if he knew what he was doing.

"Course I know what I am doin'!" he snapped back. "Now get out of my kitchen!"

"Your kitchen?!" I yelled. "Who said this was your kitchen?!"

Suddenly the place was quiet—pin drop quiet. Not good . . .not good for business.

I stepped back into the dining area and saw that all of the faces were looking at me with blank stares—even Millie. I tried to find something witty to say in that awkward moment, but my mind went blank. I then smiled apologetically and told our guests that we were having some technical difficulties and to please stand by.

They laughed. Thank God they laughed. Was it something I said? Was it the coffee?

Millie shook her head and went back to taking orders. I went back to the kitchen, and Jerome told me again to get out of *his* kitchen.

"This ain't your kitchen!" I whispered loudly.

"Well, it's mine while I'm workin' . . . now get out!" he shouted.

Then it hit me. "Jerome! You were mad, but you didn't swear—you-did-not-swear!"

I was smiling at him like an idiot waiting for his reply. And in the midst of all the confusion and chaos, he grabbed a tennis ball, squeezed it hard, stared me in the face, and told me that the day ain't over yet.

Later That Night . . . The Kindergarten Cafe

It was a peaceful night with a light breeze to keep the mosquitoes away. I was exhausted. Day one was behind us, but day two was ahead of us—and that was the problem. This café thing is so daily. It never ends. You just get through cleaning up one table and the big mess on it, and it gets dirty again. It never ends. Thank God that I had listened to Miss Maddie and decided not to offer supper. I think even Jerome and Millie are appreciating the time off, at least for starters. I know Maynard is. He told me that Millie finally came home to cook him his supper. And can a town like Bullpen support a café with three meals a day? I don't know, but the business side of me is coming out now that I am starting to watch my Ps and Qs. What is it with Ps and Qs anyway? What accountant ever came up with that phrase that really means to watch your money coming in and your money going out? Ps and Qs—go figure. What about Xs and Os or Ys and Gs?

As I pondered the reality of our first day, I would have given us a C minus as far as a letter grade. And as far as what grade we would be in school, I would say we were somewhere between kindergarten and the first grade—maybe closer to kindergarten. Had we been competing in the cities with other restaurants, we probably would have closed this afternoon.

Sorry . . . still trying to get our act together.

Thank God for Millie, who knew a little bit about running a café. Thanks to her and her previous experience, the day was not a total loss. We made close to 300 dollars ($279.52 to be exact). We made over 80 dollars alone on coffee. Is that good? It was 25 percent of our take, but I had no point of reference to know if that was good or bad. It was what it was, and we would live again to fight another day at the café tomorrow.

Thank God people around here are understanding, but I guess they don't really have a choice in the matter. It's not like they can go to Starbucks down the road or anything. We are the only show in town and I find that it's almost better to come right out and say we are new at this stuff, and let the chips fall where they may. It is almost like we are asking for their help in being understanding, rather than pretending that we are somebody we are not, imitations versus the real thing. Honesty. Is that such a bad word in business? Hey, we are who we are and we will get better. Please give us a little breathing room, and we will get it right. It's funny, but you could almost see people pulling for us. Perhaps they were desperately hoping that we could make a go if it since they had no other place to eat. Where else could they go? A pizzeria? A tavern? I couldn't see a McDonald's in Bullpen or a Subway, Burger King, Dairy Queen, or Sonic—maybe a White Castle, but definitely not Applebee's, Bob Evans, Marie Calendar's or Cracker Barrel . . . . The list goes on and on as great restaurants come to mind. What do we have to offer? Oatmeal and some soupy eggs. So what did people put up with before there was a health department? A lot, apparently.

We would get this café thing down, but right now we were the little engine that could and I was looking for T-shirts that suggested that thought. Perhaps we could wear T-shirts like Avis: We try harder . . .or . . . simply: We Try. That's reassuring for customers, isn't it? Wouldn't you just love to go to a restaurant where the people wore T-shirts that said, "We Try?" Or better yet, what if the cooks made a personal visit to each table wearing dirty, meat-stained aprons with Big, Bold, Italicized Letters that read, " We Try—We Really Do." Sounds delicious, doesn't it? Yes, someone who "really tries" is back there cooking my food. What a comforting thought. We could sell comfort food. Yes, we could franchise this concept nationwide and make millions. We could call it the "We Try" restaurants. Sorry dear, McDonald's will have to wait, because right now I am craving a burger from the "We Try" restaurant down the street.

So how did my Uncle Roy do it? I saw no instructions on how to run a café in his desk drawer where all of his papers were kept. And I still cannot find the hushpuppy pancake recipe that everyone was asking about. I guess he had made them so many times, he didn't need a recipe. Try Googling *hushpuppy pancakes* and see what you get.

And then there was this whole commotion about maple syrup—real maple syrup. I thought Aunt Jemima's was good enough, but not in Bullpen. Who eats real maple syrup nowadays? I thought Aunt Jemima was the real thing. That's what I grew up on. But I came to find out today that it's made from corn syrup—not good for the heart, as Slater Gray informed me.

"Think about that for a minute," Slater told me (as if I have a minute to spare on the first day at the café—unlike Slater who is now retired . . . You have to be careful around these retired guys. They like to talk).

"What is real maple syrup?" asked this former botany teacher—as if I am supposed to be the student who is supposed to guess the right answer. But there were others in the class today—the rest of his retired coffee buddies: George, an old military man; Pete, a retired warehouse manager; and Freddie, a retired farmer.

"Tell me," I replied.

He went on to say that, years ago, real maple syrup came from the sap of real maple trees. That sap was then boiled down to the point that when the water evaporated, it left behind the sweet maple syrup. It was used on pancakes, waffles, oatmeal, etc. But, as the demand grew for the real thing, companies began finding ways to make it cheaper by substituting artificial ingredients. Over time, they had completely substituted everything maple out of maple syrup. Then people grew up on the artificial syrup, and when they tasted the real thing, they didn't know what it was. Irony of ironies, he told us, they thought that the artificial thing was the real thing and that the real maple syrup was an imitation.

"Think about that for a minute," he said to his now curious classroom. "Think about the significance of that."

I was thinking about a lot of things at the moment—like when was Jerome going to get this oatmeal thing down, but apparently it was not the right thing to be thinking about.

"Help me out Slater," I asked him, wiping off a nearby table with a dishrag. "I'm not getting it."

"Yeah, tell us, oh learned one," George chimed in sarcastically.

Slater braced himself for the moment he had set us up for. Curiosity was his friend now, and he was milking it like a good teacher for everything it was worth. Everyone in the café was listening—especially Millie. Like a fine actor, Slater braced himself again for his delivery, cleared his throat and smiled at us all without so much as a word.

"Well, don't just sit there like a bump on a log, Slater. Tell us!" Millie cried out impatiently.

"It means that sometimes things in life are not as they seem. It means that imitations have often replaced the real thing and when he real thing does come along, we don't even recognize it," He stated proudly.

"Like fake moo-cha-chas," George blurt out laughing, then cupped his hands in front of his chest. Millie gave him a disapproving stare, but to no avail. He and the rest of the "boys" were suddenly off and running into tabloid land. Slater stared at his empty bowl of oatmeal and sighed, having suddenly lost complete control of his classroom.

His message did not go unnoticed, however. As a writer, I think back on these kinds of things—and somehow it hit me that Slater had touched upon a profound truth whose meaning had multiple levels of understanding.

Perhaps there is, after all, intelligent life in Bullpen.

June 16 . . . Our First Business Meeting

It is early Tuesday morning, and I have assembled the troops before we open at seven. I am very tired and looking for my misplaced cup of coffee. I thought it would be important to assemble the troops and talk through yesterday's events and then improve on today's. It seemed like the good manager thing to do at the time, so I had them all line up.

Don't you love Tuesdays? Tuesdays are almost Wednesdays, and Wednesdays are halfway through the week in most people's world—but not in mine. In the restaurant world, our halfway through the weekday (or hump day as some call it) is actually Thursday, since our week ends on Saturday—not Friday, like most normal people. And Jerome is already asking for a day off.

"A day off?" I confront him. "We just started!"

Next thing I know, all three of them will form a union and demand days off. And I will have to deal with a negotiator—the same one that Hormel uses at their corporate headquarter in Austin, Minnesota. I could just see a potential strike with Millie, Jared, and Jerome holding signs along Main Street, asking innocent bystanders to boycott the Bullpen Café. They would demand more and more benefits while all of my competitors would go to Mexico and China to open cafés.

I am getting my first taste of management and the real world antics of what it means to run a business—and it is, after all, unpleasant, but necessary.

"I suppose you want a day off too, huh Millie? And what about you, Jared? You want a day off too now?! Anyone else want a day off around here?! Why don't we all take a day off and retire on our 279 dollars that we made yesterday. That's it, let's all take a day off and go to Hawaii or Cancun or the Fiji Islands."

They are all smiling. They are mocking me. I get louder.

"Next thing you know, we will all be getting entitlements from our friendly federal government, because that is what we do when we don't get our way. We get on our hands and knees and cry like little babies and then blame the government for not taking care of us or bailing us out. Well, I got news for you,

General Motors—we are the government!"

They are still smiling. No one is taking me seriously. I shake my head and ask them if we need to talk about anything else before we get started.

Jerome asks me if he can now go to the bathroom. They all burst out laughing, and I don't get it. Jerome then tells me he was just kidding about the day off.

Oh, now I get it . . . . Let's push Charlie and see how far he will go on an empty tank of coffee. Oh, that's a great way to start the day.

Who called this meeting anyway?

Later That Day . . . Love is in the air

It was another red-letter day at the café. We made two dollars and thirty-three cents more than we did yesterday. At this rate we should be millionaires by 2065.

For lunch, our deli sandwiches were a little warm, or so we were told by . . . yes, you guessed it, Slater Gray, our now resident health inspector. When I asked him how long the sandwiches had been sitting on the counter before they were served, he said five minutes and forty-three seconds.

"You mean you were timing it?" I asked him.

"Of course," he replied.

Apparently, it was an efficiency study. Don't you just love guys like Slater? Next thing you know he will be bringing his own meat thermometer. He also had some suggestions for our placemats that included a botanical quiz called "Name that flower."

After he left, George called me over and told me that he has a flower that will stump even Slater.

"Oh yeah?" I asked. "What is it?"

"A red-fruited bastard toadflax," George blurted out laughing along with the boys.

"A what?" I asked him.

"A red-fruited bastard toadflax."

More laughter.

98

It is a pretty sight, really—grown, retired men sitting around a cup of coffee with nothing better to do each morning than to chew the fat and laugh at grade school stuff. Makes you want to retire early and join their ranks, doesn't it? I wouldn't have thought much of George had it not been for Slater, however. Apparently George spent a lot of time behind enemy lines on reconnaissance missions during the Viet Nam War, and he still has nightmares to prove it. Who would have thought it? Not me. It just goes to show you that you can't judge a book by its cover—any book. Ironically, it is Slater who is more proud of him than anyone else.

Homer came in again today, but he only ordered coffee in spite of our great oatmeal. He gave me a special invite to his home next week for supper and to play Crokinole. Not familiar with the game, I Googled it. I found that it's a board game made of wooden checker-sized disks that you flick with your fingers on a round, wooden board, and you score it like shuffleboard. I can't say that I have ever had a desire to play Crokinole, but next week the battle is on. I asked him how he was getting along with his lady friends, and he winked and told me that Rooster Cogburn has things well under control.

"Rooster Cogburn?" I asked.

"John Wayne," he replied. "You know, the western with Audrey Hepburn?"

I'd never seen the movie. I was suddenly tempted to ask his advice on women and what kind of engagement ring to get Karen, but I remembered that he had never been married, so what would he know apart from his playboy status in Bullpen? I was going to ask Jerome his advice, but he wasn't keen on the idea from the beginning. Then I was going to ask Millie, but I didn't want all that news floating around Bullpen. After all, Karen hadn't said yes, yet.

So I took my own advice. After work, I took off for Northfield, Minnesota, where I had found an engagement ring that I liked online. When I got there, it didn't quite look the same as on the website, but I bought it anyway. It still looks cool—an eighth of carat diamond with a simple gold band. That ought to get her attention, huh? I thought so. Then one of my bloggers blogged me earlier today and asked me if Karen herself would be reading the blog and I would be spilling the beans from my own website. Good question, but "small chance," I told her. I had never mentioned my blog to Karen in my texts, and what are the chances of her finding out? Interesting isn't it? I now have over 30 regular followers, and some of them are beginning to ask questions that I had never thought about before. It's like my life is becoming an open book—

literally. I never really thought of it that way. I simply wanted to share my experiences and thoughts about life with the blogging community in my *News from the Bullpen Café* and see if anyone was listening. It's kind of like writing a public diary that I thought might be of interest to someone, somewhere in the world, but I guess that all too apparentness comes with the writing territory. What is it about writing? You bare your soul by wearing your heart on your sleeve, and then you wait for someone to respond to what it was you wrote. Did you like it? Did you get anything from it? I remember writing groups in college that would pick apart your story, like Payton Manning would pick apart a defense, and it took three weeks to show your face again in public. Did I write that? Oops. I remember Mary Jenkins in fourth grade had a crush on me and wrote it in her diary. When it was discovered at recess, I was the talk of the fourth grade class, and she was clearly embarrassed.

I never really noticed Mary Jenkins. She was a nice girl, but not the kind you would notice in the fourth grade, and what she saw in me remains a mystery. I was not the best athlete, nor the class clown. I colored within the lines, and only occasionally was I sent to the principal's office. But there it was, right out in front of God and everybody: Mary loves Charlie and will love him till the day she dies. She sounded like Donna Reed in the movie *It's a Wonderful Life*.

I suddenly wondered what had become of Mary. I never saw her after fourth grade, and yet her words I discovered on the playground that day still linger.

Love is funny, isn't it? What is love anyway? What does it mean to *fall* in love? That's a great phrase isn't it? Why don't they call it *slipping* in love, like on a wet floor, or *parachuting* in love or *sky diving* in love? After all, isn't love a leap of faith? You put it out there and hope that the other party likes you as much as you like them. Talk about risky. Isn't marriage the biggest risk of all? I mean, you are supposed to be spending the *rest of your life* with this person. It's not like you can take back your wife for a new car each year, or treat her like a house and simply move out (well, maybe some do). Marriage has to be the leap of all leaps of faith. It's like death—you don't really know what it is like until you get there (ok, bad analogy). But do you really know what the person is really like before you marry him or her? No. How can you?

Yes, there is all this hubbub about living together before marriage, but I never bought into the idea myself. What is living together, anyways? A test? An NFL preseason game where you try things out and, if they don't work, then you look for another field goal kicker to better your team? I'm sorry, but the coach wants to see you in his office and bring your playbook. Yes, let's test this relationship out for a few months and see what happens. If things go well, then let's get married, if not, then *que sera sera*—what will be, will be. And how long do you run the test? One month? Five months? A year? Five years? Is five years enough? Or do you keep extending the due date out and then out some more, hoping to make double, no triple, no quadruple sure that this person is the real deal and that you are in fact in love? Oh yes, I am *really* in love this time. I mean *really* in love—the no kidding kind of love. Really? Real love? No, fake love, silly. Of course it's the real deal.

But can you really get to know someone in that test stage called "living together"? Can you really commit yourself and bare your soul, knowing that if you do, something you might eventually say or do might merit grounds for separation? Can you really be honest in a test like the periodic high-pitched siren that comes from the National Weather Bureau that reminds the TV viewers in the wee hours of the morning that this is only a test—repeat, only a test? So don't get too excited. Don't go running out in your PJs—this is only a test. So, are you still holding back a part of your real self for fear that the other party might find out what you are really like and then leave you? Horror of horrors—rejection. Or, they might be afraid of what you really think about them, so they are on their best behavior. So, who is really being themselves? Who is being honest? And, can you stay at the helm and weather the real storm when conflicts arise and things don't go as planned?

Houston? Do you copy?

What is love? Maybe Jerome is right. Maybe I am too young. Maybe I'm not. Maybe I am a little scared of commitment, knowing that Karen may not be the person I thought she was. That's a comforting thought, isn't it? But doesn't real love offer real commitment in spite of the conflicts and differences?

I consider the divorce rate—almost 50 percent of married couples end in divorce. Think of that. Google "divorce rate" and see for yourself what the statistics are. And women instigate 73 percent of those divorces. Does that surprise you? Why? Why is it that more women than men want a divorce? I always thought it was the other way around. Men are more entrepreneurial and wild at heart. Women, on the other hand, are more security oriented, more family oriented. If women are from Venus and men are from Mars, then would it not stand to reason that men would be more apt to want a divorce than women? So what is it that is different today about marriage? A hundred years ago you married for life. Divorce was a social taboo and I suppose there were women that suffered through a bad marriage, as Hans's wife, Gladys, had done back in 1892. (Remember Gladys? She was the mail order bride who came from Norway and then left on the boat back to Norway after Hans drank himself to death).

So, why such a high divorce rate today? Is it because there are more bad marriages today than yesterday? Or is it because more women believe they are in a bad marriage based upon their expectation of the "good life"? But what constitutes the good life? Does the world today really offer a woman any more happiness than the world did a hundred years ago? Is Paris Hilton really that much happier today than if she had been born yesterday? Do more money and more publicity and more things really make us happy and give us the security we want? Or is it all just an illusion, like a never-ending dog race around a materialistic track, where dogs chase a mechanical rabbit that is always just beyond their reach? And what happens when the dog catches the rabbit? What happens when you get all of the things you want in life? Is that what gives you joy? How long can the joy of the new house last before you need to remodel it? Or get the new car or take a longer vacation? Is the allure and gravitational pull of more and better things and more and greater prestige leading us all into a proverbial black hole?

Houston?

Are more women flooding the corporate arena in search of true happiness, true security and a true sense of belonging that has now usurped the family? But how many securities does it take to feel secure? And how much wood would a woodchuck chuck, if a woodchuck could chuck wood? And what is happiness? What is love? Have we substituted power, position and the pursuit of pretty, prestigious things for real, down-to-earth relationships, to the point that we don't recognize the real thing when it comes along? Like maple syrup, have we substituted an imitation of love for the real thing?

I wondered.

June 16 . . . Hush Puppy Pancakes

I was just about ready to shut down my laptop for the night when a blogger from North Carolina, by the name of Sweet Tea, wrote in with a hush puppy pancake recipe! There it was. This just in—a real, down-to-earth, repeat down-to-earth (*you copy that, Houston?*) recipe for hush puppy pancakes!

2 cups of Krusteaz pancake mix

1/2 cup of stone ground corn meal

3 tablespoons of sugar

1 teaspoon of salt

1 teaspoon of vanilla

1 egg

1 cup of buttermilk and enough regular milk

to give it the proper pancake texture (whatever that is).

Oh thank you, Sweat Tea from North Carolina! Thank you for the recipe!!!

After I blogged her back, I came to my senses. I have gone mad with cooking. Yes, I have gone completely mad with cooking. One month ago, I would have thought a reaction like that was a sure, telltale sign of fatigue, or of a soul gone mad from local cuisine—ranting and raving and frothing at the mouth like Mr. Hyde. Honestly . . . it is, after all, just a recipe.

Julia Child? Chef Boyardee? Would you agree?

June 17 . . . Field of Dreams

I am late for the Bullpen Rotary meeting tonight that started at seven pm. It's not actually called the "Bullpen Rotary," but I call it *that* because *that* is the only way I can get a handle on understanding what it is. I would have missed it entirely, had it not been for Millie, who reminded me of it late this afternoon. It is held at the Watkins Curiosity Shoppe along Main Street, run by Mavis Nordstrom (no relation to Nordstrom's department store, she is quick to tell me). Mavis is a middle-aged woman who wears clothes straight out of the 1890s. I don't know if that is part of her business image or if that is what she likes to wear. Apart from the red neon sign that hangs in the window, you would not think it's a business by looking at the pretty frilled window coverings. With a Curiosity Shoppe, I am curious about how she manages to stay in business in such a small town. But then again, I am curious about how we all stay in business in Bullpen. Perhaps that is what we will discuss tonight.

I am welcomed with a cold glass of apple cider and handshakes with the other prestigious members of the group, including the mayor, Terrell Paulson; Gerald Gustafson, who owns, operates the Bullpen Elevator; Rodney Holbrook, who manages Baker's Garage; Eddie Carlisle, an owner and operator of Eddie's Gas and Go (no relation to Kitty Carlisle); Abel Greendorf, who owns and operates the Grandview Laundry Mat (I have been meaning to ask him if he could fix his coin-operated dryers); Annie Peterson, owner and operator of Annie's Car Wash (and Wax); and Jake Zimmerman, who owns the welding shop in town.

It is a friendly group that kids around and catches up on Bullpen events, well past 8 o'clock.

The mayor wears a distinct Fu Manchu moustache that comes down to his chin. I ask him how long he has had it, to which he smiles and tells me, ever since he took out a billboard advertisement for his insurance business with his face on the front. One night, some kids drew a Fu Manchu moustache on his face as a testament to the art of graffiti. Trying to erase it, he only made his face look worse—and being too cheap to buy another advertisement, he left the graffiti on the billboard for the duration of his rental agreement. In time, however, people didn't recognize him without the large moustache. So, in order to save his insurance business, he grew a Fu Manchu to match the graffiti image that was portrayed of him on the billboard.

They ask about me, and I tell them that people still recognize me without a moustache. No one laughs, and I am guessing my comment wasn't that funny. After an awkward moment of silence, they then tell me how glad they are to have me in town. I then ask them how my uncle ran the café and if I am measuring up to their expectations.

"Fine," says Gerald.

They all nod in agreement, as if they can actually say anything else since I am now officially a part of the Bullpen Rotary, and having shaken hands with everyone. "You run a fine café," he repeats.

"And your uncle was a fine proprietor," states Rodney. "Very fine indeed."

They all nod in agreement again.

"But he didn't charge $2.50 for coffee," adds Mavis politely.

Despite her friendly demeanor, I sense a little tension over the price of coffee, and I ask if it is too high.

"Oh, not at all," says Eddie. "'Bout time we started raising prices around here."

Mavis disagrees.

I have hit a point of contention, and then I suddenly find myself becoming a little miffed. Is it not my restaurant? Do I need a boardroom or Rotary Club to approve the price of my coffee? Mavis seems to think so.

"So what price should I charge for coffee?" I ask Mavis.

"$1.25 at the most," she replies without hesitation, as if she had known all along that I would ask her. "Most elderly people in town are on a fixed income."

"Okay," I tell everyone, "I'll think about it."

They all nod approvingly, except Eddie.

Then it hits me how much a simple price of coffee affects a whole coffee drinking community. Throw out the supply and demand theory. What about the affordability theory? Maybe that is why Homer only orders coffee. Maybe he can't afford much else. My head is spinning with thoughts about coffee as the conversation continues around me like a blur. Who would have known that

$2.50 was too high a price for coffee in Bullpen? What were people thinking and talking about anyway? Obviously, it was the price of coffee. Yes, obviously, there was a buzz about coffee and I didn't get the corporate memo. Who knows what people were thinking and talking about behind my back? Why those scoundrels. They pay $3.50 in Dinky Town at the university, for goodness sake, and those are penny-pinching college students. Why can't they pay $2.50 for a special blend, straight from a roaster in Montgomery, Minnesota? Doesn't anyone around here appreciate a good—I mean a really good—cup of coffee? Have their taste buds been anesthetized through the years—no, generations—of drinking poor coffee? Who knows what they were drinking before? Who knows what they had grown accustomed to? Why, the hall of fame coffee cups had probably never been washed. Never been washed—yikes. Coffee stains from over twenty years ago that were still on the cup—more yikes. Where was I twenty years ago when someone had first stained his cup? I was running around in diapers. No wonder they had no appreciation for real coffee. Their taste buds had been codified like the ancient . . .

"Charlie?"

I am suddenly brought back to reality, hearing my name.

"You with us on this one, Charlie?" asks the mayor.

"Yep," I reply, having no clue as to what I just agreed to. "I'm with you all the way."

"Good, then you can be this year's chairman for the Bullpen Historical and Commerce Committee."

"The what?" I ask.

"The Bullpen Historical and Commerce Committee," they all reply.

Isn't it amazing how fast a promotion can come when you least expect it? Note to self: "I will not daydream in the Bullpen Rotary meetings anymore. I will not daydream in class anymore. I will not daydream in Miss Roberts' fourth grade class anymore because bad things can happen when you daydream. What? Oh, yes, Miss Roberts—no, no I will not daydream in your class any more, and yes, I understand that if I do it again, I will have 50 more sentences to write for tomorrow."

I had passed from the battle-ax of Miss Bartlett's third grade class to the field cannons of Miss Roberts'. She was the epitome of modern warfare with modified field artillery and multiple sentence structures to prove it. One of Miss Roberts' sentences was enough to put your writing hand out of commission for at least two days. And 50 sentences? You could kiss your recess and your wrist good-bye for at least a week.

"Due to my inability to conform to the rules of this classroom, I have hereby forfeited my right to participate in any privileges pertaining to this classroom, which I hereby have violated in accordance with the rudimentary procedures set forth in such subject matters in question, and I will not be able to engage in any such privileges as long as I stand outside the merits of this imposition that has been duly set upon me, due to my inability to conform."

Oh, but if only Miss Roberts could see me now. Oh Yeah....See where daydreaming got me now, Miss Roberts? How do you like them apples? I am the man. I am now the chairman of the Bullpen Commerce and Historical Committee—whatever that is.

The meeting continues, and I am thinking it is time to text Karen. She is coming home in two days. But the meeting lingers on and on, as we talk about ways to bring more business to Bullpen. Then suddenly, like a bolt of lightning, I am reminded of the movie *Cars*.

"We need a Lightning McQueen," I say jokingly, and the rest look at me with blank stares.

"You know . . . Lightning McQueen, from the movie, *Cars?*" I ask, then wait for any signs of life.

But there are none.

"Did you ever see the movie *Cars*? You know, that animated cartoon that Disney put out a few years ago?" I ask.

More blank stares.

"Ah," I reply disappointedly. "It was just a cartoon about a small town on historic Route 66 that had been bypassed by the interstate and . . ."

Then it hits me.

"What would you all think about having a historic town festival, Like Bullpen Days, that goes back in time to the founding fathers? We could have a baseball tournament right out there in County Road 30," I suggest to them enthusiastically.

"A baseball game in Bullpen?" asks Annie.

"Yeah, right out there in the original spot, near Ole's old bullpen. After all, isn't that how the town got its name?" I ask.

"But who would come to Bullpen to play baseball?" asks Mavis.

"*Field of Dreams*!" I shout. "*Field of Dreams*, with Kevin Costner and James Earl Jones! That's it!"

More blank stares.

"What are you talking about?" they ask, dumbfounded.

"*Field of Dreams* was a movie!" I reply excitedly. "It was about a man who built a baseball field in the middle of a cornfield and then Shoeless Joe Jackson shows up, along with the rest of the Chicago White Sox from 1912, or whatever year that was."

"Yeah, I know about Shoeless Joe Jackson," remarks Able. "He was that barefoot field goal kicker for the Miami Dolphins."

"No, that was Garo Yepremian," replies Rodney, "But I think we are on to something."

"And we don't have to have just a baseball game; we can have a horseshoe tournament," cries Gerald.

"Who plays horseshoes anymore around here?" asks the mayor.

"I don't know, but if we build it, people will come. Hey, they came to a lutefisk dinner didn't they?" I ask, looking for support. "Why can't we expect people to come to Bullpen for Bullpen Days."

"Yeah!" shouts Rodney. "Bullpen Days with caramel apples and pork on a stick and pickles on a stick and snickers candy bars on a stick and deep fried green tomatoes on a stick and . . ."

Gerald's eyes light up. "Yeah!" he bolts out. "And deep fried ice cream sandwich bars with chocolate sauce!"

"Now you're talking!" cries Rodney. "And caramel sauce!"

"Yeah, I think we are on to something big here, Charlie. By golly, if we build it, they *will* come!" chimes in the mayor, smacking his lips.

A powder keg of creative ideas suddenly explodes. There is talk of carnival rides, more deep fried foods, and lutefisk on a stick (maybe not a good idea), a five-kilometer fun run, a tractor-pulling contest, an all-city garage sale and . . .

As the conversation swirls around me, I simply sit back and observe it all, as if I am filming our discussion with an imaginary camera—for posterity's sake for course.

June 18 . . . The Contest

Thursday morning was a blur. I didn't even remember getting out of bed, but there I was at 6:00 am in the kitchen with Jerome making preparations for Hush Puppy Pancakes.

"I still don't see what's so special about Hush Puppy Pancakes," he said, stirring the batter. "Why don't people eat real food around here, like grits and fried okra and hominy and biscuits and gravy and . . . "

"Because we are not down south," I reminded him. "Besides that, this is a recipe from North Carolina, so quit your sassing."

He eyed me fiercely and continued to mix the batter. We had now placed it on all the menus—a hand-written note that looks a little tacky—but the news is out, and we are expecting a big crowd. I took Mavis Nordstrom's advice and thought through the cost of coffee. Stubborn, I still thought we could get $2.50 for a good cup of java, but I also put on the menu a cup for $1.25 that does not have the special blend. I will be interested to see what kind of response we get.

Jerome shook his head about the whole thing—pessimistic and grumpy.

"Why don't you let me do the placemats and get us some real food around here?" he interjected. "Man, everything is milk-toasty bland. Why, it's no wonder all you northerners is so constipated—you ain't got no spices up here. Oh, I forgot," he said mockingly. "Excuuuuuse me—you at least got yourselves some black pepper . . . Oooo . . . it's gettin' a little hot 'round here . . . Ooo it's gettin' hot. Oh, be careful now . . . don't you go playin' with that salt and pepper shaker, cause if you spill some of that black pepper on your hands, we'll have to take you to the hospital for third degree burns."

"That's enough," I said.

"Why, in Louisiana, we breastfeed our youngins on pepper, just to make the milk palatable."

I ignored him and added more buttermilk to the batter. He sampled it and winced.

109

"Man, this needs somethin'. This needs . . . " his eyes suddenly lit up. "Oh man, if this had a dash of nutmeg or a little red pepper, it would be good enough to slap yo momma."

"No!" I yelled. "We are going to stick to the recipe, and nobody is going to be slapping anybody's momma."

"Well, that's just it . . . no guts, no glory."

"I'm not interested in glory," I told him. "I'm interested in customers who will come back and eat here again."

I could tell he was fighting back the urge to swear, but he reached out and grabbed his tennis ball and squeezed it.

Yesterday George and the Boys were kidding Jerome about squeezing the tennis ball as a placebo for his expletives. George—a veteran in the art of foul language, and one of the military's finest examples of how colorful swearing can be—bet Jerome that, if he went a whole week without swearing, he (George) would wash dishes for a day and give Jared a day off—with pay. The original bet was to give Jerome a day off with pay, and that George would cook in Jerome's place. But Jerome wasn't going to give up his place in the kitchen for anyone or anything. But if Jerome lost, then he (Jerome) would have to wash George's windows. This was a task his wife had given him over three weeks ago, and something George hated to do more than clean toilets. Apparently he could never completely get rid of the window streaks to his wife's satisfaction, even if he used a whole bottle of Windex.

George then made a big sign with all seven days on it, and he let it be it known that anyone who caught Jerome swearing was to put an X on this homemade calendar. Any blank days would count as a no-swear day. George then put the sign up under the smiling moose (with my permission) for all to read:

Attention All Bullpen Café Patrons:

Be it known that this calendar denotes the beginning of days in the bet between Jerome Boatman and George Helford, that if anyone is to catch Jerome swearing, they are to mark on that day an X for all to see. If after one week, this calendar is blank and no one has witnessed nor heard Jerome say so much as an inkle of a swear word, then I, George Helford, will wash dishes for one day for

Jared with pay. If, on the other hand, there is but one X on this calendar, be it known that George wins the bet and Jerome is to wash my windows, without streaks, to the satisfaction of my dear wife, Clair.

Signed this 17ᵗʰ day of June

Jerome Boatman and George Helford

Their signature confirmed the covenant between the heretofore-mentioned parties, and I, knowing what was riding on that bet, began to bait Jerome over the Hush Puppy Pancake batter.

"Come on Jerome, come on," I teased him. "Just say one little swear word, just one little swear word, come on, you can do it!"

Abruptly, he threw the tennis ball at me and walked out of the kitchen. Startled, I saw that he was serious as he walked out the front door, stopped, threw down his apron, and walked toward his apartment across the street. I called to him, but to no avail. He was across the street now and entered the front door of his apartment. As I started to cross the street, I saw Millie.

"What's with Jerome?" she asked.

"I was teasing him about swearing," I said apologetically.

"You were teasing him about swearing?" she asked like a firm mother. And suddenly I felt like a little kid in trouble.

"Yeah," I admitted. "I told him to say just a little one."

"You don't know what progress he has made since he first got here. You don't know how hard he tries not to swear!" she said, scolding me in front of God and everybody.

"Do you think he likes squeezing that tennis ball all the time? Do you?" she continued, pressing me for an answer. I stammered for one as I saw Mrs. Johnson peaking behind her curtains, in her bathrobe and curlers, from her apartment across the street.

"At least he is trying to better himself, and that is a lot more than I can say about most folks," she continued. "He has a family that is coming for Christmas, and all they have ever known him to do was swear about this and swear about that. Well, he is a different man now! He is trying—and any man that tries that hard to be a better man ought to be commended—not teased! That was mean! That was just plain mean!"

Millie stormed off to the café, leaving me standing in the middle of Main Street at 6:35 in the morning, with more people on both sides of the road peaking at me through their curtains. If there was a place to hide, I would have hidden in it, but there was nowhere to hide that morning—at least not on Main Street.

Later That Morning . . . Sweet Lemon Cake

I was still feeling a little tender having taken a verbal thrashing from Mille. We were in full swing, and I was missing Jerome. Against my better judgment, I added nutmeg, but I couldn't bring myself to add red pepper to the Hush Puppy Pancakes. The morning crowd was busy, and without Jerome, I was running around like a madman, cooking and serving along with Millie and Jared. Homer came in and ordered the $1.25 cent coffee and two Hush Puppy Pancakes. After a few bites, he told me they are the best he has ever tasted. Lenny Jorgensen ordered the same, along with the mayor. Now I was thinking that maybe Mavis was right about the price of coffee. As I thought about it, more people were ordering the $1.25 cent coffee than the $2.50 coffee. I would wait to tabulate the day's earnings this evening and see how we did.

After the breakfast rush was over, I entered the kitchen and found Millie making a cake.

"What is that for?" I asked.

"Jerome." she said. "I am making him a cake to congratulate him for not swearing yesterday—and all of us are going to give it to him."

"All of us?" I asked stupidly.

"All of us!" Millie said sternly.

It was a moist lemon cake with real lemon frosting. After it cooled, Millie iced it like an artist, and when the morning crowd disappeared, a little after eleven, she, Jared, and I walked across the street to Jerome's apartment. Millie then knocked on the door.

"Jerome? You in there? You open up, you hear me?" she shouted.

Finally, the door opened and out popped Jerome's head.

"Well, don't just stand there—let us in," she demanded.

Jerome did, and we all stepped into his apartment. Millie presented him with the cake and told him that we are all proud of him—that he has gone a full day without so much as one swear word. Jerome stared at the cake for a moment, and then his eyes began to swell with tears.

It was then that I suddenly felt a deeper appreciation for Jerome than I had ever felt before. I don't know what his life was like before Bullpen. I don't know what pains he bore or the burdens he carried, but as he looked down at that cake, it was as if he was suddenly given permission to let them all go.

Millie gave him a hug, then found a plastic fork to cut the cake in the small kitchenette. We then all sat down on the wooden crates he has for chairs and dug in. The cake was the homemade kind that melts in your mouth and lingers on for what seems like eternity. It is the sweetness that overpowers the sourness, and it was like that this morning—the sweet lingering part. In an odd way, I felt as though we were all family, sitting on the makeshift chairs—all broken in ways we would never fully understand, and yet whole in ways that we could. I could only guess what had gone on in Jerome's life before Bullpen and what he had gone through. Whatever it was, it seemed to have melted away that morning as we all sat in a circle eating lemon—sweet lemon cake—together.

June 18 . . . Reaching Karen

I have a blogging buddy by the name of Ivan the Terrible. Ivan is about six years old and rides his bike to the top of Thomforde Hill to see what I am doing at night. This is the second time he has been here, in spite of the lateness of the hour.

"Don't you have to be home now?" I ask him.

He shakes his head no. What kind of parents would allow their six-year-old child to be out past 10:30 at night? I can only guess. He never wears a shirt, that I have seen, and his snotty nose is always covered with dirt. He must like to eat, because I have not seen him up here without something in his hand. Last week it was a slab of bologna—no bread, just bologna. And this week he is eating melted chocolate ice cream out of a big plastic ice cream pail. I have not seen his family at the café yet, but I have seen Ivan, and yes, he is terrible. When he comes up to see me, he leans the handlebars of his bike against the truck bed, scratching the paint. I have told him three times tonight to get off his bike and then come up to the truck, but talking to Ivan is like talking to a . . . well . . . it's like talking to a six-year-old. He is fascinated by the illuminated laptop screen and just wants to touch it.

"No, we are not going to touch the screen," I tell him, "and no, this is not a TV. This is a computer, and yes, it can play music . . . Yes, it can play video games . . . Yes, it can play videos . . . Yes, it can play movies . . . and I think you had better be going home now, Ivan. I'm sure that your father is looking for you . . ."

"My dad is in prison," he says.

"Well, I'm sure that your mom is looking for you," I reply.

"She's working," he says.

"Well, don't you have an older sister or something?" I ask.

"I have a younger brother, but he sleeps a lot," he answers.

"Well, maybe you should go down and see if he is still sleeping," I suggest.

He nods and turns his bike towards town, with one hand on the handle bar and the other on the ice cream pail that sways back and forth down the road. I watch him and make a bet with myself that he will not make it home without dropping the ice cream pail—and I am right. After coasting to the bottom of the hill, he drops it under the streetlight. He then circles around it three times, as if he can't decide whether to pick it up or not. He doesn't and rides away to what must be his home. The melted chocolate spills from the ice cream pail, leaving behind a little kid crime scene.

I have not heard from Karen in days, and I am wondering what's up. I have sent her numerous text messages, but none have come back. I know that she is due in Minneapolis Saturday morning, and my guess is that she has simply been busy with all of the travel preparations. Not sure what flight she is coming in on, and knowing how hard it is to meet someone at the airport, I have decided to meet her at our Italian restaurant near the university after she gets in.

Suddenly, I get a blog from Mary in New York.

"Hi, Mary from New York," I reply.

She asks me if all the people in Bullpen are as real and as "charming" as I describe them.

Hmmm . . . how do you answer that? I guess I never really saw them as charming before.

"Yep," I reply, "they are what they are, and they are as real and as charming as you want them to be."

How's that for an answer, fellow bloggers?

I guess it all depends on your point of view or perspective. I am reminded of the children's story about two travelers who approach a small village. The first one approaches and sees an old man sitting on the outskirts of the village. He asks him if there are any hypocrites and liars there. The old man tells him yes—so the traveler departs to another town. The second traveler comes along and asks the same old man if he will find any good people in the village. The old man tells him yes, and so he travels on into town.

Perspective is a funny thing, and stories are often used to describe it. As an English major, I had read many stories, and what always amazed me was the power they had to move us towards a particular point of view or perspective. They were in every culture and every tongue and every tribe since the beginning of time—shaping our opinions and values and beliefs. So what is so powerful about a story? Why do people go to the movies and read books? What is it about the story that captivates its audience and makes us want to stand up for the hero and strangle the villain? Perhaps it is because we can relate to the story in our own vicarious way, through our own experiences, whether of love, betrayal, hate, jealousy, nobility, cowardice, vengeance, forgiveness, happiness, or unrest. Like a still photograph, the story captures a certain element of life itself and then frames it in the context of perspective. In photography, perspective is everything, and so it is with the stories. Jesus told stories—parables—that moved the people to do what was right. The prophet Nathan used a parable when confronting David about his sin with Bathsheba. He told him a story about a man who had but one sheep that was stolen and killed by another man—referring to David's own betrayal of Uriah, one of his own commanding officers. David had slept with Uriah's wife, Bathsheba. Having been a shepherd, David was so taken by the story that he demanded that the thief be put to death. Little did David know that he had condemned himself.

Good stories are like that. They have the ability to shape our perspective and reveal truths about ourselves, whether we want them to or not.

I never really considered the people in Bullpen as charming until now. Her words suddenly got me thinking about my own perspective. Would someone else write about these same experiences with a different perspective?

I wondered.

So, what was the truth of the matter? Were the people in Bullpen really charming, or were they just ordinary? What made them charming or boring? The reader or the writer?

I wondered.

I then began to consider about perspective in the context of truth and whether a perspective could be right or wrong . . . and who was to say what was right and what was wrong? By what standards were we to measure?

It always amazed me to think that two people could see the same thing from two different perspectives and arrive at completely different opinions about a topic or a situation, based on their previous experiences and perspectives of life.

So who was right and who was wrong? And by whose standard were we to measure? Could someone living under an illusion of grandeur see life for what it really was? Or did that illusion cloud his or her point of view?

I suddenly thought of the dog races that my grandfather had taken me to in Phoenix when I was a kid. I remember watching greyhounds chasing mechanical rabbits around the track and thinking, "Why don't they get it?

Why don't those dogs see that the rabbit is not real, but only a figment of their imagination?" Illusions do that. They cloud our better judgment to the truth of the matter.

So, what is truth? Can there be any lie or illusions in truth? No—otherwise, it would not be truth. Is truth all knowing? It would have to be, for it would have to know everything in order to judge everything as to whether it was true or not. And it could not do so if it was not omnipresent; it would not be able to expose the lie.

My whole upbringing was predicated upon the truth. My father made his living by discovering the truth, as do most courtroom attorneys. How many times had my father asked the witness to "tell the truth, the whole truth and nothing but the truth, so help me God," as if God himself knew the truth or was truth himself.

So, if a person committed a crime and no one saw him do it, does that mean that the crime was never committed? No, something had to be there to see it—something called truth. It was a witness. It was there at the scene of the crime, making it all knowing or omniscient. And try as it might, the lie could never keep the truth from being exposed, no more than darkness could keep itself from fleeing in the presence of light. No, light was always more powerful than darkness, as truth was always more powerful than the lie, making it all-powerful or omnipotent.

"Sorry, Mary from New York, but my legal and analytical genes have just gotten the better of me . . . So what was your question again?"

"I think you answered it," she responds. "Thanks."

"No. Thank *you*—Mary from New York."

Isn't blogging amazing? I get a little snapshot of someone's life in New York, and I don't even know her. It's like we are communicating on this surface level, without really knowing each other, as I blog my thoughts about life in Bullpen and life in general. Can you really get to know someone on the Internet or through a blog?

I wondered.

Can people ever be something other than what you thought they really were? And how do you really know who they are, apart from words.

Her question suddenly gets me thinking in a different direction, and all I can think of is how you fellow bloggers perceive me—and how you perceive

Bullpen. Do you see what I see? How can you? You only have my words to describe what the town is like. "Charming" she calls the people here.

"Charming?" I ask myself. "Are they really that charming?"

As I finish typing and get ready to shut down my laptop, I see Karen's text message come across my cell phone.

"Charlie?"

"Missing you Karen," I reply. "Been trying to reach you the last few days, but no response. How are you doing?"

"Good," she answers. "I need to see you."

"Me too," I reply. "What time do you get in?"

"Early Saturday morning."

"What about dinner at our restaurant near the university at seven pm?" I ask.

"Yes," she replies.

"Can't wait to see you," I tell her.

XOXO

Charlie

A floodgate of memories suddenly hits me and I pull up a picture of the two of us on my laptop. Don't you just love her smile? Her hair is blowing in the wind, and her eyes are vivid, almost looking beyond the camera. We are standing on the dock. Behind us is her parents' palatial lake home and her playhouse that is barely visible behind her head. I Google Sting on YouTube and hear our song "Fields of Gold" play over and over again. I'm lost in the two of us as we drive among the amber waves of grain on long-forgotten highways. I then pull out the ring that I have been carrying in my pocket for the last few days. I just want to look at it again, and the more I see it sparkle against the night sky, the more I am in love with Karen.

June 20 . . . Fields of Gold

We would meet at an Italian restaurant near the University. It was the place I had taken her on our first "official" date. I had rehearsed my marriage proposal no less than 50 times earlier this afternoon and still wondered what I would say in the clutch. Would I use the more formal approach? . . . "Karen, will you marry me?" Or the *Rocky* approach? . . . "Ah—say, Karen, what are you doing the rest of your life, huh?" Or the non-threatening, non-evasive, nonchalant approach: "Say, ah, what about getting married?"

As I stood in front of the bathroom mirror, I wasn't sure if I should propose on one knee or two. I jockeyed back and forth between the distinctly different styles: first one knee and then two knees and then back to one and then back to two—up and down and up and down. Who knew which one was best? I thought about Googling which approach was more accepted, but decided that a real man should be able to decide this for himself. So I did: getting down on two knees—hence, the "two-kneed approach"—seemed too humiliating, as if you are begging someone to marry you. No, I liked the one-knee approach. It seemed more athletic or noble, like being knighted or something. But as I got down on one knee to rehearse again, I pulled my hamstring. Not good.

I hobbled over to the dresser and put on the shirt that she had made for me in college. It was a little tight in the chest—and a little long in the sleeves—but maybe that is how she sees me.

How does she see me?

I guess I never asked. I then put the engagement ring in its jewelry box and stuffed it into my pocket for safekeeping. I had chosen to drive my Toyota instead of my uncle's truck. The Toyota has a CD player, and I brought along the song, "Fields of Gold." We would play it all night as we drove along forgotten country roads, just as we had done before we graduated. Pretty romantic, huh? I took one last look in the mirror and glanced at my watch. It was Showtime.

I arrived early and sat in the back and waited. She was late in coming, and I had ordered a raspberry ice tea. After I drank the second one, I had to rush off to the bathroom.

119

When I got back—she was there.

Wow! . . . Karen, you . . . you look great! Wow! . . . So how was Frankly . . . . I mean Italy? . . . Really, your great grandfather still okay? . . . Oh yeah, that's right, he's dead. I meant your grandfather . . . That's good . . . That's real good. It's so good to hear your voice.

I felt for the engagement ring in my pocket to make sure it was still there. I moved my right leg to get it—the one with the pulled hamstring—and it was very tender. I was wondering how I would get down on one knee and then get back up after I proposed. My heart was pounding, and I could barely hear a word she was saying. And then it dawned on me that she was pointing to her ring finger. She was wearing a simple silver band. Suddenly she rotated it to reveal a monstrous diamond.

She was engaged.

Her face was bright and alive with excitement as she described the man she met in Italy—the man who proposed to her in Italy, the man who took her heart in Italy . . . a friend of the family for years . . . His great grandfather fought with her great grandfathers . . . His grandfather did business with Onassis . . . His family owns a winery south of . . .

I found myself nodding, as if trying to comprehend it all, as if trying to get my arms and head and heart around it all.

Suddenly, she was getting up from the table and then kissing me on the cheek and telling me she would never forget me.

"But Karen . . . " I stammered.

She put her hand up as if to stop me. She had tears in her eyes. She then turned and walked away.

I followed her out the door and saw her get into her father's red Ferrari.

"But Karen," I said again.

But she was driving away, and I was left standing on the sidewalk, watching her license plate fade into a blur of city lights.

My heart had just been ripped apart and I was trying to find it among amber waves of grain that swelled like an ocean tide, but I could not find it. It was lost where Karen and I had once walked in fields of gold . . .

June 21 . . . Saving Private Charlie

. . . machine-gun fire from Italian bunkers opens up and peppers the beachhead before me like heavy rain. It is wet and cold and I cannot find Karen's ring along the sand as soldiers yell at me to take cover. Suddenly, an incoming shell explodes, and the percussion sends me reeling back into a makeshift foxhole. I am missing an arm. I cannot find my arm. My head is spinning, and everything is a blur. Suddenly the pain is intense, and I find myself throwing up. From out of nowhere comes a Black soldier, and he carries me back behind our own lines, yelling for a medic. . . .

. . . When I awaken, my head is still throbbing and I am moaning. It's hard to focus. Beside me sits someone rocking in my uncle's chair.

"That's it, Charlie. You gonna be alright…you gonna be alright."

Things are fuzzy. My head aches. I see shafts of light break through my uncle's curtains. And slowly, things come back into focus, like the lens of a camera. I am lying on a sofa, watching Jerome rock back and forth in my uncle's chair.

"You gonna make it, Charlie. Oh yeah, you gonna make it . . . Now why'd you go and tie one on like that last night, huh? Over a woman? Didn't I tell you that she ain't for you? Huh? But did you listen to Jerome? No way, and then you go proposing like that? You ain't nothin' but a blind man, looking for some sorry damsel or dumb sell or whatever you want to call her. That ain't for you. Why, she ain't nothing but an illusion. And to think you could a killed yourself over some illusion, drinkin' all that tequila! Man, no wonder you are sicker than a dog!"

I rub my head and beg him not to yell so loud. But he doesn't listen. Stubborn as ever, he continues to yell.

"Tequila! Man, that stuff will kill you if you drink enough of it. And all over some woman! So you gonna kill yourself over some woman?"

"I wasn't trying to kill myself," I shout. "And could you stop yelling! Ouch—my head."

121

"Now, a real woman would see what she's got in her man—not some illusionary woman, lost in some fairy-god-spell. Here now take this."

He holds up a glass filled with orange and red stuff that is moving.

"What is it?" I ask him.

"It's called 'The Look-out,'" he says. "Now drink it up. Believe me, it will help that hangover."

"Why do you call it the look-out?" I ask.

"Cause you gots to tell your stomach to look out, cause it's comin'."

"What?" I ask him. But like a stubborn coach, he is determined to get it down my throat. I oblige him and gag at the first taste. It is hot and terrible.

"Oh man, man what is in this thing?" I stammer.

"Two raw eggs, tomato juice, cayenne pepper, black pepper, chili pepper, dill pickle juice . . . "

"Stop! Ouch . . . my head . . . I don't want to know what's in it," I tell him.

He pushes the glass up to my mouth, and I down it quickly. After I gag, then gasp for air, he nods approvingly.

"There," he says at last. "Now that'll do it. Now just don't go and puke it up and you should be good in about 25 minutes. Otherwise, we got to use Fire-in-the-Hole."

"Fire-in-the-Hole?" I ask.

"Oh, you don't wanna know what's in Fire-in-the-Hole."

I can only imagine. As my stomach begins to rumble, I ask him how he knows about last night.

"Well, let's just see if we can figure this one out," he says mockingly. "We got ourselves a car parked up on the hill at 2:30 in the morning, blastin' some stupid song on repeat, wakin' up half of Bullpen county, a diamond ring sitting on the dashboard, and a half-empty bottle of Tequila. The man done puked all over his shirt and then knocked himself out and is snorin' up against the window, soundin' like a man sawin' logs desperate to heat his home in winter. So, you tell me what happened? Man, you could a drowned in your own vomit—like Jimmy Hendricks or Janice Joplin or my good friend Willie when he done lost his home to Hurricane Katrina. Man, if I hadn't a gotten up and opened up my balcony door to get some air last night, I never would a heard that song blastin' away and seen your car sittin' all by its lonesome up on top of Thomforde Hill. And throwin' up—all of it over some woman . . . And then haulin' you back here was like haulin' a sack of potatoes. But can we make it all the way into town without you pukin' your guts out? No sir…we gots to stop every 50 feet so you can puke it all out. That's right, Charlie. You just keep pukin'. Oh—oh, and then fightin' you to put on a clean shirt was nuttin' short of World War Three."

"So you brought me here?"

"Oh, yeah! And had to watch you all night. I lost one friend who drank himself to death. I ain't about to lose another."

Tears well up in his eyes, and he begins to rock faster, staring down at the floor. My stomach is still churning and continues to rumble. I feel like throwing up, and my head begins to spin again. I am exhausted and lie back down as his spoken words begin to pound inside my head as if he is yelling inside a 55-gallon steel drum.

As I doze off to sleep, the only word that continues to resonate inside the drum is "friend."

Later That Afternoon . . . Miss Maddie

Needless to say, we missed church this morning. When I woke up it was two pm, and yes, Jerome was still there rocking next to me.

I sat up on the sofa and began to rub my eyes. He told me I was going to be all right.

But I wasn't. There was a hole in my heart.

He told me he had parked the Toyota behind the café and had to plug his nose the whole way down when he drove it, since I had thrown up on the dashboard as well as my shirt.

"Yeah, and you gonna have to clean out that heater too, cause come fall when it gets cold and that heater fires up for the first time, you is gonna smell it all over again," he informed me.

"How would you know that?" I questioned.

"A little bird told me. And what's more is that you got yourself another complimentary ticket," He replied.

"Expired tabs?" I asked.

"Expired tabs," he affirmed. "Just thank God you wasn't in the car when he pulled over and gave you a ticket or you'd have gotten yourself thrown in the slammer. Then you would'a had to get you a good attorney to get you out. You know any good attorneys that can get you out of jail?" he asked with a big smile.

"I wasn't drinking while I was driving," I said. "I'm not that stupid."

"We can debate that later," he said.

He cooked us some oatmeal and we both ate it. It was awful. I asked him if he put some Fire-in-the-Hole in it and he laughed.

It was good to hear Jerome laugh. We talked for a while longer. When he left, I suddenly felt lonely. I always hated late Sunday afternoons—and this one was the worst. Late Sunday afternoons were the times when you had to get ready for the up-and-coming week—whether you liked it or not. Late Sunday afternoons felt as bad as late Friday afternoons felt good—if that makes sense. But I guess I'm not making a whole lot of sense right now.

I then had a notion to visit Miss Maddie. I just wanted to talk to someone. I hesitated about seeing her again, wondering what other weird prayer she might pray over me. But deep down inside, I was missing her company.

When I arrived at her home in my uncle's truck, her dog, Flint, came to meet me. His bark echoed across the yard, and she came out to investigate.

When I stepped out of the truck, I saw her standing there looking all proper in her Sunday clothes. It dawned on me that she reminded me of my great grandmother, the sweet one, the one that used to rock me to sleep after hellish, little-kid nightmares.

I don't know why I started crying when I saw her, but I did. And without so much as a word, she came over and simply put her arms around me and hugged me, for what seemed like eternity . . .

June 24 . . . The Dark Side of the Moon

It's been a couple of days since I have written, and I apologize to any of you fellow bloggers out there that have been wondering what is going on in Bullpen.

Haven't felt much like writing, lately. Sorry.

When I opened up the blog, I noticed that there are a string of messages. Thanks for blogging. Thanks for some of your kind responses and thanks for some of your advice and opinions about Karen—not that I agree or disagree. Right now, it doesn't matter what anyone's opinion of her is—including my own. It's funny, but it seems like a part of me is missing. I guess it's like that when there is a separation. I have thought much about what has happened—and for the life of me, I cannot figure out where I went wrong. More than anything else, it is a lonely feeling. Jerome and Millie made me a lemon cake yesterday, and I thought that was nice. Although I ate some, I haven't been feeling real hungry lately. Millie calls it depression. I call it loss. She tells me I will be all right in time, and I know what she says is true, but for now, things still hurt. Part of me still thinks Karen is out there in cyberspace, somewhere in the hills of Italy, trying to text me. Like Apollo 13, I am orbiting the dark side of the moon, and there is still no word from Karen, and I have lost all sense of hope.

Houston…Are you out there? It's so lonely in space.

June 26 . . . The Tennis Ball Trophy

The Boys have been making a big to-do about the swear word contest between George and Jerome, and to date, there is not one X on the calendar, which means that Jerome has gone a whole week without a swear word. Maybe he swears in his apartment. I don't know. But no one has heard him swear publicly, and he is within striking distance to claim his reward. Slater is the official timekeeper, and this morning it seems that most of the town is in for breakfast to witness the grand event. With 15 fateful minutes to go on the clock, the Boys are doing their utmost to get Jerome to swear. But Jerome just sits on the piano bench with his dirty apron and smiles without a word, as the clock ticks down.

I told him the least he could do was to put on a clean apron, but no, he has to pick the dirty one on this day, of all days, when the café is standing room only. Not good for public relations.

As the clock clicks down to three minutes, George and the Boys put on war paint, feathers, and cowboy hats, dancing before him like wild banshees. The town laughs and Jerome continues to sit in silence, like a proud Indian chief, as the ranting and the raging around him intensifies into what appears to be a mock western battle.

With 20 seconds left on the clock, George stops and yells out, "Damn it, Jerome, can't you give a war veteran a fighting chance? Double or nothing, huh?"

The crowd boos.

"Triple or nothing," he cries in desperation.

More boos, and then Slater steps on top of the counter and announces, "Jerome is the winner."

The café erupts with laughter.

George laughs and pats Jerome on the back, along with the other patrons. A few decide to play up the moment and hoist Jerome up on their shoulders. The children scream with delight, and adults, young and old, begin to clap in rhythm as Jerome raises his arms like Rocky. As they circle the cafe for the second time, you can see their shoulders strain to keep Jerome's big frame up in the air. They finally set him on the piano bench and yell, "Speech!"

Jerome stands on the piano bench like a great orator, then clears his throat. Silence fills the room.

"Oh, man," he says at last, as if trying to catch his breath. "It was tuuuuuuuff," he declares, drawing out the word to its fullest possible extent. "Man, it was like hell not being able to say even so much as a . . ."

Jerome catches himself and starts to laugh along with the crowd.

"By golly, Boatman," George shouts. "You did it—you went the whole week without a swear word. You're a better man than I."

As the crowd continues to laugh, George's tiny wife, Clair, breaks through, holding a bottle of Windex and a roll of paper towels.

"Bout time you started on those windows, George," she states, handing George the Windex. Everyone laughs, and George smirks and then heads for the door, but the event is not over. Millie shoots a sharp whistle, and the café is suddenly silent. She motions to her husband, Marvin, who then comes forward, carrying a paper bag.

Millie grabs the bag, and all eyes are fixed upon her. She then reaches inside and pulls out a makeshift stand in which inverted nails protrude through a small wooden plate, resembling a tiny display of miniature flagpoles in a circular formation. She then reaches inside and pulls out a fluorescent yellow tennis ball—the kind Jerome used to squeeze. As she places the tennis ball on the protruding nails, the crowd begins to laugh.

"This trophy is awarded to Jerome Boatman for a job well done!" she announces.

The cafe suddenly erupts in applause, then laughter, as people start patting Jerome on the back and shaking his hand—the first being George himself. Then, like a receding tide, the café soon empties. And when the breakfast rush is finally over, Millie—as if holding a piece of fine china—carefully takes the mounted tennis ball and places it on the trophy hall of fame, next to the hole-in-one golf ball that is elevated on an aerosol can cover. The tennis ball is but one thread in the tapestry of Bullpen's historical events, whose stories are told in the yellow newspaper clippings, old photographs, and little-kid drawings that span more years than there are different kinds of crayons. As tacky as Jerome's trophy looks in the midst of the community billboard, it is a tribute to a great effort, and I can only wonder what significance lies behind all of the other homemade trophies.

Later That Night . . . Supper with Homer

I am invited to Homer's home this evening for supper, and I am not sure what to expect. What do bachelor farmers eat for supper? Bacon and eggs?

When I arrive at the house, I step up to the front door and ring the broken doorbell. I am standing on the porch of an old Victorian home that is in need of a couple coats of paint and some scrapping. The porch underneath my feet seems to sag in the middle, so I step to one side to keep from falling, should it collapse under my weight. As I wait outside, I peek through the curtains and see Homer inside, placing the last few plates around a small dining room table. He then scurries to the front door, wearing an apron. Suddenly, he stops and turns around. Realizing what he must look like, he pulls off the apron and then stuffs it under a nearby sofa seat cushion. I smile, thinking that someday he will find that apron when he least expects to and will wonder how it got there. When he finally opens the door, he is a little disheveled, but all smiles. He reminds me of Einstein in his latter years.

"Oh, come in, come in," he says excitedly.

I do and shake his hand. I am met with an assortment of aromas and smells. It is an odd mixture—deep heating muscle ointment, a musty odor, and burnt food.

"Come over here; come over here," he says anxiously and directs me into the dining room.

"Nice place you have, Homer," I say, looking about the dining room that is filled with boxes, old photographs, a grandfather clock, and a dining room table as long as the kind you might find in a corporate boardroom. One end of the table is clear; the other end is covered with more boxes and knickknacks. It looks as though he is still unpacking—and has been for years.

"Oh, I like the place," he says, moving about like an anxious host. "Do you like waffles?" he asks.

"I love waffles," I tell him.

"Good, because that's what we're having," he replies.

He hobbles into the smoke-filled kitchen and comes back with a plate full of burnt waffles, burnt bacon, and soggy eggs. Getting right down to business, he hands me the plate and tells me to sit down.

I do.

He then sits down and begins to serve himself. Suddenly, he shoots up from his chair and tells me that he forgot the syrup and the milk. He then hobbles back into the kitchen and brings back a plastic bottle of maple syrup, along with two glasses of milk.

"There," he says at last. "Waffles will never do without syrup, and you can't have waffles without milk."

I agree.

He sits down, bows his head, and offers a prayer of thanks to God for the food. Finished, he smiles at me, as if that is my cue to start eating. I do, and so does Homer, but not before he takes his napkin and carefully tucks it under the collar of his shirt, like a bib. Then, with uncharacteristic passion, he begins to wolf down his food as fast as he can and then washes it down with his milk in the same manner. Finished, he smiles at me with a milk moustache, blinking his eyes in rapid succession, and tells me how much he loves milk. Then, with a certain air of dignity, he wipes his mouth with his napkin and tells me that he and his brother were dairy farmers.

"Tell me about your brother," I say, and he does—in great length. He and his brother, Clarence, had farmed the family farm for over 40 years. Clarence was the elder brother and was the responsible one, he says, winking at me.

"Clarence never dated in his life," he goes on to say. "He was married to the farm, you know, and a wife would have slowed him down. And me? I am still trying to find the right one," he says.

"Well, be sure and take your time," I tell him, waiting to see if he has caught my sense of humor.

"Oh, I will," he replies matter-of-factly. "You know that Miss Farcus is a real looker, don't you?"

Miss Farcus . . . ? For the life of me I cannot recall what she looks like. All I know is that she has to be old like Homer, and to me all old people look alike—like all babies look alike. To me, babies only take on distinct features as they get older. And then when they get really old, like over 70 years of age, they all start to look alike again. But apparently that is not the case, at least not with Homer.

"So, tell me about Miss Farcus," I tell him. "How long have you known her?"

Homer stops to think and then tells me it's been over 15 years—ever since her husband died.

"Well, why don't you ask her out?" I question.

But he is quick to put down the notion, shaking his head as if I had said the unspeakable.

"Oh, I couldn't do that. Imagine how left out those other widows would feel," he states with conviction. "But secretly," he continues, smiling like a giddy little school boy, "secretly, I have told her that she is the cutest of them all."

And then it occurs to me that old people can still fall in love, just like young people.

We talk for what seems like another hour about everything under the sun. He then asks me if I have anyone special that I am "seeing." I tell him I had a girlfriend by the name of Karen and proceed to tell him what happened. He nods as if he understands and then tells me about a woman he once knew when he was young who had left him for another man.

"A pig farmer," he cries, shaking his fist in the air. "She married a pig farmer!" He shakes his head, then continues. "I should have fought for her. Oh, I should have fought for her, but how was I to know she liked pigs?"

I can only nod.

He grows quiet and stares down at the floor. I can only guess what he is thinking. We now have something in common, and for a brief moment, we share the silence that is broken only by the steady, hypnotic rhythm of the grandfather clock that ticks beside us.

I begin to wonder what a young Homer was like, and what his "girlfriend" was like. But there are no pictures of him or her on the wall. Was she pretty? Was she kind? Was he strong and fierce like a warrior, or had he always been kind and courteous and somewhat timid? As the clock continues to beat in those solitary moments between us, I wonder if time had been good to Homer. Or had it worn down his optimistic outlook on life, like ocean waves that relentlessly pound upon the once-sharp edges of jettisoned rock, year after year.

He smiles as we talk some more. I am expecting the evening to be through, but I am wrong. Suddenly, he glances at me with a competitive glare and asks if I have ever played Crokinole before. I tell him no. He then stands up and uncovers the board game from under the boxes at the end of the table.

He has come alive now and quickly explains the rules as if I have played the game before and the mere mention of them is only a formality prior to the eminent battle before us. He then slides the board to me and hands me my "shooters," he calls them—ten, quarter-sized discs that resemble wooden checkers that you flick with your finger, "shooting" them across the board. It's scored like a shuffle board game with each side taking turns.

We start playing without so much as a practice round, and I soon begin to realize that, to Homer, it is not just a game—it is a war, and he is Michael "not-in-my-house" Jordan. Yes, the kind-hearted, mild-mannered (did I mention courteous?) Dr. Jekyll has suddenly turned into Mr. Hyde. He then begins to jerk, fuss, contrive, squirm, and squint across the board like a disgruntled field general, blinking profusely. He then moans and cajoles about his hideous angles of attack.

"That will never do," he bellows to himself, as if disgusted with his performance. "That will never do."

He then fires off a series of shots in a wild, ephemeral fury and collapses into his chair—exhausted.

I don't remember the won-loss record between us that night. What I remembered on the way home was the calm after the storm—when you could hear the faint ticking of the grandfather clock as the tension on Homer's face began to recede like an ocean tide full of memories of a body once young. And when a smile finally broke across his face, I knew that Homer's Ulysses had returned from the battle of Troy—and with him, the kind-hearted Homer.

June 28 . . . Dinner at Lenny's

I am invited to Lenny's farm for dinner this afternoon. I'm trying to remember how I got out there before, but as I continue to drive along the country roads, it begins to come back to me. It was less than a month ago that I was on my way to Lenny's farm to pick up my uncle's truck and was greeted by his wife, LuAnn, with a plate of homemade caramel rolls. I am hoping that she will make them for dinner, and I'm getting hungry.

As I pull into the long driveway, Lenny's two dogs meet me—George and Gracie. They are golden retrievers that do not bark but only wag their tails. I have always liked golden retrievers and wished that I had one as a kid, but my mother told me that they shed too much.

As I get out of the truck, they continue to wag their tails, and George nuzzles his nose up to my hand as if telling me to pet him. I do. Then Gracie—not to be outdone—does the same. They continue to walk beside me as I approach their large white farmhouse. In the front, there is a wrap-around porch that is secured by an all-white, wooden railing that opens in the front to make room for the steps. Surrounding the porch is a long, lazy lawn of fresh-cut grass. I love the smell of cut grass and stop to enjoy it as I look beyond to the windbreak of cedar trees, buffering the land from the never-ending rows of waist-high corn. As I look at the barn and adjacent outbuildings, I am reminded of an implement dealer who once told me that, when selling farm equipment and farm-related services, you need to sell to the one wearing the pants in the family. If the house is neater than the barn or out-buildings, you sell to the wife. If the barn and outbuildings are neater than the house, you sell to the husband. In this case, I guess it would be a tie. As I stand there admiring the orderliness of it all, I feel the wet noses of George and Gracie rub up against my hand as if still vying for my attention. Attention deficit disorder is a common problem among golden retrievers.

As I approach the porch, LuAnn opens the door and greets me with a hug. Lenny follows close behind and shakes my hand. They invite me in, and I am met with the most wonderful of smells. It is Thanksgiving in June with the

132

smell of freshly baked bread, turkey, mashed potatoes and gravy, rhubarb and pumpkin pie coming from the kitchen. I kid Lenny that he is not fatter than he is with all that good cooking going on around him. Lenny laughs and offers me something to drink. We sit down in the living room and talk about the weather and politics and farming while LuAnn is busy in the kitchen.

It has been a great year for farming, and with an early spring, the crops are ahead of schedule. Lenny then offers me a tour of the house, and I accept. The home was built at the turn of the century by his great grandfather, and it has been in the family for over four generations, with each generation adding its own additions and flavor to the home. When I ask about the pictures of his four kids on the wall, he tells me that his two daughters are married. One lives in Wisconsin, the other in Connecticut. His oldest son is engaged and is visiting his fiancé for the weekend, while his youngest son is canoeing in the boundary waters of Minnesota. "Kind of quiet," he tells me as he points to their empty rooms.

The tour is cut short when LuAnn calls us down for dinner. And just as I had anticipated, we have caramel rolls and freshly baked bread. I tell her that she needs to bake for the café, and she laughs, shaking her head no. That means she would have to get up early in the morning, and that is simply not going to happen.

"I thought all farmers and their wives get up early in the morning," I tell them.

Lenny laughs. "Not LuAnn. She's a night owl. It's a wonder how we ever got married. Ain't it dear?" he says across the dining room table.

She nods and tells me that they have worked out a lot of things since they've been married.

Finished with dinner, LuAnn brings out the two pies, and I eat until I can eat no more. Lenny finishes his pie and then leans forward and stares at his empty plate as if wondering what to say next—and suddenly he is at a loss for words. There is an awkward moment of silence between us, and I am a little confused as to the change in atmosphere. He then forces a smile as he taps his fork on the table. Then he tells LuAnn to go get the checkbook.

I'm a little taken back by the request, but I continue to sit there while Lenny grows quiet and reflective. I wonder what is going on. LuAnn returns, holding a three-ring binder full of checks and stubs for the family farm, then writes out a check and hands it to Lenny, who hands it to me.

There are tears in Lenny's eyes, and I am confused. He tries to explain what is going on with his hands but is too choked up and beckons for LuAnn to finish what he himself cannot.

"This is a check for $7,500," she tells me. "There is more, but this is a good start. Your uncle loaned us some money about three years ago when things were pretty bad for us. We had some unexpected bills, and there was a terrible drought that year. We had overextended ourselves with new equipment and new land and had nothing to pay the bank. We had leveraged everything, including our home. Six months after the foreclosure notice, the bank was ready to take our home, and that's when your uncle gave us the money. . . . We always thought we would be able to pay him back, but . . . "

There are tears in her eyes now.

"If it wasn't for Roy," Lenny adds, "we would have lost our farm."

I stare at the check for $7,500 made out to me, and I'm dumbfounded.

"Why me?" I ask. "Why was the check made out to me? Why not his estate or the Bullpen Café or . . . "

"I think Roy would have wanted it that way," she says. "He talked a lot about his nephew Charlie."

"But I never really knew him," I say.

"Well, he must have known you, 'cause he would talk about you quite often."

"Really?" I reply, somewhat shocked. "So, tell me about my uncle. Why did he settle down in Bullpen?"

"Suzanne's father used to own the Bullpen Cafe," LuAnn begins to explain.

"Who was Suzanne?" I ask.

"Why, your aunt," replies LuAnn. "You didn't know you had an aunt?"

"No," I reply sheepishly.

"Why yes," states LuAnn. "She was working there the day Roy came in to ask for directions. Apparently he had gotten lost while driving."

"It must have been love at first sight," Lenny interjects, "because they were married that summer, and then she died the following spring from complications."

"Complications?" I ask. "From what?"

"Childbirth. She died in childbirth," answers LuAnn.

"So what happened to the baby?" I ask.

134

"She died too," Lenny replies. "It was a little girl—Kirsten is what your uncle named her. They are buried in the cemetery behind the church."

"I had a cousin?"

"Yes," replies LuAnn. "You had a beautiful little cousin."

Astonished and bewildered, I am suddenly lost in thought about an aunt and a cousin I never knew. My mind begins to race back into the mental archives of time, searching for clues, anything that might shed light on what seemed to have been purposely lost and then forgotten among members of my own family.

"So, what else do you know about my uncle?" I finally ask.

"It's hard to imagine what this town would have been like without him," offers Lenny. "I guess only God knows how many people he helped and how many lives he touched."

Later That Night . . . My Uncle's Letters

I looked through the file drawers tonight when I got home and found my uncle's marriage license. It was tucked away behind the profit-and-loss statements of the café. It was nothing more than ink on paper, but it was enough to reveal a part of my uncle that I had never known—perhaps would never have known had I not come to Bullpen. Why had not my own father told me about my aunt? Why had he not told me about Kirsten? Did he know about Kirsten? What was it between them that had created such a rift? Was there a rift? I had more questions than I had answers. I thought about talking to him, but all I could see was more of the Finstune family glare. "Damn the Finstune glare," I said out loud. I had a right to know about my own family, and if there were secrets, it was not my fault.

As I dug through the rest of the file cabinets, I began to wonder if my uncle had wrestled about coming to Bullpen as I had. Perhaps he had been even more encumbered by the weight of tradition that had marked him for a promising and prestigious career in law. Since Roy was the oldest of the Finstune brothers, it must have been a shock to my grandpa when he came to the realization that his number one son would not be graduating from law school. I could only imagine the disappointment on my grandfather's face when he realized the full impact of my uncle's decision. Would my grandfather lose his status among his fellow colleagues whose sons and daughters were enroute to some noble and equally prestigious profession? What could be more noble than law or medicine or research and development? But a café owner in small town USA? A scandalous affair might have been easier to bear for my proud grandfather, who had probably saved a place for his beloved son beside him at the firm. I can only imagine what silent pains my grandfather must have borne, having always wanted—according to my own father—to have his two sons beside him, practicing law. It was his dream, his unending passion. What a disappointment it must have been to hear the news. How he must have tried to persuade Uncle Roy to weigh the evidence and reconsider his verdict. But it seems as if his prosecuting evidence fell on deaf ears, as the jury—his own son—ruled in favor of a small-town life as opposed to a prominent career with one of the most high-powered attorneys in the state. Perhaps it would have been better if Roy had died. Then there would have been an excuse. But Roy had not died; he had chosen a path completely opposite from the scripted life that had been laid out before he was born.

As I continued to dig through the endless files of mindless paper, I found a whole file of photographs called "My Brother." I stopped and stared at a handful of old pictures of my uncle and my father camping together, swimming together, eating together. There were silly photos and not-so-silly photos that all suggested a great love they had for each other—once upon a time.

As my fingers began to sort through more files, I discovered it. Tucked behind an unmarked manila folder in the back was a letter in his own jagged but legible handwriting, to Suzanne. As I pulled the envelope from behind the file, I saw that it was addressed to Suzanne Walters. The return address was that of his former home in Minneapolis. As I pulled the letter from the envelope, I began to realize that he had been about the same age as I was now when he wrote it, and suddenly I was there with him:

Suzanne, I wanted to write and tell you that I am not going back to law school next fall. I am coming to Bullpen to be with you. I am alive with the thought of you, and that is more than I can say about any jurisprudence or hearing or objection. If there is any motive that embodies and empowers the great Constitution upon which the laws of our land are built, it is love, the love for freedom, and that is what I am with you. I am free to be as I am—without shame and without consequence of the race I have run my entire life—a race that has no winners—only victims. I am suddenly alive, Suzanne; I am suddenly and completely and carelessly alive and in love with the most beautiful woman in the world. Against all odds, I found you tucked away inside a sleepy little town, a back eddy from the swift and powerful current that claims the lives of those who chose to chase the ephemeral pursuit of a prestigious career. Yes, I was lost that afternoon when I came upon you at your father's café—lost in more ways than you can imagine. But, like a prisoner whose rudimentary life has given way to passion, I now see the most complex of attributes in the simplest of notions that spill carelessly over with the fullness of themselves like the smell of cherry blossom trees in spring.

Oh, how I have wrestled against reason, weighing all aspects of my decision. But in the end, I cannot turn back from what I know is true. I believe it was God that brought me here, guiding my hand that guided the wheel that led me to ask you for direction that fateful day, and direction I have found.

Against all odds, I found you, Suzanne. Against all odds, I have chosen us and all that our future may hold together. Against all odds, I am choosing the road less traveled as I had done the first day I met you. Two roads diverged in a yellow wood and I? I have taken the road less traveled, and that has made all the difference.

I sat amazed, looking into the heart and soul of the articulate and passionate man whom I never knew, much less understood. It is my uncle's heart that bares itself upon the page, like indelible ink that cannot or will not deny its affection or itself, standing against the forces that sought to take its soul. It is the heartfelt cry of a man who defies all others with his own sense of identity, who is neither enamored by the fear of man nor adjudicated by the love of mankind. As I read and reread the letter, I was lost in time and felt as if I was just beginning to see my uncle with clarity. It was then I searched for other clues that could draw me closer to his inherent nature, but I found none among the needless paperwork and mundane files that lay within the cabinet.

It was then I looked above the desk where I suddenly saw the score to the song "Fire and Rain" by James Taylor, encapsulated in a simple black frame upon the wall. The frame looked crooked against the linear composition of the rest of the pictures, as if it was somehow taken down more than the others. As I reached to straighten it, I noticed for the first time that it protruded beyond how a normal picture would hang. Pulling it off the wall, I found a letter neatly tucked inside the matting. It was a letter worn along the edges and authored again by my uncle's own hand. I opened it carefully and began to read:

Tonight, Lord Jesus, my heart is broken and the pain is too heavy for me to bear. I am undone and cannot stand. I have lost you, Suzanne. I cry out for you, but you lie silent upon your bed, your lifeless hands so cold to the touch. You—who made my heart alive—now lie upon your own bed, asleep with our daughter. Oh, if you could wake again and speak to me. Wasn't it yesterday that we had made our plans together? Are we not still a family tonight? I hold your hands not wanting to let go, but in the break of day I see your quiet, beautiful face for the last time, before they take you and our child away, down the long and empty corridor.

Lord, help me. I am undone and cannot stand.

I drive to the top of Thomforde Hill. It is 1:49 in the morning, and all is quiet. I Google James Taylor on YouTube and listen to him playing "Fire and Rain." I listen to the heart-felt cry of an artist who had captured his own pain through a simple, but profound song—the same song that had epitomized my uncle's pain.

The song is suddenly over, and I am left in my own silence, wondering about my uncle.

June 29 . . . Ivan the Terrible

We now offer donuts, Bismarcks, and long johns from a local bakery that delivers to us in the wee hours of the morning. Donuts and pastries are much-sought-after items, and we have decided to incorporate them into our breakfast menu. I love donuts, and so does Jerome—the glazed kind with the sweet, sticky sugar coating that gums up your fingers until you lick them clean. Then there are the Bismarcks—the ones with the chocolate icing and the Bavarian crème filling—not to mention the cinnamon rolls and other pastry items. They all go great with coffee, and they are the talk of the town. In doing the math, I find that Mavis Nordstrom, the Watkins lady, was right. Offering a lower price for coffee seems to be paying bigger dividends than offering higher-priced coffee. It's funny what and how people perceive prices. They now spend more at the café buying donuts but pay less for coffee. I guess they justify the additional expense by perceiving the rest of the menu as a good deal and, therefore, order more off the menu. It's all about marketing. And marketing is all about perception. How do we perceive what we buy? If you take a simple desk lamp made with reasonable quality and sell it at Wal-Mart, you pay a certain price, but if you take the same lamp and sell it at Macy's, people will be willing to pay twice as much.

It's all about perception.

Selling is as much a psychological phenomenon and an art form as it is a science. I remember when a local restaurant called the Old Country Buffet had decided to lower the price of their all-you-can-eat meal and then charge separately for the beverages. It all used to be one price for everything, but now they had two separate prices: one for the meal and the other for the beverages. Although they had dropped the price of the meal, they were charging extra for the beverage, and people perceived that negatively, even though they had dropped the price on the meal.

Marketing is crucial. It was originally Walt Disney that came up with the idea of charging one flat fee for Disneyland. In other words, one fee paid for as many rides as you could fit into one day, rather than having to pay for each individual ride over and over again like they do at the Minnesota State Fair. The perception at Disneyland was that you could make that fee as good a deal as you wanted to by taking advantage of as many rides as you could in one day. Charging one flat fee put the choice back in the people's hands, giving them a sense of control. The perception was that, if they wanted more, then they could come earlier and ride more or come at a time when not everyone was there so they didn't have to stand in line forever. The decision was theirs as to the value of the Disney Experience. With Old Country Buffet, however, that option was no longer present. Since most people wanted something to drink with their meal besides water, they were forced to pay "extra" for a beverage, and even though the meal was less, together it was perceived as more, and that perception—as justified as it was—was not positively perceived.

At the café, I still offer high-priced coffee, but it is only ordered 20 percent of the time. Hmmm . . . what does that say? I don't know, but what I do know is that the donuts are going like hotcakes, and it will be interesting to see if they supplant the oatmeal. And if so, what will be the net financial result?

As I am serving Slater a Bismarck, Ivan the Terrible walks in without a shirt and shoes. I tell him that, if he has no shirt and no shoes, then he will get no service. Looking confused, he nods, but he doesn't get it. I tell him again, but he still doesn't understand. He simply points at the Bismarck and tells me he wants it. He then gives me a dime, and I tell him that he doesn't have enough money to buy one. We have a little conversation about the difference between what he has and what he needs in order to buy it, but I am not getting through. So, I decide to give him the Bismarck as a promotional item and chalk up the difference as an advertising expense.

Yes, an advertising expense. That's it. I now have an advertising budget to promote my new items on the menu, and how better to promote them than with Ivan—my walking "little-kid" billboard. It's a brilliant idea. Surely the power of suggestion will hit others as they watch Ivan walking around town, eating his Bismarck, because little kids don't lie—they eat what they like. Grownups know that. Surely, if Ivan is promoting something by simply eating it, then whatever it is has to be good, right? And wouldn't they want the same thing Ivan has? It's all about perception and the power of advertising. And it only cost me the difference between the regular price of the Bismarck and Ivan's dime.

It's a brilliant idea, if I say so myself.

He takes one bite of the Bavarian crème Bismarck and, just like that, asks me where the bathroom is. I point to the bathroom, next to the kitchen, and he marches off, dripping Bavarian crème on the floor as he goes.

It's funny, but I don't really remember seeing him come out. Being distracted with cleaning the tables and bussing dishes and taking orders and helping Millie behind the cash register, I wonder what has happened to the little guy. It is then I hear Jerome yell.

"Mayday—Mayday! We gots ourselves a gusher and it's comin' fast and furious."

I suddenly see a steady stream of water leading up to the bathroom, and I rush over to the door.

"Ivan!" I yell. "What are you doing in there?"

I hear the toilet flush.

"Ivan!" I yell again, reaching for the doorknob, but it is locked. "Ivan, open the door!"

I hear the toilet flush again and then a sloshing sound of feet as the water continues to flow out from under the door.

"Ivan!!!"

Jerome is suddenly with me. He tries to force the door open with his shoulder, but to no avail.

"Man, we gots to get this thing turned off or else get ourselves an ark," he cries.

The toilet flushes again, and another burst of water gushes out from under the door.

"Ivan!" I holler. "Stop flushing the toilet and open the door!"

Jerome runs into the kitchen, comes back with a long bread knife, and tries to chisel his way through the door handle—again to no avail. Suddenly, I hear little clicking sounds from inside and then the familiar sound of the latch letting go of its stubborn position. Just as Jerome pulls back his knife, the door flings open and there stands Ivan, blinking like an idiot with chocolate smeared across his face. Jerome rushes to the toilet, grabs the plunger, and starts plunging like a madman.

"Come on!" he yells. "COME ON—FLUSH YOU PIECE OF . . ." And as if on cue, the toilet bowl begins to swirl, and I hear the heavenly sound of flowing water running down into the pipes below. As I stare and watch to make sure that it drains, Jerome holds up the end of the plunger. Lodged inside of it is the last of Ivan's Bavarian cream-filled Bismarck.

"Ivan," I yell, "what were you thinking?"

He is still blinking profusely as if confused by the whole matter. He then wipes the side of his mouth and tells me that he doesn't like the crème in the donut, so he flushed it down the toilet.

"Well, that explains everything," Jerome says, shaking his head.

As Millie, Jared, and the rest of the customers grab towels to mop up the wet floor, the health inspector shows up unannounced.

What do you tell the health inspector at a time like that? You tell him that Ivan the Terrible flushed a Bavarian cream-filled Bismarck down the toilet, and you look for the plunger to prove it, but you can't find it.

"It was here just a minute ago," I tell him. Then, as I look out the window, I see it in the hands of Ivan as he crosses the street towards home.

"There!" I shout like a madman. "There is the culprit! He is the one responsible for this mess. He tried to flush a whole Bismarck down the toilet because he didn't like the Bavarian crème filling and . . . "

I suddenly find myself salivating like a rabid dog. I reach down trying to find my composure, but it has suddenly slipped away with Ivan.

"He is the culprit!" I continue to yell, pleading my case like a man on trial for his life. "Don't you see him walking down the street with the plunger?"

I continue to point, but the health inspector is not even looking in Ivan's direction. Before he leaves, he hands me a list of citations—most of which include the bathroom. And then it dawns on me that the cost of Ivan's ten-cent Bismarck was more than just the cost of an advertising expense. Yes, my walking, talking "little-kid" billboard is out there plunging everything in sight. Brilliant.

June 30 . . . A Community Billboard

I am reading through the numerous blogs that have come in the last few days, and I am amazed to see what I call a mild following. Thank you for kind words about my uncle and for taking time to share your thoughts about the loss of someone in your own life.

One of you had a brother who died when his Volkswagen flipped over and threw him from his car. He was an English major in college, and you think of him every time you see his name written on his books he loved to read or hear a song that he loved to play on the piano or hear his name in public.

Bill from Maryland writes that he can still hear his wife's encouraging voice in the recesses of his mind, even though she died over 24 years ago.

One of you, by the name of Gloria, still grieves over your friend who lost his life in the Vietnam War—and you go to the Veterans Memorial Wall every year on his birthday with a white carnation—the kind he had given you on your first date. You, too, continue to listen to "Fire and Rain."

And Mary from New York tells about the loss of her parents and how she and her younger brother had to move from Minnesota to New York over 11 years ago to live with grandparents.

There are other stories, and as I read all of them aloud, I find myself sharing in their grief as they had shared in my uncle's. Suddenly, I realize that this site is bigger than I am. It is a little like a community billboard—like the one at the café—and I am but a catalyst that has triggered a following of people who have begun to write and share stories of their own.

July 1 . . . Bullpen Days Are Full Steam Ahead

I arrived late to the Bullpen Rotary meeting that was held at Mavis Nordstrom's Curiosity Shoppe and there was electricity in the air. I was met again with a cup of warm cider and eager nods from the fellow members. Since I had missed the last meeting, I was behind the eight ball in terms of the new developments regarding "Bullpen Days." Just as I began to take my first sip of cider, Eddie Carlisle patted me on the back and started to fill me in with a preliminary schedule of events. But before he could finish, the mayor cut him off and told him it was time to officially start the meeting.

The meeting them came to order with the secretary, Mavis Nordstrom, reading her notes from last session's meeting. It was unanimously approved that Bullpen would invest all $1,258 in the Bullpen Rotarian Fund to push the event forward in a massive marketing campaign that would reach tens, if not hundreds of thousands, of hungry Bullpen "wanna-be's." In the end, it would be our finest hour, trumping even the apex of Bullpen's glory days and the infamous baseball game of 1893. Yes, Bullpen Days would bring about a renewed sense of pride, not to mention money, to our long-forgotten community. People would no longer think of Bullpen as the armpit of civilization. No. They would now come and see us for what we really were: hard working, honest, intelligent people who cared about a town that was not even mentioned on most state maps. We would no longer have to play second fiddle to larger communities like Northfield or Zumbrota or Wanamingo—or even Zumbro Falls. Bullpen would, in fact, rekindle its own sense of identity that had been snuffed out when Bullpen's own beloved high school had merged with the nearby farming communities of Chesterfield and Clair Valley (the once proud home of the Clair Valley Blossoms) into what is now known as the Tri-town Independent School District.

And to commemorate the union of the new district, a new high school was built. It was called the "School of Tomorrow," featuring every imaginable modern technological gadget and wizardry that the Tri-town Independent School District could borrow—and borrow it did—building a massive educational complex

144

that was exactly twenty-five miles and twenty-five minutes from each township. It was right in the middle of a cornfield, simply because the visionary members of the Tri-town School Board (having seen the movie *Field of Dreams*) believed that if they built the school there, people would come. Yes, it was only a matter of time before the Tri-town Independent School District would grow into a metropolitan community, so large that it would soon dominate the prestigious Zumbro Valley Athletic Conference and produce more championship teams than a kid could count on his or her fingers at recess.

But the communities didn't grow. And over the years, the once-proud independent school district's only claim to fame was a mere consolation trophy for women's wrestling.

Then adding insult to injury, it came out in the 2000 census that most of the townsfolk from the surrounding communities were geriatrics, and it was the geriatrics that defeated the new referendum that was designed to increase property taxes to pay for yet another gymnasium. Immediately after the referendum fell short of the goal line, the school board reconvened. With egg still fresh on their face and desperate for anything that might bolster the fledgling district that had begun to falter on its loans, the Tri-town School Board did the only plausible thing it could do to restore their rightful standing among the other more prominent communities. It voted unanimously to hire a good football coach. And good he was, but not at football. And after two winless seasons and three affairs, the school board ran him out of town on a rail.

Cumulatively, all of these effects on Bullpen were simply trivial matters of concern. The real devastation—according to the mayor—was that over time, the Bullpen students began to blend in to the non-descript melting pot of the new high school—looking and acting and talking like the other students from Chesterfield and Clair Valley. There was no difference between them. Even the once-proud Norwegian accent—the hallmark of Bullpen's identity—was being prostrated by the more distinct German, Irish, Polish, Finish and Swedish accents. And to make matters worse, the Tri-town Independent School District had imposed desegregation through forced bussing. Yes, the tentacles of the racial tension that was responsible for Rosa Parks and the Montgomery Alabama Bus Boycott of the 1950s had finally found its way north into southeastern Minnesota. Now Swedes had to sit next to Fins and Germans next to Poles and Irish next to Norwegians for a full 25 minutes—one way. And to make matters worse, they had begun to share their lunches, swapping Irish soda bread for lefse and Swedish meatballs for wiener schnitzel.

145

As Mavis continued to read the major events surrounding Bullpen Days, I glanced at the clock on the wall.

There was to be a five-kilometer race, a commemorative baseball game, a tractor-pulling contest, a bake-off, a pig roast, a wiener roast, an all-town scavenger hunt, potluck supper, beer garden, blue-grass contest, acrobatics . . .

"Acrobatics?!" I blurted out, spilling cider on my clean shirt. "What kind of acrobatics?"

Apparently, it was a stupid question, and I could tell by the looks of my fellow Rotarians that they now had to stop and educate the new guy.

"Methune Fuliedy" (pronounced full-I-dee), Able replied matter-of-factly. Then Mavis continued reading.

"Wait!" I interrupted. "Who is Methune Fuliedy?"

Apparently, that too was a stupid question.

"You don't know Methune Fuliedy?" They asked me.

"No—I'm sorry, but I don't know Methune Fuliedy. Who is Methune Fuliedy?'

The mayor interceded and told me that Methune is a local stunt man who is known for getting shot out of a cannon.

"Oh," I found myself saying, " . . . like an Evel Knievel kind of guy."

"Exactly!" said the mayor. "Only Methune can fly up to 300 feet before landing."

"300 feet!?" I cried out.

They all nodded.

"So, when did you get this guy?" I asked.

"Last week." replied Gerald. "Oh, you have to book him far in advance, but he just so happened to be free for the last weekend in August. So we booked him."

"You booked him? How much does he cost?" I asked.

"Five thousand dollars a shot, plus insurance," replied the mayor. "Last year he missed the target and ended up in the hospital."

"Five thousand dollars a shot—plus insurance?!" I cried out.

"Oh, he normally charges ten thousand," explained Jake. "But since he is a second cousin to a friend of Eddie's wife, he gave us a sweet deal."

"Oh, that is just sweet," I said sarcastically. "So, where are we going to come up with $5,000 to pay him and his insurance company when we only have a little over $1,200 in the bank?" I questioned.

"Ticket sales," replied Rodney Holbrook smugly, as if he was just waiting for my question. "We will presell tickets, and all of the money we make in presales will help us pay not only for Methune but also the rest of the event, including Johnny Dugan and the Rascals."

"Who's Johnny Dugan?" I asked.

"You ain't never heard of Johnny Dugan?" replied Gerald.

Then they stared at me as if I had just said a four-letter word.

"No," I replied.

"Why he is the hottest country western singer in southeastern Minnesota, and we got him," shouted Eddie.

"So, we are going to sell tickets to Johnny Dugan, and that will cover this cannon guy and Johnny Dugan too?"

They nodded.

"So, how are we going to monitor the tickets?" I asked them.

"Simple," replied the mayor. "We're going to rope off an area just down the block from the Bullpen Café and have a beer garden and live music with Johnny Dugan and the Rascals."

"And how much are we going to charge for tickets?" I inquired.

"Five dollars for kids under five years old, and ten dollars for kids over five years old. Adults will be twelve dollars," they replied.

"Twelve dollars!" I shouted. "What adult in their right mind is going to spend twelve dollars to see this Methune guy get shot out of a cannon and this Johnny Dugan guy?"

The room was suddenly quiet—and I, being the astute observer of human nature that I am, quickly came to the realization that I was out of order or, should I say, out of sync with the rest of the Bullpen Rotarians. I was being shot down with nasty glares, so being the bright college-educated graduate that I am, I shut my mouth and conformed to their all-too-apparent irrational judgment. This was, after all, Civics 101, and I was the rookie in town—the new guy—and what does the new guy know, anyway?

And who knows? Maybe, just maybe, this Johnny Dugan fellow will be a hit and this cannon guy will bring down the house—and preferably not with his own body.

July 4 . . . Fireworks in Rochester, Minnesota

After the last of the lunch rush had left the café, Mille sat down on the counter and asked Jerome, Jared, and me if we wanted to go with her and Maynard to Rochester for the big fireworks display. Having nothing else to do that night, we all agreed. So it was settled. Maynard and Mille would pick us up at six pm, and we would go out to eat at a Mongolian café in Rochester, then go to the fireworks afterwards.

At fifteen minutes to six, Maynard and Mille pulled up in front of the café. To my surprise, Maynard was driving a brand new Cadillac and smiling from ear to ear. He had bought it three months ago as a present he had promised himself when he retired from the post office. Like a little kid at Christmas, he couldn't stop talking about all of its special features, including the rearview camera that shows you what is behind you when you back up. To demonstrate, he pointed to Bullpen's only light pole, put the car in reverse, and told us to look on the dashboard monitor and watch it come into view. And it did—much too quickly, however. After hitting the post, the Cadillac lurched to a sudden stop. A look of terror shot across Maynard's face. He jumped out of the car to survey the damage as Millie gave him a verbal thrashing. But as he inspected the bumper, a smile broke across his face. Looking pleased with himself, he told Millie not to worry—just a little paint smear from the silver lamppost. As Millie shook her head, Maynard jumped back into the driver's seat, giddy with excitement. And just like that, he pulled a U turn in the middle of main street, barely missing two parked cars—and off we went like a herd of turtles with Jared seated in the middle of the back seat and Jerome and me on both sides of him. Maynard then locked the doors, and as we began to roll down Main Street, I suddenly felt like a little kid going on a family vacation.

But it was no vacation driving with Maynard.

As he gave us the play-by-play and the accompanying demonstration of the car's new features, we started to veer over the dividing line and into the oncoming lane. When an 18-wheel semi approached us and honked his horn, Millie simply told Maynard to get back in his lane. He did so with the greatest of ease, narrowly avoiding a head-on collision.

We almost had four head-on collisions that evening on the way to Rochester.

Jared was his usual quiet self as he simply watched the near-death experiences pass us in the other lane while listening to music on his earphones. However, Jerome was clearly beside himself, squeezing anything he could get his hands on. And Millie? She was as calm as calm could be, as if these near misses were a normal part of "driving with Maynard." She had either become immune or calloused to the aspect of death—or God himself had given her a special dispensation of grace to ride with Mr. Magoo. It was then I began to wonder about Maynard and guardian angels in general. I wondered if there was a special task force that had been assigned to Maynard at birth, and if so, did they get extra combat pay? And how many other near-death experiences had this special task force kept him from during his life? I wondered if we would make it out alive every time he looked back at us, taking his eyes off the road while describing more of the special features of his new car as it would begin to veer into the oncoming traffic.

"Maynard," Millie would say again, "keep your eyes on the road."

And slowly, Maynard's head would turn toward the road ahead of him—and the car, as if pushed by unseen angels, would veer back into its own lane—just in time.

We arrived at the restaurant unscathed, but Jerome looked ill. Maynard, still talking about the Cadillac's new features, unlocked the doors with his keyless remote—and like a paroled convict, I felt a sudden sense of freedom. Jerome, however, was still incarcerated, as he simply stared out the passenger window until Maynard opened his door and helped him out.

"There now," Maynard said at last. "I'd say we made pretty good time, huh?"

Jerome nodded sheepishly and managed to roll himself out of the car. Jared followed, and I came around from the other side. Millie took Maynard's hand, and the two of them walked to the front door of the restaurant, like an old couple in love. Jerome, however, was clearly hurting. As I waited for him to catch up, I jokingly offered my hand. To my surprise, he took it, leaning on me like a battle-scarred soldier. As the two of us hobbled to the front door, he began to squeeze my hand as if it were a tennis ball.

"Don't let him drive home," he pleaded. "Charlie, you gots to promise me you ain't gonna let him drive home."

Like an old army buddy, I promised him I wouldn't.

As we entered the Mongolian café, the smell of stir-fry was in the air, and it was good. Suddenly Jerome came alive, like a boxer who had caught a whiff of smelling salts, and he began to lick his lips as the waitress escorted us to our seat.

As we squeezed around the table, Maynard was still standing, and like a proud sea-faring captain, told us that the dinner was on him. I told him it wasn't necessary to treat us, but he insisted, nodding affirmatively again and again, as if trying to convince himself of what he had just done. When Millie looked up at him like an admiring first mate, it reaffirmed his decision, and his nods became more definitive. We all thanked him, and he sat down, grinning from ear to ear.

When the waitress came, she described the setup and how we were to get our own food from the salad bar, place it on our plate, and give it to the chef who would fry it up on the large round grill at the front of the restaurant. Her directions were easy enough to follow, and follow we did, as Maynard and Millie led the way. Jared went next, followed by me and then Jerome.

It was a smorgasbord of choices at the salad bar: green peppers, black olives, mushrooms, fresh tomatoes, and raw beef, chicken, and pork. Sprouts, carrots, garbanzo beans, and a variety of greens populated the rows of serving trays along the bar. Jerome was now fully alive, trying to keep the mound of food he had piled on his plate from spilling on to the floor. Jared was doing the same. We then gave the young, Asian chef our plate and he fried our culinary choices for us on the grill, splashing various bottles of marinade upon the heaping mound of fresh food. The oils from the marinade sizzled, then snapped, and then jumped upwards on the hot grill as the sweet and tangy smell of vinegars and fruit juices permeated the front of the restaurant. When the tiny fires erupted again and again, it was as if we had our own display of fireworks as the flames jettisoned upwards in a brilliant display of blues and oranges, doused by another splash of marinade. In the midst of all the sizzling and smoking fury were the flashing knives in the chef's skilled and articulate hands, slashing, then scooping, then tossing the stir-fry upwards. The jumbled food hung suspended for a moment, then came crashing down in all directions, with carrots and garbanzo beans and mushrooms skidding across the grill. But before they had come to a complete stop, they were herded, then hurled upwards, again and again, in the same meticulous fashion of artistry. Finished, the chef took his knives and spun them about in his hands as if performing an encore. As the sharp knives flashed like a rapid succession of strobe lights, the people clapped. The young chef came to an abrupt halt and, facing the crowd around him, smiled graciously and began to fry the next plate of food. What was more fascinating than the chef's exacting hands, however, was the expression on Jerome's face as he studied the master. He seemed lost in a trance as he nodded and swayed, shaking his head in rhythm to the chef's movements being played out before him. When he suddenly came to, he saw that Jared and I were smiling at him. Self-conscious, he scowled.

"Well, ain't you never seen a man at work?" he retorted.

"Not like that," I said.

"Well, just you wait till Jerome gets that knife thing down," he said. "Just you wait."

Yes, I could hardly wait. I could hardly wait to wrap his hands in Band-Aids and tape his hands in gauze—and then clean up all the blood from his "knife practice." And when I told him so, he shook his head.

After dinner, we went and sat on the grass in the midst of an open field near the Rochester municipal pool and waited for the fireworks. Millie knew just where to go and had brought a large flannel blanket and a cooler. After we sat down, she passed out cold cans of root beer and bags of kettle corn. Slowly, the field became crowded with thousands of others as the darkness began to descend.

Having the need to go to the bathroom, I excused myself and found the Satellites (out-door toilets) lined up in a neat row like kiosks near the pool. Already, there was a long line, and as I stood there waiting my turn, I happened to see Jeff Gordon, a fraternity brother from the university. I walked over and surprised him. We shook hands and laughed and we talked briefly before his turn for the toilet. When he came out the door, I was still standing in line.

"We are having a reunion this summer," he said. "If you have any ideas on where to host it, let me know."

"I have just the place," I told him. "I'm running a restaurant in Bullpen, Minnesota."

"Bullpen?" He asked, looking like a dog at a new pan.

"Yeah, Bullpen," I said. "I took over my uncle's restaurant for a year."

"So, no law school?" he asked.

"I'm going to Harvard next year," I replied.

"That's good," he said slapping me on the back. "You had me worried there for a minute, Charlie. Hey, give me a call and we can set this thing up."

I agreed.

We chatted for a few more moments; then as my turn in the Satellite came up, we shook hands and he slipped back into the crowd.

When I stepped out of the Satellite, the words "next year" suddenly hit me. They had come out of my own mouth so spontaneously, so matter-of-fact—like a knee-jerk reaction. What would next spring hold? Had law school become so much a part of me that it was an unconscionable act not to consider it? I wondered, looking up into the twilight sky.

"*Houston?* You still out there?" I said out loud.

A teenage kid, overhearing my own conversation, looked at me as if I was crazy. Perhaps I was. I nodded to him, but he shook his head and walked away. As I looked skyward again, I realized that next year was really not that far away. It seemed as if time itself had begun to accelerate—and before you knew it, next year would be here. So what would my future hold?

Houston?

I thought about Karen, and I suddenly missed her. What was she doing now? What did American people do in Italy on the Fourth of July? Then I thought about my parents and wondered what they were doing. Every Fourth of July, up until two years ago, had been spent at Grandpa's boathouse near Hudson, Wisconsin—just across the river—until he sold it and retired permanently to Arizona. I suddenly missed my Grandpa—my piss-and-vinegar Grandpa—and the times we spent fishing together on the river in Wisconsin.

Just as I made it back to the blanket, the first of the rocket's red glares shot across the skyline in a burst of ephemeral glory. The young kids ooed and awed at the splendor above, then covered their ears as the percussion of booming shells exploded one after another. Next came multicolored weeping willows and dragon tails and smiley-faced starbursts. It was a Fourth of July that I had never experienced before as we all huddled together sharing root beer and kettle corn with our nearby Hmong, Caucasian, Mexican, and African-American neighbors. When one little kid started to wander off, Millie simply guided the child back to her parents, but only after she gave her a tootsie roll. Soon there were other kids pushing their way to our blanket for tootsie rolls, and Millie had plenty to go around. As I saw the multiracial hands reaching out for the candy, I saw our own blanket as a little melting pot, just like America itself. And as the fireworks burst above us, I saw the American flag flying near the pool, as if it was waving its approval; and suddenly, I was more proud of America than I had ever been before.

After the fireworks had ended, we simply continued to sit on the blanket, eat the remaining kettle corn, and enjoy each other's company until the last of the lights went out around us. We then walked to Maynard's car—not far from the grounds—and just before he unlocked the doors, I told him that I would drive home. He was about ready to protest, but Millie agreed.

"You boys can have the front seat. and Maynard and I will have the back," she said reassuringly.

Jerome breathed a sigh of relief while I examined all of the new gadgets. And by the time I finally figured out how to start the car, Maynard and Millie were asleep in each other's arms—and remained so all the way back to Bullpen.

Later That Night . . . Once There was a Way to Get Back Home

It was a peaceful night, and I was melancholy. The words "next year" kept coming back, and I could not let them go. What would my future hold? I missed Karen. Maybe you are like me, feeling like a tiny skiff on the vast expanse of a never-ending ocean or like a lunar module struggling to get your frame of reference in the vast, black hole of space.

Houston, do you copy?

Where am I going? Why am I here? Why was I born for such a time as this? These are questions that have plagued mankind since the beginning of time, and tonight I was among the skeptics of a never-ending and impersonal universe. Is there life on other planets? If so, what secrets lie in the distant galaxies beyond our own? Was life fabricated by random chance, or did its infinite complexity demand a greater explanation from an infinite mind?

I wondered.

When I was in Sunday School, one of my teachers told me that God always was—that He had no beginning and no end. As a kid that very thought scared me, because I could not get my mind around that infinite thought, and today it is no different. I don't know what eternity means or what it holds. I don't know what was before me or what will come after me. I only know the moment and in this moment, I felt the gentle breeze against my face, heard the orchestration of summer sounds and smelled the surrounding earthy smelling fields of pastureland.

What would my future hold . . . Houston?

As a child, I never thought about the future as I had never thought about the past. I only thought about supper and a place called home. Once there was a way to get back home, but as I grew older, I found it was impossible to return. I had come to the realization that, ever since birth, I was destined to leave the once-familiar setting and find my own way on this path called life. And like young eagles that were pushed from the nest, I have struggled to fly.

Perhaps some of you fellow bloggers are like me. Perhaps some of you have crashed and others of you have soared, but either way, something changed. The home you once knew would never be the same. Nothing ever is the same, and that realization suddenly brought pain. Where are my friends from the old neighborhood? Where are my classmates from school? Is life simply a series of hellos and goodbyes? If there is a big-bang theory, then are we not all shot out of the same institutional cannon at once, like brilliant but ephemeral fireworks that will one day fade away into the vast expanse of time and space? What then? If we came into this world alone, will we not leave it alone? Who am I? And what will my future hold? Does my life have purpose, or is it simply a random evolutionary coincidence in a cruel game called chance?

Houston, do you copy?

Is there a Houston that beacons us? Is there a Houston that gives us a point of reference from which we are to turn as we come around the far side of the moon—a reference that guides us through the vast expanse of an endless universe in an attempt to bring us closer to our own destiny?

I wondered if there was a God who knew my name. I wondered if there was a God who knew me before I was born—a God who knew whether I would choose a road less traveled or a congested highway. And if there is a God, is He like the gods of ancient Greece—uninvolved and unattached? Or is He a God who continues to take a special interest in his own creation?

I wondered.

As I was about to close down for the night, I got an email from Mary from New York.

"I couldn't sleep tonight and saw that you had posted your 'News from the Bullpen Cafe.' I smiled as I read about Millie and Marvin. They reminded me so much of my own grandparents who are now gone. My grandparents were such wonderful people, and I thank God they were there to raise my brother and me after our parents died. My brother is now in the military and stationed in Afghanistan. Besides a cousin in Florida, he is all I have. Tonight he is protecting our freedom on foreign soil by putting himself in harm's way— simply because he chose to do so. His life is so vulnerable out there on the front line—like a candle in the wind. Like you, I never thought about the future or the past, but now I miss the days we had together as children. I pray for him as I pray for the others around him—that God will protect them as they protect us on this Fourth of July.

"Thank you for listening…

"Mary from New York."

July 5 . . . The Sunday School Superintendent

Jerome and I went to church on Sunday only after Jerome pounded on my door for what seemed like hours. Reluctantly, I got dressed, and miraculously, we made it on time, even going through the proper channels to enter through the back of the church like normal people.

I am now proud to say that for the last three weeks we have been singing all four verses (and sometimes five) of songs in the *Lutheran Hymnal*, thanks to Jerome, who now prides himself on such a feat. And now that we have done so for three consecutive Sundays, it has become a "custom." It is common knowledge among Lutherans that, if you can do anything in the church service for three consecutive Sundays, it becomes a "custom." And if you do it for more than five Sundays in a row, it becomes a "tradition." And if you go a month and half, it becomes doctrine—full-fledged, sanctified, Martin Lutherized doctrine. And to put it mildly, we are all excited about the possibility of it becoming just that—doctrine—especially Jerome.

The rest of the service was short and sweet. Afterwards—when I was on my way out the door and minding my own business—I saw her coming out of the corner of my eye.

It was Mrs. Sherburne, the Superintendent of Sunday School.

Now Mrs. Sherburne is an older lady in her mid 60s, but she moves about with a dogged determination like that of a military drill sergeant. She was heading my way, and the moment I saw her, I knew intuitively that she was after me. Superintendents of Sunday School have but one agenda: to find able-bodied members that are willing to teach Sunday School for the rest of their lives. Yes, once a Sunday School teacher, always a Sunday School teacher. And once *pegged* as such, you can never retire—ever. I had seen the battle-scarred, glassy-eyed veterans as a kid in my own church. There was Mrs. Winkler, the fourth and fifth grade Sunday School teacher that had been there since the church was founded in 1910. She was wheeled into the classroom and then wheeled out by her great grandson who would often come early to help interpret her hand signals, since she could no longer talk. And then there was

Jacob Farley (the ghost of Christmas past, we called him), who had enlisted in the service of his church when he turned 18. He, too, had served faithfully for over 52 years and had never gone AWOL. Think about that—he had never gone AWOL. Jacob Farley was a Sunday School icon and a hero by anyone's standard, faithfully teaching the same curriculum for 52 unbroken years. Count them—52 faithful years, whether he knew what he was talking about or not. Then there were Mrs. Fleming and Mrs. Coburn and Mr. Arnold (need I mention more?) whose eight-by-ten-inch black-and-white photographs lined the hallowed basement walls on the Sunday School Hall of Fame—but not one of them was smiling.

And it all began with a seemly innocent question: Will you teach Sunday School?

"But I am not qualified," was always the objection.

That was no problem to the Sunday School superintendent. After all, what did qualifications have to do with anything? If you could fog a mirror, you were drafted, and that was that. Yep, kiss your civilian life good-bye, because you were now property of the Church Sunday School Division and would report directly to the Superintendent of Sunday School Education herself.

This morning the Superintendent was clearly on a recruiting mission and had but one objective: and I was it. I knew that intuitively by the way she continued to pursue me as if she was stalking some kind of prey.

I pushed ahead through the crowd—she followed. I doubled back—she doubled forward. I ducked into the bathroom—she waited outside. I waited inside—she waited longer. At last I found my chance and followed an innocent parishioner out the bathroom door, using his body as a human shield. But she was on to me. She was a crafty one, that Mrs. Sherburne, but worse yet, she was determined.

As I made one last ditch effort to shake her off my tail, I shot for the exit and saw what appeared to be an opening big enough to drive a truck through. But to my dismay, the hole closed as quickly as it had opened and I was stuck in the middle—and she was coming.

"Oh, Charlie . . . you whooo . . . Charlie," she yelled out unashamedly.

I tried politely to wedge my way past the mayor, who was discussing pertinent issues about Bullpen Days with another parishioner, in one last effort to avoid her. Seeing it was impossible to squeeze past him, I ducked my head behind his—but when I looked back to see if I had lost her, we made eye contact.

Horror of horrors.

"Charlie? Oh, Charlie? There you are," she said.

"Yes, here I am—hiding behind the mayor," I thought to myself.

"Do you have a minute?" she asked me.

"I'm sorry, Mrs. Sherburne, but I have to get back and . . . and . . . and ah . . ."

"Oh, it won't take but a minute. As you probably know, Mrs. Jamison has just gotten back from the hospital and won't be back to teach the first and second grade class. Would you like to take that class for a while, Charlie? I have heard you would make a great teacher and . . ."

What do you say in a moment like that? You think carefully about what plausible excuse superintendents have never heard before—the one that is not found in that surly superintendent's handbook of excuses. And if you can't think of any excuse? Well, then you stammer like an idiot.

"Ah . . . well, ah . . . well . . . have you thought of Jerome?" I asked stupidly.

"Well, I asked Jerome, but he suggested you and thought you would make a great teacher given your . . ."

So, Jerome had pushed her on to me, I thought to myself. Why that spineless fraction of a man. That scoundrel, that weasel, that . . .

"THAT SON OF A B— " Oops. I had spoken those last words of thought out loud. Horror of horrors. Suddenly, the whole congregation stopped talking and turned towards me, staring at me as if wondering what the next word would be that came out of my mouth. Thank God I had caught myself in mid-sentence, but now I wondered what would come out of my mouth. Think, Charlie—think! How would I finish that sentence? My next word was crucial and it had to start with a "B." In that millisecond of time and eternity I searched for a "B" word that would appease my audience. Then it came to me: Blessing.

"Why, that son of a blessing," I said matter of factly, forcing a smile. Suddenly, it was as if the whole congregation breathed a sigh of relief—especially the superintendent in search of a potential Sunday School teacher.

Why I told Mrs. Sherburne that I would take over Mrs. Jamison's first and second grade Sunday School class remains a mystery, but I did it. Perhaps I thought it would be a peace offering, considering that I had almost sworn in church. Whatever the reason, she was delighted to have someone—anyone—teach that class. As she continued to thank me, she kept bowing like the plump Austrian lady who accepts third prize in the Austrian Music Festival competition in the movie *The Sound of Music*. Did she know something that I didn't? Who were these kids? And why had it been so difficult to find a teacher for them all these weeks?

I wondered.

When I arrived at the truck in the church parking lot after giving Mrs. Sherburne my acceptance, I found Jerome leaning against the passenger door, sleeping. Upset with the way he had set me up, I opened his door, and he fell out. He came up fighting mad, but I was more so.

"What in Sam Hill did you do that for?" he yelled, getting ready to swing.

"What in Sam Hill did you volunteer me for?" I yelled back.

A smile broke across his face, and then he started laughing.

"What's so funny?" I asked him.

"Let's just say—ah, that class you got?" he continued.

"Yeah?" I replied. "Well, let's just say, from what folks was tellin' me, you got your hands full," he stated.

"So you pawned them off on me—thanks, pal," I replied.

"Hey, you're younger than me—you got more energy to deal with them kids—especially Ivan," he retorted.

"Ivan the Terrible?" I asked.

Jerome nodded emphatically.

Suddenly, it all made sense.

Later That Day . . . Pruning

I had been invited to Miss Maddie's for lunch that afternoon, and when I first arrived, I had a sudden notion of Karen, missing her all over again. The last time I was here, I had cried like a baby, and the pain in my heart was still there.

As I got out of my uncle's truck, however, I had no time to think of Karen, for Miss Maddie met me broadside with pruning shears, putting me straight to work trimming her hedges and pruning more of her rose bushes. She owns 45 acres of land, most of which is an apple orchard that overlooks the Zumbro Valley and the sleepy town of Bullpen.

I enjoy the physical work outdoors, and the rewards are even more enjoyable—Miss Maddie's cooking. For lunch she had prepared an avocado salad with walnuts and fresh spinach. There were also strawberries, fresh rhubarb bread, and real lemonade. As a kid, I used to hate avocados and walnuts and salads in general, but not now. Perhaps my taste buds have changed. Now, I appreciate all kinds of foods and their various flavors and combinations. Right proportions can make or break a dish, and that is what separates the good cooks from mere food handlers. A good cook can eat something and tell you what it needs—perhaps more salt or garlic or thyme or pepper—and how much, depending on the dish. It is the art of cooking, and it is as much an art as finding the right words is for a writer. It is all about discernment in the littlest of details that separates the good from the great. Why does a great interior decorator look at a room and tell you what it needs for color and comfort when someone else cannot? Why does a musician hear a piece of music and tell you where you need to put the next stanza when someone else cannot? Discernment. It's knowing what works and what doesn't. Sometimes it comes with experience, but often it comes with a premonition. Miss Maddie calls it a gift from God—an anointing. I am not sure what I would call it, but it is the reason why some can draw and some cannot. It is the reason why some can throw a fastball 95 miles an hour and some cannot. It is the reason why some are tone deaf and some are not.

It is easy to talk with Miss Maddie about anything it seems. She asked me about Karen, and I told her that the memory of her still stings. She nodded as if she understood. She then shared with me about her own life—her tragedies and her triumphs—and I came to realize that the depth of her suffering has brought her to a greater understanding and empathy for others.

Finished with lunch, she donned her "Audrey Hepburn" hat, and we headed to the orchard for more pruning. Although it was beyond the pruning season for apple trees, she told me it is never too late to get rid of a few unproductive branches. Flint, her dog, accompanied us. As we walked among the rows, the apple trees appeared to fall in line like a military roll call under the careful scrutiny of her watchful eyes. It was as if each tree was to give an account of its fruit that it has begun to bear these last few weeks. If no fruit was visible, she told me where to prune and how—as only an experienced vinedresser could.

When we reached the end of the row, she did an about-face and then began the next series of inspections on the other side of the row. She was meticulous, stopping every ten feet or so, gazing up at the soldier-tree that was standing at attention. Flint stopped and sat down by her side, as if he was doing the same. She looked comical, examining the large apple trees wearing her straw hat and oversized leather gloves. She then moved off center, holding her hands behind her back like a field general as her eyes continued to scour the tree for any deficiencies. Satisfied, she moved on with Flint following close behind her like a private.

It was late afternoon by the time we finished inspecting and pruning all the ranks, and I was hungry. So was Flint. As we head back to the house, Miss Maddie suddenly stopped. Out of the blue, she told me that God is pruning me, whether I know it or not.

I was not sure how to respond to a statement like that, and I asked her what that meant.

"It means that some things have to be taken away to make room for more," she replied. "Our lives are to bear fruit, Charlie. Good fruit. Do you know what the most productive apple trees are?"

"No," I admit.

"They are the ones that are humbled. They are the ones who are cut way back in the fall and look like an old woman with a bad hairdo."

She laughed.

"Like me in the morning," she said. "But they are the ones that produce. The other ones look pretty, but that's the problem. They are full of beautiful leaves that take the precious sap that should be used to produce fruit. They are so full of themselves that they cannot be used for anything else. Bear fruit, Charlie. God has called you to bear fruit, and that often means you will look much different than the rest of the world."

I was not sure what to think about her statements.

We continued talking, and then we stopped just a few yards short of the porch.

"What does it means to bear fruit?" I questioned.

"Cut away all of the branches and debris that clutters your life, and what do you have left?" she asked me.

"I'm not sure," I told her.

"The truth," she replied. "Only when you see the truth can you understand that it is not *what* you were created for, but *who* you were created for. It's a relationship, Charlie—a heart-felt, honest relationship with the one who created you and calls you by name. Knowing and having that relationship will give you purpose and meaning . . . and fruit."

Flint was patiently wagging his tail, looking up at her with his big brown eyes.

"Yes, I know you're hungry," she said to him.

"Well, that's enough for one day, Charlie. Come on, it's supper time."

"Suppertime," I said out loud as she and Flint headed up the steps into the house.

My mind suddenly slipped back to my freshman year, and I was standing outside a home where a family had gathered for supper. I was hoping they would see me and invite me to join them. Then I saw Miss Maddie, moving about her kitchen in preparation for the meal at hand. And when my eyes finally met hers, she motioned for me to come inside, and I did.

It was suppertime.

July 8 . . . The Truman Show

It is a windy night up here on the hill, and it is enough to keep the mosquitoes away as I sit in the back of the truck, blogging. Tonight I received a voice mail from my mother, reminding me about my dad's up and coming fiftieth birthday party this Saturday night. Apparently, she had left a message before, but I didn't get it. It's a party on a Mississippi riverboat, the Delta Queen. She has invited many of Dad's colleagues and other associates, along with board members from the agricultural conglomerate that she represents. My brother Karl will also be there, flying in from Boston where he is interning with a reputable law firm. It is a formal affair, the kind in which my mother excels, and it is as high brass as you can get in Minnesota. And me? I am told not to embarrass my father. Why the sudden concern? Have I ever embarrassed him before? Apparently so. Perhaps it was the time when he had to come and get Jerome and me out of jail a few weeks ago. Perhaps it is because I have not made any attempt to come home after a month's "experience" running the Bullpen Café. Or maybe the real issue is that I am an embarrassment to my mother, and she doesn't have the courage to say so directly.

Why *did* she choose the words "Don't embarrass your father"? As I thought about it, it occurred to me that it was a backhanded warning. It implied that she is looking out for him, protecting him from any adverse effects of an "embarrassing son" (AKA Charlie Finstune). But the truth of the matter is that my mother is issuing a personal threat by trying to leverage my relationship with my own father in order to get what she wants. It is manipulation—and it is a brilliant and powerful tactic. After all, who in their right mind would want to deliberately embarrass their own father? No one. So what are these threats all about? Attempts to control this embarrassing son? And if so, where does this need to control come from?

I wondered.

And if I am such an embarrassment, then why am I invited? Well, not to invite me would be even more embarrassing. It is, after all, my father's fiftieth birthday, and all his family should be invited.

"Please come, but don't embarrass your father. Love, Mom."

Makes you want to just get in the car and run home to her outstretched arms, doesn't it? Come to think of it, I have never seen my mother with outstretched arms? I have never seen her hug my father for that matter. So, why the sudden need to support him now? Is it simply because it is his fiftieth birthday party—or does it go deeper than that?

I suddenly wondered how our family had become so dysfunctional.

I thought we were normal growing up. The neighbors always thought so and told us what a great family we were. We mowed our lawn and took out our garbage as all good neighbors did. We attended church on Sundays and were amiable enough, or so I thought. I got good grades, or relatively good grades, or . . . in some cases, not so good grades. But my brother Karl was a straight "A" student and the captain of the debate team. So weren't we a good family?

What is normal? What is abnormal or dysfunctional? If you grow up in a dysfunctional home, how can you tell what normal is unless someone or something tells you the truth about your abnormality? Take for example the movie *The Truman Show,* with Jim Carry. It is a great story about perspective and self-discovery. For you fellow bloggers that have not seen the movie, it is about a man by the name of Truman Burbank, who is the star of one of the most popular shows in television history. The only thing is—he doesn't know it. He doesn't know anything. An entire world has been fabricated for him in a special Hollywood studio to simulate a small town called Sea Haven, where he has lived since birth. Truman's only perspective of life since a baby has been one that the director/producer/creator, Ed Harris, has scripted for him. All Truman knows to be true is the make-believe world in which he lives—until one day a young woman tries to tell him the truth about his life. Left wondering what she meant, he decides to take a few detours from his normal routine and discovers cameras in the strangest of places—and camera crews scurrying to recover from his "unscripted" actions. Over time, he begins to discover that the world he has grown up in is not real or normal. But, because it is the only world he has ever known, he thought it was.

So how do we know the truth about our own situation? How do we know if we have been living in a dysfunctional home unless someone tells us? The answer is, we can't, until someone or something tells us otherwise.

The fish friends of Bruce—the killer shark from the movie *Finding Nemo*—call it intervention.

Fellow bloggers, would you agree?

July 11 . . . Rolling Down the River

It is Saturday night, and I am driving along the pier, trying to find a place where I can change from my suit into a tuxedo that my mother had ordered for me for the special occasion. I thought the suit would be good enough—but apparently I was wrong. So all I need to do now is to find a men's bathroom or something to change in, and I will be set for the evening. But after driving around for ten minutes, the closest thing I find is a local—very local—bar.

It is a crusty kind of bar near the pier, and I feel out of place in my suit and tie, holding my tuxedo as I push though the smoke-filled haze enroute to the bartender to get directions to the "men's" room. I am suddenly the center of attention as those sitting around the bar eye me sarcastically and smile—some with teeth and some without. I am suddenly feeling very "yuppie," and as I approach the counter, I ask the bartender if I can use the bathroom to change my clothes. He is a bearded, stocky man with no neck, around forty years old, and upon my request he gives me the once-over stare, then simply nods his head towards the back.

"It's my dad's fiftieth birthday," I tell him, as if trying to explain why I'm there, "and I need a place to change."

He continues to stare at me as if irritated, as if that is the only thing he does all day is to direct guys like me to the "men's" room. I thank him and work my way to the back of the smoky haze until I find it. Suddenly, it occurs to me why the bartender has had to direct so many men to the men's room. On the wall adjacent to the bathroom door hangs a painting of a scantily dressed, full-bodied woman. I am guessing that it was a former waitress, and I can only imagine why someone had the audacity to take a black magic marker and draw a moustache on her face. "This really is a rough part of town," I say to myself, but then I realize that most men probably wouldn't notice her moustache anyway. But that's just a guess.

After I say good-bye to the former waitress on the wall, I step into the bathroom, and I see that it has not been cleaned in the last 20 years—and smells like it. There are two closed stalls and one urinal. One of the two stalls is occupied,

165

so I take the other—the one without the dents. As I shut and lock the door behind me, I find that the stall is tighter quarters than I had anticipated, and I can barely turn around. Surrounded by graffiti—some graphic, some written—I carefully place the tuxedo on top of the water tank, above the toilet. I notice that the toilet itself has no seat cover. Perhaps it was used as a battering ram during a recent barroom brawl. Perhaps. As I turn around and start to loosen my tie, the unthinkable happens. I bump the tuxedo bag, and all its contents spill into toilet.

Horror of horrors!

My life flashes before me as I quickly fish the bag out of the toilet. To my surprise the dry cleaning bag has miraculously shielded most of the tuxedo from the water.

"There is a God!" I say out loud, but as I hold the bag up, I notice that the bow tie has taken on water.

"Son of a . . ." I stop and catch myself mid-sentence, then try to reassure myself there is no more collateral damage.

"You okay in there?" comes a guttural voice from the adjacent stall.

Oops . . . I forgot I'm not alone, and I now have an audience in the next stall.

"Ah, yeah . . . I just dropped my tuxedo in the toilet," I tell the voice next door—as if he needed an explanation—as if I needed to give him the play-by-play of what has just happened.

He laughs. I suddenly laugh with him . . . we are laughing together. Who is this man? I am not sure I want to find out, so I continue to dress quickly, banging along the stall walls as I try to put on my pants, shirt, and shoes.

"So, do you think you could keep it down in there?" he says.

"No problem," I reply and then decide to finish dressing outside the stall. Having put on the pants, shirt, and cummerbund, I wrestle with the cufflinks, then stare at myself in the cracked mirror. Not bad for a quick change. Now, for the bow tie. I rinse it under the faucet to clean it off and in the process splash water all over the front of my pants. They will dry, I tell myself. I then look about for a paper towel—anything to dry off the bow tie, but there is nothing. So I squeeze the bowtie and let the water drain down the sink. I then put it around my neck and adjust it as best I can. It will have to do. I am running late.

As I pull into the pier, I notice that my mother is waving to me. It is not a friendly wave. It is an urgent wave, and I am tempted to wave back, but I realize this is not time to be funny—they are waiting *for me*. The whole boat is waiting for me, and yes, I have done the unthinkable—the very thing my mother warned me not to do—I have embarrassed my father in front of his peers. As I park the car, I grab my father's birthday gift, a box of expensive cigars, and then make a mad dash to the plank. I am greeted by the captain and my mother, who careens me into an unseen corner near the bathrooms. Her face says it all—disgust, disappointment, urgency, embarrassment—did I mention anger? She is fussing over me now, and I feel like a little boy getting ready for Sunday School. She grabs my bow tie and yanks it back and forth as my head jerks in the same directions. Apparently, I had not done a good enough job adjusting it myself.

"My God, Charles—what took you so long? And your bowtie! It's all wet!" she whispers loudly. Then she cringes and starts to sniff me. "My God! What's that rancid smell?"

Oops. In my brilliant attempt to dry off my bowtie and pants, I had done the unthinkable—I had turned on the heater to speed up the drying process, and to my own horror, the stench of vomit from my tequila party a few weeks ago, had permeated the Toyota. Yes, I had cleaned everything but the heater. Jerome had warned me that turning the heater on in the winter would trigger the stench—and he was right.

So, what do you tell your mother in a moment like that? . . . Well, Mom, I had a little pity-party after I had heard about Karen's engagement to this Italian guy whose family owns some winery near Sicily, and then I took a bottle of tequila and got drunk listening to Sting and then puked all over the dashboard—some of which ran down into the heater that I could not clean without removing the dashboard. And then when my bow tie fell in the toilet while I was getting dressed in the men's room of this distinguished tavern down the road, I came up with the brilliant idea of trying to use the heater to dry it off so I wouldn't have to explain all of this to you if and when you decided to adjust it.

"I'm not sure," I reply. "My guess is that the guy before me had a bachelor's party and the tuxedo wasn't cleaned."

She shakes her head, steps back to look at me, and then notices my wet pants.

"And your pants are wet, too!" she exclaims. "My God, Charles. You look like you just peed in your pants! Can't you do anything right? You stay here until you dry off while I find something for that smell of yours—good God."

She does an about-face, then breaks into an instant smile as one of the lady guests greets her, asking if everything is okay.

"Oh yes," she tells the other lady, smiling cordially. She then laughs and takes the other woman's arm in hers, and the two of them walk down the hallway like old friends until their voices are swallowed up by the Dixieland music playing above.

And me? I am feeling like a bad dog in need of a bath. I have been quarantined until further notice.

As the Dixieland band continues to play above me, I walk about my two-foot-by-four-foot kennel. It is a perfect night, and I watch the huge paddle wheel circle about in an almost hypnotic fashion, with each blade dipping into the mighty Mississippi, as we are propelled steadily forward and away from shore. On each side of the banks are city lampposts that line the boardwalk where couples stroll arm-in-arm—and I am suddenly missing Karen.

I wait for another ten minutes for my mother, but she is nowhere to be seen. My bow tie seems dry enough and so do my pants, and I no longer smell rancid—at least that I can tell. So, I venture upstairs where the Dixieland band is filling the air with Louisiana jazz and suddenly think of Jerome. He would love this kind of music. When they start playing "When the Saints Go Marching In," people milling about the food bar drift on to the dance floor and begin to march in rhythm to the familiar tune. The champagne lady passes me, and I take a glass and start to gulp it down. Hungry, I move to the food bar and spot my brother talking to a distinguished-looking, middle-aged man with silver hair. They appear to be engaged in an intense conversation, so I choose to wait to see him later. I am looking for my mother, but she is nowhere to be seen, and neither is my dad. So I hone in on the hors d'oeuvres and down three stuffed mushroom and two bacon-and-cheese wraps on a toothpick. I grab another glass of champagne from the bar and then down another mushroom. As I am standing there minding my own business, I am approached by a number of my father's colleagues who shake my hand and ask me about my future.

"Charles! . . . I understand you are going to Harvard next fall."

"Yes, I am."

"Great school—when I was there we . . ."

"You must be Charles. Glad to see you again, Charles. Do you remember me? I used to work with your dad on tort litigation, years ago . . ."

"Hello, Charles. I used to work with your father at his law firm in Minneapolis. So I understand you are going to law school next fall, is that right?"

"Yes."

"Atta boy. You won't regret the discipline and it will open so many doors for new opportunities. I was just telling my son the other day that if he wants to get ahead . . ."

Get ahead of whom? I didn't know that we were racing.

"More champagne, Sir?"

"Yes, please."

"You must be Charles."

"Yes, I am."

"So your father tells me you graduated with an English major from the University"

"Yes."

"And just what kind of a job does that land a fellow nowadays with an English major—a junior high teaching job?"

"More champagne, Sir?"

"Yes, thank you."

"So tell me, Charles, have you decided what kind of law you will specialize in? Divorce is a great field now. Over 50 percent of marriages end up in divorce courts. Of course, bankruptcy is always a good alternative, if you can stomach all those sorry-ass excuses. But if you were to ask me, I'd say personal injury is the cleanest way to go. You get a third of every case you win, and let me tell you, some of these cases can be in the millions. Even an English major can figure out it doesn't take too many cases like that and you're set for life…"

"More champagne, Sir?"

"Yes, more champagne, please."

"Hello Charles. I remember you when you were just a little guy . . ."

The room is starting to spin, and I need to sit down.…no, I need to throw up.

"Excuse me, but I need to go to the bathroom."

"More champagne, Sir?"

"No, no thank you."

I am moving quickly now through a blur of moving bodies that are dancing on the Delta Queen. I find an opening and then stagger downstairs where I am alone—thank God, I'm alone . . . Now where is the men's room? Too much champagne . . . too fast . . . Now where is the men's room again?

"Captain? . . . Oh, Captaaaain! . . . Doesn't anyone around here know where the men's room is? Captaaaain! Oh, there it is . . . Oh . . . I-I'm so s-sorry, madam. I . . . I thought this was the men's room. Say, do you n-n-need some help with your butt, I mean button? . . . No, no p-p-please don't yell . . . I'm leaving. See? I'm leaving. Say, can you tell me how to get to the men's room? Oh yeah—next door—g-got it . . . Sorry . . . . Come on Charlie, it's time to go . . . It's time to go and leave this nice lady alone . . . . Come on Charlie, you can make it . . ."

And I do.

As I sit in the stall, the riverboat engines slow and then stop. We are turning around, and I decide to wait out the storm of dizzy spells. When my head finally clears, I wash my face and hands in the sink. It is dusk now, and I step outside and smell the fresh air. Upstairs, the party is in full swing with alcohol flowing more freely than the river itself.

I am enroute to wishing my dad a happy birthday and slide in and out of little pockets of people carrying on intimate conversations. The band has come back after taking a break, and I spot my brother talking with my dad. My dad has his arm around my brother's shoulder as the two of them talk freely in front of the stage. He then pats Karl on the back in an "atta boy" moment and steps in my direction. Suddenly, our eyes meet from across the room. He simply stares at me, and without so much as a word, he turns and walks away. I am suddenly standing there wondering what to do. I feel like an uninvited guest to my dad's own party. Was it the champagne? Was it the fact that I held up the boat? Was it the fact that he had to get me out of jail a few weeks ago that made him turn away—or was it something deeper?

I am tempted to follow after him, but my heart is suddenly heavy from rejection. I then look about for my mother, as if I could find some kind of comfort there, but she is nowhere to be seen, and I am guessing that it really doesn't matter anymore. I resign myself to the bottom of the boat for the remainder of the party—out of sight and out of mind.

When the riverboat docks, I am the first one off. And as I drive away, I see out of my rearview mirror the myriad smiling and laughing faces that are exiting the Delta Queen. As I approach the road leading home, I see the same bar that I had used earlier that evening to change clothes. I decide to stop in, and I find that the same bartender is on duty. As our eyes meet, he motions me to the bathroom in the back as he had done before, but I shake my head no.

"I'd like to order a drink," I tell him.

"What'll it be?" he replies.

"Tequila," I say. "Lots of tequila."

July 12 . . . The Mad Scribbler

I had suddenly awakened this morning and found myself sleeping on the couch of my uncle's apartment. How I got there remains a mystery, but as I looked at my watch, there was a nagging thought that plagued me. It was the notion that I was to be somewhere this morning, but where? Then it hit me.

I had forgotten about Sunday School!

Sunday school starts an hour before church, and I was late. I had no time to change, so I ran to the bathroom in my tuxedo, smelling a faint, rancid odor. Did I turn on the Toyota's heater last night on the way home, or had I thrown up again? I grabbed a can of Gillette deodorant and quickly sprayed the aerosol all over me to conceal any rancid smell, grabbed a stick of gum in the kitchen, and combed my hair en route to the church. Who was it that signed me up for this teaching thing again?

As I wheeled into the parking lot, I saw that there were only a few cars there—one of which was Mrs. Sherburne's blue Buick. As I entered the main door, she was standing there to meet me.

"Good morning, Mrs. Sherburne," I said briskly.

"Good morning, Charles. I trust you had a good night's sleep?" she asked.

"Couldn't have slept better," I told her.

She eyed me suspiciously, as if I had just broken one of the 11 commandments—no, 10 commandments—"Thou shalt not lie"—and then she sniffed about me. She suddenly eyed the tuxedo with a questioning air, suspicious of everything now. But I had the upper hand and she knew it. She needed me more than I needed her, and if she fired me on the spot, then so be it. I would rather sleep in on Sunday anyway. But she is a crafty one, that Mrs. Sherburne. She knows just how far she can play her cards. She knew that I know that she knows that I know that I have the upper hand and that, if she pushes me too far, I just might resign—and right then, I was more than willing to do so. And if I did resign? Who would teach the class? Who would teach Ivan then, huh? Put that in your pipe and smoke it, Mrs. Sherburne. Go ahead

171

and threaten me and see how far that gets you.

As we continued to play this little cat and mouse game, I decided to have a little fun and tell her outright what happened last night and test her reaction. I decided to tell her the truth, the whole truth, and nothing but the truth, so help me God.

"To be honest, Mrs. Sherburne," I began, "I was out drinking last night after I left my father's fiftieth birthday party. I must have gotten rip-roaring drunk, because I don't remember how I got home. All I know is that, when I woke up on the couch this morning, it dawned on me that I had to teach Sunday School. So, I hopped in the truck in my tuxedo, and here I am."

I was smiling. I had played my trump card and waited for her to fold. But she didn't fold. All she did was stare at me, so I continued.

"To be honest, Mrs. Sherburne, I'm not the kind of person that should be teaching these kids, anyway. Just look at me. Now if you want a real teacher, Jerome would be . . ."

"Nonsense, Charles," she said, interrupting me. "You are perfect for the task—absolutely perfect. You're honest and forthright, and that is half the battle nowadays. Just try to find someone who is that honest. I believe it is one of the finest characteristics that is needed to be a great teacher today. Honesty and humility—not thinking of yourself more highly than you ought. The apostle Paul thought so, and I could not agree with him more. Charles, you will make a great teacher!"

I was dumfounded. The crafty Mrs. Sherburne had just called my bluff and had laid down a straight flush of her own. So, what do you do when someone has just trumped your own poker hand? You take it like a good soldier. You nod politely and then proceed down the hallway to the combat zone . . .

The minute I entered the class, I saw six seemingly innocent children sitting quietly at their desks, and I was impressed. Suddenly, one of the kids told me that I looked funny in my clothes, and I told her that I was wearing a tuxedo. I then started to tell the class what a tuxedo is. Out of the blue, little Edgar Willis shouted out that I looked like Tennessee Tuxedo.

"Who is Tennessee Tuxedo?" I asked him.

He told me that Tennessee Tuxedo is an old cartoon that he saw at his grandmother's house in Northfield. Once he called me the name, it stuck—and all six voices, including Ivan the Terrible, chimed in, shouting "Tennessee Tuxedo! Tennessee Tuxedo!" As they continued to chant my name over and over, I found it useless to fight it, so I embraced it. I then went about restoring order to the chaos created over my newly christened name.

We next proceeded to start the lesson on Noah, and I got out the crayons to color the ark.

All was well until I went looking for a broom to clean up the crackers that Ivan had brought for treat time. (*It's funny, but I don't remember having a "treat time" in Sunday school growing up as a kid—and for a brief moment, I had this silly notion that I had been taken advantage of by first and second graders. I had meant to ask Mrs. Sherburne afterwards about "treat time," but she was suspiciously absent*). When I came back with the broom, I found them all coloring the basement window with crayons, as if it was a group art project. After a brief inquisition, I discovered that it was Ivan who had initiated the mural and had done most of the scribbling himself, earning the prestigious "mad scribbler" award by his fellow classmates. The interesting thing is that, if you look at the mural against the light of day, it actually looks like a stained glass window of the gathering storm before the flood. I was half tempted to write to the publisher of the Sunday School curriculum, suggesting that they include a stain glass art project with their lesson on Noah, along with some suggestions on "treat time," stressing that a teacher should never, ever, under any circumstance, leave his or her first-and-second-grade class unattended.

By the time the Sunday School class from hell had ended, Tennessee Tuxedo was on a search and destroy mission—looking for Jerome, the one who had volunteered me for the job. But, like the crafty Mrs. Sherburne, he was suspiciously absent.

July 12 . . . The Big Kahuna

It is a windy night up here on the hill, and I am perusing through a plethora of blogs that some of you have sent me. Thank you for your words of encouragement, fellow bloggers. Yes, I was having another pity party at the bar last night—and yes, it was stupid driving home under the influence—and yes, I should have been arrested—and yes, I apologize to all the Mothers Against Drunk Drivers that I was not arrested and thrown in jail, in which case my dad probably would have had to bail me out—again—not that he would have minded on his birthday.

And for those of you who thought tequila was a bad choice to drown out my sorrows—I agree. Vodka would have been a much better choice. And to all the "wanna be" psychologists who wrote in—yes, there are definitely some deep, dysfunctional issues within the Finstune family lineage that date back to my great-great-great-great-great-great-great grandfather, Thaddeus Finstune, who had issues with his own father, Isaac, who had given his much younger brother—Joseph—a coat of many colors before he was extradited to Egypt.

And to all you former "Marine Corp" psychiatrists out there, I agree—it's time I grew up and buckled up and took rejection like a real man. Instead of resorting to alcohol, next time I will try and remember to either kick someone's butt or throw someone overboard.

Again, thank you for your words of encouragement.

I guess I should at least be grateful I have a dad. I realize that some kids don't even have fathers. So, is not having a physically present father any better than having an emotionally absent father? I don't know. I wonder about all the kids nowadays, growing up without a father, like Ivan the Terrible, whose father remains in prison—or so I have been told. *So what is it about fathers, anyway?* Why is it that 90 percent of kids in penal institutions don't have a father figure in their life? Why does Hallmark sell far more Mothers' Day cards than Fathers' Day cards? Karl seems to have no problem relating to my dad. Why was I the black sheep? Who authored this life of mine, anyway? And do I have a choice in my destiny, or was it all planned out before I was born? Ah, that is the never-ending, proverbial, "let's-pontificate-till-two-in-the-morning" college question that never ends with a definitive answer. So, there you have it. We are back at square one without any greater understanding of life.

It's always easy to second-guess your situation in life, as it is to complain about your situation. I had stopped in at Miss Maddie's this afternoon to talk about that very subject, but I ended up mowing her lawn. Stubborn as she is, she was determined to do it herself. But, as you would expect from an 82-year-old woman, her eyesight is getting progressively worse. Nobody the age of 82 ought to be mowing a lawn. When I arrived, she had already clipped off three of her smaller bushes coming around the side of her house and had made significant inroads to her begonias. After much coaxing, she finally took the riding mower out of gear, took off her Audrey Hepburn hat, and decided to let me give it a whirl. And whirl I did, taking out another begonia patch until I got the steering thing down. When I came in for lunch, I asked her point blank why she always worked on Sunday. After all, wasn't it supposed to be a day of rest? She told me that it was the only day she could work with me, knowing that I would probably stop over. How did she know that? And had God given her a special dispensation, like the kind given to the NFL players, the clerks at Wal-Mart, the phone operators, ambulance drivers, doctors, gas station attendants, or anyone else that had to work on Sunday? And why me?

"Because I am supposed to impart some things into your life from your heavenly Father," she said matter-of-factly.

"Oh, really," I replied sarcastically. "So did the Big Kahuna tell you that?"

She laughed out loud.

"Big Kahuna? I've heard God called a lot of things, but never Big Kahuna," she said.

I was suddenly feeling special, as in "especially" deficient, knowing that only God himself can help me. "Yep, there's that Finstune boy, and God help him." Help him with what? What does God need to impart into me that I don't already have? Patience? Common sense? (*OK, maybe some common sense— after all, it was my grandpa who used to tell me that common sense wasn't so common, and looking back, I could have said no to the champagne lady last night.*) Compassion? Understanding? Wisdom? All of the above? So, if I am so deficient of "something," then who was she to impart it?

"Do you think it was an accident that I came to Bullpen?" I asked her.

"Oh, no," she said, as if I had uttered blasphemy. "There are no accidents with God. The shepherds and wise men didn't just *accidentally* come upon a babe lying in a manger."

175

"Great," I said. "So, how did you know that I would be over to help this afternoon? Did the Big Kahuna tell you that?"

"Nope," she replied. "I took a guess."

So, why *had* I gone to Miss Maddie's this afternoon? Had something compelled me, or was it because there is nowhere else to go on a Sunday afternoon in Bullpen?

Jerome does nothing on Sundays but rock in his rocking chair on his apartment balcony overlooking Main Street. I had asked him why, and he told me that he likes to sit and think—and that Sunday is his only day to do so without an interruption.

"Think about what?" I had asked him.

"Stuff," he said defensively. So I left it at that.

Millie and Maynard go out driving on Sunday in Maynard's new Cadillac, and by the grace of God, they have always come back alive.

And Jared—I have no idea what Jared does. Jared is a mystery. He is a good worker, but he is a mystery and keeps to himself. Jerome has tried to pull him out of his "shell"—but without success. All Jared does is listen to music, choosing not to engage in conversation. I caught him off guard last week, eating lunch without his headphones, and I asked him if he liked to do anything beside wash dishes and listen to music. He told me he thought he might like working on cars like his dad. That was a surprise. So he *does* have an interest. And, he *does* have a dad, who I came to find out later is a mechanic in Portland.

"So why don't you go and live with him?" I asked him.

"He's remarried and doesn't want me hanging around his new family," he told me.

"When did he tell you that?" I asked.

"Last time I went out there to meet him," he replied.

What kind of father would not want his own son to hang out with his family? What kind of father would not want to spend time with his own son and get to know him? Suddenly, I had caught a glimpse into Jared's heart, and I wasn't sure what to say. I only knew that it was broken, and I sensed that he was yearning for affection and affirmation from his own father. He had gone all the way to Portland and had put himself out there like a trapeze artist, flying through the air, hoping that his dad was at the other end. But he wasn't.

To all you "wanna be" psychologists and "Marine Corp" psychiatrists, what do you say to a kid who has no one out there to catch him?

July 15 . . . My Uncle's Fiddle

It is Wednesday—one of the coldest days on record for July in Minnesota, and the café is buzzing with excitement. Bullpen Days are only four weeks away, and the town is brimming with pride over the up and coming event. As a publicity stunt, the Bullpen Rotary Club had put out the call for a creative design for the official "Bullpen Days Insignia," and contestants from all over southern Minnesota had entered the competition, including Bullpen's own Slater Gray, whose flamboyant interpretation of Bullpen's history didn't earn him the award, but did earn him the reputation as an avant-garde artisan. Slater had painted a historical montage of Bullpen's own colorful past (and present) with such voracity and transparency that it had shocked even members of the Rotary Club. It was, in fact, a rather large painting (54 by 48 inches)—a portion of which featured the historical softball game of 1893, with Slater's own depiction of Ole Gunderson and Pap Farkas shaking hands across a little creek. It was like the early depiction of the Minnesota Twins Baseball Insignia of two Twins shaking hands across the river that separated Minneapolis from St. Paul. Also included on that same half was the Bullpen Café, the Lutheran church, a few of Ole Gunderson's draft horses, the bear he shot in Wisconsin, a boat heading back to Norway (apparently representing Hans Running's wife Gladys's trip back to the mainland), a lone apple-blossom tree in spring that Hans had written about in his letter to Gladys (which described Bullpen as a "pink prairie"), more draft horses, an old disc plow, and then a few new tractors and combines to represent Bullpen's entrance into the 21st Century.

But what had startled the committee, however, was the other half of the montage. Slater, as if lost in an artistic frenzy, had clearly stepped over the boundaries of discretion with his depiction of Sven and Ole's brief but memorable trip to Racine, where they had stopped at a nightclub to see a few showgirls while en route to the Chicago World's Fair of 1894. It was argued that the number of less-than-fully-dressed dancing girls depicted was clearly disproportional to the actual number that Sven and Ole would have seen on stage. But worse, Slater himself had taken this historic event and had given it his own dramatic interpretation—much to the dismay of Mrs. Nordstrom, who called it smut. Slater, however, called it art. To resolve the issue, it was moved in the committee that, if the painting was to be displayed at the Café as an original, commemorative work from one of Bullpen's own "artists in residence," then Slater would have to paint some more clothes on the showgirls. As the proprietor of the Bullpen Café, I wisely seconded the motion. When a vote was cast, common sense prevailed, and the motion passed, becoming the final ruling of the committee.

The insignia that had won the contest, however, was from a female art student who had answered an ad in the Rochester paper. The student had drawn a picture of an old baseball lying in a foreground of tall grass. Several yards behind the baseball she had portrayed a bull with an inquisitive look on his face, staring in the direction of the lost ball. As the first place prize, she was to receive a complimentary lunch at the Bullpen Café and was to ride in the parade in George's 1967 convertible Mustang (as opposed to the Allis Chalmers combine that was originally suggested). During discussion over whether or not that compensation was adequate, it was moved, and then seconded, that the notoriety alone from such an award would be enough to bolster her fledgling artistic career.

In order to commemorate the first annual event, the mayor then authorized the Bullpen's official insignia to be placed on everything: place mats, napkins, T-shirts, caps, coffee cups, helium balloons, and cheap promotional pens. The women's auxiliary agreed to make a full-fledged banner that is to extend from one side of the street to the other and is able to withstand any element that Mother Nature can throw against it.

And now individuals and organizations that I never thought existed in Bullpen are starting to come out of the woodwork to offer their help, expertise, and resources. It is a little like the story "Stone Soup" with everyone contributing something to the community stew—whether it's welcomed by the committee or not.

In the end it will be Bullpen's finest hour, showcasing to the world Bullpen's former splendor and present day glory, however short lived that might be.

Posters have now been printed and placed around Bullpen and other surrounding towns, advertising all events: the tractor-pulling contest, a horseshoe contest, and a fire-fighting contest with fire hoses that will use competing water pressures to push a barrel back and forth on a high steel cable. There will also be a baking competition with various fields of entries: breads, pies, and cakes—all with the same judging standards as the Minnesota State Fair itself. There will be a softball tournament that is to be played on the very same field as the first game in 1893, a five kilometer fun-run, a fiddle and bluegrass contest, and then the crème de la crème—the human cannon ball. Fireworks will be added if the budget permits.

Now that the bluegrass competition is official, the Bullpen Bluegrass Ensemble is looking for a fiddle player, and on this cold July morning, Gary enters and asks me if I would consider playing. He recalls a conversation we had weeks ago, up on Thomforde Hill, about how I played the violin in fourth grade. He remembers that I had told him it would have to be a cold day in July before that happens.

"Well," he says with a smile on his face, "it's a cold day in July."

"That it is," I tell him.

"Then you'll play?" he asks me.

I am thinking this conversation is private, but nothing is private in the café. George overhears my conversation and yells out, "Of course he'll play the fiddle! It's about time we had some decent music around here."

"Well, don't get your hopes up," I tell him and the Boys. "Last time I played was in fourth grade, and the only song I knew then was 'Mary had a Little Lamb.'"

"I once knew a Mary," shouts George. "And she had more than a just a little lamb!"

The Boys laugh, along with Slater, who is basking in his new-found fame as Bullpen's own artist in residence. His illustrious painting now hangs proudly under the smiling moose (it was George's idea to put it there, as if to give the moose something more to smile about).

Curious about the commotion, Jerome comes out from the kitchen and asks what is going on. George fills him in on Gary's proposal. Jerome then turns to Gary, tells him, "He'll do it," and then turns back to the kitchen as if he were my agent.

"Last time I played the fiddle was in fourth grade, and I sounded worse than Jack Benny on steroids. Besides, I don't have a fiddle," I tell Gary.

But he won't give up.

"How about your uncle's fiddle?" he asks.

I am running out of excuses and begin to realize that Gary is just as crafty as Mrs. Sherburne. I wondered if he had ever been a Sunday School teacher under her tutelage.

"I'll think about it," I tell him.

And I do.

That night I take my uncle's fiddle from its stand and dust it off. It seems strange holding a musical instrument that my uncle had once played. As I run my fingers across the strings, I hear myself playing "Mary had a Little Lamb"—and it sounds as bad in my mind now as it did then.

But when I pick up the bow, it is as if a flood of memories has suddenly been unleashed, and I am back in fourth grade, playing in the living room, hearing the sound of the dishwashing machine finish its wash cycle in the kitchen. There is a momentary pause before the rinse cycle begins, and I run the bow across the strings, the sound permeating throughout the empty house as if it were my only friend, my violin trying as best it can to sing. All of a sudden, there in that living room, it is as if I can hear a chorus of heavenly voices and an entire orchestra of stringed instruments playing a "Hallelujah Chorus." And suddenly, I am no longer alone as I continue to run my bow across the strings, lost in the mystery and company of music.

Back in the present, I pick up the bow to my uncle's violin and run it across the strings, and the sound of squealing pigs pierces the silence of the apartment. I grind out "Mary had a Little Lamb" again and again, until it all sounds the same. It is 2:00 in the morning before I lay down my bow—and I am exhausted.

July 18 . . . Charlie Daniels on Steroids

I have just finished practicing with the Bullpen Bluegrass Ensemble. The oldest man in the group is Cecil Armstrong and has been playing the guitar since he was 13. He is now 67 and doesn't miss a beat. The young banjo player in the group is Willie Backstrum, and he is only 15—a natural at the banjo. The elderly lady is Vivian Chester, who lives in Zumbrota and drives all the way to Bullpen to play. She has a witty sense of humor that keeps everyone smiling, including Gary, who plays the mandolin and is the leader of the group. And me? I am Charlie Daniels on steroids. I am as much the "mad fiddler" as Ivan the Terrible is the "mad scribbler."

It's all coming back to me now: "The Tennessee Waltz" and "Mary had a Little Lamb." But after watching Charlie Daniels play "The Devil Went Down to Georgia" on You Tube, I have been inspired by a living legend, and have decided to play that song when and wherever I can—serenading poor, helpless Bullpen Café patrons that are at the mercy of my fiddle.

"Charlie, you put that blasted thing down, you hear me?' George yelled this morning.

"Not till you hear 'The Devil Went Down to Georgia' one more time," I replied.

"Oh, is that what that song is?" he asked mockingly.

The Boys laughed, but George was serious.

"Damn it, Charlie, if you play that song one more time I'll . . ."

"You'll what?" I asked him, challenging his bluff. "Just what will you do, George?"

This time I laughed.

"Hey," I continued, "if you hadn't volunteered me, you and the Boys wouldn't have the privilege of hearing me practice,"

"I'd rather hear a donkey bray at midnight," Slater remarked.

181

"I'd rather hear a jackass," replied George.

He gave me a mock salute, but I continued to play. Jerome has resorted to earplugs, Jared to head phones, and Millie to ear wax. The rest of the clientele are a captive audience until Bullpen Days.

What is important, however, is not what George and everyone else at the Café thinks, but what my fellow musicians think. And right now they think I am making progress. When I hit a few wrong notes tonight, they were all very supportive; and Gary mentioned more than once that it's not about the competition.

And he is right. It's not about the competition. But personally, I think we have a great chance of winning it all. Move over Charlie Daniels.

July 19 . . . The Bible Alphabet Game

This morning I decided to continue to play out the reputation that was given to me by my beloved first and second grade class as "Tennessee Tuxedo." Yes, I went to Sunday School bright and early wearing the same tuxedo—only this time it had been dry-cleaned. I decided to buy the tuxedo. I am not sure why I decided to buy it. Maybe it was pride—or defiance. Whatever it was, the tuxedo was now mine. When Jerome asked me after church why on God's green earth I bought a tuxedo, I told him it was because I could—and left it at that. He was about to ask me another self-incriminating question, but I beat him to the punch line and told him that any time he wanted to take over my Sunday school class, he was more than welcome to do so. He was strangely silent after that.

The kids, however, seem proud of the fact that Tennessee Tuxedo is teaching them, and they can't wait to point me out to their parents in the hallway. Yep, that's me—the one wearing the tuxedo. Mrs. Sherburne thinks it's a great idea, and there has not been so much attention about Sunday School since Albert Shoemaker lit a cigar in the boy's room ten years ago. The tux may be a little over the top, and perhaps a little theatrical, but I need all the help I can get in teaching these little monsters.

This morning Ivan came in with a bag of powdered doughnuts (and yes we did have treat time—how can you not have treat time with powdered doughnuts—and no, I did not leave the classroom to get a broom). Needless to say, I had one doughnut; and needless to say, I spilled powdered sugar on my tuxedo; and needless to say, I had difficulty getting the powdered sugar out.

We didn't touch our lesson at all this morning because I hadn't read it, and I figured what Mrs. Sherburne doesn't know won't hurt her—at least to my knowledge. What we did do was to sit around in a big cozy circle and share about our favorite family vacation. I thought it would be a great way to get their attention and take some time off the clock, and it did—until one of the students told the class that his favorite part of their vacation was watching their neighbors swim naked in the lake up north under a full moon (emphasis on the full moon). Needless to say, it was all good until the word "naked" came out.

Houston, we have a problem…

"Naked" is a funny word to say by itself, but a entire classroom full of first and second graders yelling it over and over and laughing at the same time gives a whole new meaning to the word. (*As a side note, something that should be put in all Lutheran Sunday School teaching manuals is "safe questions"—right next to the page on Noah's basement window mural. All teaching manuals should have at least a full page, if not a whole chapter, on "safe questions."*)

It was then that I suddenly imagined myself standing before the District Lutheran Sunday School Board, trying to explain why my kids are yelling "naked" in the hallways, parking lot and sanctuary. So what explanation do you give to Mrs. Sherburne and the rest of the Sunday School board members? Well, for starters, you tell them that Adam and Eve were naked in the Garden of Eden and hope that that is sufficient.

"OK class, enough with the naked word! Let's play a different game, like the . . . the ah . . . alphabet game. Yeah, let's all go around the circle and think of Bible animals that start with all the letters of the alphabet," I told them.

It was a brilliant idea. I mean, what could go wrong with a Bible game like that? And calling it the "Bible Animal Name Game" gave it just the right amount of religiousness that would appease even Mrs. Sherburne. So, I explained the rules and told them as an example, for the letter "C" you could use the word "camel."

"So, who has a Bible animal that starts with the letter 'A'?" I asked them.

Little Toby Christiansen raised his hand, but before I could call on him, he blurted out the word, "ASS."

"Okay," I replied. "That's another name for donkey."

But as quickly as Toby volunteered the word "ass," Edgar Willis chimed in with his own version of the word.

"Yeah, I'm going to kick your ass," replied Edgar, as if the word had just triggered a knee-jerk reaction within the neurons of his limited but descriptive vocabulary. "That's what my dad said to Mr. Kramer last week."

"Well," I reassured him, "he was probably referring to Mr. Kramer's donkey or something."

"He doesn't have a donkey. He just has two dogs that keep pooping in our yard," remarked Edgar.

"They poop in our yard, too," cried little Abby McBride.

"Well, I'm sure that Mr. Kra . . ."

"But Mr. Kramer said that he was going to kick my dad's ass," continued Edgar.

Soon utter chaos erupted and the whole class was involved in the great debate over whose ass was going to get kicked.

As the voices continued to escalate, I found myself weary of the all-too-apparent notion that things were spiraling out of control.

"Class . . . Class? . . . CLASS!" I yelled. "NOBODY IS GOING TO KICK ANY BODY'S ASS!!"

The room suddenly got quiet—too quiet.

Houston, we have a problem.

The faces of terrified first and second graders stared at me as if I was some kind of monster. "What have I become?" I asked myself. But in the same moment it took to evaluate my outburst, the all-too-apparent realization hit me that if I didn't diffuse the bomb, little Abby McBride would burst into tears, and that would mean an appearance before the Superintendent and the National Lutheran Sunday School Board to give an account of myself, as Martin Luther had tried to do before the Diet of Worms. In the end it would mean scandal and rumors and excommunication.

Houston, do you copy?

I forced a laugh, then told them that that is what all the donkey riders yell at each other when they are riding their rented mules.

Their expressions of fear turned to bewilderment, and for a moment I had altered their focus, diverting a possible catastrophe.

"Haven't you ever heard donkey riders yell that at each other when they get close?" I asked them.

They shook their heads no.

"Well, you . . . you just need to listen more carefully. They just kind of yell it out so everyone can hear it."

I cupped my hands as if yelling into a canyon and shouted, "Hey! Nobody is going to kick my donkey!" Then I brayed like a donkey at midnight: "Hee haw—hee haw."

A few of the kids giggled, and Abby smiled, and I realized that I had just dodged a bullet. Thank God I had dodged the bullet. Breathing more easily, I proceeded with the next letter of the alphabet.

"Okay, so let's go on to the next letter. Does anyone have a Bible animal for the letter 'B'? Ivan? You got a Bible animal that starts with the letter 'B'?" I asked.

"Bullsh-"

Before Ivan could finish the word, I yelled "Recess!" drowning out his voice with mine.

"But we've never had recess," declared Toby.

"Well, we do now!" I shouted as I quickly whisked them out the door so that I could reevaluate my choice of games. As the class exited, Ivan stayed behind.

"What is it, Ivan?" I asked him.

"What's a bullsheep?" he asked.

"You mean, that was your word?" I asked him.

"Yeah, it's what my mom calls some of the sheep."

"What kinds of sheep?" I asked.

"The ones with horns," he said.

"Oh . . . I bet that is what your mom calls the male rams," I told him. "Bullsheep. That's a great animal name that starts with 'B,' Ivan. Nice job."

Ivan smiled as if he had just made a great contribution to our class—and he had. I just wish I had seen it coming, along with everything else that morning. And now that the classroom was completely empty with thirty-nine minutes left on the clock, I just wished I knew where I could find my students.

July 20 . . .
"I Know What Love Is": Forest Gump

It's a cool night here on top of Thomforde Hill, and I am finally alone after one of the cars left just moments ago. Homer told me earlier this week that years ago they used to call this place Necking Hill. When I asked him what necking meant, he told me that it meant to kiss face. So when I asked him when was the last time he had been necking up on Thomforde Hill, his face turned three shades of red, and then he changed the subject.

End of discussion

He had, however, invited me over earlier in the week for yet another game of Crokinole and then waffles. Those were some of the best I had ever had, and when I asked him about the recipe, he looked at me as if to ask how I dare have the audacity to ask him for it. What is it with some people and their recipes? It's like pulling teeth to get them to share their secret ingredient(s). It is as if they are donating blood or giving away one of their kidneys for a transplant. Jerome, on the other hand, is willing to give away both his kidneys and then some. He wears his recipes on his sleeve, like some guys wear their heart on their sleeve, and lately he has been trying to persuade me to allow him to cook some Cajun food for Bullpen Days. The thought of dirty rice, however, is still unsettling, but he assures me that it will all turn out all right in the end. That's a comforting thought, isn't it? We might burn down the café, but in the end, it will all be okay. And there I will be, sitting on top of Thomforde Hill at 2:00 in the morning, watching the last of the fire trucks leave the café. In the end, however, Jerome's persistence prevailed, and I decided to let him try out a dish or two if he would stop nagging me.

Jerome is funny. Apart from researching recipes and cooking in the kitchen, the rest of his time is spent rocking in his rocking chair up on his balcony, where he thinks about stuff. Last week, however, he got a letter from his kids and spent all Sunday afternoon in his rocking chair, reading and rereading it again and again. He told me that he doesn't know where his ex-wife is, but

187

his kids are now staying with his sister in Charlotte, North Carolina. He is hoping that they can come for Christmas—and, if possible, come and live with him. That's his dream, and ever since he got the letter, it seems that that is all he thinks about and talks about, apart from his recipes. It's a simple dream, really—one that most people take for granted. He told me the other day that a man has to have a dream, something that he can believe in, or he just floats downstream like any dead fish. I have to give him credit; when most people are complaining about what they don't have, Jerome is just grateful for what he does have. He told me that that is the key to happiness. Frustration is the difference between what a person actually has and what he thinks he should have. Sounds like an entitlement, doesn't it? If you focus all your energies on the difference between the two, he told me, you will never be happy. He calls it "the great divide"; it is a constant state of comparing yourself to someone or something else. It is an unmerited (my definition) expectation that is always just out of reach—and because you are always pursuing the future possession of it, you don't have time to enjoy the present.

Simple enough.

To be honest, I was surprised at his depth of understanding. I asked him if he thought of that all by himself, and he said that it came to him a few years ago. He said that white people have that problem more than Black people, because they compare themselves to each other more than Black people do. I disagreed, but that didn't stop him from telling me his opinion. He said that, if a white person succeeds, other white people get all jealous, and the gap between where they are and where they think they should be just gets bigger—hence the great divide. He said when Black people succeed, however, other Black people are on the sidelines rooting for them.

"Is that so?" I asked him.

"Yep," he told me "—it's so."

So when I asked him what the difference was between a dream and an unfulfilled expectation, he folded his arms like some resident guru and told me that a dream is from God and is something worth pursuing, while an unmerited expectation is from the devil himself, and it is between you and the world. It is designed to keep you focused on the wrong thing and running in the wrong direction as you constantly compare yourself to others and what they are doing or what they have. "Got to get ahead of the next guy to feel good about yourself," he told me. "That is straight from the pit of hell, because it keeps you focused on what you don't have, and then you feel like you are always behind and need to catch up. God forbid that you ever get behind and lose status with your neighbor," he told me. "If your neighbor is your standard and feeling good about yourself comes by being better than him, then you are as lost as a coon dog chasing his own scent." And that, according to Jerome, is the problem with most white people. Even when you tell them they are chasing the wrong scent, they won't change because they can't admit that they have wasted most of their lives doing so. It's no different than climbing the wrong ladder when they should have been pursuing God's dream for their lives instead. It's called "pride" he told me, and it will destroy a man if he continues to chase it.

It's hard to argue with Jerome once he makes up his mind—and his mind is obviously made up on this matter. Perhaps there is some truth in it, but I don't believe that white people have a greater problem with pride than Black people—after all, people are people, and jealousy knows no color boundary.

It is, however, interesting that we had this discussion after I had sent out emails to my fraternity buddies telling them that we could host our reunion here in Bullpen. After my encounter with Jeff Gordon during the Fourth of July celebration in Rochester, I decided to host our fraternity party at the café.

It would be great to see the guys again and catch up on what is going on in their lives. I felt a little hesitant about sending out the invitations, however. Some of my frat buddies are interning at prestigious laws firms, while others will be attending law school this fall, and still others are en route to a promising career. Since I will be attending law school next fall, I felt I could justify my lowly position here in Bullpen as one of "life's experiences." I am young enough and can get by with it for now. But I imagine that, the older I get, the more that grace period shrinks. It's like a baby. You think they are so cute and cuddly as infants, but when they get older, more is expected from them. I can get by with being a small restaurant owner for now, but what if I stay on like my uncle? God forbid. How could I show myself at my high school reunion? Would I be the butt end of small-town jokes? And if I showed up in my uncle's pickup truck, how would that be perceived? What is perception? What if I had decided to spend my life as a carry-out boy for the local grocery store in North Cedar where I grew up? Or a janitor? Or a garbage collector? How would I be perceived by my classmates? And if I cared about that perception, would I not be like some coon dog "chasing his own scent"?

189

Who cares what others think of you? Apparently, a lot of people, including myself—if I am honest. And take, for example, my parents. For those of us growing up in North Cedar, there was an undefined but powerful force that permeated our community at large. It was a standard that was pushed upon me whether I liked it or not. And when I had fallen short of that standard—I had failed my parents. That is what I sensed from my own father the other night at his birthday party. I had failed him. I had not measured up to this standard, and I was to feel his shame through abandonment. It was becoming clear to me now. It was a disciplinary stick that was meant to put me back in line to where I belonged—among the rank and file—and I had felt its sting.

But the real question in all this is not about getting back in line; it is a question about love. Am I loved simply because I do as I am told and conform to my parents' standard and that of the community in which I grew up? Is love based on some outward behavior? Or is based on who I am as a person?

I wonder.

I am suddenly reminded of a line in the movie *Forest Gump*, with Tom Hanks: "I might not be very smart, but I know what love is."

I might not be the smartest kid going to law school next fall, but I know what love is. I know what affirmation is, and if I am honest with myself, I still crave it from my father.

I envy Karl and hate him at the same time. Karl is the "good boy" who has never deviated from his faithful role as the elder son and the respectability that comes with it. He is the epitome of what a good son should be—and I am not. The question is, would my father love him any less if he were different? And what about my own father's father? If my own father was the "good boy" in my grandfather's eyes, then what did that make my uncle?

July 22 . . . Fishing with Gary

Jerome and I went fishing with Gary after work this afternoon. Gary took the day off and did some work around the house, then took Jerome and me to his favorite spot on Beaver Lake. It was a great little lake and a great day to fish—a little cloudy and a little cool for July. We entered on the south side of the lake in Gary's 16-foot Lund boat.

Gary started his Johnson 25 horsepower motor, and we shot across the lake while he continued to eye his depth finder.

"We are looking for structure," Gary said. "Sudden drop-offs with a weedy bottom, about 15 to 20 feet deep—that is where you will find the walleyes."

As we reached a halfway point across the lake, he slowed, then cut the motor and dropped the anchor.

"This is it," he told us. "This is the spot for walleyes."

He handed us each a pole. I asked what they had been biting on, and he told me the last fish he caught here was on a sinking Rapala. That sounded good to me, so I asked for the same thing, then hooked mine up and dropped it into the water.

Jerome, however, had brought his own bait in a glass jar. It was dark brown and slimy . . . and above all else, it was stinky. No, on second whiff, it wasn't just stinky—it was nasty stinky. It was the kind of smell that could make a grown man cry—or at least gag—if he had caught the smell. I was suddenly reminded of Jerome's hangover concoction that he had given me weeks ago after my tequila party on top of Thomforde Hill. What on earth had he put in that thing? Even Gary winced when he caught the scent of the mysterious bait.

"What is that stuff?" I asked Jerome.

He told me that I didn't want to know—and I didn't. I just plugged my nose as I saw him handle the bait with his bare hands, thinking that those are the same hands that have to handle food on a daily basis. Bleach was all that I could think of as Jerome pushed his stinky bait through a plain-Jane hook. Then he plopped it into the water.

191

"That ought to do it," he said. "Why, if they don't take that bait, they just ain't hungry."

I laughed out loud. "Yeah," I told him, "I bet they are down there right now just fighting over that stinky bait."

"Yep," he said, "and may the biggest fish win."

Gary smiled, and I laughed, but no sooner had I done so than we all saw his line jump down into the water—and just like that, Jerome had caught his first taste of fishing in southern Minnesota.

"I gots one!" he yelled. "Oh, I gots me the mother lode! Oooo wee! Oh, just look at that old Dan Tucker pullin' on this here line . . . Come on now, you son of sea biscuit. You can run, but you can't hide."

And run the fish did, but Jerome was determined to haul him back.

"Now you stop that, and you get yourself in this here boat, you hear me?" Then he shifted into what sounded like a transmission overdrive, accelerating his verbiage while shouting at the fish in a deep, incoherent southern-Louisiana jargon all its own—none of which I could comprehend.

After the fifth time he had repeated this incantation, I told him that if he stopped speaking Southern and started speaking Yankee, the fish just might cooperate.

But no sooner had I said it than the fish jumped out of the water and then dived back into the deep.

"Why, you get yourself in this here boat!" he cried. "You hear me, you no good sea dog!"

I told him to speak a little louder since fish are hard of hearing in Minnesota.

But no sooner had I said that than the fish started jerking the pole in all different directions—and Jerome fought on as if his very life depended on it, sweating and swirling and spitting—that's right, spitting—like a wild banshee, nearly tipping the boat over again and again—and he would have if Gary and I hadn't been holding on to the other side to counterbalance his weight.

"Now, you get yourself in this here boat—I'm warning you! You hear me, you old sea dog?!"

And then he stood up and continued to yell at the fish in that same southern Louisiana mumbo drawl. As the boat rocked back and forth in jeopardy of capsizing, we both yelled at Jerome to sit down before he swamped us all. But it was no use. Jerome was lost in a fit of anger, blurting out more southern

Louisiana obscenities, and just when it looked as though all was lost, just when it looked like Jerome was going to fall in the lake and take us all with him, the fish jumped right into the boat, as if it understood every word Jerome had muttered.

"Well, I'll be!" shouted Gary.

But no sooner had Gary gotten out the words than Jerome jumped on the fish and pinned it to the bottom of the boat like a wrestler. And me? I was still watching the show, hanging on to the gunnels for dear life, wondering how on God's green earth did this all happen.

But there it was—bigger than life—caught in Jerome's big hands and looking "plum tuckered out," as Jerome later described him.

It was nothing short of a miracle, according to Gary, who had never seen anything like it before.

"Well, if that doesn't beat everything I have ever seen!" he cried. "I thought you'd never land it. Why that fish just hopped right in the boat, Jerome—no net. Why that must be a ten-pound walleye."

"I'd say it's closer to twelve," replied Jerome.

But Gary just continued to shake his head in disbelief. And Jerome? He was smiling from ear to ear.

"Oh, you of little faith," he finally said to Gary, then me. "Oh, you of little faith."

When we finally did weigh it, the fish tipped the scale at a whopping eleven and three-quarter pounds. Jerome was going to fry it up in some Cajun spices, but Gary and I finally convinced him to have it mounted next to the smiling moose. The only exception would be the mounted lure. I wasn't going to have Jerome's stinky bait coming anywhere near the Bullpen Café.

July 23.....The Sunday School Fiasco

I got a call today from Mrs. Sherburne and she wanted to meet me after her Wednesday night leaders meeting at the church. She was discretely coy about the topic, but from the tone of her voice, it was urgent. She preferred to meet me in my Sunday school room and we did, shortly after her meeting.

When I met her she was very friendly, but uneasy. She smiled politely and asked if I would have a seat. I did so in the small toddlers chair that pushed my long knees up to my chest when I sat down.

I had a floodgate of memories sitting in that chair, which reminded me of all the time I had spent in the principal's office at Creek Valley Elementary School. It was that sinking feeling that had always come upon me as I waited to speak with the assistant principal—and in some of the more serious cases, the assistant principle, the principal, my mother, my father and other members of the school board-—and not necessarily in that order.

"Well Charlie," she began, "I want to thank you for volunteering for the first and second Sunday School class. I think that you are trying to do a good job and I am sure that you are trying very hard to teach, to the best of your abilities, but we have had a few concerns that were brought to my attention these last few weeks, and I thought that it would be best to get them out into the open, to see if we could to resolve some of these issues."

"What issues?" I asked.

She stared at the floor for what seemed like an eternity, as if trying to find more politically correct words to say. She was clearly struggling with the great weight of conviction that was upon her, and through the process of osmosis, I too, was beginning to take on the same burden—whatever it was. I shifted uneasily in my tiny chair, as I had done in the presence of Mr. Wallace, the assistant principal at Creek Valley, when I had put a frog in Debbie Dolbeck's rubber boot. When Debbie had put on her boot for recess that rainy April day in third grade, the frog jumped out—miraculously unscathed. But Debbie was traumatized by the event and all she could do was

194

scream—and she kept on screaming for no less than a half hour, according to Timmy Reynolds, who had timed her. Debbie was a true environmentalist, and pricked with a pin, she would bleed green. Yes, Debbie was a tree hugger in every sense of the word and loved frogs almost as much as trees. Her father was the head of environmental studies at one of the local colleges and she was destined to follow in his footsteps, until that frightful day. Her parents sued (and won) the school district charging them for their blatant mismanagement of unsupervised children. And for the punitive damages, her family recovered all of their expenses for all her psychiatric treatments and linguistic tutorials that had finally helped her speak again.

"Charlie," began Mrs. Sherburne, "some of the parents have complained to me that their kids have come back home saying words that are…perhaps… inappropriate for Sunday School?"

"What kind of words?" I asked.

Mrs. Sherburne fidgeted in her chair for a moment and then turned three shades of red—and then she blushed.

"Ah, well…ah," she stammered. "Words like "naked," for one."

"Oh?" I said as if surprised.

"Yes, apparently some of the kids have been coming home telling their parents that the 'naked' word has been used more than once in class."

"Well, I have an explanation for that," I assured her. But she looked far from interested in hearing it at that moment.

"There were other words, as well…words like…like 'ass'. Then Mrs. Hallstead told me that she overheard you yelling in class and when she looked out her door, she found that most of your kids were running through the hallways, unsupervised—31 minutes before the end of class, to be exact."

So it was Mrs. Hallstead that had squealed on me, I thought to myself. Mrs. Hallstead was a battle-ax of a woman, perfect for the fourth and fifth graders with her militant style and self-righteous perpetuity that could cause even a drunken sailor to blush.

"She told me that she heard everything through these walls last week," Mrs. Sherburne continued. "Tell me, Charlie, are you using your curriculum?"

"No, Mrs. Sherburne," I confessed. "To be honest, I only took a look at it this past week, and to be even more honest, it is that same material we used 15 years ago in our church. I'll bet it's at least that old."

"Older," she interjected. "But it's the only curriculum that has been approved by the counsel."

"Well, to be frank, Mrs. Sherburne, it is a very boring curriculum—safe, but boring. I have a very rambunctious class, as you well know. Granted, I have not come prepared these last few weeks, but looking at the material, I can't help but think that it might be a contributing cause to the problem with this class."

"So, how did the words 'ass' and 'naked' come up last Sunday?" she asked me.

"The naked word came up when I asked the kids about their favorite summer vacation and one of the children talked about seeing their neighbors swimming naked in the lake. The ass word came when I thought it best to go on to a new word game and I asked the kids what Bible animals started with the various letters of the alphabet."

She nodded, as if she knew where I was going. "So, the letter A was for ass, is that correct?" she asked me.

"That's correct," I replied. "That was the word someone had used to describe a donkey and then someone else put their own political spin on the word—and well, then things kind of spiraled out of control. That is when I yelled what I yelled."

"And what was it that you yelled, Charlie?" she questioned.

"That nobody was going to kick anybody's ass," I said sheepishly.

She nodded as if she understood.

"Then," I continued, "I thought it best to take a little recess, but I forgot that we still had 32, I mean 31 minutes left of class. And then I had some trouble trying to find them. It was like they all thought it was a game of hide and seek—hence I guess the kids were running wild through the church."

She nodded again.

"Charlie," she began. "I can't fire you. After all, you and I both know there would be no one else to take your place."

"Well, there's Jero—" I tried to interject.

But she, being the crafty one, cut me off and continued, putting her hand upon my knee like a grandmother would.

"We both know that this is a thankless job," she began. "And yes, the curriculum is boring—but in some small way I think that we are making a difference in their lives. You have no idea where some of these kids come from, or what they have been through, or what they have seen. A lot of these families today are broken and fractured. I don't even know who drops them off on most Sundays. But what I do know is, that they come."

She then looked about the small room and wiped her eyes with a handkerchief.

"They come, Charlie—they come in spite of everything else going on in their lives. For some parents, all we are is a free daycare center, so they can do what they want on Sunday mornings. For others, we are simply an extension of the public school to teach them something spiritual rather than academic; and who knows what the other reasons are that people use to bring them here. All I know is that they come. And if we can impart some kind of kindness or acceptance or something of eternal significance—then in some small way, I believe that we have done what the good Lord would have us do—and for that—well, for that, you can't thank me enough for such an opportunity."

She smiled at me and I nodded.

"You will do just fine, Charlie," she says at last. "The kids like you and that's a good thing. Follow the curriculum as best you can—but above all else, pray—pray for these kids—they need it."

She then patted my knee and turned and walked out the door. Sitting there alone, I looked about the room filled with broken crayons and scissors and a tub full of colored paper. As my eyes gazed upwards, I saw the mad scribbler's artistic rendition that he and his fellow classmates had drawn on the basement window only a few Sundays ago.

If I were a Grinch in Whoville, my heart would have grown three sizes that day. Yes, Mrs. Sherburne was a crafty one, but what I discovered that evening was her heart. She loved these kids and actually believed that what she and the other Sunday school teachers were doing was making a difference in their lives.

Oddly enough, sitting there in my own tiny little chair, I suddenly felt as if I was making a difference, too.

July 24 . . . Jerome's Stinky Bait Incorporated

I have been receiving a number of requests from you fishermen (and women) out there asking for Jerome's stinky bait recipe. It's funny, but when I asked Jerome earlier about giving it to me, he was as tight to the chest about his recipe as bark on a tree. I found it funny that a man that wears his Cajun recipes on his sleeve is as secretive about his stinky bait recipe as the KGB is about the Kremlin.

I had told him about my blog site called, *News from the Bullpen Café,* in which I describe events that are happening here in Bullpen. Then I told him that I had written about the fish he caught with his stinky bait and how people had blogged in, asking for the recipe. I then told him that one blogger surnamed "Far Quart" (from the movie, *Shrek*?), is willing to pay good money for his bait. And, if it actually works, I told him, he wants to market it, or better yet, is willing to buy your first franchise, if it will be available.

"Franchise the stinky bait?" he asked.

"Yep," I told him. "Can't you just see the golden arches?"

"Yeah," he replied, as if dollar signs were spinning around in his head. "Just like McDonalds."

"Yeah," I said. "Just like McDonalds with a big sign out front that reads, 'Stinky Bait: billions and billions served.'"

I was kidding.

He wasn't.

"So, how do I write back to them people?" he asked. "I don't have a computer."

"You don't have to," I told him. "They can send their requests snail mail to Bullpen, Minnesota, in care of Jerome's Stinky Bait Factory, and you can send out your orders from here."

"Yeah," he said, as if lost in his own entrepreneurial world. "Yep, that'd work."

"Yep," I agreed. "Just get yourself some plastic bottles for shipping and . . ."

"Oh, no," he retorted, stopping me in mid sentence. "It would have to be shipped out in glass to keep 'em from gettin' contaminated."

"Contaminated?" I asked. "If you ask me, Stinky Bait is the essence of contamination."

He eyed me fiercely, as if I had just profaned his sacred product.

"Well, then you will need to find some good shipping materials to put that glass in." I told him. "The last thing you want is to have those bottles break en route to some desperate fisherman. If it ever did break," I continued, "you would have the post office on your door in a heartbeat—and you would then have to reclassify Stinky Bait as hazardous material."

It really didn't matter what I said after that, Jerome had slipped into millionaire land and had wanted to put canning jars on our weekly shopping list for the café. He then asked me what price he should charge, and I told him $19.95 for a half pint, which would include shipping and handling. He agreed, and next trip into Rochester for groceries and supplies, we would pick up half pint canning jars. When I asked him if we needed to pick up any stuff to make Stinky Bait, he got defensive and told me that he had that part covered. I then asked him if he could mass-produce his "recipe" for Bullpen Days, and he told me that he would have to think about that. But that is what Jerome does best—think.

So, Mr. Far Quart and you others that have blogged in, asking about the recipe to Jerome's stinky bait, just send in a check made out to Jerome Boatman for $19.95 to cover shipping and handling. Mail it to: Jerome's Stinky Bait Factory, in care of Bullpen, Minnesota . . . and may the biggest fish win.

July 26 . . . Sunday School 202

I was a little hesitant about Sunday school today, still a little tender, I guess, about the kids going home and telling their parent or parents (or whoever else might be responsible for them) about everything we do in class. Even though I probably end up knowing more about them than they do about me, I can't go and complain to Mrs. Sherburne about their private lives.

Ivan was absent this morning, and that strikes me as odd. I have not seen him at the café in the last few days buying donuts, either. Oddly enough, I have started to miss the little guy.

In our deeply theological discussion this morning, I was asked the question "Does God have a beard?" by Abby McBride.

"I don't know," I told her. "Why do you ask?"

"I want to know if there is any shaving cream in heaven," she replied.

Hmmm . . . shaving cream in heaven . . . I had never thought much about shaving cream in heaven—and to be honest, I had never thought much about heaven. Is it a real place like Chicago or New York or London? And if so, is there also a hell to shun?

Without Ivan, class was relatively quiet. I did find some old animal crackers in one of the cupboards, so we had treat time, which seems to be the biggest event of the class right now, next to coloring. I have decided not to wear my tuxedo any more. It's too cumbersome and too hard to put on in less than five minutes, should I happen to oversleep. Besides, they all know me by now as Tennessee Tuxedo.

Later that Afternoon . . . Blueberry Picking

Miss Maddie asked me after church if I would take her blueberry picking in one of her favorite spots in southern Wisconsin—about an hour's drive from Bullpen. I agreed and then asked Jerome if he wanted to come along for the ride. He agreed, so we piled into the pickup truck after church and headed west. It was a pretty drive, winding through all of the rolling hills as we journeyed to Miss Maddie's favorite spot. Wearing her big wide brimmed sunbonnet, she sat between Jerome and me and kept patting him on the knee while talking to him. Every now and then the brim of her hat would obscure my vision of the road, and I would have to tell her to lean back so I could see.

She would laugh, but she never took off the hat.

When lost, she would have me pull over on the side of the road and take her index finger and place it in the middle of her forehead, like a honing device or some sort of GPS system, and after getting her bearings, she would smile and point in a particular direction.

"That way," she would tell me. And off we would go again, winding through the back hills of the blue highways, as they were pictured on most state maps. I figured that we had crossed and re-crossed the mighty Mississippi River no less than three times looking for Blueberry Road—and if I had not known better, I would have thought that she was getting lost on purpose and enjoying every minute of it. We finally found our way onto Highway 35 on the Wisconsin side of the river, across from Lake Pepin. Then we turned on to County Road A to Maiden Rock where we pulled into a blueberry farm called Blueberry River Produce.

"Oh, this is it," she cried as we drove up to what looked like an old farm house.

It was a pretty area with gentle rolling hills that overlooked the deep green valley beyond the river. Just beyond the farmhouse were rows upon rows of full-blooming orchids and heather in hues of purple, pink, and red. The hum of honeybees could be heard above the warm gentle breeze as they sucked nectar from adjacent poppy seeds. The farm was alive with life, and like the bees, Miss Maddie was smelling everything in sight. When finished, she placed her hands on her hips and arched her back.

"Okay boys, this is where we start picking," she said, stretching all her backbones. "Oh, and what a great day to pick, huh?" She laughed like a giddy little schoolgirl and then marched to the back of the pickup, handing Jerome and me our own plastic ice cream pails for picking. She then introduced us to the owners—a cordial, old married couple, as down to earth as the farm itself. We talked for what seemed like half an hour as they asked Miss Maddie about what had transpired since they saw her last. And she covered all the highlights, telling them how Jerome and I had come to Bullpen and were now helping her pick berries. Eventually, the conversation ended and they pointed us in the right direction, and we were off with our ice cream buckets in search of blueberries. Jerome grabbed his bucket and was off to the races, sampling more in his mouth than he could put in the bucket.

"Why, we hit the mother lode!" he shouted with a mouth full of blueberries. "Just look at 'em all!"

And we had. The bushes were full of ripe, juicy berries that were sweet to the taste. Suddenly, Jerome stopped and grabbed two blueberries and placed one in each eye. Then he scrunched his face together to keep them from rolling away, looking like a little kid with bulging, blueberry eyes.

"Oh, get those perfectly good blueberries out of your eyes," Miss Maddie said, pretending to scold him.

Then like a little kid herself, she took and placed a large blueberry on one of her front teeth, and then smiled at us, giving her the appearance of a toothless old woman. We both looked at her and laughed.

"Well, look at you, Miss Maddie. Ain't you just a child at heart," Jerome said laughing.

And she was—giggling and laughing and smelling and looking and eating and picking all the way down the countless rows of blueberry bushes, finding the clusters of berries that that were nestled beside and within the green, leafy bushes.

At the end of the day we had compiled no fewer than six big buckets of berries. It was a feast by anyone's standards. On the way home we stopped at Dairy Queen in Lake City and ordered vanilla ice cream, topping it off with— of course—blueberries.

It was late by the time we got back to Bullpen. The sun was setting across the Zumbro Valley, making deep, dark shadows throughout Miss Maddie's apple orchard. When we pulled into her driveway, Flint began to bark and Miss Maddie awakened from her nap. When the truck stopped, Jerome got out and offered his hand as he said goodnight to Miss Maddie—but the night was far from over. After stepping out, she took one look at the two of us, adjusted the brim on her hat, and with blueberry stains all over her lips, she told us "boys" to come on in for supper.

And we did. We had cold chicken, baked beans, potato salad, fresh bread, and more vanilla ice cream—with blueberries. Then after supper, she put us to work, rolling out dough for her countless blueberry pies. We had an assembly line going that night with her measuring, Jerome mixing and kneading, and me rolling. Then Maddie did the cutting, shaping and filling of each pie plate with the fruits of our labor from that afternoon. After the first pie had come off the assembly line, she popped it in the oven. One hour later we were again enjoying fresh blueberry pie as we sat on her porch looking at the stars above.

"Now ain't this the life?" stated Jerome, gazing up at the stars. "And to think that God calls all them stars by name."

Miss Maddie nodded.

"Why, we is lookin' at the same stars that Abraham saw when making a covenant with God. Why just look at 'em all—and the Bible says that Abraham's descendants would be as many as them stars. Why, there gots to be billions of them stars. Can you imagine havin' that many kinfolk?"

Miss Maddie shook her head. "You sound like you know a lot about the Bible, Jerome."

"Oh, my Daddy was a preacher man," he replied.

"Tell us about your daddy," she said.

"Well, I don't 'member much about 'em. I was the youngest of twelve children, and he died when I was eight years old. He died right after he done got through preaching on Sunday afternoon—giving a "sermon on the mount," my momma told me. After they did an autopsy, they told my momma that it was a miracle he done lived past his fifteenth birthday. They told my momma that he had one of the smallest hearts they had ever seen for a man his size. But we all knew different. Our daddy had the biggest heart you ever seen. Folks lined up for three blocks to pay their respects after he died. He was a good man, Miss Maddie, and we was just grateful he lived as long as he did—otherwise, I might not be here."

Miss Maddie smiled, and Jerome started to continue. "Sometimes I just . . . I . . ."

Miss Maddie suddenly got up and grabbed his hand, holding on to it without so much as a word, until Jerome's big frame began to shake. Suddenly there were tears streaming down the sides of his face. He wiped them with the back of his hand, as if embarrassed.

"Tears are nothing to be ashamed of, Jerome," she stated. "Nothing to be ashamed of."

He nodded.

"You will see him again someday," she said, still holding his hand. "Heaven is a place—like a city—that God has prepared for those who love him—and that is where your Daddy is."

Jerome nodded.

"So, how many kids do you have?" she asked.

The question seemed to startle Jerome.

"Four, Ma'am," he replied.

"And you miss them, don't you?" she stated, as if it was a rhetorical question.

"Yes Ma'am," he answered.

"Do you ever feel like a failure 'cause you couldn't provide for them like you thought you should?" she asked.

He nodded.

"You will, Jerome—you will," she told him reassuringly. "And before the year is out, I believe you will be reunited with your kids."

His big frame began to shake as more tears streamed down the sides of his face.

"You're not a failure, Jerome," she reassured him, holding his hand. "God calls you a great man, just like your Daddy. Don't you ever forget that."

Jerome was quiet on the way back home. I could only guess what was going through his mind and heart as we came down Thomforde Hill into Bullpen. When he stepped out of the truck, he told me thanks and made his way up into his apartment as if to relish the words that had been spoken over him. They were dream words, and he was holding them tightly to his chest as if they were in jeopardy of being lost or stolen.

I suddenly smiled, seeing a mental image of Jerome playing around in the blueberry patch as he had done earlier that afternoon. He had grabbed two blueberries and placed one over each eye and then scrunched his face together, looking like a blind man with bulging, blueberry eyes.

Then I saw Miss Maddie holding a single blueberry up to her front tooth in a playful manner, as she too had done that afternoon, pretending she was a toothless old woman—the same woman that had grabbed and held Jerome's hand later that night, helping him see something he could not see for himself.

July 29 . . . Frat Party Preparations

I had gotten word back from my frat brothers:

It was official—the Bullpen Café had been chosen as this year's annual convention site and would host the annual fraternity dinner one week after Bullpen Days. It was a toss-up among New York, Chicago, and the café, but with all the news surrounding Bullpen (that I had conveyed to my frat buddy during my brief discussion while waiting to use the urinal at the Rochester fireworks display this past Fourth of July), the delegates ruled in my favor. I anticipate around 25 of us that night. Jerome has volunteered to make us a special Cajun dinner with gumbo shrimp and Popeye's biscuit twins—and, of course, dirty rice. I was told to get a keg of beer for the event, and I will do so next Wednesday, after Bullpen Days, when Jerome and I go to Rochester for groceries and supplies. We may need all the liquid refreshment we can get if Jerome's Cajun cooking is as hot as he says it is.

With only a week and a half before Bullpen Days, the town is in full swing, preparing for the big event. I continue practicing my violin daily at the café, and I'm told by my patrons that I am making a lot more interesting sounds, which can only mean one thing—I'm making progress. This afternoon, however, the Bullpen Committee had called for an emergency session after hearing the news that our main speaker, Slater Gray, had developed a severe case of laryngitis. Slater had first tried to make his announcement this afternoon at the café with hand signals. When no one knew what he was trying to say, he began to clutch his throat. Homer thought he was choking and shouted out his errant assumption. No sooner had he done so than George and the Boys began performing the Heimlich maneuver on Slater, nearly crushing his fragile frame. When Slater came to after having had the wind knocked out of him, he motioned for a pen and a place mat. When they were given to him, he managed to scribble out the words "I have laryngitis and cannot speak." He then passed out, but no one noticed for several minutes since everyone was busy trying to decipher what he had written on the place mat. George called it the most "unintelligible" piece of writing he had ever seen. When it was finally discovered that Slater had laryngitis, word was quickly given to the mayor, who then called for an emergency session. At that session, suggestions for a new and perhaps more notable speaker ranged from former governor Al Quie to Dick Cheney, to former Minnesota Twins baseball star Kent Hrbeck, to Gump Worsley—one of the first goalies of the once-proud Minnesota North Stars, before they were sold to Dallas under the dubious ownership of Mr. Norm Green. Gump was of the old school and never wore a facemask during his entire NHL career. When asked if Worsley had ever been hit in the head with a hockey puck, the mayor (who had suggested Gump), got a little defensive and told the committee that Gump had not lost any of his marbles and was as good a speaker as any—and much more reasonable than Donny Osmond.

Mrs. Nordstrom disagreed.

An argument ensued, then more arguments, then more yelling and then more blaming for tasks that remained undone. It was civics at its finest, with everyone getting into the act, including the mayor. But in the end, everyone apologized, and there were hugs and tears and all kinds of reciprocating gestures of kindness. And as quickly as the fires of disagreement had ignited, they had been extinguished—until the mayor brought up Gump Worsley again.

That's all the news I have from the Bullpen Café, fellow bloggers.

PS

If any of you happen to be in the vicinity of Bullpen, Minnesota, a week from this coming Saturday, I am taking this moment to extend a personal invitation to come and be our guest. I cannot guarantee Bullpen Days will be fun, but I can guarantee that it will be interesting.

August 5 . . .
T minus 72 hours to Bullpen Days

There was another emergency meeting this afternoon with the Bullpen Committee to discuss some recent issues surrounding Bullpen Days. Apparently, some of you bloggers have been calling the mayor's office with prank phone calls, asking the whereabouts of some housing accommodations in Bullpen.

Housing accommodations in Bullpen?

No, I would suggest hotel accommodations in Rochester—about 30 minutes from here. But thank you for your calls anyway. Now the mayor is asking me about my blog and is all interested in marketing Bullpen to the world. He told me that he has always had higher aspirations for politics than just being a mayor and has had his eye on a state-wide gubernatorial position for more than three months now.

And now that the cat is out of the bag (not that it was ever in the bag): the mayor and the rest of the committee are fascinated by the onslaught of publicity from my *News from the Bullpen Café* WordPress blog site.

"It's just a blog," I told them. "I just describe the events that happen in Bullpen and report them to the world at large. I just sent an invitation out to all my fellow bloggers that they are more than welcome to come to the event. How was I to know that so many of you would call in checking for accommodations?"

Mavis suggested that those coming from far away could stay at people's homes like they do at the motorcycle rally in Sturgis, South Dakota, in August.

Eddie asked her how she knew about the Sturgis rally, and she told him that she had heard about it one time from a biker that was passing through and wanted some Watkins' vanilla for his mother.

And we all believed her.

Needless to say, the word is out that we are in need of some housing accommodations, and people in town are mowing their lawns, painting their fences, and cleaning up any and every available spare room they can find—or at least some of them are, including Millie and Maynard.

I have come to find out that Maynard is cleaning out his garage and filling it with two double beds and a hammock. Millie told me later this afternoon that he is pulling out all the stops with a microwave, two floor fans, a nightlight, a sprinkler out back, and, of course, a commode—all for the incredibly low price of just 25 dollars a night, including the spare bedroom on the second floor. I told her that Best Western, Marriott, and other hotel chains had nothing on him.

All in all, I am surprised to find that no one really asked or cared about what I had been writing about on the site. All they seemed to care about were accommodations and the new-fangled publicity—and for that, they were all grateful.

So, fellow bloggers, thanks to you, there is now an official sign-up sheet (as opposed to an electronic sign-up sheet) listing all the various homes that have offered rooms or garages that you can rent for the night. Just continue to call the mayor's office to let him know what you are looking for and to find out what is available. And also, please let him know that you're not a prank caller.

August 6 . . . The Excitement Never Ends

It's a mad frenzy here in Bullpen. People have gone mad, stark raving mad with fame and fortune—especially Jerome. He has been up until three am the last three nights, preparing and bottling two special Cajun recipes that are so secret that even he's having trouble remembering what's in them. When I asked him why he had suddenly become so secretive about his Cajun recipes, he told me that these were the only two that were just his—and it had taken him years—years—to get the right combinations of ingredients and proportions. Personally, I think it had taken him seconds—seconds—to realize there may be some money to be made off his secret recipes.

In addition to bottling his Louisiana hot sauce, he is also mass-producing his stinky bait concoction in the half-pint jars that we had gotten during our grocery and supply run in Rochester last week. With the time crunch upon us, he hired Jared to help him, but only after he had sworn him to secrecy. Once Jared was fully sworn in, Jerome showed him what part of the dumpster in which to find his raw material. So, for the last three nights, both he and Jared have been dumpster diving with rubber boots, homemade gas masks, flashlights, and garden spades—and I can only imagine what they look like. Jerome's inspiration for his "filthy rich business" (as he now calls it) was fueled by the first check he received in the mail for $19.95, from someone who plans on entering a fishing tournament in Arkansas (was that you, Far Quart?).

To promote Stinky Bait, Jerome is placing a large 24-by-36-inch sign underneath the walleye that is now mounted near the smiling moose. When I asked him if he had gotten permission to do so, he told me Millie thought it would be okay. When I asked Millie who was in charge, she told me that Jerome needed all the help he could get to promote his sales—as if that was the answer I was looking for. It was a homemade sign and looked tacky, so I told him to clean it up and at least get Millie to do the lettering. He did, and now the ad reads:

This Bad Boy was caught on Stinky Bait.
Only $19.95
Get yours while supplies last.
And may the biggest fish win.

He plans on selling both his Cajun hot sauce and his fish bait at the same table, underneath the sign. I warned him, however, that, if I ever caught so much as a whiff of that stinky bait in the café, he would be out of a job.

He reassured me that he had everything under control—and I am trying my best to believe him.

For those of you fellow bloggers that may be here on Saturday—please come and see me. I would love to meet you. And now, without further ado—Ladies and Gentlemen of web world, I present to you the official schedule of the Bullpen Days events:

Saturday:

6:00 am there will be a five-K run/walk that will start and end at the café with contestants making a big loop around County Road 30 and then returning down Thomforde Hill.

8:00 am the cafe will be hosting a waffle-eating contest for $3 per person, with all the milk you can drink for free, thanks to the American Dairy Association. Homer and others have offered their waffle irons as back-ups.

9:00 the hunt for the Bullpen Medallion begins after a brief introductory speech by our honored speaker—Maynard. There had been some confusion a few days ago as to who was to invite whom, and in the end, no one had contacted Gump Worsley, much to the dismay of the mayor. Looking for a fill-in speaker, Millie suggested Maynard, who had represented the local mail carrier's union (also known as the National Association of Letter Carriers) over 15 years ago. With their backs against the wall, the committee had no other choice than to approve Maynard, with only one vote in abstention.

9:30 in front of the Watkins Curiosity shop, the local 4H is running and judging a bread-baking contest, a cookie-baking contest, and a pie-baking contest.

10:00 am the bluegrass competition will start in front of the café, with volunteer judges selected from surrounding communities.

Noon marks the start of the official baseball tournament that features eight local teams that will be playing on the original field of the famous game of 1893. Lenny Jorgenson and other farmers helped prepare the pasture to its original condition and size. I call it the Field of Dreams. And teams will be using old baseballs, old leather mitts, and old bats to commemorate the event.

4:00 pm is the tractor-pulling contest near Felix Manion's farm, off of County Road 30.

5:30 pm is when Methune Fuliedy—the human cannon ball—will be shot out of a cannon.

6:30 is the all-town potluck supper—free for all guests, with the town providing the meal.

8:00 pm to midnight will feature Johnny Dugan and the Rascals in the Beer Garden.

Sunday:

8:00 am to 9:00 am is a pancake breakfast at the Lutheran church, $3.00 a person.

9:00 am is the worship service at the Lutheran church.

11:00 am—Final rounds for the tractor pulling contest.

August 7 . . . T minus 7 hours and Counting

We had another emergency session this morning to rehearse any and every possible contingency plan for an event that may not exactly go as planned. To date, we have all the bases covered, and food vendors have set up shop, ready for tomorrow's big day. The café will be open at 8:00 am for the waffle-eating contest and then will feature its regular menu the rest of the morning, with Jerome serving his original Cajun food in the afternoon. Since I will be occupied with other events, I asked Millie to cover for me and get some additional help. She recruited Melissa Magnuson and a few of her friends to man the store while I'm gone. I think we are good. The weather calls for rain—another concern. Sitting in the pickup tonight, I have seen a few sprinkles on the windshield, but that is all. If the weather holds, tomorrow may be good after all.

As I look down into Bullpen through the windshield of my uncle's truck, I see the sleepy little town that has come alive with anticipation of tomorrow's big event. Across Main Street hangs a thick canvas banner that was made by the Ladies Auxiliary. They are as proud of it as the rest of the town, and it serves as a testimony to Bullpen's willingness to work together for a common goal—even to the point of sacrifice. The committee put out a survey earlier in the week to see if Bullpen's residents would be willing to provide an evening meal, free of charge, for the guests that attended Bullpen Days—and the response was an overwhelming 'yes.' The mayor called it a miracle and wondered if bond issues could be passed the same way. The committee then organized who was to bring what dishes, desserts, salads, and drinks. "If in doubt," wrote the mayor in his town-wide memo, "bring something."

Since then, others have come forward and offered their services in ways no one expected. George and the Boys took it upon themselves to clean the streets surrounding the town—like Minnesota's Adopt a Highway program. The Ladies Auxiliary, not content with the banner alone, went out and bought little American flags to distribute for a small donation which will be sent to the Armed Forces oversees. The Lutheran Church members set up their own canopy

212

and are offering free ice cream cones and Gideon Bibles. Lenny Jorgensen and other farmers spent most of yesterday grooming the baseball field and hauling folding chairs and tables from the local high school. Others are pitching in here and there—some noticed, some not. It is the story "Stone Soup" all over again, with members of the town giving what they have for a greater good. It is the movie *Field of Dreams*—if you build it and announce it and plan for it, they will help—and they will come. And the people are coming, seeking lodging from local families for the price of a memory of an event as unpredictable as the weather itself.

Regardless of what tomorrow may bring, fellow bloggers, tonight I am quite simply amazed. It is, after all, a study of faith: simple, childlike faith.

August 8 . . . Bullpen Days Are Upon Us

I staggered out of bed at five am, searching for coffee and finding none. What kind of man owns a café and runs out of coffee for himself?

I had to drag myself into the shower and out into the wild blue yonder. To be honest, I had forgotten what an early morning looked like—a real early morning like this one with the glimmer of sunlight piercing the horizon, like a game of peek-a-boo. And as I drove down Main Street to my official position halfway along County Road 30 to man the water break station, I saw a plethora of different ages and sizes and shapes stretching and jogging and warming up for this ungodly event—the five-K run/walk. Who signed me up for this thing anyway?

Mrs. Sherburne—crafty Mrs. Sherburne.

Personally, I never understood jogging or running for that matter—moving down a path, a dirt road, or a high-school track to obtain a trinket, a plastic little trophy or ribbon that you could place above your nightstand. There were joggers at the frat house telling us non-joggers about the feeling of utopia when you get your second wind (as opposed to your third wind) and coasting effortlessly along the road with one foot in front of the other in a mindless, mechanical exertion of the will.

Who cares.

The end never justified the means of punishing your frame for those relentless miles. Was it not Jim Marshal, one of the famous defensive linemen of the Vikings years ago, that once told a reporter (who had asked him why he didn't work out in the off season) that there was only so much tread on the tire? Atta Boy, Jim.

The rain had held off, and the cloud cover provided a cool morning for the contest. When the first jogger came by at 6:41, I handed him a cup of cold water. He smiled, and I smiled back, quickly replenishing my cup of spent water on the table as only a good water-break station manager would do. I could have been a better water-station manager had I not fallen asleep at my post. I was then awakened a few minutes later by the sound of slurping,

214

guzzling, out-of-breath and out-of-their-mind participants. When I saw Lenny and his wife run up to the table, however, I quickly repented of every bad thing I had muttered about joggers.

At 8:00 am it was on to the waffle-eating contest at the café. There were no less than 80 contestants—some of which were joggers. Millie was busy collecting fees while the Ladies Auxiliary was busy making waffles in the back, with no less than 10 extension cords running across the floor. I could only hope that we wouldn't blow a fuse—but we did.

Jerome was quick on the spot, however, and ran next door, and thankfully the mayor was there to help. Like an Indy Pit Crew, they had electricity back in operation in no less than 2.5 minutes, and the Ladies Auxiliary and the contestants breathed a sigh of relief. As I was moving about the event, I was stopped by no fewer than five people who asked me if I was Charlie Finstune. And after I told them I was, they told me how much they enjoy reading my blog. I told them I'm honored, shook their hands, and thanked them for coming to Bullpen Days. I was feeling like a rock star until the third waffle iron blew another fuse downstairs, and we were now down to nine irons, including Homer's. But the tide turned as the waffle eaters were now slowing down—even Homer, who could not resist entering the contest. Thirty minutes into the event, it came down to two contestants—a thin, middle-aged man from Claremont and a young, heavyset man from Dodge Center. The thin man—as I call him—lay on his back as his heavy-set wife stood over him, feeding him waffles like fellow convicts fed Paul Newman eggs in the move *Cool Hand Luke*. In the end, the thin man won, and his bigger wife hoisted him up on her shoulders as he was declared the victor. She then carried him into the bathroom and encouraged him to stick his finger down his throat to throw it all up.

"You'll feel better, Honey," she told him. "Believe me, you'll feel better."

As if she would know . . . . Homer couldn't stop laughing.

At nine o'clock the hunt for the medallion was announced, and there were no fewer than 300 people in attendance. They crowded in front of the Watkins Curiosity Shoppe as Maynard stepped onto the podium and tested his bullhorn. He then thanked everyone for coming and gave an introduction to Bullpen Days with a background history of "our beloved community." However, when he added how important it is to support unions and postal employees that represent the backbone of the greatest postal system in the world, the mayor threatened to take his bullhorn away. So Maynard dutifully launched into the rules and clues accompanying the event at hand, while holding up a picture of the medallion. He mistakenly told his captive audience where not to look and, in the process, accidentally gave out a major clue to the medallion's whereabouts. Before he could finish speaking, a 12-year-old girl came up and handed him the medallion.

"Why, look here," he shouted into the bullhorn. "My, what a sharp little girl you are. I guess that ends the hunt for the medallion, ladies and gentlemen."

A cry of disgruntlement (if that is such a word) rang out, and the mayor, quick to improvise—as any good politician should do—told the unruly medallion seekers them the committee would re-hide the medallion and give out another prize in 10 minutes, with new clues to accompany its whereabouts. As he quickly whisked Maynard off the podium, he called for another emergency session of the committee to reconvene at the insurance building.

We did. First and foremost on the agenda was to make sure that Maynard did not set foot onto that podium again.

Agreed.

The mayor then pulled out his notes from previous meetings and told the committee that we would hide the medallion in the area we had originally planned. He then deciphered his notes on the clues that had gone along with that original site.

Eddie Carlisle was then asked to hide the new medallion and slipped out the back in a clandestine manner. Mavis then typed up the new set of clues from the mayor's previous notes and printed them on his copy machine.

Apart from the misspellings, it was a brilliant contingency plan, one that even Collin Powell would have been proud of. Nine minutes and 39 seconds later, the mayor stepped onto the podium as the rest of us passed out the new clues, and he announced the new rules for the medallion search. He then waved the checkered flag, and the hunt was on.

The rest of the morning ran without a hitch. The bake sale had an unexpected winner, however, for pies and cookies. It was Slater Gray, of all people, who had won both events, much to the chagrin of the ladies in town. He accredited his two victories to the Betty Crocker Cookbook, much to the further chagrin of the disgruntled ladies in town. A woman from Rochester, however, won the bread-baking contest—thank goodness.

The bluegrass competition started right at 10:00, and I was a little nervous. I had nailed "Mary had a Little Lamb" just that morning while practicing between events in the basement of the café. Needless to say, when it was all over, we came in fifth out of five, but as Gary said over and over again, it is not about the competition. The winning group was out of Zumbrota, Minnesota. Called the Sweet Tooth BlueGrass Band, it was made up of five teenage boys. I was impressed. They continued to play throughout the day, along with the other groups.

At noon, eight teams went down to the original baseball field to compete in the first annual baseball contest using old bats and gloves. In the fifth inning of the second game, one of the payers hit a foul ball deep into a pasture, never to be found—just like the baseball of 1893. Again, the mayor was on the spot, throwing out a second baseball like the President at a major league game.

At four o'clock the tractor-pulling contest began just outside of town on Felix's farm. A dirt track 300 feet long had been prepared, and I was told that the winning tractor would pull a weighted sled the furthest distance down the track. The sled had four wheels at the back and a ground friction skid on the front. As the tractor moved forward, the weight on the sled shifted from the wheels to the skid, making it harder to pull. I had never seen a tractor-pulling contest before, and like in the movie *Those Magnificent Men and their Flying Machines*, each tractor was accompanied by a pit crew of ready-made believers, most of them family. It was like watching monsters of the midway as men and machine snorted and growled and fumed, spewing jet black smoke as they thundered down the dirt track en route to the winner's circle. In each contest, the big machine simply came to a halt, spinning its wheels in the ground as if frustrated that it could go no further. In the end, Lenny Jorgenson's John Deere came within two feet from beating a farmer from Racine, Wisconsin, who drove a Massey Ferguson 6.5 twin fuel pump diesel engine—whatever that is. After the contest, the two shook hands and talked at length, as if comparing notes on tractors or conferring about farming.

It was five o'clock when I came back to the café. And looking at the floor fans and the open door, I had a sneaking suspicion that something had gone awry—and it had. The worst was confirmed when I got within 50 feet of the café and caught a whiff of the stinky bait.

"Doggone it!" I yelled.

Millie, Jerome, Jared, and Melissa were scurrying about inside with mops and pails and rags and brooms and—worse yet—masks.

"It's a pickle, Charlie!" cried Melissa. "It's a pickle!"

"When I get hold of that Ivan kid, I'm gonna skin him alive," cried Jerome.

"Ivan the Terrible?" I shouted. "Doggone it all!"

217

According to Millie, Jerome had made a valiant attempt to save the glass jar that Ivan had dropped. The boy had opened it in the café to see what it smelled like. When Jerome caught a whiff of the scent, he yelled. That startled Ivan, who then bobbled the jar and, like a slow-motion instant replay, it bobbled out of his hands and fell towards the floor. Jerome had dived to save it from crashing and had actually caught it in the palm of his hands, but he too bobbled it. It broke when it hit the floor.

"Thank God it happened at closing time," said Melissa. "Had it happened earlier in the day, we may have had a stampede to the door, and someone could have been maimed or killed."

The others all agreed, which was no less comforting. For the next 20 minutes we bleached the floor, the tables, the mops and anything else within a ten-foot radius of the crash site. We then put out two more floor fans and propped open the door as wide as possible.

Just before the human cannonball was announced, the smell had subsided.

All five of us then stepped outside, and there, in the middle of Main Street, must have been 500 people waiting for the event. It was packed. Even Millie had never seen Bullpen this crowded. People had come with their lawn chairs and blankets, sitting down right in the street to see the rocket man fly over their heads, as they would view an airliner in flight. He was to be shot from one side of the town to the other and land in a 20-by-20-foot air mattress.

I had never seen a human cannon before. When the rocket man stepped out of his trailer and put on his helmet, I had a sinking feeling that the odds of his hitting the air pad were less than good.

But who was I to judge?

This was, after all, what he does for a living—$10,000 a pop (and we were getting a deal at $5,000). Being the businessman, all I could see were dollar signs flying through the air, but if all 500-plus people decided to stay for the pot luck and then the beer garden, I guessed that it would be more than enough to pay for his launch.

His female assistant came out and introduced him as Minnesota's one and only "Rocket Man," building up his past achievements with a passionate crescendo. The audience was clearly aroused and clapping with each accolade. Rocket Man, as he was commonly referred to, was carrying what looked like an early 1930s leather football helmet, as if that, too, was part of the act. When he finally put it on, the crowd erupted in a huge cheer, and they kept on cheering as he somersaulted into the cannon, offering more theatrics to the already heightened event.

Then came the long countdown, from 60, down to 30, down to 15 seconds, and then in unison the crowd finished the countdown from 10 to 5 to 4 to 3 to 2 to 1—and nothing happened.

"No!" I said out loud, thinking people were going to demand some kind for refund. It was a dud, like a firecracker that had never exploded.

The female assistant, uncertain of what to do, began the countdown again, this time from 30 down to zero—but again, nothing.

The crowd was a little unsettled. His assistant fiddled with something on the cannon. It was clear they were having technical difficulties. Again, the mayor came to the rescue with fun facts about human cannonballs, never missing a beat. As Rocket Man and his female assistant reexamined the cannon, the mayor began asking people in the crowd who had come the farthest and how they had heard about us. He had everyone raise hands, and starting at 100 miles, 70 percent of the audience lowered their hands. Then he went to 500 miles, and more dropped their hands. When he got to 2000 miles, one old lady was still holding up her hand. He called to her in the crowd with his bullhorn and asked her to come up to the podium where he stood.

"Yes, ma'am," he said, "and where do you come from?"

"Alaska" she replied.

"Alaska!" cried the mayor. "What brings you to Bullpen?"

I thought she was the lady who had given me my first lutefisk recipe on the blog site a few month ago—Queen Crab—but no such thing. She was visiting a friend at the Mayo Clinic and heard about our Bullpen Days from a nurse, who had read about us in the paper.

Interesting.

The mayor continued to quiz the audience until Rocket Man and his assistant seemed confident, having adjusted some kind of mechanical device on the cannon.

This time the mayor started the countdown on his bullhorn, and the crowd joined in unison from 30 to 15, to 10, to 5, to 4, to 3, 2, 1—blast off!

A sonic boom filled the air, and suddenly Rocket Man shot out of the cannon and began to soar fearlessly through space, like Flash Gordon with his arms tucked at his side, wearing his flight goggles and looking as if he was propelled by an unseen force or some mystical kind of jet fuel.

And he continued to soar—higher and higher. Watching him fly over the crowd was nothing less than breath-taking—until he kept soaring and soaring. In that split second of time you could see that he was clearly going to overshoot his landing site—and he did. Rocket man was now going where no man had gone before. The crowd gasped as he began to descend into the great abyss. Suddenly, thoughts of hospital bills and lawsuits and every imaginable catastrophe that could begat mankind filled my mind.

"No!" I yelled, and just as I said it, he landed, smack dab in the middle of the Beer Garden tent, taking down three poles and a few tent stakes.

The crowd rushed to the scene, wondering if he was still alive—and he was—miraculously. When he began to struggle to free himself, the tension eased. Then, as only Rocket Man could do, he jumped up and out of the tent, took off his helmet, and took a bow. The crowd erupted into a thunderous applause and started chanting, "ROCKET MAN, ROCKET MAN, ROCKET MAN" over and over and over again. He continued to take his bows, holding hands with his female assistant.

"Wow, that was cool!" I heard Jared say.

"Yeah," I replied sarcastically, knowing all too well what could have happened.

Soon members of the committee tended to the broken tent, while other town members began to prepare for the "all-town" potluck supper.

It was logistics at its finest, with men taking the tables from along the street and laying them end to end, while the women and children brought out the various dishes. Signs were placed over each section of tables: main dishes, salads, desserts, and drinks. It was like clockwork—like an ant colony simply going about its business—with chairs being erected around the remaining tables.

In minutes it was all ready, and the pastor blessed the food, thanking God for His provision, protection, and blessing—and for keeping Rocket Man alive. When he finished, suppertime was underway. There were hot dishes and cold dishes and cakes and pies and salads upon salads. There were mashed potatoes and chili and tacos and corn dogs and dishes for every other imaginable taste. The lines flowed smoothly from both directions, feeding into the serving tables, then back out into the seating area, like streams of free flowing traffic. Hungry children stood over the various smorgasbords with fidgety hands and big-eyed smiles as they waited in anticipation for their turn in line. Suddenly, I noticed one little girl reach up and take a single piece of bread and eat it with delight—and then it struck me how precious it was to simply watch a totally dependent child enjoying what had been freely given to her. It was hunger fulfilled and innocence personified.

After we had all finished eating, everyone pitched in to take down the tables and chairs and help cleanup—including our guests. As we all began to work together, the line that separated the guests from the town hosts began to blur. And then it hit me: they had suddenly become part of us by simply helping—by serving rather than being served—and in doing so, they had taken ownership to the event themselves. Suddenly, Bullpen Days was no longer like Jesse James Days or the St. Paul Winter Carnival or the Taste of Minnesota, where the vendors did nothing more than cater to guests, which had defined the relationship as such. But not here. The lines had been unconsciously blurred through the simple notion of a free meal and the need to help clean it up. The once-silly notion of a potluck supper and the family-style dining had unknowingly become the apex that would differentiate Bullpen Days from all other festivals. It was a lesson on marketing, management, and ownership—perceived or actual—and it was built upon the ageless notion of serving others, with nothing more than a free meal and giving them the opportunity to help in return. And, unbeknownst to us at the time, it was brilliant.

By the time we had finished cleaning Main Street, I had counted no fewer than 30 people who had come up to me thanking me for the invitation on my blog. One young man had brought his grandfather and told me that he had never been invited to a free meal like this before. As I shook their hands, I began to see the power of a simple invitation as opposed to an advertisement. An advertisement implies that you are trying to sell someone something, and that, by itself, defines a separation between buyers and sellers, with one side trying to get as much for an item as possible and the other side trying to pay as little as possible. A true invitation, however, implies giving something away without expecting anything in return. As I pondered the thought of whether we were trying to sell people on Bullpen Days or were simply trying to include them as part of our own event, Jerome came up and asked me if he still had a job, knowing how I had warned him about the stinky bait. He had put on his best apology face, and I found myself nodding yes.

A big, wide grin then broke across his face.

"See, I knows you weren't really gonna fire me, now was you?" he said.

"Well, don't press your luck—the night is still young," I replied. "So, how did your sales go today?" I asked.

"Hey, I'm makin' big money now," he said. "Pretty soon I'm gonna get me one a them fast-food restaurants and serve Cajun, 24/7."

"You do that," I told him. "In the meantime, do me a favor and see if you can land me another corn dog, will you?"

He nodded and then came back with two of them. He handed me one, kept the other, and then went back towards the café. When I turned around, I saw a young woman approach me from out of the crowd.

"Are you Charlie Finstune?" she asked me.

"Yes," I replied.

"I want to tell you how much I enjoy your blog," she told me.

"Well, thank you," I stated. "I'm sorry . . . but I didn't get your name."

"Mary," she said.

"Well, hi, Mary. Have you had a good time in Bullpen?" I asked, eating my corn dog.

"Yes," she replied. "I've eaten waffles, I've listened to some bluegrass music, I've seen an old-fashioned baseball game, and I've even played a few games of Crokinole with Homer Robertson."

"Did you win?" I asked.

She smiled and shook her head.

"No, Homer's Ulysses beat me after coming back from Troy."

I smiled.

"So, you *have* been reading my blog. That's great," I said. "So, who else have you met?"

"Everyone but Miss Maddie. I can't seem to find her," she replied.

"Well, she's got to be around here someplace," I assured her. "So, what brings you to Bullpen?"

"Your blog, primarily," she said. "I've done some writing on my own, and I think you have a great idea for a story here. I think it touches upon the very issues that define our generation."

"How is that?" I asked.

"I think our generation is trying to find what is real," she replied. "And I think we are trying to discover what real relationships are in the midst of all our technology—Facebook and Twitter and text messaging—the Internet."

"Are we succeeding?" I asked.

She smiled. "I don't know."

I smiled.

"It's funny," she continued, "but when I read your blog, I read it in real time, and it's as if I'm a part of it—it's as if we are all a part of it and have the ability to change its direction, like an interactive video game. It's an interesting concept—that real people in real time can affect the outcome of your story."

"Perhaps it's not just my story anymore," I told her.

"Perhaps not," she replied. "But there is also something romantic here in Bullpen."

"Well, I don't know if I would call it romantic," I said, looking at the floor fans blowing the stinky bait smell out of the café.

"I would," she stated. "And I guess that's why I came. I wanted to see for myself if it was real."

"Well, it is," I blurted out like an idiot, pointing to the town. "It's all real."

She nodded and smiled and then looked down at the ground, as if embarrassed, and I suddenly saw something about Mary that was shy and innocent and beautiful.

"Do I know you?" I asked.

She seemed to blush at the notion, and I sensed an awkwardness in the moment. Suddenly, she reached out and shook my hand.

"I'm sorry, but I have to go," she said. "It was a pleasure to meet you, Charlie from Bullpen."

And as quickly as she had appeared, she turned and slipped back into the crowd.

I don't know why, but for a moment, I was tempted to follow after her—but having no apparent reason to do so, I simply watched the back of her blouse fade into the colorful kaleidoscope of clothing that was all around us. And suddenly she was gone.

When I turned around, Millie was standing there next to me, as if she had been eavesdropping on our conversation the whole time.

"Nice girl, that Mary," she said to me.

"Do you know her?" I asked.

"She rented a room from us last night."

"Really." I said. "Where is she from?"

"New York," replied Millie. "She called herself Mary from New York."

August 12 . . . A Honeymoon with Destiny

The town is settling down after a "Honeymoon with Destiny"—a phrase used to describe the success of last weekend. "A Honeymoon with Destiny" has a nice ring to it, doesn't it? The mayor said he thought of that phrase all by himself as he and the rest of the town continued to bask in the afterglow of Bullpen Days. Next year, he vowed, the event will be bigger and better, and there will be a carnival and parades with high school bands and Shriners and clowns and motorcades and other kinds of parade stuff. Regarding the guest speaker, he told us that Gump Worsley would be called well in advance, and if his busy schedule didn't permit him to attend, then the committee would be free to contact other notables, such as Donny Osmond or Dick Cheney. Maynard, however, is still a little miffed that he was ushered off the podium as fast as he was. He felt rushed and hadn't gotten through all of his notes—especially those regarding the history of the Pony Express and the first mail train.

The Beer Garden was a financial success, with Johnny Dugan and his "little" Rascals playing well past midnight. Only one fight had ensued, and it was between two members of his own band for reasons that remain unknown. George, however, speculated that Spanky—the littlest of the Rascals—started it by handing out a few "spankings" of his own (Homer thought that was funny). And speaking of spankings, the Minnesota Twins baseball team seems to be taking a few more than they have been giving out lately—and that is a cause of great concern to most of the café patrons.

Slater Gray is now basking in more glory, as not only the Artist in Residence, but the Baker as well. George and the Boys now call him "Thin Man Crocker" after he single-handedly absconded with two out of three blue baking ribbons, snatching them from the jaws of irate women, using nothing more than a "*Betty Crocker Cookbook*, of all things" (to quote Melissa Magnuson). His two blue ribbons now hang proudly to the right of the smiling moose and are a constant eyesore to the once proud, bodacious, beautiful bevy of bakers from Bullpen, who had to concede the prize. Millie has threatened to take them down herself if I don't. I'm in a quandary, hoping the agony of defeat will soon pass. Otherwise, I will be forced to remove this contentious point of contention in the baking war between the sexes.

The hottest story circulating the café, however, has been about Rocket Man. Apparently, Rocket Man's female assistant had been assisting Rocket Man in more ways than the Ladies Auxiliary thought were necessary. It was a complete misunderstanding, according to the mayor. But while George and the Boys have been milking the story dry, the Ladies Auxiliary filed an official statewide boycott of all his future appearances.

Other than that, things are pretty quiet around town. Jerome made 250 dollars on his stinky bait and Cajun Spice sales, while the café made over 500 dollars on the Cajun dinners he served from 11:00 to 4:30.

This afternoon, we went into Rochester to get our weekly supply of groceries and a keg of beer, along with gumbo shrimp and dirty rice for our frat dinner on Saturday. I'm looking forward to the event.

It is a peaceful night with a little drizzle, and it's nights like these that I miss Karen. I wonder how she is doing, and my guess is that she has long since been married. Was she now on her own "honeymoon with destiny"? Perhaps, but I guess in the end it doesn't really matter what I think.

But as I stare out the window, I'm suddenly melancholy, thinking of our times spent together at the university. In a few days I will see some frat brothers, and I'm certain that the topic of Karen will come up. I'm not sure how I will handle it. I should be happy for her, but I'm not—I miss her, and wish she had never gone to Italy. If she had died in a car accident, then missing her would take on a whole different dimension than being rejected. She chose someone else, and there is a gnawing sensation that I was not good enough to win her heart.

I suddenly hear a siren approaching, and soon a sheriff's car zooms past me, then down into Bullpen and beyond. We don't see much action going through Bullpen, and I wonder what the emergency is? Domestic violence? An accident? The red flashing lights soon fade out of sight, and it's quiet once again. As I glance down at my laptop, I notice that a few of you have written in.

Blondie tells me there will be better days ahead.

I have still not heard back from Far Quart . . . Was that you that ordered stinky bait from Jerome? If so, did it arrive in one piece, or did some little kid accidentally open it before you had a chance to use it in your fishing tournament?

Frozen Tundra has just written in to say he had a great time at Bullpen Days.

See? I'm telling you fellow bloggers that you missed the show. It was one of Bullpen's finest hours.

Any other comments? If not, I'm signing off and going to bed.

PS

I am not sure who you are—Mary from New York—but I understand it was you that came on Friday night and stayed with Millie and Maynard. Thanks for coming. I don't know why you had to leave so suddenly—maybe you had to catch a flight back to New York. If it was anything I said, please let me know.

August 15 . . . Frat Night

It was 5:00 when Jeff Gordon and Tony Williams pulled into the café and helped set up for the annual dinner. Tony brought in the fraternity candelabra, which will be notched again this year to represent its presence among the brethren.

Here! Here!

Jeff brought the usual box of cheap cigars, and we'll smoke them on into the night, stinking up the café and my uncle's apartment. I figure we have until Monday to air out the café before the patrons come back for breakfast.

As they look about the café, Jeff and Tony both laugh at the coffee cup hall of fame and all of the various trophies, knickknacks, crayon drawings, and old newspaper clippings along the wall. They kid me about the smiling moose and ask me the story behind it, but I don't have an answer. They then look at the walleye and Jerome's sign that I had decided to leave up to help him with his local sales. I had decided to take it down for the night, but had lost track of time.

This Bad Boy was caught on Stinky Bait.

Only $19.95

Get yours while supplies last.

And may the biggest fish win.

Jeff asks me about the stinky bait, and I tell him the story behind it. He laughs, as if I had made up the story, but Jerome, who is preparing food in the kitchen, comes out to set the record straight.

"So who's the one that don't think that I caught this fish on stinky bait?" he asks.

"I am," replies Jeff.

"Well, Charlie was in the boat and saw the whole thing—ain't that right, Charlie?"

I nod. "Yep, I saw the whole thing. If you do any fishing, Jeff, you ought to buy some of that stuff."

"Really," he laughs sarcastically.

"Really," I reply.

I then introduce Jerome, and they shake his hands. I tell them that Jerome will be cooking a real Cajun treat for us tonight. They smile.

Soon others arrive: Frank Simmons, who had graduated two years ago last May; then Jeremy Asher, Bill Bright, and Conrad "Easy on the Sugar" Johnson. Conrad was a big boy who decided to go on a sugar fast last fall. Three days into the fast, however, we found him sitting naked in the bathtub, eating a box of cherry Jell-O, devouring it like a mad dog. When we tried to take it away—he growled. Conrad was never the same after that. He had become a complete sugarholic, eating everything and anything that had even the remotest portion of high fructose corn syrup, sugar, artificial sweetener, or any derivative thereof. It mattered not to Conrad what it was, as long as it was sweet. And now that his sweet sensors had been acutely attuned to sugar and all its various forms, he had become like a shark that could smell blood from miles away. Nothing was safe anymore, and nothing was sacred—not your secret stash of mints, not your Crunch Bar, not your Snickers, and certainly not your Almond Joy. It was enough to ruin your whole day to find out that he had taken and eaten it all. We frat brothers had been patient, trying to understand his addiction, but none of us dared confront him until the day he single-handedly drank all 24 cans of the Mountain Dew in our refrigerator that had been designated for our frat party.

Enough was enough.

We brought him in, surrounded him and confronted him with the problem. After he began to growl, we wrestled him to the ground and told him he had a problem with sugar. He denied it and kept on denying it. He had become a perpetual denier in a perpetual state of denial, until we tied his hands behind his back, sat him in a chair, and placed two Milky Way bars in front of him, challenging him to keep from salivating.

He couldn't.

And that realization was the beginning of the end of Conrad's addiction. He finally realized he had a problem and committed himself to rehab three days later. Four weeks later, he came out a new man—and there was peace in his eyes—yes, peace.

Then others begin to arrive: Jeremy Caskel; Terry Jones, the computer geek; Bobby Fisher, the golf guru; and Thomas Edwards, the video game expert.

As the noise grows louder in the café, I tell them there is beer upstairs in the apartment. And like the snap of geese, there is sudden exodus to the keg. More continue to come, however—stragglers who have had difficulty finding Bullpen on the state map or MapQuest or their own GPS. But they come: Trent Anderson; Tucker Armstrong; and Gabe Loucious, the bombardier—the one who could launch a water balloon over 500 feet with his surgical tubing slingshot with relative (emphasis on relative) accuracy. There was only one smashed window that was attributed to his cannon fire, and even that had been unconfirmed.

I greet them all and show them to the apartment upstairs. Soon there is singing and stomping on the floor of my uncle's apartment while the ceiling shakes below in the café. They are singing one of our theme songs: "Buffalo Gals, Won't You Come Out Tonight."

I check with Jerome to see if he needs any help, and he tells me he has all under control. So, when the last of the boys arrive, I join them in the apartment upstairs for a glass of beer and a cigar.

I have forgotten how stinky cigars can be, especially when everyone is smoking them. I open a few windows and the balcony door, where a few of the boys are standing and admiring the view of Main Street. Gabe is calculating distances for his water balloon, estimating how far it would take to reach the top of Thomforde Hill. I tell him about the hill and how that is the only place for phone or Internet reception. Back inside, a few of the boys are shooting pool, and the smoke is so thick that I can barely make out who is playing from across the room.

There is more laughter—and singing and stories and tales of the glories that seem to have gotten a little more dramatic and bigger than I originally recalled them. Distilling our own alcohol is one of them—a story they have all heard before, but it's worth repeating and repeating and repeating—especially the part about cutting down the tree in the midst of our environmentally friendly classmates after we had formed the copper coil for our condenser.

There are other frat adventures, including those surrounding Mickey Emkovic, the fireworks expert and pyro-technician, who had rigged one of the nearby women's sororities with "explosives" on their first night of orientation. After detonating the fireworks at 2:00 in the morning, he and a few others that were watching on the west side of the dormitory claim they saw some of the women running out of the building wearing less than their sleepwear, but that too had been unconfirmed. When it was discovered that it had been Emkovic who had rigged the event, he was suspended for a week. When he came back to the frat house after his suspension, he was heralded as a war hero and received the highest award any frat brother could attain while serving in the line of duty—the "Valiant Stogie," an expensive cigar which he has yet to smoke.

We continue to share in the history of the frat, memorializing past greats such as Emery Langston—an Eagle Scout who had gone on to graduate school at Yale and was now up for election into the Rhode Island House of Representatives. Also discussed are Theodore J. Loftiness, a member of the distinguished Loftiness Brothers Investment Firm, and Willie Lombard, who had invented one of the sleep-omatics with the adjustable sleep number. As more notables are mentioned, we all toast their accomplishments with, of course, more beer. After what seems like hours, Jerome calls from downstairs that dinner is ready. There is again a mass exodus to the café below, and as the boys are seated on the benches and stools and worn out chairs, there is an undercurrent of joking going on as to whether the chairs will support them.

They do.

Once we are all seated, Jerome comes out and serves us a feast: gumbo shrimp and the Popeye's biscuit twin and dirty rice and other Cajun delicacies, some of which are a surprise even to me. When the boys finish eating, they cheer for Jerome, and he comes out smiling. But when he tries selling them his Cajun sauces and stinky bait, I cut him off.

It is then that our President, Jeff Gordon, stands up. He is clearly drunk and offers a toast to the frat, and we all cheer him. He then calls for the sacred candelabra and matches. When he finally lights the candelabra on the seventh match, we all stand up and began singing "Home on the Range," which Jeff leads with great gusto, like a choir director. Finished, we sit down, and he begins with an alumni and frat business briefing, discussing up-and-coming events and the importance of supporting next year's frat, along with the bank account and other necessary but boring stuff. He staggers through it just fine, and we applaud him when he finishes.

He then raises his glass of beer and thanks me for hosting the event. There was more applause. I stand up and thank them for coming to Bullpen and ask if they had trouble finding it.

They did.

Then, like a comedian, Jeff starts in on Bullpen and asks if anyone would be able to find their way back home. The frat boys laugh. He then begins to mock the smiling moose and Slater's blue baking ribbons and the crayon drawings on the wall, asking if they had been done by seniors at some senior center. The irony is that a few of them had been. Then he rips into the dented malt maker and the various trophies, like Don Rickles. And the boys continue to laugh, raising their beer mugs with each new attack. He is on a roll, cutting down everything in sight and slurring his speech to add emphasis to his sarcastic tone. When he points out Jerome's stinky bait sign, he begins to giggle, and the anticipation of what he is going to say has the drunken frat boys in a stupor. He can say at this point anything and they will laugh—it's not what he says, but how he says it. And when he calls the stinky bait a bargain for only $19.95, he drops his jaw, as if mimicking a frantic shopper and calls it a real day-after-Thanksgiving door buster.

As the grown men burst out laughing, Jeff realizes he is on a roll and pushes his momentum, calling for the frat to camp out at the café on that black Friday, making sure we could beat the rush and get our stinky bait on sale before anyone else did. Then he begins to lisp like a little kid who can't pronounce the letter *s*. It is no longer stinky bait, but "thinky bait." His slurred, drunken stupor adds to his comical presentation.

"Thinky bait," he says again and again, each time working the mispronounced word into a more exaggerated pitch, until he has everyone chanting it with the same lisp. "THINKY BAIT, THINKY BAIT," we all cry, caught up in a comic frenzy. He then raises his hands, motioning for everyone to be quiet. And then in a loud whisper he states, "That's eathy for you to thay."

Cheers ring out, and then Jeff starts in on the trophies, mocking each one with his own fabricated version. When he gets to Jerome's tennis ball trophy, he coddles it like a fine piece of artwork and then kisses it.

"The Stanley Cup of trophies," he cries out, asking if any of the boys have ever seen such fine craftsmanship. He then asks me about the award, and I tell him. His face then goes ballistic with comic contortions. As the room erupts into more laughter, I suddenly feel defensive. He then calls for Jerome, but Jerome, fully capable of hearing every word from the kitchen, won't answer.

"Come on out, Jerome," Jeff yells. "Let's hear just one little swear word for old time's sake, huh?"

It is then I suddenly feel protective of Jerome and all the other Bullpen awards as the room continues to chant, "JEROME."

When Jerome finally comes out, the room cheers, anticipating a swear word or flurry of expletives, but there are none. He simply stands there without expression, looking out into the frenzied crowd. When our eyes meet, he looks at me, not with anger or contempt, but with sorrow, as if wounded—and I am abruptly cut to the heart, as if I have betrayed him and the rest of the town.

It is at that moment I realize how much I have changed and how I now stand in direct polarity to the misguided perception that is running rampant all around me. I don't know why, but all I can remember is Millie reading me the riot act only weeks before right out in the middle of Main Street. We had discussed this very topic—and suddenly I hear her very same words coming out of my mouth, as much a surprise to me as anyone else.

"You don't know what this man went through to get it," I begin, looking out among my colleagues.

The room suddenly becomes quiet when they sense I am no longer laughing with them. I go up to Jeff and take the trophy out of his hand and turn to Jerome, who is simply staring at me.

"I'm proud of my friend and what he had to do to stop swearing. If you all knew what kind of background he has come from and what kind of hell he went through after Hurricane Katrina, you would be proud of him too. I salute you, Jerome," I say at last. "I salute you."

And I do.

There is a brief and awkward silence that has come over the room. But suddenly it is broken by a strong voice coming from the back

"Well said," shouts Frank Simmons. And soon there is a second to the motion and then a third.

As I place the trophy back on the shelf, there comes a motion to adjourn to the smoking room upstairs to continue our festivities. The motion carries and we trickle up to the apartment to pontificate and tell more stories and smoke more cigars and drink more beer and shoot more pool.

Towards the end of the night, I have a chance to talk with Frank Simmons. I always liked Frank. He was an upper classman but never acted like one. When I was a sophomore, he was a senior, and I remembered the times when we would simply sit and talk about stuff into the wee hours of the morning. He was like an older brother.

He asks me if I have any coffee and tells me that he needs some caffeine for the road. We go downstairs, and I make him a batch of the good stuff, and we drink a cup together on the counter. He eyes the coffee cup hall of fame and then smiles.

"Kim and I are finally getting married," he says at last.

"Congratulations," I tell him. "When is the wedding?"

"Next summer," he says smiling. He then hesitates. "She's inviting Karen and her husband to the wedding . . . and you'll be invited as well."

My heart is suddenly walking in "Fields of Gold."

"I hope you will come," he says.

I hesitate.

"I will," I finally tell him.

"As you probably know, Kim was a bridesmaid at Karen's wedding."

"I figured that," I tell him. "They were good friends."

"Apparently, it was quite the wedding," he says. "Karen flew the whole wedding party to Italy, and they spent a week touring the countryside together."

"Wow," I find myself saying.

"Kim took a bunch of pictures, and some of them are on Facebook," he continues.

I nod, and he looks about as if there is something else on his mind.

"It's funny, Charlie, but Kim came back from the wedding and was all impressed by *everything*. It was all perfect."

"It sounds that way," I tell him.

"But looking back, she told me that it was too perfect."

"I don't understand," I tell him.

"It was a fairy-tale wedding, Charlie, and knowing how close you two were . . . well . . ."

"Well, what?" I ask him.

"Well, maybe it's just me, but I think Karen is living in a dream world. Have you seen her parents' home on the lake?"

"Yes."

"Have you ever seen her dollhouse?"

"Yeah, it's huge." I reply.

"Well, that's just it. It's huge. People in third world countries could live in that thing. And do you know what it's filled with?"

"Barbie and Ken dolls," I tell him.

"Yeah," he replies. Frank grimaces and then continues.

"Kim said that the reception hall was decorated just like her dollhouse. And on the wedding cake were a Barbie and a Ken doll. I don't mean to read into something that's not there," he continues, "but I could never see Karen as a lawyer. She always struck me as the kind of person who was on the lookout for some other kind of life."

"I guess she found it in Italy," I say.

"Maybe, Charlie," Frank continues, "but Kim said that Karen was different in Italy. She was just different—not like herself. I can see the wedding, maybe with all of the excitement, but the whole week she was not like her usual self. Even now, Kim has a hard time communicating with her. I think Barbie had finally met Ken, the man who would bring her the happiness she always wanted as a child. Call it what you want, Charlie, but I think she's living in a fairy-tale world—and sooner or later that fairy tale will come to an end."

I stare at the stains on the coffee cups along the wall, lost in thought.

"I hope it isn't so, Charlie," he says at last. "But I think sometimes people can want something so badly in life that they become blinded from seeing what is real."

My mind is suddenly racing in a thousand different directions. Was it true? And if so, why couldn't I have seen the illusion? Maybe, like Karen, I had been living in a dream world of my own.

Frank and I continue talking into the wee hours of the night as we had done in college. When he and the last of the frat boys leave, I stand outside and watch their taillights fade into the tiniest notion of a memory. When I look across the street, I see Jerome sitting in his rocking chair out on his balcony.

When he sees that I see him, he stops rocking, rises to his feet—and salutes me. Not knowing quite what to do, I salute him back.

August 23 . . . Sunday School Prayer Balloons

This morning Mrs. Sherburne sent me a helper to help with my class. It was a twelve-year-old girl named Maria who said she wanted to help teach Sunday school. Apparently, Mrs. Sherburne thought that it might be in my best interest to have a helper, and I am wondering why. Maria, however, is a cute little girl with a lot of energy and curly hair to match, but what is most important is that she loves the kids and loves to help, always asking me what she can do next. Since Mrs. Sherburne had given me some vague parameters within which to follow my boring—emphasis on boring—Sunday School curriculum, I thought I would take advantage of it and apply some of my own creativity to the mix. The lesson today was about Daniel and the lion's den, how he had prayed to God and how God had answered his prayer and delivered him.

Good enough lesson I guess. So I took the liberty of taking a few of the helium balloons that had been left over from Bullpen Days (with our official insignia I might add), attaching a prayer request from members of our notorious class, and sending them up to God and letting the chips fall where they may. Cool, huh? I thought so. So Maria and I began our project by helping the kids write down their prayer requests on a three-by-five note cards and then stapling the card to a string that was attached to the balloon and then letting them go into the upper stratosphere at the end of class to demonstrate how our prayers go up to God.

It is interesting what a first and second graders think is important to God. Edgar Willis asked if he could give back his younger sister and get a puppy instead. That seemed like a reasonable exchange, I told him, but wouldn't he miss his little sister?

"No," he replied.

"Okay, well, let's see if there is something else that we can pray to God about. Do you have anything else you want to pray about?" I asked him.

"When my brother leaves for college, I want to get his room." he said.

"Sounds good," I told him. "Let's write that down."

"Next," I said.

Little Abby stepped up to the plate, and I asked her what kind of prayer request she wanted to bring to God. She told me that she wanted a pony and a stable to go with it—and a big swimming pool.

"Okay," I found myself saying, "but what if we prayed for someone? Do you have anyone that you want to pray for?"

"My grandpa is not feeling well," she said.

"How about if we pray for him instead?" I suggested.

She agreed, and we put it on the card and stapled it to the balloon string. I was feeling a little like Santa's helper as the requests kept coming in. Abby asked me if God had a beard like Santa, and I told her I wasn't sure. I guess she is still fixated on beards.

When the kids had all finished writing their prayers on the three-by-five cards, you could cut the excitement in the room with a knife. Maria then handed me her cards and balloons, and I asked the kids if they were ready to launch them. Ivan was the first to shout, "Yes!" As we were about ready to mass exit out the door, I gave them specific instructions to be quiet as we went down the hall, but they were too excited. Just before we were about ready to leave, Maria asked me if I had a return phone number or anything on the cards in case someone found them.

I had never thought of that. I just had the ethereal notion that these helium balloons would ascend into the never-ending abyss of space and never come back. The thought that they might actually come down and that someone might actually find them, actually read them, and actually respond to them had never actually occurred to me. It was—after all—simply an object lesson for today's session on prayer and nothing more.

"But someone might find them, and wouldn't you want them to know about who you are and where you are from?" she asked me.

"Ah . . . yeah . . . good point," I said, taking mental notes from my twelve-year-old assistant. "Good point."

So, she and I put the names of the kids and my phone number on each prayer card, just in case the object lesson might become something more than just an object lesson. We also put Bullpen, Minnesota, on the cards to let people know how far they had come if they found them.

"Smart thinking, Maria," I said.

She smiled, and off we went with our left-over helium "Bullpen-Day-Balloon" prayer cards—with my accompanying cell phone number on the back.

It was a perfect Sunday morning with a few overhanging clouds. The helium balloons with the official Bullpen Days insignia were just moments away from launch time. Like Rocket Man, we began the count down, and each child held his or her own balloon tightly. When we reached zero, the children let them go, and off the balloons went, sailing higher and higher into the wild blue yonder while the kids cheered. We must have watched them for a good ten minutes until the last of them were but a few specks in space. Then the kids all ran back into the church—all but Ivan, who just stood there staring into the clouds, still holding his balloon.

"Aren't you going to launch your balloon, Ivan?" I asked him.

"I want to make sure that God gets my prayer," he said.

"I'm sure he will," I told him. "He's a big God. What do you say we let go of our balloon and go back inside, huh?"

But he simply stood there, clutching the string of his balloon with a tight fist and staring hard up at the sky. Just as I was getting impatient trying to think of something clever to get him inside, he began pointing straight up as if he had finally found what he had been looking for.

"I see his hand!" he said excitedly. "I see God's hand up there!"

I looked up, and, sure enough, I saw what appeared to be a *hand-shaped cloud* reaching across the sky.

"Yeah," I said. "Let it go, Ivan."

And he did.

His balloon shot up into the white cumulus fingers with its string tail wagging back and forth like an excited little puppy, carrying Ivan's three-by-five prayer card. When it finally disappeared from sight—and when Ivan was finally content that his request had been received by God—he reached out and took my hand, and together we walked back into the church.

August 30 . . . Brunch at the Café

September will soon upon us, and summer will be officially over on Monday—Labor Day. I am tempted to make my annual pilgrimage to the Minnesota State Fair this weekend, but thoughts on cleaning up the café seem to be more prevalent at this point—and knowing I probably won't be attending the fair, I am already missing the corn dogs and anything that else that could be deep fried on a stick, including a deep-fried Snickers candy bar. I don't know how they do it, and neither do I care. All I know is that it rates right up there with a pork chop on a stick.

I invite Miss Maddie, Millie and Maynard, Jared, Jerome, and Homer over for Sunday hamburgers on the grill. Miss Maddie brings two blueberry pies, and Millie brings crescent rolls. We eat in the café since the upstairs is still airing out from all the cigar smoke from Frat Night over a week ago.

It is a leisurely Sunday dinner, and after we finish eating, Millie suggests we all take a walk around town, and we do—all seven of us, walking en mass around Bullpen, looking like the Italian family that was chaperoning Al Pacino and his Sicilian fiancé in the movie *The Godfather*. Maynard suggests a Sunday drive in the country and thinks he can squeeze everyone in his new Cadillac, but Jerome is the first to petition against the idea, having nearly lost his appetite and his life on our previous outing with Mr. Magoo.

Millie taps Maynard's shoulder with a gentle word of encouragement and tells him that perhaps another time would be better. He nods, as if he too thinks it best to wait, and then with his confidence restored, he reaches over and takes her hand as they walk together down the street in the warm late-summer sun. Homer and Miss Maddie seem to be lost in their own world as they converse in gentle overtones, while Jared remains lost in his music. I ponder the effects of music on the brain twenty-four hours, seven days a week, and wonder if it is like an addiction, like sugar was for Conrad "Easy on the Sugar" Johnson. I ask Jerome if he was ever addicted to anything, and he nods and tells me that swearing was like that for him. It feels good at first, and then it just kind of takes over and doesn't pay rent.

He calls an addiction "an uninvited guest that has stayed beyond its welcome." He then tells me that he and his former wife had addictions—alcohol for her, tobacco for him.

"Is that what destroyed your marriage?" I ask him.

He nods. "Addiction is like dealing with a whole other person besides the one you know," he says. "And eventually, that other person will turn on you."

"Do you miss her?" I ask him.

"Yeah," he replies. "I miss the sober Mrs. Boatman. She was a beauty."

It is the first time I have heard him talk about his wife, and I try to ask him more questions, but he is tightlipped, like a veteran who refuses to talk about the war. I can only imagine what he is thinking, but knowing that it is not for me to pry into his personal marriage, I don't bring it up again, and we walk through town without another word between us.

The entourage soon comes full circle, having seen a few sugar maples that have started to turn color in what looks like an early fall. Jerome and I are the last to step back into the café, and just before we do, he stops and turns to me as if he has been pondering a certain matter for a long time.

"Wait for a good woman," he finally says. "One that's gonna be there for you and your kids through thick and thin."

September 1 . . . First Day of School

It's a misty, rainy night up here on the hill, and I am the only one in sight. School started today here in Bullpen, along with every other public school in the state. It seemed funny to see the yellow school bus roll into town and pick up my Sunday school class along with all the other kids. As the bus drove away, Edgar, Abby, and Ivan waved to me out the back window. And as I waved back, it was as if I was saying good-bye to my own kids. I stood there in the middle of Main Street and watched them roll out of sight. I have many fond memories of my own school days when Gerty would drop Karl and me off at the corner and wait with us until the bus arrived. Like my Sunday School kids, I too waved from the back window, only I was waving at Gerty—and she, of course, was waving back at me.

It's funny what you remember as a kid, but one thing I will never forget was that Michael Davies always brought his Spiderman lunch box with him on the bus. His mother, his own flesh and blood, had always made him liverwurst sandwiches with pickles. What mother in her right mind would ever make her child eat liverwurst sandwiches? I could see one day a week or two, but five? Count 'em—five days—Monday through Friday—liverwurst and dill pickle sandwiches—two of them, side by side, next to his Hostess cupcake. We all thought she made those sandwiches because liverwurst had some kind of medicinal purpose. Tim Belcher told us that, if Michael Davies didn't eat it, he would die—and we believed him because Michael was a thin, fragile-looking boy who used to always wheeze and sneeze and cough and swallow phlegm. He was the kind of kid that always had a hanky over his face—and we're not just talking about that little Minnesota Twins Homer Hanky either. It was the big one—the fourteen-by-eighteen-inch hanky with the monogrammed initials of Michael Davies the Third—MD3. He carried that thing with him like Linus carried his blanket; and it was big enough to be his blanket when you spread the thing end to end. No, you didn't want to mess with Michael Davies' Spiderman lunchbox because, if you did—if he didn't get his daily

240

supply of liver—he would croak right there in the cafeteria, and how would you explain that to Miss Bates?

But enough about liverwurst.

Far Quart suddenly writes in to tell me that he was the one who had ordered Jerome's Stinky Bait.

So, it *was* Far Quart who had ordered the bait a number of weeks ago. He says he prefers to remain anonymous, for obvious reasons, and will contact me again in October after he has tried the bait in a few more tournaments. He tells me there may be some dollars involved if the bait is really that good. I have decided to wait to tell Jerome until the bait has proven itself—no sense in counting your chickens before they hatch, or your fish before they bite. But the notion that you could actually make money off of Stinky Bait amazes me. Only in America…only in America…

Queen Crab writes in after a long-forgotten spell and tells me she loves liverwurst and can't get enough of it in Alaska. It rates right up there with salmon pate.

I wouldn't go that far, I tell her . . . lutefisk maybe, but not salmon pate.

Then Sweet Tea from North Carolina asks Queen Crab if she has a good recipe for liver pate, and suddenly the game is on. I introduce the two of them and let them talk liver to their hearts content. Then others chime in with their own special liver recipes and "fond" memories of family reunions with liverwurst sandwiches with pickles, liver and onions, beef liver stew, chicken liver mousse, and . . .

Who would have thought liverwurst was such a hot item, anyway? And all these years I just thought of it as medicine—the kind that could keep Michael Davies alive for just one more day.

September 2 . . . Jared's Guess

It had been raining and misting and cloudy since Monday. Rain makes everyone miserable and grumpy after a while, and I was no exception. Not seeing the numbers come in, and seeing the till drop in dollars, is always a little alarming for an owner. This was among the worst weeks on record, with people staying away from the café in droves. I had thought it might be the residue from the stinky bait in combination with the cigar smell from Frat Night, but I when I asked others, they couldn't smell it.

George went to the VA Hospital up in Minneapolis this week to look into some stomach problems he has been having since Sunday. I hope it wasn't anything he ate at the café.

The café is not the same without George. The Boys need a ringleader—a catalyst to instigate all the rumors in town. Even Slater was getting a little lost without him. The Boys have continued to come each day, but they cannot exact a punch or demand an audience like George. To be honest, I miss him too, not just because he is a good and regular patron, but because there is something endearing about George, in spite of his rough demeanor.

Since the café was empty, I decided to let Jared go early, and he nodded. Jerome had already left earlier to take care of some personal business. When Jared was finished sweeping, I asked him if he had any plans for this fall now that he had graduated from high school.

"Is there anything you like to do?" I asked him.

"Auto mechanics, I guess," he told me.

"Well, why don't you go to school?" I asked him.

He hemmed and hawed and never really answered.

"Do you like café work?" I asked him.

"Not really," he said. "Washing dishes is okay, I guess, but—yeah, it's okay, I guess," he said, as if trying to catch himself about telling his boss what he really felt about his job.

"When do classes start?" I asked him.

"Sometime this fall, I guess," he stated.

"So, if you did go to school, where would you go?" I asked.

"The vo-tech school, I guess," he replied.

"That's where you would like to go?"

"I guess."

"Is it just a guess, or do you really want to go there?" I asked him.

"I guess I would like to go," he replied.

"How much does it cost?" I asked him.

"Over a thousand dollars."

"Do you have the money?" I asked him.

"No."

"So, since you don't have the money, I guess you can't go—is that it?" I questioned.

"I guess not," he replied.

"I guess there is a lot of guessing going on around here," I said jokingly.

He nodded sheepishly.

"If you had the money, would you go?"

"I guess."

It was at that moment I remembered that Lenny had given me $7,500 that my uncle had loaned them. And that was not the half of it, according to Lenny. I knew I had at least that in the bank account, and if he wanted, I could help him with the tuition.

"If you had the money, would you go?" I asked again.

"I guess," he said.

"Then let's do it," I said. "I'll help with the tuition."

"Why would you want to do that?" he asked me.

"I think you would make a great mechanic, and when you get real good," I continued, "you can take off my Toyota's dashboard and clean the heater."

"Is it that dirty?" he asked me.

"Very," I told him.

He had stuffed his hands into his pockets and was staring at the floor.

"Find out what this vo-tech school would cost," I continued, "and get back to me, and let's see if we can't get you into school this fall, huh?"

"I guess," he said.

He made a motion for the back door but stopped. He turned around and hesitated as if he was trying to say something—anything. But Jared wasn't much for words, and sensing his uneasiness, I decided to say something in his stead.

"It's not that I don't want to keep you as our rock-star dishwasher," I said, breaking the silence.

He nodded.

"It's just that I think that if that's what you want to do, then I guess that's what you should do. And I guess that if a guy can help out another guy, then I guess he should," I said jokingly, using all the *guesses* I could.

But it was as if he had simply not heard the humor between the lines. I don't think I had ever heard Jared joke around, play a trick, or make a sarcastic comment to or about anyone. Like words, Jared took life at face value, nothing more and nothing less—and I guess that was okay.

"Thanks, Charlie," he said at last.

He then looked at me and started to say something else but stopped, as if he was trying to express something more than his own words could convey. Finally, he just nodded, shoved his hands into his pockets, and walked out the door.

I guess I will never really know what else he was going to say to me that afternoon. I thought about it afterwards, but it was—after all—just a guess. Later that day, as I was thinking about Jared, I began to realize that we humans are a continuous work in progress—full of past histories that cloud our present and future perspectives of life—sometimes for the best and sometimes for the worst. But at the end of the day, when all is said and done, it is simply amazing that we communicate as much as we do—even when we are at a loss for words.

September 4 . . . George

It is a rainy night here in Bullpen, and my heart is heavy. George has been diagnosed with colon cancer and will go in for surgery on Wednesday. News reached the Bullpen Café early this morning, and the Boys took it hard, along with Slater and Homer and everyone else in town. The doctors give him less than a month to live, and they are being generous with that. Of all the people that have taken the news hard, it is Jerome that has taken it the hardest. He has done nothing but rock in his rocking chair ever since he heard the news—and now, even as I write, he sits on his balcony in the rain, refusing to go inside. And adding insult to injury, the rain continues to pound all around us, like impatient feet running endlessly across a wooden floor.

I am told that cancer is a disease that is not recognized as an enemy of the body. It lives right beside the good cells and continues to grow and be fed like all the other healthy cells. If left unchallenged, it eventually takes the life of its host—and in doing so, it kills itself. Cancer is ironic that way—it kills itself by taking the life of the very thing that had once given it life. In one sense, it is like the communism George had fought so hard to prevent in Vietnam. The fight was unsuccessful: Vietnam—along with Cambodia—fell victim to "The Killing Fields," the cancer that not only took the heart but also the soul of the very thing that had once given it life.

Being a Vietnam Veteran, George is at the Veterans' Hospital in Minneapolis, and I plan on seeing him tomorrow after work. I have decided to stop by and see my parents as well, since the VA Hospital is not that much farther from home. The notion of being home is suddenly compelling.

Don't we all desire a place to call home? Is there not a universal notion of home in the heart and soul of all of us? Were we not all born into a family and grew up in a family (or the facsimile thereof) and have a deep-seated longing to return? If there is no place like home, then tell me what other place is there? Home . . . I'm going home . . . . It is Dorothy in the *Wizard of OZ* when she pleads with the wizard to take her back to Kansas. It is Currier and Ives' majestic sleigh ride over the river and through the woods. It is the Budweiser Clydesdales trotting down a carpeted path of freshly fallen snow en route to a place where family and friends have gathered to greet you at the door with open arms. It is the Norman Rockwell painting of a family gathered around the dining room table in anticipation of the Thanksgiving dinner where grandfather will carve the fatted calf or the roasted turkey. It is the romantic place that never grows old and never grows dim. It is the neighborhood that remains forever etched in time eternal, where friends are always there and always ready to play. Yes, I am going home tomorrow.

As I finish writing for the night, I see various blogs coming in from you late night bloggers, and suddenly I don't feel so alone.

Bazooka Bill writes in to tell me that home is nothing more than a state of mind, that growing up as a military brat, you have no place to call home when your father is transferred to a different base each year. The military is your home.

Good point.

"And how old are you?" I ask.

Thirty-eight is his reply, and he tells me that he has been in the military all his life and now has three kids of his own.

"Just like you?" I ask.

"Just like me," he writes back.

Then Candlestick writes in and tells me that the farm she grew up on will always be home to her.

"And how old are you, Candlestick?" I ask.

"Eighty-nine," she replies.

"When did you start blogging?" I ask her.

She says it was two months ago. And now that she has been properly introduced to blogging, she tells me that she is trying to make up for lost time.

"Cool," I tell her. "Any grandchildren?"

"Thirteen grandchildren and twenty-one great grandchildren," she replies, "and none of them live on a farm."

"Well, thanks for joining us tonight, Candlestick. May your flame continue to shine brightly."

She makes a smiley face and tells me she has plenty of wax left.

I agree.

Others comment about their own homes while others offer prayers for George. I am amazed at their compassion and tell them thanks. And as I do, I suddenly wonder about Mary—Mary from New York. Are you still out there, Mary? I haven't heard from you in weeks. If you are, what do you call home?

September 5 . . . A Visit to the VA Hospital

I asked Jerome if he wanted to go with me to the hospital after work to see George, but he told me he hated hospitals, so I decided to go by myself. But as I was getting ready to leave, I received a call from Miss Maddie, who told me that she needed to go with me.

As I pulled into her driveway, I could see a few of the apple trees beginning to change color. And as I looked out over the Zumbro Valley, I could see one lone tree in the distance bearing streaks of amber leaves. I could only imagine what the Valley would look like in a few weeks as the advent of autumn descends upon Bullpen.

Before the truck had come to a full stop, Miss Maddie came out carrying a knapsack and a picnic basket, dressed in her Sunday best. When I got out and offered to carry her things, she protested and then heaved them into the bed of the pickup. She then climbed into her passenger seat, looking disheveled and tired, as if she had been up all night. And she had, I was to find out later. She had been up all night praying for George, and she had a lot more praying to do. Then she told me to step on the gas, like I was some kind of get-away-driver. I had never heard the expression before and was about ready to kid her, but I sensed that she was not in a kidding mood.

As I stepped on the gas, we shot past Flint, who was sitting at the end of the driveway looking as if he was wondering what was going on.

"I'll be back, Flint—you watch the farm," Miss Maddie yelled out her window, and then she turned to me.

"We got business to do, Charlie," she said as we gathered speed down the county road. "This ain't no time to be lolly gaggin'."

I thought I was doing pretty well when I looked down at my speedometer, but apparently that wasn't good enough for Miss Maddie, as she hounded me again to "get the lead out." Then she began praying in what she called an unknown tongue, but to me it sounded more like gibberish. Her eyes were shut and focused as she dived into her own little prayer world while mumbling funny-sounding syllables. A look of concern then swept across her face, and she was all business now—whatever business that business might be.

247

And me? I was thinking that that was a fine how-do-you-do. I mean, she didn't even have the courtesy to say hello or thanks for picking her up. Hey, if it wasn't for me, she wouldn't be going to see George.

But no sooner had I thought those thoughts than she suddenly stopped praying, opened her eyes, thanked me for picking her up, and apologized for not thanking me earlier.

"No problem," I said, but my words had fallen on deaf ears since Miss Maddie had dived back into "prayer world," rocking back and forth, looking hard and intense, as if trying to focus on a tiny spot on the wall while she continued to ramble on in her unknown tongue.

"Thank you, Lord," she suddenly said in English. "Thank you Lord."

None of it made sense to me as we went zooming down the county road.

When we arrived at the hospital, I pulled up to the front door, and Miss Maddie scooted out of the truck. She told me that she would meet me in George's room and that I was to bring all of her stuff. She then walked through the main entrance, leaving me to park the truck and carry her belongings.

When I walked through the main door carrying the picnic basket and knapsack, I was met with an "oh-no-you-don't" stare from an older security guard. He asked me for the knapsack and picnic basket, emptying them both right in front of God and everyone. From the knapsack he pulled out three Bibles, a concordance, a Webster's 1828 dictionary, note pads, a flashlight, and a jar of cold cream.

He looked at me with a questioning glare when he examined the cold cream. I simply shrugged.

"It's Granny's," I told him. "You know—the lady that came through here just a few moments ago?"

He nodded as if he understood, then went about searching through the picnic basket, telling me that it is against security measures to allow food in the building.

Again I shrugged my shoulders and told him it was Granny's idea. I then asked him if he would like some fresh-baked cookies.

Tempted, he looked as if he was wrestling within himself as to what to do. He then asked me what kind of cookies, and I told him that they were chocolate chip and that her homemade chocolate chip cookies put Keebler to shame—and to be sure to take a few extra for break time in case he got hungry.

The temptation was simply more than he could bear as we both caught a whiff of *Granny's* fresh-baked cookies. After he had finally resolved his internal quandary, he told me he thought he could make an exception, knowing that *Granny* had made them—but he would have to keep the picnic basket locked up from the big, bad wolf.

I told him that Little Red Riding Hood would be proud of him, and he smiled for the first time since we had met. He then took the goods from the basket, and using his body as a human shield, placed them in the knapsack out of view of the security camera across the room, keeping a few cookies for himself. Then in full view of the camera, he took the empty picnic basket and placed it behind his chair.

I thanked him, and he nodded—and off I went in search of George's room.

When I found it, I saw that Miss Maddie and George's wife, Clair, were talking quietly near George's bed. As I stepped inside the room, I could smell the fresh flowers that were lined up along the windowsill. Suddenly Clair saw me, then reached out and gave me a hug and thanked me for coming.

"You're welcome," I found myself saying, looking at George, who was sound asleep on his bed. I then told her that I had never seen George so quiet before. She smiled. I then handed Miss Maddie her knapsack and told her that the picnic basket had been taken by security, but there was still food in the bag. I then came over and stood beside George, studying all the various intravenous tubes running in and out of his body and leading to a vacillating monitor that measured his heart rate and other vitals. But as I stood there watching the monitors, I suddenly wondered what they didn't or couldn't measure.

It's hard seeing a man fighting for his life. Dressed in his hospital gown, he suddenly looked so vulnerable—like a candle in the wind that could be extinguished with one sudden gust. As Clair and Miss Maddie continued talking, I took his hand while I watched his chest rise and fall with each breath. I suddenly wondered, if his chest stopped rising—if he suddenly stopped breathing—where would he be? In a "Clean, Well-Lit Place"? In eternal darkness? In eternal light? What was beyond his last breath? What was beyond this world?

"George," I whispered. "You have to come back to the café. It's been too quiet without you. The Boys are lost without their fearless leader . . . and Slater, well, Slater thinks he's now a poet in residence with his ode to the bastard toadflax."

I was hoping he would smile, but all he did was breathe.

"Keep breathing," I told him. "Just keep breathing."

It was then that Clair began crying and Miss Maddie reached out and held her in her arms. Then she began to sob as if she had finally been given permission to cry.

"It's okay, child," Miss Maddie said, holding her in her arms, "It's okay."

I don't know how long Miss Maddie held her, but it was long enough to calm her shaking body as her sobs began to recede back into an ocean of spent emotions, waiting for the next wave to hit the shores. Then it would start all over as her shoulders began to shake in spastic movements, calmed only by the steady hand of Miss Maddie, who continued to stroke the back of her hair.

"It's okay, child," she said over and over. "It's going to be okay."

When the last wave of sadness receded, his wife sat down next to George and rubbed his arm. Miss Maddie then took out her Bible and other materials and sat down in a chair beside George on the other side of the bed.

"George," Miss Maddie began. "I'm going to pray for you, and we are going to beseech heaven. Do you understand what I am saying?"

George continued to sleep.

"Good," she replied. "Now I want you to agree with me. I want you to agree with me that God's word has final authority here—not the doctor's word, not the hospital's word, not the nurse's word, not the cancer diagnosis—nothing—do you hear me?"

George continued to sleep.

"Good," she said again and then began thumbing through the pages of her Bible. She started quoting scripture after scripture, vacillating between all three Bibles that she had brought along.

Clair and I simply sat back and watched as she continued to quote God's Word, then pray, then quote more of God's Word. When the charge nurse came in and checked on George's vitals, Miss Maddie continued to pray—never missing a beat, much to the disapproval of the nurse.

"Doctors know a lot, but they don't know everything, George," she continued. "You and I are just going to continue to believe his promises. Do you hear me? . . . Good."

It was as if the hair on the back of the nurse's neck began to bristle. She was a battle-ax of a woman, and sensing that Miss Maddie was encroaching on her territory, she asked her to leave. But Miss Maddie—half her size—wouldn't budge. It was a stalemate between two stubborn wills, with each one vying for position, until George's wife told the charge nurse that it was okay—Miss Maddie was a dear friend. Eyeing Miss Maddie like a formidable foe, she finally nodded and told her that she would be back to wake up George in a few minutes to give him his medications. Clearly disgruntled, she left the room in a huff. Miss Maddie then knelt down beside the bed and continued praying.

I waited a good half hour, but the charge nurse never came back. Clair looked tired, and Miss Maddie told her to go to the visitors' lounge and lie down and get some sleep. If George ever came to, she would come and get her, Miss Maddie assured her. Reluctantly, she agreed and left the room. Miss Maddie then told me I could do the same if I wanted to.

"How long are we staying?" I asked.

"As long as it takes," she replied. "I'm not leaving until we get the victory."

"I was thinking about going home for a visit, as long as we were here. Do you mind if I come back a little later tonight?' I asked.

"No," she replied. "Visiting your family would be a good thing."

"I'll be back later, then," I told her.

She nodded and then began praying. As I left the room, I walked past the nurses' station where a few of them eyed me suspiciously as if I was an accomplice to one causing all the commotion in George's room. I smiled at them, and they politely smiled back. When I reached the main lobby, I nodded to the security guard, who also nodded back.

"Don't forget your picnic basket," he said, handing it to me.

"Thanks," I replied, and headed out the door.

As I got in the truck, the thought of going home suddenly struck me as an odd notion. How many months had it been since I was home? It seemed like eternity.

When I pulled onto Erin Avenue, I could see the familiar neighborhood, and suddenly there was a flood of memories. Tim Belcher and Jeff Petrus were two faces that immediately came to mind. Where were they now? I then passed Huggins' house and eyed the garage where Andy Huggins, Tim, Jeff, and I had hidden from the student-driving instructor. He had chased us after we cut into his mobile device that was used to communicate to his student drivers while they were driving around the parking lot of the nearby junior high school. Andy Huggins was an electronic wizard and had rigged up a Radio Shack device that could intercept the two-way communication system that operated between the instructor and the student driver's car. Since the driver's education class was held at the junior high each year, students were taking the course en masse, with multiple cars moving around the parking lot at the instruction of the teacher, whose radio frequency could communicate to all the student drivers in the parking lot. When Andy was able to patch his way into the student drivers' cars with the same clarity as their own audio system, he could interrupt the teacher's instructions with a few of his own. When he told car number three that he was driving like an old lady, the driver then sped up. Andy then did the same to cars number four and five, with both cars nearly colliding. The instructor was able to hear the whole conversation and was wondering what was happening. When he saw four little heads laughing on the other side of Valley View Road, he knew immediately what the problem was and gave chase. We all ran for our lives and hid in Huggins' garage, thinking we were safe, until he came in and heard us murmuring inside Huggins' old boat.

Andy was grounded for a week from electric gadgetry, but Tim, Jeff, and I got off relatively easy after the instructor, a football coach at the high school, recognized Jeff— whose brother had started on the football team.

As I passed Jeff's house, I could clearly see the hot-air balloon that we had made from plastic straws, birthday candles, some Scotch tape, and the largest dry cleaning bag we could find. As if it was yesterday, I could see it floating over St Patrick's church parking lot, stopping thirty feet off the ground, and attracting cars from Valley View Road. Hovering there in the parking lot, with its sixteen birthday candles keeping it aloft, it had born a striking resemblance to some sort of incantation or visitation from Mary herself.

As I rounded the corner, I came upon our home. It had a large backyard that butted up to the fourteenth hole of the adjacent country club golf course. Being a member of the country club, my father had his own golf cart parked in the garage and would often phone ahead—and if time and space permitted, he would hop in the cart and play a few rounds. The golf course was a great convenience that way, and it provided easy access to a cross-country ski course in the winter as well. When not playing himself, he would often sit on the patio and critique other golfers, mumbling to himself about how not to putt or chip onto the green.

Our home was a large home, along with all the others in the neighborhood. It was a stucco house with an English Tudor design that gave it an old European look and feel. The cobblestone driveway had a slow curve that accentuated the depth of the front yard. There were two oak trees that Karl and I had planted, with Gerty's help, when I was in kindergarten. Gerty had wanted pine trees, but my mother thought differently. The rest of the landscape was a mix of an old English butterfly garden that had surpassed the equinox of its blooming season—lilies and heather and marigolds were all in fast decline. As I drove up the driveway, I could see that the house was empty.

I had a key to the front door, but feeling like an uninvited guest, I didn't enter. I had considered calling earlier but thought it best to simply stop by unannounced. I got out of the truck and peered inside the lifeless, empty rooms that had always been home to me ever since I could remember, and suddenly I missed Gerty. Her real name was Gertrude Reider, but Gertrude was too formal of a name for her.

She had died when I was in junior in high school, and her funeral was held at a German church in St. Paul that was attended by many of her old German friends. Gerty was an immigrant. She and her husband had lived in the German-speaking portion of northern Yugoslavia before the war. And since they lived close to the Austrian border, her husband had been drafted into Hitler's army through no fault of this own. After the war, Russia occupied their old homeland and allowed the safe return of all Yugoslavian soldiers that had been forced to serve under Hitler. There was peace during the Russian occupation, but when the Russians left, Tito and his communist's regime—who had fought against Hitler during the war—exacted revenge on the Yugoslavian solders that had been forced to fight with the Nazis. There was a terrible retribution, with frequent incidental murders in retaliation among those German-speaking Yugoslavian soldiers that had fought with Hitler, and Gerty's husband was no exception. One night they dragged him from his bed, stripped him naked, and beat him ruthlessly until he died. She would never forget it, nor would I ever forget her telling me the story. It's funny what you remember as a child. The image of her husband being beaten to death was horrifying to the imagination of a young boy. It was always hard for her to talk about her life in Yugoslavia, but every time she did, I was right there with her in my mind.

"Ve don't always know vat za future holds, but ve know who holds za future," she would often say after recalling her life in Europe. I never really knew what that meant as a kid, but I liked the sound of the sentence in her thick German accent. It had a seesaw rhythm to it, and I would often go about imitating the accent, much to her chagrin. At night she would pray with Karl and me before bedtime and tell us that Jesus loved us, whether we knew it or not.

As I stood outside looking into the dining room, I thought of the countless evening meals she had served: beef stroganoff with homemade noodles and butterkipful cookies. She had even attempted lutefisk one Christmas Eve but failed miserably, as if anyone could actually fail at making lutefisk. She then threw it in the garbage out in the garage, but I often wondered if she had done it on purpose in order to serve something else that night.

Perhaps.

She was an integral part of our family. She loved to play cards, cook and bake, laugh, and read to us as children, often setting Karl and me on her lap to read us stories from *Grimm's Fairy Tales* and other children's books.

"So vat is za moral of za story, Charlie?" she would ask me.

"I don't know," I would reply.

And she would explain it to me again, and yet again, as her thick German accent added still another fascinating dimension to her ability to tell stories. Her passion and enthusiasm for drama was unparalleled as she read each page with great expression and feeling. It was later in college that I attributed my desire to write stories to Gerty.

"I miss you, Gerty," I said out loud.

I missed the way she would remove her false teeth and show Karl and me her gums and the roof of her mouth as only little kids would want to see. I missed the way she would sip her coffee with a spoonful of sugar and then add the cream. I missed the way she would point at us with her crooked finger when she was upset. It was the same finger that she used to rub our foreheads at night when we had a fever.

I then glanced at my watch and noticed it was late, so I decided it was time to head back to the hospital.

When I arrived, Miss Maddie was waiting for me at the front entrance, smiling from ear to ear.

"He's going to be okay," she said.

"What are you talking about?" I asked.

"I got the victory," she said, holding the Bible up in the air. "I got the victory."

I wasn't sure what she meant by that, but who was I to argue—and besides, she was already three steps ahead of me on the way to the truck—and it was all I could do to get the lead out and keep up.

September 7 . . . Get Well Cards

It is a rainy Monday morning at the café, and the news that George has survived the night after a rough five-hour surgery is good news. Clair called to tell us that his heart had stopped three times on the operating table and the doctors can't figure out why he is still alive. "Critical but stable" is his present condition, and the report is a breath of fresh air in Bullpen as people shuffle in and out of the café to catch updates on his progress. In a way, it reminds me of the movie *Cinderella Man*, as listeners gathered around the radio to hear the play-by-play account of James Braddock in his fight with heavy-weight champion Max Baer during the Great Depression of the 1930s. Only this is not a fight for a boxing title or a prized purse, but a fight for life—and for now, George may be down, but he's not out. Even the pastor took time during his sermon to pray for George, along with the whole congregation, and Mrs. Sherburne had all of the Sunday school classes make him get-well cards.

Ivan had drawn a heart for his get-well card and, with the help of Maria, on it he told George that he would give him some of his own blood if he needed it. When I asked him about giving blood, Ivan told me he gives his younger brother blood all the time. It got me thinking about his home life, and when I asked Mrs. Sherburne about it afterwards, she told me that his younger brother needs a blood transfusion every three to four weeks and Ivan has the same, rare blood type as his brother. I never knew that—and I'm beginning to realize that there are a lot of things I don't know about Ivan—or the rest of the kids, for that matter.

At the end of class, we had seven cards, and four of them were addressed to Santa. I thought I had made myself clear about the assignment, but who knows what kids really hear. It makes me wonder if they hear anything I say, and if I have anything worth saying—a writer's worst nightmare. I had put my heart and soul into explaining their assignment, engaging them with stories about the importance of our get-well cards and what that would mean to George, especially stories about George and concepts of God and prayer. And just when I had their undivided attention with nodding heads and attentive eyes, just when I thought I was making a deep, spiritual connection with the heart and soul of each child, Abby blurted out that she had gotten new shoes. I guess it was no wonder that Santa Claus had somehow gotten thrown into the mix after that. But knowing George, I decided to send the Santa letters, anyway, thinking that if or when he does recover, they may just add some levity to the doldrums of hospital life. It was then I decided to write a letter of my own, and when I thought about his life hanging in the balance, I got choked up knowing there was a strong possibility that I might not ever see him again.

I hope you are smiling when you read this card, George. I tried as best I could to tell my Sunday School class that these were not letters to Santa—but somewhere along the line there was a disconnect between my objective and theirs. I guess I am not as good at giving orders as I thought. Maybe I need some of your military experience, or at least a contingency plan. I miss you George. We all miss you and pray that you keep on fighting and come back home. If you don't, who else will eat my day-old donuts for half price?

Charlie

September 8 . . . Miracles

It is a warm September night, and I am not alone up here on Thomforde Hill. There are at least three other cars parked along the side of the road this evening. The days are getting shorter as the sun has now begun to cast its shadow deeper and deeper into Bullpen earlier each night.

Jared enrolled last week at the vo-tech in Rochester and will be taking auto mechanics classes starting this Thursday. He was able to get in with a late registration and needed a car to get to Rochester and back, so I told him he could use my Toyota. He will continue working at the café on Saturdays, and in the meantime, I have hired Melissa Magnuson to take his place during the week. To be honest, I was surprised that he had taken the initiative to enroll once he knew he had the money to do so. I gave him a check for the entire term, and when he thanked me, he had struggled for words as he had done before.

"It's okay, Jared," I told him. "You have thanked me more than enough. Just make sure that you fix the stinky heater in the Toyota when you get good at all that mechanic stuff."

He nodded and smiled. When I told him that he could continue to wash dishes until Thursday, his smile suddenly disappeared. I guess he was hoping to take a few days off before starting classes. But when I told him he could find someone to take his place until then, his smile returned. Later that afternoon, however, he told me that he couldn't find anyone—and by this time the smile had all but disappeared beneath a long and drawn out face. When I told him that Jerome and I could do it for him until then, his smile miraculously returned.

I will miss Jared during the weekdays. I will miss his "little-mouse-in-the-corner-not-even-knowing-he-is-there" presence—if you can actually miss someone that you don't even know is there most of the time. I just hope now that Melissa and Millie can stay out of each other's hair.

Jerome is more of himself lately, as each day passes with more good news of

George's slow but steady recovery. The café is still news central, and the doctors at the VA have upped his chances of survival to fifteen percent, as opposed to one percent. Slater and the Boys are breathing more easily as well, knowing that George seems to be making progress. The doctors have warned, however, that we are not to get our hopes up. His apparent "recovery" could come before the crash, predicting his demise like a stock market analyst reporting on the Dow-Jones. I have come to the conclusion that the doctors really don't know what's going on when it comes to George. It is as though they are shooting in the dark as to what odds to give him, like a bookie on game day, discrediting the notion that maybe God can still do miracles. And horror of horrors, if God does do a miracle, then how could they ever expect to get credit for his recovery? But maybe that is why miracles are called miracles—because they fall outside the realm of human understanding or human reasoning or human credit.

How much do we really know about miracles? Who can explain why a baby at birth cannot live in air one moment and then not live without air the next? And how does a cell reproduce itself? How does a heart cell know how to be a heart cell and not a lung cell? And how did all these cells come together to form this complex human being with all these parts that have to work together, with each playing a distinctly separate, but equally important, role in order to sustain life? The complex DNA molecule alone has our own unique characteristic and identifies us from anyone else's DNA to the point that it is now used as evidence in court.

There are more questions than there are answers, which tells me that we know very little about what goes on in our own world—and the universe at large.

As I blog these thoughts, Big Kahuna from Texas writes to say that miracles are only a state of mind.

"How so?" I ask.

"It's all a matter of perception," he writes back. "It's all about how our mind chooses to interpret the never-ending stream of photons bombarding our optic nerves. We never actually see with our optic nerve. We see with our minds, which interpret the information that our optic nerves provide," he states.

"The mind's sole job is to make sense of the world around us, and it has limited tools with which to do so," he continues. "As an example, it must differentiate one photon from another—and with an almost infinite number of photons assaulting our optic nerves each nanosecond, the mind goes into overload and can only assimilate a small fraction of the photons. It is like having a billion pixels racing towards a monitor that can only handle a hundred—so in the process, it filters out vast quantities of other photons by taking only those which it can handle and then categorizing and grouping them into cognitive associations and patterns. It is these patterns and associations that are left for interpretation by our mind. What we don't see is the infinite number of photons that never get past our optic nerve, leaving us with only a fraction of the total picture. The incomplete data of what we perceive is, in reality, only a fraction of the truth."

"You lost me there, Big Kahuna," I write back. "So what does that have to do with miracles?" I ask.

"They are happening all the time," he responds, "but our mind doesn't perceive them as such because it only has a limited perspective of reality. In other words, when something out of the ordinary happens—something that is really happening all the time, but we don't perceive it as such—we call it a miracle. But it is no such thing. It is only a common, everyday occurrence that is suddenly brought to our attention."

"So help me understand," I reply. "So, what you are saying is that there is an unseen realm that is creating 'miracles' around us all the time that we cannot perceive? Is that correct?"

"Precisely," he replies.

"So there is no external force that intervenes on our behalf to change the course of reality as we know it?' I ask.

"Nothing of the sort," he replies.

"So how do we know if these miracles—or newly discovered perceptions, as you describe them—are good or bad?" I ask.

"There is no such thing as good or bad. There only is," he states.

"So if somebody beats you up, is that good or bad?" I ask.

"It is neither good or bad nor right or wrong. Life only exists as it is—nothing more, nothing less," he replies.

"So, if there is no right or wrong, then are there any absolute truths?" I ask him.

"None," he replies. "It's all relative."

"But isn't the notion that there are no absolute truths an absolute truth in and of itself?" I ask him.

There is no reply.

"Big Kahuna? . . . You out there? . . . Did I lose you?"

Houston, do you copy that?

Somewhere out there is a man who doesn't believe in the absolute truths but only in a vague, ethereal notion that life simply *is*—and because life simply *is*, it doesn't really matter what we do or what we live for, because there is no right or wrong—and consequently, there are no consequences for our actions or decisions. In the end, we are but dust, nothing more and nothing less, with the confines of morality suspiciously absent—and subsequently, justice. And that is the inherent error found in relativism. There is no justice because there are no absolutes of right or wrong. There only "is," and whatever meaning "is" has is only relative to what we define "is" to be.

But this philosophy buries its head in the sand like an ostrich, ignoring the reality around it in the hope that, by its doing so, the reality will conform to its way of thinking or perspective. The problem is that an ostrich never has, nor ever will, change the reality of the world around it by burying its head in the sand. Life has rights and wrongs and the consequences thereof. If it didn't, we would have anarchy, with every man doing what was "right" in his own eyes—arbitrarily deciding what the world should be apart from the social and physical and moral truths that surround us.

If the French philosopher Camus was right in his book *The Stranger* . . . if Camus' presupposition about life was that it was meaningless and that it was free from any constraints of right or wrong and moral absolutes, then why have a justice system at all? Why have laws? If life simply is, then why don't we all just do as we please—without regret and without consequences? And if we did, what kind of society would we have?

These were exactly the kinds of conversations we had had at night at the frat house, as we pontificated great thoughts into the wee hours of the night while carefully avoiding any notion of absolute truths or moral objectivity with our own ad-hoc philosophies—and beer. Because, if we had acknowledged any absolute truths, then we would have to be accountable to them and consequently to the one who created them—and that would put a cramp in our ethereal notion of freedom.

No, the reason society functions as well as it does is because there has to be a moral guidepost within mankind that knows right from wrong—internal rules and boundaries by which to live. We knew, growing up, that when we lied, it was wrong, and we knew when we took something that did not belong to us, that too was wrong. We all knew when we had done wrong—no matter how many times we or society had tried to convince us otherwise—because inside us was a conscience and a written moral absolute based on the *Golden Rule*: "Do unto others as we would have them do unto us." That premise was eternal and had lived in the heart and soul of every human being since the beginning of time. It was the same premise that was recognized by our own Founding Fathers who created the basis of our government—"*We hold these truths to be self-evident . . .*"

Suddenly, the question was no longer did "self-evident" truths exist, but how did they get here? Who put them here? Was there a creator? Were we an accident or simply a derivative of a sophisticated plasma that evolved from some big-bang theory, as most of my college professors surmised?

No, I concluded, there had to be a creator, a lawgiver who had written intrinsic, self-evident laws within our hearts that every attorney understood. Life was not an existential, meaningless existence as Camus and others had believed. There were moral absolutes that only a creator could put inside each and every man's heart—and that alone was nothing less than a miracle.

September 13 . . . The Christmas Star

This morning in church, we prayed again for George, and the news is that he will be coming back home next week. There was a round of applause as the pastor stood up before the congregation and told us so. Jerome was smiling from ear to ear, then stood up clapping—and soon the rest of the congregation followed and stood to their feet as well.

Jerome then cried out, "Let's sing us a hymn, Pastor! Let's sing all three verses of 'Amazing Grace.'" And the congregation laughed.

In the end, we sang all four verses, and nobody sang them louder, or more off key, than Jerome. I asked him after church how it was that a man who loved to sing as much as he did could sing so off key.

"Now that's a walkin' paradox for a Black man, ain't it?" he said.

I was about to agree, but I caught myself.

"No," I said. "Now look who's prejudiced. Just because a man is Black doesn't mean he can sing, and just because a man's white doesn't mean he can't dance."

"Oh, now you is jumpin' into water way over your head, and you don't even know how to swim," he said. "You better just drop it right here and now, Charlie, 'cause every Black man knows how to dance, and that's just the gospel truth of the matter. All white men do is wiggle them hips like Elvis, but a Black man—now he was born dancin' in his mama's womb."

"Is that right?" I asked him sarcastically.

"Yep, that's right," he replied, as if the case was closed.

He had that "don't-mess-with-me" look about him, and I decided to obey the look and let him carry that theory to the grave if need be. It was, after all, Sunday—a day, according to Jerome, that the good Lord had set aside as a day of rest.

In the meantime, however, the whole congregation had been invited to Miss Maddie's for a fall picnic and an opportunity to pick and eat apples.

It was a perfect Sunday afternoon as we drove out to Miss Maddie's, along the gravel road to her farm. The haze of the late summer sun was beating down on the adjacent cornfields that were ripe for harvest, while honeybees were busy buzzing about gathering the nectar for the long, inevitable winter.

"It's a funny thing about bees," Miss Maddie told Jerome and me as we came within sight of her farm. "The scouting bees go out miles from the nest, and when they come back, they stand before their own congregation and do a little dance. [Jerome told us that those were the *black* bees, and Miss Maddie laughed.] That dance is what tells the other bees where to find nectar. Bees are amazing—pollinating the cornfields, honeysuckle fields, apple blossoms, and cherry blossoms each spring, entirely unaware of the critical role they play in the pollination of the eco-cycle. On hot days, they will use their wings as fans to cool the larvae beds. In winter, they huddle together in a massive ball, continually rotating from the outside in, then from the inside out, so they all stay warm. When threatened, they will fight to the death to protect their colony and their queen. They are a perfect study in community," Miss Maddie concluded. Jerome and I agreed.

As we pulled into the driveway, Flint came out to meet us. I then parked the truck, and Jerome and I took out a few of the tables that we had borrowed from the church for the picnic, setting them up on the porch overlooking the apple orchard. Other cars pulled up behind us, and soon there was a mass exodus to the front porch where the ladies began to place all of the various dishes, desserts, and salads on the tables. But when Slater arrived with his Betty Crocker sour cream raspberry bran muffins, all of the older ladies' heads began to turn as he placed them at the head of the table—under their careful scrutiny. There was a sudden awkwardness about the moment, but everyone pretended to be polite. And everyone was until Slater started grinning from ear to ear as if bubbling with pride over his latest batch of Betty Crocker sour cream raspberry bran muffins. Suddenly, the sting of the blue ribbons that he had stolen out from under the bodacious bevy of beautiful bakers from Bullpen had suddenly been rekindled after the jealous, smoldering embers had all but died down only a few weeks ago.

"What's that you got there, Slater?" asked one of the ladies, forcing a smile,

"Oh, nothing but a few sour cream raspberry bran muffins," he replied.

You could suddenly cut the tension with a knife as a few of the ladies began to migrate toward his muffins, eyeing them suspiciously.

"Yeah, I decided to try these with some sour cream," he continued, "even though the recipe called for milk."

It was as if the President himself had spoken. There was a sudden uncomfortable silence as they all leaned in to listen to what other secret ingredients he had used.

"Then I decided to use honey as opposed to sugar, so they stay moist," he continued.

"Is that so?" a few of the ladies replied, inching their way closer to the muffins.

"Oh, yeah," replied Slater, seemingly unaware of this surreptitious interrogation. "I used honey instead of sugar, just like I did when I won the blue rib—"

"Slater," I shouted, knowing I had to say something before he entered the city limits of Bragville. "Could I get your help with a few chairs?"

"Why, Charlie," he said enthusiastically. "I was just telling the ladies here about my award winning—"

"Right over here, Slater!" I yelled, shaking his hand while pulling him away from the table at the same time. "I need some help moving chairs right over here."

It's funny, but I don't believe Slater ever knew what hit him—or what was going to hit him, for that matter. Blinded by his own preoccupation and reputation for award winning recipes, he was destined for a land mine and didn't even know it. I was suddenly reminded of a time when someone had gone into my car and turned off my car lights after I had forgotten to turn them off. Thinking that someone was breaking into my car, I asked him what he was doing. "Turning off your car lights," came the reply. Someone had saved me from a drained battery, and I would never have known it apart from the fact that I had asked. How many other times had I been spared the trouble of a dead battery or an unforeseen land mine? . . . Enough to be grateful.

Slater may never know why he was suddenly asked to help set up chairs, but I did—and if a guy can help another guy stay out of Bragville in the midst of an ill-tempered audience of older women, then he ought to. After all, sometimes a guy just needs a helping hand—literally.

After lunch our bluegrass band played out on the porch as the late afternoon sun began to settle across the valley below. In the distance was the tall white steeple of the Zumbro Church which was nestled in and among the green, amber, and crimson-colored leaves of the distant valley. It was a pretty site, the kind you would see in a poster or a post card. As the bluegrass band played, I got a few nods from the other members, particularly during the "Tennessee Waltz." Gary said afterwards that it actually sounded like the "Tennessee Waltz"—the best compliment I have yet to receive.

When we finished, we all gathered at the orchard and began picking apples—Haralson, Honey Crisp, and Macintosh apples. Members of the church and their families picked and gathered as many apples as their baskets and pockets could hold. And when I looked over at Miss Maddie, I saw that she was smiling from ear to ear, wearing her wide-brim Audrey Hepburn hat.

When she saw me, she smiled and said two words: "Good fruit."

I too smiled. Then Abby came up to me with her own little basket and handed me a Honey Crisp apple, twice as big as her little hand.

"Here you are, Mr. Tuxedo," she said, as if pleased that she could offer me something of her own.

"Thanks," I replied.

It was then Jerome came over and asked if he could cut the apple in half. I agreed, and under Abby's watchful eye, he separated the top half from the bottom and pointed to the star inside.

"Ya know what this is, young lady?" he asked Abby.

"No," she replied.

"See them five seeds all spread out like a star?" he asked her.

"Yes," she replied.

"Why, this here ain't no ordinary star," he said, winking at her. "Why this here is the Christmas star. Now go ahead and eat it," he said, handing her half the apple and then handing me the other.

We both ate the halves together, and when I saw the juice dribble down the sides of her cheeks, I laughed—and she did the same with me. Then we both wiped the juice with the back of our hands. When we had finished, Jerome began to nod as if he had been waiting to tell us the rest of the story.

"Now you knows where to find the Christmas star," he said. "And it'll never steer ya wrong."

September 19 . . . A Soldier's Homecoming

It was a hero's welcome this morning with most of, if not the entire, town there to meet George when he arrived. Like Ulysses, he had retuned triumphant, as banners and signs welcomed him home while kids' hands waved at his car that slowly made its way down Main Street. Although George was under strict orders to get plenty of rest and to stay low, his wife had arranged a homecoming party with Millie and Melissa, who, along with every other lady in town, had made every imaginable cake possible. When the car finally stopped at the café, the mayor opened the passenger door and greeted George with a hug. Looking weak and fragile, George could only smile and wave to the rest of the town. Lenny and the Boys then took the wheelchair out of the trunk and helped him ease his bony body into the seat. Then they rolled him into the café as the crowd cheered. Once inside, the wily old veteran asked to be rolled over to the coffee cup hall of fame, and once there, he motioned for his cup on the wall. Slater reached up and gave it to him, and when he had secured the cup in his hands, the crowd began to clap.

There were tears in his eyes as he looked out over the sea of people crowded about him. He then raised his cup in the air and stammered, "It's about time I got a decent cup of coffee."

We all laughed, and suddenly George was at a loss for words, choked up with emotion. No one had ever seen him at a loss for words before, and soon everyone was encouraging him to continue, but all he did was raise his hand as if to let us know that he was going to be all right.

"This is a damned honorable welcome," he said at last. "Damned honorable . . . Thanks for all the flowers and cards and prayers."

The crowd nodded, and George continued, his voice straining under the weight of his weakened physical and emotional state: "I had the privilege to talk with a few Vietnam veterans while I was at the VA Hospital," he said, "and they could have only wished for a welcome like this. As some of you may know, the Vietnam War was not a popular war, and those of us who finally did come home were spit on for serving our own country."

A sudden hush fell upon us all—a shaming, uncomfortable hush, as George reached for a handkerchief in his front packet to wipe his eyes. "I can't begin to tell you," he stammered at last with quivering lips, "I can't begin to tell you how much this means to me."

He then gave a salute, and we applauded him.

After that, we had cake, and George was the first to finish his with the help of his wife. After she had wiped the crumbs from around his mouth, the Boys helped him drink his coffee. It was the good stuff. It was a fresh cup made from a special blend of Millar's wood-roasted coffee—a small way in which to honor a man who had deserved so much more.

September 25 . . . A Community Harvest

It is a cool night up on top of the hill, and I am alone in the truck as I recall the events that have happened the last few days in Bullpen. Felix Manion was farming north of town and got his hand caught in a combine two days ago. He would have bled to death if it wasn't for his wife, who had come to bring him lunch out in the field. Although Felix had gone into a state of shock, she managed to keep her cool, applying a tourniquet, using his own belt. She then phoned for help. The Mayo One helicopter then evacuated him to St Mary's Hospital in Rochester where he remains in critical but stable condition.

Melissa organized a food committee, and women have been bringing food in shifts out to their home in the country. Felix is a younger farmer, in his thirties, and has three kids: two little girls and an older son about eight years old. Since neither Felix nor his wife has any other family nearby, Millie and Maynard have been staying at their farm to care for the kids while his wife, Kim, stays at the hospital. Although they have no shortage of food for the next several days (if not weeks), people continue to bring more, wanting to help in any way they can.

What I found to be even more impressive, however, was that late this morning, Lenny and eight other farmers in and around the area took time from harvesting their own crops and drove their combines right down Main Street en route to Felix's soybean fields. Seeing all nine combines roll into Bullpen was like watching an old film clip of General Patton's tanks roll into liberated France toward the end of WWII. People were waving at the caravan from both sides of the street as the power of the huge earth-shaking machines rolled on by. When they reached Felix's soybean fields, all nine harvesters began to work in tandem, like a choreographed dance line, assembling themselves in a V-formation with Lenny's combine leading the pack. The other eight harvesters flanked him, four on each side. Then they moved across the field as one large harvesting machine, mowing down a huge swath of soybeans with each pass, leaving nothing behind but a cloud of dust and a wake of stubble.

After numerous passes, they would stop and empty their combines into a caravan of waiting trucks that then hauled the beans to the grain elevator just south of town. They worked late into the night with their huge searchlights flooding the fields before them, casting monstrous shadows through an unfiltered haze of milled soybeans while they continued to advance, devouring huge chunks of acreage like locusts.

It was community in action with each person playing a crucial role. Women brought baskets of sandwiches, thermoses of coffee, and plastic bins of cakes and cookies, while men ate in between shifts as their combines heaved a sigh of relief, emptying themselves of their abundance of amber grain into the eagerly waiting trucks. Younger kids—some in their pajamas—played tag and other games while older kids seemed to mimic their parents and those around them by offering each other coffee or sandwiches. Although it was way past their bedtimes, no one said anything about going home, as if the adults all knew that this experience of communal giving was worth far more than the educational experience their children could have learned from any classroom the next day.

To them it was Life 101, and if you had not been there, if you had missed it, you would have somehow felt as though you had failed the exam.

September 27 . . . The Spirit of God

It was a great fall afternoon, and I asked Miss Maddie if there was anything I could do to help her get ready for winter.

"Plenty," she replied.

I don't know what she would have done had I not asked. When I arrived, there were dead bushes to cut and straw bales to place around the perimeter of the farmhouse for insulation, and logs to split for her fireplace. By the time I was done with all the odd jobs around the farm, it was getting dark, so we decided to call it a day and went inside.

As always, she had fixed supper for me. This time it was chili and homemade cornbread with blueberry pie for dessert. Just eating the pie brought back memories of berry picking this past summer. We ate in the kitchen, and when we were done, we went into the living room. I gathered up some of the wood I had split that afternoon and then lit a fire in the fireplace. We then just sat and watched it together without so much as a word. I was always amazed by fire and the way it consumed the wood before your very eyes, and then I broke the silence and told her so. Then she told me an Old Testament story about Elijah and the prophets of Baal in I Kings, chapter 18. It was a showdown to prove whose God was greater—the God of heaven or the god of Baal. The contest consisted of a sacrificial offering lying on the altar, and the god who answered by fire was the true and greater God.

It was the prophets of Baal who had the first shot at it, calling out to their god. They did so all morning and all afternoon—all 400 of them. And when their god did not answer them, they cut themselves and cried louder. When their god had failed to hear them, Elijah stepped up to the plate like Babe Ruth had done in the 1932 World Series when he called his shot, pointing into center field and declaring that it was there where he would hit a home run—and he did on the very next pitch, parking it 440 feet to the deepest part of center field. In theatrical display of power, Elijah asked that not one but three barrels of water be poured on the offering—in spite of the drought in the land.

Then Elijah called on the God of Israel—and fire came down, consuming not only the sacrificial offering, but also the water, licking it dry. And the people cried out in fear, having never seen the power of God demonstrated like that before.

When I asked Miss Maddie about God's power, she told me that the power of His Word holds all things together—every atom, every molecule, every proton and neutron and cell and tissue. The very fact that we are alive depicts the power of God, she said. Without its presence, the body dies.

I had never really thought much about why a body lives and why it dies. The last time I thought about it was in Mr. Allen's ninth grade biology class when we dissected fetal pigs that had been perfectly preserved. I remember thinking that one moment that pig was alive and the next it was dead. Why?

"What was missing? What was it that had gone from its body to cause it to die?" I asked her.

"The spirit of God," she replied.

I should have known. Everything about Miss Maddie comes back to God. And if it doesn't, she'd find a way to make it come back to God.

"Don't you ever think about anything other than God?" I asked her.

"Scrabble," she said smiling. "I love to play Scrabble."

"So, how did you know that George was going to be all right?" I asked her. "After all, the doctors said that his chances of survival were—"

"God told me," she said.

"Okay," I said sarcastically and then laughed. "So how come he didn't tell me?"

"I don't know," she responded. "Were you listening?"

"Was I supposed to be listening?" I asked.

"Well, if you expect to hear from God, you are," she replied.

"So, how do you know when he speaks to you?" I asked.

"If you had a son, wouldn't it be strange if you never spoke to him?" she asked.

"I guess," I replied. "So how does God speak to us? And if so, how do we know it's him and not something else?" I asked.

"There are many voices out there competing for our attention, but only one of them is God. Jesus said that my sheep will know my voice, but the voice of a stranger they will not follow. If you spend time with the shepherd, you

271

will know his voice—sheep do, and so will we. The irony is that sometimes God speaks to us and we don't even know it. I would venture to say that he was speaking to you about coming to Bullpen—and you didn't even know it."

"That's pretty presumptuous," I said.

All she did was smile—like she knew something I didn't. I had the sense that I could argue all I wanted with Miss Maddie and come back to the same conclusion: her word versus mine. Like a good attorney, I would make a case that George's recovery—as miraculous as it was—was purely coincidental and that there was no other evidence to support the contrary. And the day she came out of the hospital declaring that she had the "victory" before George had actually recovered was like New York Jets' quarterback Joe Namath declaring victory against the heavily favored Baltimore Colts in Super Bowl III two weeks before the game. So what if he did? He was lucky, and so was Babe Ruth, and so was Miss Maddie. But what I continued to wrestle with, fellow bloggers, is that George lived—just as she said he would—in spite of the diagnosis to the contrary by medical experts.

We talked about a number of things after that. And toward the end of the evening when the wood had all been consumed, leaving behind a mere skeletal frame of glowing red coals, Miss Maddie began to open up about the death of her husband and the deaths of her two sons in Vietnam. It started with a simple question: "What was your husband like?" And it ended two hours later as she described the love of her life and their two sons.

It was difficult for her to talk at times, and when she was through, tears began to stream down the sides of her face, glistening in the reflection of the dying red embers.

Suddenly, I knew that it was my turn to hold her hand.

And I did.

As we sat there together in silence, I wondered how long she had been holding onto the pain of the distant past. Then I thought about Robert Frost who once wrote that wood warms you twice, once when you cut it and once when you sit and feel its warmth from a glowing fire. If the Old Testament story was right, then maybe, just maybe, God had shown up that night as he had done with the sacrifice on the altar with Elijah—licking dry the tears upon Miss Maddie's face, taking away her secret pain of loss and sorrow with an all-consuming fire.

October 7 . . . A Letter to the Editor

George has been making great strides in his recovery since coming back to Bullpen and is beginning to feel like his old self. It is good to hear laughter again in the café, and we can thank George for that. His entourage of "wily old sea dogs"—as he now calls the Boys—is continually at his (Majesty's) service as they respond to his every whim and fancy, pushing him about the café in his wheelchair. His wife told Millie yesterday that he doesn't really need the wheelchair and that he is walking just fine at home, but apparently he is milking his present condition as long as he can, ordering himself about like old man Potter in the movie *It's a Wonderful Life*. The Boys don't seem to mind, however, and rather pride themselves on taking care of the old General, as he is now affectionately called after he was given a corncob pipe and an army surplus officer's cap. I have to admit that there are times when George bears a striking resemblance to photographs of the famous World War II General Douglas MacArthur.

The latest story in Bullpen, however, has been the news about the soon-to-be-fired head football coach at Tri Town High School. Apparently, he had the same problem as his predecessor—extracurricular activities stemming from various inappropriate relationships with female teachers. This has been a major event in the community, with letters to the editor pouring into *The Beacon* at an unprecedented rate. Then there was an announcement of an emergency school board meeting that has been planned to discuss a possible replacement. George, however, suggested hiring a female head coach to eliminate any future notions of what he called "hanky-panky." He even went so far as to write his own letter (to the editor) to that effect. It was meant as a joke, but when the Boys dared him to send it in, he did. And to his and everyone else's surprise, it was published the following week. The owner and editor of *The Beacon* (a man who had never cared much for football and thought that all the hubbub of hiring and firing of coaches over their scandalous "extracurricular activities" these last two years had taken center stage in the community's gossip column far too long) had decided to personally chide the community by publishing

George's letter, along with his own comments on how the game of football had gotten out of control, becoming an obsession in the community—and nation—with more important subjects like politics, economics, and crossword puzzles taking a back seat.

Oops.

Much to the editor's own chagrin, a backlash of angry readers flooded *The Beacon* with personal threats and boycotts of the paper unless he recanted from his "self-righteous" position. As a result, last week's edition of the newspaper broke all previous sales records in the history of the newspaper as readers rushed to see if the editor had done so. And like a smart business owner, he had—right there on the front page—in big, bold *New York Times* print:

Editor Apologizes for Lack of Better Judgment

George, however, is now enjoying his celebrity status and is known community-wide as the catalyst that started the whole riotous public notion of hiring a female head football coach in the first place.

But the real breaking news is that George's fame isn't just among the immediate communities that subscribe to *The Beacon*. His notoriety as a champion of women's rights has now begun to extend into the far corners of feminist groups nationwide. These activist organizations have been looking for a poster child to champion their cause ever since they lost face and faith in Bill Clinton after his incident with Monica Lewinski, and they apparently decided that George might be the one. However, their main concern—according to George—was that, before endorsing him as their candidate, they wanted to make sure that he had no Monica Lewinskis lurking in his own closet.

In addressing such a delicate issue, George called upon the Boys to help him craft a careful response to their most eminent concern. The Boys were to check for spelling and grammatical mistakes, while George, on the other hand, was responsible for its content.

Dear Activists:

I am deeply honored that you have considered me for such a prestigious position as spokesman—excuse me spokesperson—in an attempt to help women everywhere obtain a fair and equitable shot at any football coaching position or career on a local or national level—including the NFL. I am well aware of the short and long comings of Bill Clinton, and I understand that the majority of you voted for him hoping that he would, in turn, honor you as a woman should be honored. I regret to say, however, that our former President—a once proud champion of women's rights—took the Constitution too literally when it came to life, liberty, and the pursuit of happiness by taking liberty with one of your own in pursuit of his own happiness. "That's life," he would later say in his own defense. Or was it mutual consent? In either case, I assure you that I have no Monica Lewinskis lurking in my closet that I know of. My wife will vouch for that, as our closet is rather small and my portion of it is even smaller and could by no means hide a woman of Monica's stature or constitution—no pun intended. If I can be of any further assistance, please let me know.

Sincerely,

George Whitman

Although George and the Boys copied and mailed out a letter to every activist organization that had sent an inquiry, to date there has been no reply.

October 20...

An Eligible Bachelor in Bullpen

It is 8:30 pm up on Thomforde Hill, fellow bloggers, and it has been a number of days since I have written any news from the Bullpen Café, and things are relatively quiet. With Halloween coming up in a little over a week, Millie and Melissa have put up various Halloween figures on the walls and windows, while I had a few Halloween placemats printed up for the occasion. Slater asked if he could put the flower of the month on it as well—a rare Thailand Parrot Flower—and I told him I had no objections. It looks like an orchid, but it's not; but since it looks like one, he is sure that it will throw off any would-be guessers—as if anyone in Bullpen would actually take time and guess what it really was anyway. I then decided to put in a few questions of my own about Bullpen—past, present and future, including birthdays and other pertinent information—on the placemat. As an example, Homer will be turning 90 in two days, and we will be having a celebration here at the café for him at noon featuring his favorite cake—carrot. I never really asked Homer what kind of cake he liked until he told me to ask. After I had asked him, I got to thinking about the idea of offering cake here at the café in place of donuts since it would be harder to flush cake down the toilet than a donut. As of late, the toilet has been free of any hitches, Bismarks, or long johns because Ivan has not been there to flush them down it. Three weeks ago, Ivan flushed down another long john, but Jerome was quick on the plunger and had the toilet free flowing before the rising water could spill over the edge.

Zealous to keep it that way, Jerome made a drawing of a donut with a circle and a line through it above what looked like a toilet with four legs and a stick figure sitting on the seat. He then drew arrows from the donut to the stick man, making the inference that donuts were not to be flushed down the toilet. But inferences are hard to draw when the drawing itself is in crayon and posted outside the bathroom door for Ivan and the rest of the world to see. But the fact that he made the drawing in crayon, made the picture look as if a little kid had drawn it. George, meanwhile, thought it looked like a jockey on a horse in the winner's circle, waiting to be crowned with a wreath of roses at Belmont or the

Kentucky Derby. Jerome, a little defensive of his artwork, insisted that it meant that no donuts were to be flushed down the toilet. In the end, the drawing raised more questions than answers as people using the bathroom began to ask which kid had won the coloring contest. Jerome, now a little more defensive of his artwork, argued that anyone could clearly see it was a toilet and not a horse, but George and the Boys disagreed. A bet ensued, and George—eager to redeem the bet he had lost this summer to Jerome—placed a cardboard shoebox near the cash register in order to prove his point. Slater was to act as the moderator to ensure a fair election, as Minnesota's own Secretary of State, Mark Ritchie, had done with comedian Al Franken in his race with Norm Coleman for the US Senate seat in 2008. Voters were given a slip of paper to vote for either the Belmont jockey or toilet man. To date, it is 71 for the jockey and 59 for toilet man, and Jerome, needless to say, is not happy—regardless of the outcome.

So, where *is* Ivan the Terrible? His conspicuous absence speaks volumes, and it has sparked a note of apprehension in spite of the fact that things are nice and quiet around town. But that's just it—they are too nice and too quiet.

When, after Ivan had missed his second consecutive week, I asked my Sunday School class where he had been, I received a plethora of answers—none of which answered my original question. When I asked a second time if anyone knew Ivan's whereabouts, little Edgar's hand shot up. When I called on him, he eagerly pulled out a crumpled receipt from his back pocket for a mousetrap he bought at Cumberland's in Owatonna, Minnesota, for $2.17. He was going to get the coyote call for $9.95, but his allowance ran out. He told me he is now a proud member of the Minnesota Trappers Association and has a mousetrap to prove it.

"So, you gonna trap mice?" I asked him.

"Yep," he replied.

I assumed that trapping mice was only the beginning of a long and arduous career, like an entry-level position followed by bigger rodents, like rats, then muskrats, then ferrets, then squirrels, and finally coyotes. I then asked him why he just didn't buy a cat to catch mice instead, but he just stared at me as if I had just blasphemed the whole Minnesota Trappers Association. When he realized that I was just kidding, he smiled.

It's funny, but when kids know that you are joking with them, their eyes light up as though they think that they have you all figured out. When that happens, they feel that they have been elevated to the status of an adult and are now competing in a mental sparring match on equal footing. And if they can keep up with you, then they start to believe that they are "all-that-and-a-bag-of-chips." And the funny thing is—more often than not—they are.

But after all was said and done, the question still remained: where was Ivan? Should I pay him a visit? Suddenly, my better judgment kicked in. Yes, reason asked me why I would ever want to know where Ivan was. After all, life is good. Why would I want to go looking for trouble? Have I gone mad? The mere thought of Ivan coming into the café conjures up a gunslinger coming into an old western saloon—evoking fear in the heart of the proprietor, who is all too aware of the eminent gunfight or barroom brawl that is about to ensue.

So where is the little gunslinger anyway?

Houston?

Natasha Uno writes in and asks me if I have any plans for Halloween. If not, she would like to come to Bullpen to meet me.

"Ah . . . wow, thanks, Natasha Uno. I'm flattered, and I'm not sure what to say . . ."

"You don't need to say anything," she tells me. "I don't even have to talk. We can simply sit in an open field together and gather the mystic forces of energy on this most sacred of Halloweens."

Houston? We have a problem.

"Sounds like a great date," I reply.

"So when can I meet you?" she asks me unashamedly.

"What do you say we just slow this down a bit," I tell her. "I don't know much about you."

"I live in a community that honors nature the way it should be honored," she replies. "Anything else you want to know?"

"What kind of community is that?" I ask stupidly. I am then met with a montage of Mother Earth news, and suddenly I'm thinking that my biosphere and hers are not necessarily in sync.

"Perhaps another Halloween that isn't so sacred . . ." I tell her, not trying to be rude.

And suddenly there is a floodgate of other offers, and I am feeling like Homer, the most eligible of eligible bachelors. Knowing what an uncomfortable situation this could be for all of us, I thank the ladies for their interest, but at this point I am not looking for a date on Halloween.

"Valentine's Day?" asks one of the ladies.

"Perhaps Valentine's Day," I reply—after I find Ivan . . ."

Houston? You copy that?

October 23 . . . Ivan

It was a gray, overcast afternoon, and after a few inquires, I found Ivan's home just north of town in the trailer court—number 15. His trailer was as run-down as you could imagine. The windows were covered by tattered blankets, and I could only guess what lay behind them. Outside on a grassless brown lawn were two ashtrays full of cigarette butts, while empty Diet Coke cans lay scattered about in all directions. It was an eyesore by any standard, and it was the bleakest trailer in the trailer court, with one dented side stuffed inward while the adjacent side jetted outward in a lopsided fashion, as if leaning on an imaginary axis. What looked like a front porch was comprised of rotten planks that protruded from the front and only door, and it seemed to convey the subtle message that visitors should enter at their own risk. Ivan's bike was leaning against the side of the trailer, and a battered tricycle sat next to it, looking upwards like a squatting dog next to its master. The red horn on the tricycle was the only bright color that stood out against the depression-gray trailer. Beside me, near one of the Diet Coke cans, lay one of Ivan's tennis shoes, looking like a Cinderella slipper that had been lost in a hasty departure.

I had never seen such poverty before, and I wondered how I had been so amiss in understanding his predisposition. As I stared in awe at the dwelling, part of me was tugging in the other direction, as if wanting to run away.

Houston? . . . Houston, why had I come here again?

I had come for Ivan—yes, Ivan the Terrible, Ivan the Mad Scribbler, Ivan the Mess Maker and Stinky Bait Dropper, Ivan the Truck Scratcher and Ivan the Toilet Plugger.

When I knocked at the door, there was a strange sensation that someone was in there but refused to answer. I knocked again and again, until the lady next door peered through her own curtains as if wondering who I was. As I continued to knock, she finally came out and recognized me from the café. Her name was Beatrice Johnson, and we carried on a brief conversation about the weather until I asked the whereabouts of Ivan and his family.

279

I knew that his father had been incarcerated, but what I didn't know was the depravity of their situation. Without money and without food, they had simply left. She confirmed not only their plight but also the fact that Ivan's little brother, Joey, was suffering from a rare heart disease and would probably not live to see his next birthday.

"But Ivan didn't even take his bike," I said to Beatrice.

"They must have left during the night, and I suppose they either missed it or didn't have room," she said.

We talked a few more minutes, and then she excused herself and went inside. As I stood there staring at the vacated property, I couldn't help but recall the first day of school and watching him wave at me from the back of the bus until it disappeared out of sight, as if foreshadowing things to come. I recalled the first time I had met Ivan on the top of Thomforde Hill. Curious, he had kept asking about my laptop that illuminated the darkness around us. I could see it now. It was as if he was drawn to the light that had begun to pierce his own darkened world.

As I stood there looking at the depravity of the vacant trailer home—and the gray, overcast sky behind it—my heart began to sink.

Ivan the Terrible was gone.

October 31 . . . Halloween

Halloween came and went in Bullpen. We had our own Halloween party up in the apartment where Jerome, Millie, Marvin, Jared, Melissa, and John (her husband) came over to help pass out candy. Earlier that afternoon, we had all made signs and put them out in front of the café, pointing to the back stairway that that comes out from the alley. It would have been easier simply to have passed out candy from the front of the café along Main Street, but the thought of decorating the outside stairway was too good of an idea to pass up, according to the ladies. In the end, I don't know who had more fun decorating—Jerome or Millie and Melissa. In addition to the one huge pumpkin that they had placed at the top of the steps, they draped no less than four white bed sheets over the stair railings to serve as a kind of ghost tunnel. If you were less than 43 inches tall, you had no problem climbing the stairway. But if you were taller than 43 inches, you had to bend over all the way up—or crawl. The little kids thought it was cool. The big kids thought it was a pain in the neck—literally—as they hunched over while climbing all twenty-three steps to the top. But once there, they were rewarded with trick-or-treaters' pay dirt—chocolate candy bars: Nestle Crunch bars, Almond Joys, 100,000 Dollar Bars, Butter Fingers, Milky Ways and Snickers.

As a former trick-or-treater, I had determined that, if I was ever going to pass out candy of my own, I wasn't going to pass out the cheap stuff. No, kids were to remember my apartment as the place that passed out the big candy bars. As a kid, I distinctly remember the homes that didn't scrimp on candy—specifically chocolate. The Ashenbachs were notorious for the big Nestle Crunch bar—not just one year, but every year. It was the kind of candy bar that made the big thumping sound when it hit the bottom of your bag. No, old man Ashenbach never scrimped at Halloween when it came to candy. And if you timed your visit to his front door with other trick-or-treaters, you could just kind of hang around with the other bags and then just keep sticking your bag into the mix, holding it out there along with all the other bags, and hope that old man Ashenbach would lose track of which bag was which and give you extra Nestle Crunch bars. Being the last one to pull your bag away was the real trick to trick-or-treating. One year he dropped three Crunch bars into my bag simply because I kept it out there until all the others had pulled theirs away. And when Karl and I counted our booty at the end of the night, I had beaten him by one extra Crunch bar. Beating Karl was one of the greatest triumphs in my trick-or-treating career. The next year I had vowed to do it again, and when we tied, I decided to put on a different costume and go back to old man Ashenbach's. As I was in the bathroom putting on mom's black eyeliner for a beard, Gerty came up the steps—and the moment I heard her, I knew I was in trouble.

"Vat are you doing, Charlie?" she asked.

Karl, not wanting to be beaten for a second straight year, spilled the beans and told Gerty that I was going out as a bum for another round of trick-or-treating.

I never did get another candy bar from old man Ashenbach that night. All I remember was standing there with my head under the faucet, gasping for air, while Gerty kept scrubbing my face trying to remove my black beard. Since it never came completely off, I was to live with the "beard of shame" for the next week, knowing all too well that it was okay to ask for seconds at the dinner table but not during trick-or-treating.

Halfway through the night, Abby and Edgar came up through the white-sheeted tunnel of ghostly goblins. They had been trick-or-treating together as Spiderman and Cinderella. And when I asked Edgar if he was using his webbing to scale all the tall buildings in Bullpen, he nodded.

Jerome, who had been on a power trip handing out candy ever since he had been duly assigned to such a post at the beginning of the evening, suddenly decided to pull rank and thought it to be of the utmost importance for them to sing a song before they got their chocolate bar. It was a cruel demand by anyone's standards—and what's more, it was against the Geneva Convention's International Articles of Trick-or-Treating. In spite of the fact that I told him so, he continued to demand a song, holding them hostage to his own inhumanely whimsical notion.

Edgar and Abby laughed and thought he was kidding, but he wasn't. Jerome was serious, and then he held out the chocolate bar—just out of reach—to make sure he got his song. After deliberating for a few minutes, they agreed on "Twinkle, Twinkle, Little Star." But Jerome thought they could do better and held out for more. When they finally convinced him that they couldn't think of anything better, he asked them if they knew the song "When Crawdad Daddy Met Polecat Momma." They looked at him like a dog at a new pan, and after a brief internal deliberation, he decided to sing it for them.

I had never heard such howling and fussing and carrying on over some old mangy polecat and crusty old crawdad. But Jerome was clearly enjoying himself, bellowing out all kinds of Cajun-Bijou-Louisiana-mumbo-jumbo-shrimp-type words that I could barely understand, much less pronounce. And as he continued singing, the song began to build momentum, verse after awful verse, like a locomotive heading downhill with nothing to stop it. And suddenly I had flashbacks to our old church with 87-year-old Mrs. Jensen behind the wheel, driving our old pipe organ beyond the recommended factory settings, with fingers that jettisoned upwards and downwards, then upwards along the keyboard in a dramatic crescendo of passion and fury, hitting just enough of the right notes to give familiarity to the hymn, thus allowing the reticent congregation to sing along.

Jerome's song had begun to peak in the same terrible manner with nothing to stop it. Then suddenly he shifted gears and sped past the earthly sphere of cognitive reasoning into an ethereal, out-of-body experience. His eyes glazed over, and his voice rose higher and higher, whining like a toothless old tomcat while he worked himself into a linguistic lather—spitting and sputtering like a whirling dervish—then nothing—nothing but absolute silence. It was as if the bottom had dropped right out of the song, and my guess was that Crawdad Daddy had finally met Polecat Mamma. And for a moment we all just stood there, absolutely amazed that a human voice could replicate sounds beyond the vocal limitations of the human body. We then began to clap, and as I stood there blinking like an idiot, Jerome broke out into a smile of his own.

"That," he said at last to Spiderman and Cinderella, "is 'When Crawdad Daddy Met Polecat Momma.'"

Then, taking up his duly appointed authority as Candy Man, he plopped three candy bars into each of their bags.

"Thanks, Mr. Boatman," they said. "That was kind of cool." Then they turned to me and asked me if I had anything besides chocolate candy bars. I told them no, that they were getting the best I had. With that they thanked me and turned and headed down the white-sheeted tunnel of ghostly goblins.

I stood at the top of the landing and watched Spiderman and Cinderella walk down the steps together. Once they had disappeared from view, I looked down and saw that Cinderella's coach had suddenly been turned back into a Halloween pumpkin. The magic of the moment had been swallowed up by the stark realization that someone was missing. When I glanced down at the welcome mat in front of the door, I thought about Ivan's shoe that had been left behind in haste, like Cinderella's slipper. I then looked up at the sky. It was a clear, crisp night, and the stars had begun to spread out upon a canopy of infinite and unfathomable distances, as they had done since the beginning of time. It was the Milky Way, and as I gazed up at its milky white aura, I suddenly felt insignificantly small, and I wondered if Ivan had felt the same.

"Where are you tonight, Ivan?" I found myself saying out loud. "You forgot your slipper."

November 1 . . .
Reflections on the Prodigal Son

The sermon in church today was on the prodigal son. I don't normally listen to sermons. I usually sleep through them, but this one caught my ear for some reason. Perhaps it was because there were two brothers in this parable—just as there are two brothers in my own family: my older brother, Karl, and me.

The gist of the story is that the younger brother asks for his inheritance, then goes off to a distant land and squanders it all on a raucous lifestyle. Without money or friends, he supports himself as a hired hand for a pig farmer—and after a momentary lapse of better judgment, and knowing that his father's servants are eating better than he is, he returns home, hoping his father will accept him when he does. To his surprise, the father not only accepts him back into the family but also kills the fatted calf and then provides a huge feast in honor of his return. All is well until the judgmental older brother arrives and finds that a feast has been given in honor of his younger brother—the scoundrel, the blasphemer, the family fool. Furious that nothing had ever been done like that for him, he berates his father in public and refuses to join in the celebration. After all, he was the good boy—the one who followed all the rules only to be beaten to the punch by his wayward little brother.

It is an interesting story and got me to thinking. Am I like the prodigal son? Am I the one who bucks his position in life while Karl—the dutiful older brother—is on the fast track toward a promising career? I was the naughty boy. Karl was the good boy. I challenged authority. Karl adhered to authority. For Karl, life's path was nothing more than cause and effect. You put in your time and learned the ropes. It was that simple, and it was that direct. Life gave back to you what you had put into it—nothing more and nothing less. And if you abided by the rules, then you were *owed* the "good life" because you did what you were told. And if life didn't give you what you thought it owed you, or gave to others more than they deserved, then *it* was unjust—not you. *It* was unfair—not you. You were merely its victim. And as the victim, you had become more righteous than the law itself because you adhered to justice and justice didn't.

285

Where was the justice when the father took back your younger brother? Did he not deserve to live with the servants? Where was the justice when the father killed the fatted calf and made a feast for him and his friends? Did he not deserve to eat with pigs? And where was the justice when the father forgave him after he had shamed the family with his gluttonous, unethical lifestyle? Did he not deserve condemnation? No, there was no justice in forgiveness, nor would there ever be.

The mind is a complicated thing that tries to reach beyond its own intellectual capability while seeking to make sense of the world around it. From birth it seeks to make meaning out of causes and effects. If you touch a hot stove, then you get burned. If you leave your toys out in the rain, then they rust. There were consequences to life's actions and every action and reaction provided the guideposts and standards upon which our philosophies and perspectives of life had been built. And you either lived according to those standards or you defied your conscience and lived contrary to them. Right or wrong, they justified our presuppositions and predispositions of life. And if and when they changed—as they had for the older brother when a new standard was introduced into the mix—it would rattle our most sacred cows and most cherished beliefs.

It was only natural for the elder brother to lash out in anger. Everything he had known from birth had pointed to the causes and effects of justice—the consequences of sin. No one was to get off scot-free. It was the unwritten law. But now, his own father had done the unthinkable, the most unjust and unlawful act ever imaginable: he had forgiven the younger brother—blasphemy of blasphemies. And in doing so, he had turned the older brother's self-righteous world upside down. Like the astronauts onboard Apollo 13, the older brother had lost sight of his only point of reference and was now heading off into the dark eternity of space, forever angry and forever lost, apart from divine intervention.

Houston, do you copy?

As I think about next spring, I think about law school and about following in the path of my father and his father and his father before him. It is, after all, a Finstune family tradition of causes and effects—and justice. Spend your time in law school and expect membership into the good life, a prestigious community of your own peers—because you earned it, you worked for it, you deserved it.

And if we do all that we know to do, all that is in our power to do, all that we are supposed to do in accord with those who tell us *what* to do . . . then what happens if we are not rewarded for what we did do—or, worse yet, rewarded for what we didn't do?

If only the father had played by the same set of rules . . .

286

November 9 . . .
Mad Deer Fever Disease (MDFD)

It is an unsafe world in Bullpen and the surrounding communities nowadays. If you stand outside the café, you can hear random gun shots in the distance, as grown men—sane most times of the year—have now gone stark raving mad with mad deer fever disease—commonly known as MDFD. It starts out with just a little temperature—98.7. But then it grows over night to a sweltering 105 to 108 degrees. They tell me it strikes harder than mad cow disease and can leave behind a wake of Slim Jims and chocolate candy bar wrappers—which are only the first of many signs to come. The last sign often requires professional counseling for cases in which once happy and cheerful families are suddenly left destitute without the mental presence or faculties of their own father. In some recorded cases, victims of MDFD could not even remember the names of their own children, much less their wives. Once the tentacles of MDFD wrap themselves around its victims, there is nothing more that can be done to save them. There is no cure for MDFD, only remedies—over-the-counter laxatives and cough syrup. It is a nasty bug that lies dormant for months on end, and then in the fall, when the leaves begin to change and the weather turns cold, it resurges with vengeance, like a latent tapeworm.

Every county in Minnesota has its own chilling tale to tell of the effects of MDFD, but in Bullpen, grown men have been known to have suffered the severest of pains while trying to relieve themselves in the most untimely of times. Yes, let's not forget when that 20-point buck wandered aimlessly into their own private bathroom, only to turn away after catching a whiff of more than just the bone-chilling November winds. It was a hunter's worse nightmare—to be relieving himself just at the time when that 20-point buck comes rutting beside his stand. Oh, the misery of it all to sit silently against the tall tree like a statue with your pants on the ground and your beloved shotgun just out of reach. Oh, the agony of it all—not the pain of sitting still for so long with your pants on the ground while contracting a severe case of frostbite where the sun never shines—but the agony of knowing that you were only nineteen-and-a-half inches away from your trusty Remington—and couldn't move.

Maybe it was coincidental, but MDFD always accompanied deer season. Studies indicated the two went hand in hand, like Abbot and Costello or the Dooby Brothers. And to some, deer season was more sacred than their own anniversary (or any other holiday) as they took pride in donning their bright orange vests and bright orange hats and bright orange socks and bright orange gloves—the Orangemen (and women), they called themselves, taking to the fields and streams and whatnots, leaving behind a ghostly wake of vacated local businesses that had to weather the financial recession on their own.

Where I came from, golf was the more apropos game of choice. It was, after all, a more civilized sport than stalking, shooting, gutting, hauling, mauling, and processing deer—and probably less expensive. In golf, you simply hit a white ball and then chased it. If it landed in water, you threw out another. And if it was lost it in the woods, you did the same. There was definitiveness about golf. You knew exactly how far you were from the clubhouse and how many holes you had left to play. It was a gentleman's game, but not so with deer hunting. Not so in Bullpen. Shooting the biggest deer was as much about competition as it was about bragging rights for the next year.

In all honesty, I thought the Bullpen Café was immune to MDFD. I thought the Bullpen Café would be the Grand Central Station where hunters from around the world would flock to get a taste of real food and real coffee—as opposed to Slim Jims and chocolate candy bars. Not so. We were no more immune to the financial recession in Bullpen than any other local business. And when Millie asked me if she could take off a few days to go hunting with Maynard, the worst of my fears were confirmed.

"You too?" I asked.

It was the first time I had seen Millie cower before me. She looked timid and afraid, like a naughty little school girl before the principal. I was about ready to pull rank as proprietor of the restaurant when Melissa asked if she too could go hunting with Marvin.

"With Maynard?" I asked stupidly.

"Yes, with Maynard," they replied.

Hunting with Maynard. Sounds like a TV show, doesn't it? One can only wonder what hunting with Maynard will entail. If it is anything like driving with Maynard, then God help the Orangemen (and orange women) out there, because no one was safe from a randomly discharged slug.

"Maynard?" I asked again stupidly.

It was then Jerome got into the act, dramatizing Maynard out in the wilderness, walking one way and looking back to see if everyone was comfortable. Oops . . . I guess the gun accidentally discharged.

Hunting with Maynard . . . hmmmm . . . no thanks. Not today . . . or tomorrow . . . or ever.

That was my initial position anyway, until Millie kept telling me about the joys of hunting and the thrill of it all. Like a pesky, persistent telemarketer, she wore me down, and over time I found myself beginning to catch the symptoms of MDFD. That night I took my own temperature, and sure enough it was 98.7—the telltale sign of the disease. I tried to put the thought out of my mind. I even got up to get a cold glass of water, but when I took my temperature again at midnight, it had gone up to 98.8. Horror of horrors! Before I knew it, I had caught a full-blown case of MDFD. What was I to do? Since Bullpen had now become a ghost town and Homer was the only patron who had frequented the café during these trying times, I decided against my own better judgment to go hunting with Maynard and close the café down for a couple of days.

I then asked Jerome if he wanted to join us, but to him, the thought of Maynard with a shotgun in his hand seemed even more lethal than a steering wheel. Besides, he wanted to sit and rock and think about stuff on the balcony before the late autumn snows would come upon us.

So I went.

It was a sunny but cold November afternoon when I arrived at Maynard's house. Maynard had an extra shotgun and orange wear, and before I knew what was going on, I was among the ranks of the Orangemen. It was funny to see Millie and Melissa in their hunting gear as well. It was as though we were all going out to clean up the highway or something.

But then Maynard handed me my shotgun.

It was more than a simple firearm—it was the Remington 870 pump action, left-handed 12 gage shotgun with the 28-inch vent-rib, bead-sighted barrel that was milled from a solid billet of steel for maximum strength and reliability, like the one I had seen in the classic movie *The Christmas Story*. . . . No, it was more than that. As I ran my fingers across the silky-smooth twin-action bars and no-frills laminate stock and fore-end, the latent thrill of shooting such a piece of artwork surpassed anything that I had imagined. Even Ralphie from *A Christmas Story*—who had coveted a Red Rider 200-shot carbine action-range-model air rifle with a compass and this thing which tells time built right in the stock—would have drooled over Maynard's brand new Remington 870 pump action, left-handed 12-gage shotgun with the 28-inch vent-rib, bead-sighted barrel that was milled from a solid billet of steel for maximum strength and reliability. Like his Cadillac, Maynard had spared no expense when he bought this bad boy. The only problem was . . . it was left-handed.

The last time I had been out hunting was with my grandpa on his houseboat near Hudson, Wisconsin. He taught me how to shoot coot (pronounced "koot"—*say "shoot coot" 50 times in a row as fast as you can, fellow bloggers*). When he was sure that we were alone, he would take out his shotgun and place it parallel to the water and aim in the direction of the coot, then fire. We would watch the BBs skip across the smooth surface and then, sure enough, one coot's head would drop, and then another. Then I would try it with the same results. According to my Grandpa, we never actually killed the birds; we just stunned them. And when we were through shooting, he carefully put the shotgun back into its case and then got out a shot of brandy to celebrate. It was the first time I had tasted anything so bitter and so awful.

"Look at this baby," I said to Maynard, trying out my new-fangled lingo as if I had been hunting all my life. "This ought to do the job."

Maynard agreed.

We then drove about a mile outside of town to a clearing surrounded by woods. Maynard's friend owned the land, and it was a hunter's paradise, according to Maynard, with cornfields less than a hundred yards away on the right and a dairy farm on the left. Maynard parked along the side of the road and, taking out our shotguns from his trunk, we walked to the clearing. When we got there, he positioned me near the edge, just south of a nearby dairy farm. I was to wait there while he and the girls drove the deer my way on foot. Maynard told me to shoot at any deer that came out of clearing.

I agreed.

He and the women then went to the other side of the woods and began driving them my way. Now, waiting for a deer to hop out of the woods in the cold November air, even with the sun out, can be hard on your extremities like your toes and hands—especially your hands. And since I was just standing there, I got a little cold, so I decided to take off my gloves and warm my hands inside my pockets. I must have been warming my hands for a good ten minutes when, all of a sudden, I heard the rustle of deer coming through the woods. I don't say that I didn't panic and I don't say that I did, but when I saw two huge white-tailed bucks bounding my way while I was standing there with my hands in my pockets, it did something to my insides. Grappling for my gun, I turned around to see them pass no fewer than ten yards from where I was standing. Ten yards! I was desperate and grabbed the shot gun and whirled about, trying to figure out how to release the safety as the deer jumped past me heading toward the herd of grazing dairy cows. When I finally did release the safety, I struggled to aim the left handed barrel—and then I fired two shots at the now very distant deer with my Remington 870 pump-action, left-handed 12-gauge shotgun with the 28-inch vent-rib, bead-sighted barrel that was milled from a solid billet of steel for maximum strength and reliability.

And just like that—just like the coot that I had dropped when I fired across the lake with my grandpa in the houseboat years ago—I saw the big animal drop, way off in the distance.

I was beside myself with joy. No, I was ecstatic. Suddenly those primitive ancestral hunting genes had been resurrected from the dead and were kicking inside my belly—my very being. I let out a war whoop and then another and another. I had done it. I had bagged my first big game!

Maynard and the girls came running out of the woods as I continued to whoop and holler.

"I got one," I yelled at the top of my lungs as I saw them rush across the open field.

"Where?" cried Maynard.

"There," cried I, pointing in the direction of the barn over two hundred yards away.

I don't know who laughed first—Maynard or the girls—as they came in sight of the big game trophy. Nor did I know what they were laughing at—until I saw it for myself.

Horror of horrors . . . I had shot and killed a dairy cow—a big brown Guernsey.

It was bad enough that Maynard, Millie, and Melissa asked me to pose beside my prized cow for a photo with my Remington 870 pump-action, left-handed 12-gage shotgun with the 28-inch vent-rib, bead-sighted barrel that was milled from a solid billet of steel for maximum strength and reliability. It was bad enough that I did it, smiling and playing along with them and acting as though I was proud of my accomplishment. It was bad enough that the irate farmer, whom I had never met, came out and cussed at me with words that would have made even Jerome blush. It was bad enough that he had to bring out his four-wheeler and haul the dead carcass to the locker and have it dressed. It was bad enough that the rest of his dairy herd failed to produce milk that night due to the trauma of losing one of their own comrades. And it was bad enough that the farmer charged me double for his prized cow (so he said) along with what he had calculated for his loss in milk production due to the trauma.

As bad as all those things were, the worst came a few days later when I found myself on the front page of *The Beacon*, looking proud as a peacock standing over the dead dairy cow with my trusty Remington 870 pump-action left-handed 12-gage shotgun with the 28-inch vent-rib, bead-sighted barrel that was milled from a solid billet of steel for maximum strength and reliability.

Local Deer Hunter Bags His First Cow on Sheffield's Dairy Farm

There it was in big, bold *New York Times* print along with the eight-by-ten photo that accompanied the article.

At least I hadn't shot my eye out with a Red Rider pellet gun.

And just how that picture ended up at *The Beacon* is a mystery—or a secret. Millie claims that she and Melissa had nothing to do with it, and George continues to plead innocent. Regardless of who did it among the usual suspects, I am now referred to as the "Big Game Hunter." And to add insult to injury, the Boys framed the article where it now sits on top of the piano for all to see.

Do any of you bloggers have any good recipes for wild Guernsey burgers?

November 12 . . . Humble Pie

Okay, fellow bloggers, that's enough. Thanks for all the great hamburger recipes, but I now have enough to last me through the winter. Thanks for your shepherd's pie recipe, Queen Crab. And Sweet Tea, thanks for your recipe for Humble Pie—literally. I thought you were kidding until I tried it:

1 lb. lean ground beef
1 can chicken gumbo soup
1 bell pepper
1 onion
1 can black olives
1 tomato
Mozzarella cheese
1 tube Pillsbury Country Style biscuits

Arrange biscuits in greased pie pan; pat down. Brown ground beef, bell pepper, and onion. Add gumbo soup; simmer until thickened. Pour soup mixture over unbaked biscuits. Top with sliced tomatoes, olives, and cheese. Bake at 350 degrees until done. Let cool before cutting.

I've had humble pie on numerous occasions, but this one was actually quite filling. Isn't hamburger great? It goes with everything, like a white dress shirt, and now that we have three freezers full of it, Jerome wants to add hamburgers to the afternoon menu.

I couldn't agree more.

On a serious note, I want to take the time to thank you all for blogging in. It continues to amaze me the number of you fellow bloggers that continue to follow *News from the Bullpen Café*. Although I don't know all of you personally, I am grateful for your interest in what takes place here. With more of you hitting the site, it keeps getting harder to respond to all of you personally and tell about the events that have transpired here at the same time. Thank you for your hamburger recipes. It was pretty cute to read them—especially a hamburger helper recipe from a nine-year-old girl in Topeka, Kansas, named Little Loretta Lynn and, last but not least, a recipe of yours, Candlestick. I feel better knowing that I am not the only one who has shot a dairy cow while deer hunting. If you ever get a chance to come to Bullpen, please do. I would love to meet you and all the rest of you fellow bloggers—and I mean it. I met a few of you this summer during Bullpen Days, including Mary from New York.

I hope you are okay, Mary. I have not heard anything from you since this summer—and if truth be told, I miss your thoughts.

As for you, Far Quart, thanks for updating me on Jerome's Stinky Bait. I understand it failed to land you the big trophy fish you wanted in the Arkansas tournament. I will break the bad news gently to Jerome. He has already spent his royalties from the multimillion-dollar-big-fish-deal he thought he would land because of Stinky Bait. I guess if someone has to break the news to him, it might just as well be me. After all, I'm the one responsible for putting visions of grandeur in his head. If it wasn't for me, he might not have bought all those canning jars, gas mask filters, totes, five-gallon pails, squeegees, spray bottles, rubber gloves, rubber galoshes, nylons, protective eye wear, (nylons?), scoopers, bleach, rain slickers and matching pants, two step ladders (one for getting into the dumpster and one for getting out), plastic tarps, and smelling salts—all the necessities of going into business for yourself.

I too thought that this might be his big break—the franchising opportunity of a lifetime. Perhaps it's better this way. I couldn't see residents from Bullpen mass-producing Stinky Bait, working three shifts around the clock. Although it would boost the local economy, imagine what the factory would look like, let alone smell like. Eventually, property values would drop like they did in Pittsburgh, and those with sinus problems or asthma or arthritis would be forced to move out. And where would they go? Worse yet, Bullpen would be known as the Stinky Bait capital of the world, like Austin, Minnesota, is known as the Spam capital of the world.

But, enough about Jerome.

The winter weather is inching its way closer to Bullpen these last few days, and it seems that Old Man Winter is finally beginning to retaliate after the long Indian summer we've had this fall. That means that the Alberta Clipper is on the way. Alberta Clipper—sounds like a hockey team from Canada, doesn't it? But here in Minnesota, it is by far the most beloved and most popular phrase among the local weather forecasters. It is the phrase that that all weathermen default to when they have lost their place on the teleprompter. Alberta Clipper. It was the first term they had learned in weather broadcasting school, and it was also the last. Just the sound of it brings shivers down your spine because we have all been classically conditioned in Minnesota to shiver at the sound of it—like Pavlov's dog had been conditioned to salivate at the sound of a dinner bell. It was no accident that the weather forecasters said it, and said it often, manipulating our very biorhythms with psychosomatic chills—especially in summer. Just yell the words "Alberta Clipper" in the middle of July and watch us dive for our winter parkas in a knee-jerk reaction. "Alberta Clipper." It's kind of fun to say, and Slater says it with more gusto and more passion than anyone else in Bullpen. George even thinks he sounds like Sven Sundgaard, the local TV weatherman for KARE 11, who made it to the big leagues and now serves as a role model for Norwegians and Swedes everywhere— demonstrating that we too can make it big despite our Scandinavian heritage.

I agreed. We all agreed. And that was the problem—we all agreed.

But, enough about the Alberta Clipper and Sven and weather forecasters and Scandinavian role models.

With the advent of colder weather—and Halloween behind us—Christmas is in the air here in Bullpen, as members of the Rotary club have put up the annual Christmas stars along Main Street.

Apparently, there had been a debate a few years ago as to whether or not to put them up after Thanksgiving or before, but since you don't buy gifts for Thanksgiving—and being the materialistic society that we have become with business everywhere depending on that one special day of the year for their financial stability—the Rotary club decided to place the annual Christmas stars out before Thanksgiving in hopes that it would spur on the spirit of gift giving like an appetizer would spur on an appetite. So far, however, the decorations have not produced any results, but that may be because Christmas is over a month away and Thanksgiving is just around the corner.

My mother called yesterday and invited me to Thanksgiving dinner. She was the most chipper I had heard her in a long time. Maybe it was because Karl now has a girlfriend. That's right, a girlfriend, and he is bringing her home for Thanksgiving. Karl never had a girlfriend in junior high or high school or even college—and my mother seems elated. Apparently, it is serious. He met her at Harvard, and they have been dating now for over a month. Her name is Hillary, and mother can't wait to meet her—nor can I. There is a part of me, however, that dreads going home. And I have asked myself on more than one occasion, "What kind of person would dread going home for Thanksgiving?"

A Big Game Hunter for one . . .

November 21 . . . Southern Style Scrabble

Miss Maddie invited Jerome and me to her home this Saturday for supper and for a game of Scrabble. She had been looking forward to our coming all week and had made a special supper: roasted chicken, mashed potatoes and gravy, green beans with buttered bacon, homemade biscuits with strawberry jam and honey, real lemonade, and apple pie (did I forget the blueberry pie?).

But what started out as a great evening ended in nothing less than a disaster. It all began when Miss Maddie and I agreed that Southern words could be used during the course of Scrabble. Why? I don't know, but we did. Jerome called it Southern Scrabble, and it was the only kind of Scrabble he knew, so like good Yankees, we obliged him.

How many of you fellow bloggers have ever played Scrabble—Southern Style?

I have a word for you, and it's worth at least 47 points: the word is "don't." That's right, don't even think about playing Southern Scrabble, or even consider it, because you can't win. The deck is stacked against you if you're a Yankee, because it defies all logic with words you ain't never heard before—and probably never will again. So how do you know that they are real words? You don't. You just oblige your southern friend(s) and be the Yankee gentleman and lady you always thought you were. So when Jerome laid down his first word—"gussied"—I was polite and rather pleasant.

"Gussied?" I asked him.

"Gussied," he replied. "You know, like 'he got all gussied up for the dance.'"

Actually, I didn't know. Have any of you fellow bloggers ever heard of "gussied" before? Or how about "lawg" or "nearbout" or "septin" or "wuhd" or a "goozle" or "yousta"?

. . . Neither had I.

But these were just a smidgeon of the words that he continued to play every time it was his turn. And where was Miss Maddie during all these shenanigans? She would simply nod and smile as if it was part of the game. Not me. I figured that someone had to act as a fraud squad, so if Miss Maddie was going to relinquish her responsibilities, then in all fairness to the integrity of the game, I took it upon myself to be the Scrabble Police, since my conscience would not allow me to do otherwise.

In the beginning of the game I considered myself a reasonable man. I like to give a guy a chance as much as anyone, but when Jerome started occupying the double words spaces and triple letters spaces and finally the triple word score spaces with his unorthodox southern wordplay, it was too much for anyone, let alone a wordsmith, to forgive. As a gentleman, I had let all of his sanctimonious efforts pass unchallenged, but when he laid down a seven-letter word that he attached to the "X" on the board, I could sit silent no longer.

The word was "flambeaux," and in a passionate fit of competitive rage, what had been brewing and stewing the whole game suddenly erupted in one loud explosion.

"I challenge that!" I yelled, frothing at the mouth like a rabid dog. "I challenge that!"

Suddenly, I felt as if I was looking at myself outside my body, like an out-of-body experience. Who was this mad man? Who was this Mr. Hyde who was flicking his finger at Jerome's now empty little letter plate holder thingamabob and challenging his 87-point triple word score and seven-letter bonus? I wondered. Had Southern-Style Scrabble scrambled my own better judgment? Slowly, I began to come back to myself, and as I regained consciousness, I forced a laugh.

But as much as I tried to make light of my competitive outburst, I could not recant my objection. And horror of horrors, I was to find out that "flambeaux" was—after all—a real word that meant "torch."

With just a few letters left in the Scrabble pouch, and a loss of a turn due to the unsuccessful challenge, it was curtains for me, and I found myself conceding like John McCain had done in the 2008 Presidential Election. Slowly, the stark reality began to sink in: Charles Robert Finstune—the English major—had been beaten in Scrabble.

"Well, let's just see what all this comes to now," Jerome stated pompously, adding up all his points, knowing full well he had just kicked both our butts. Then adding insult to injury, he began adding them again—out loud—as if to make sure that we didn't accuse him of cheating.

Only later did I realize that Jerome had only laid down seven letters (excluding the "X" on the board) of the nine letter word "flambeaux"—leaving out the "u." I was actually going to accuse him of cheating on the way home, but by that time it was water over the dam.

Moral of the story fellow bloggers:

1. Forget about being a gentleman or a lady when it comes to Scrabble. 2. Challenge every word up front—even if it may lead to dissension. Remember: it's a tough job, but someone has to be the Scrabble Police. 3. Stand your ground, and don't be bullied just because someone might call you a "Yankee" or "Carpet Bagger."

And finally, if playing with someone from Louisiana or thereabouts, gol darn it, be sure not to play Southern Scrabble. And if you do succumb to the peer pressure, at least get yourself a Southern-to-English dictionary—just to keep the "cut up" from getting' all "highfalutin."

November 26 . . . Thanksgiving

It was a long ride to Minneapolis this morning, and it was cold, freezing cold. We had decided to close down the café for two days for Thanksgiving and Black Friday, as they now call it. With Christmas shoppers all about, it seemed only natural to give everyone a day off. Jerome didn't seem to mind, and neither did Millie nor Melissa. Apparently, the two of them shop in Rochester the day after Thanksgiving and have even been known to camp out in their car before the stores open at five am. Even Homer said he wouldn't be there for Thanksgiving since he has been invited to no fewer than six dinner engagements that day.

"Six?" I asked him.

"Six," he replied with a grimace on his face.

Poor Homer. The thought of his downing six Thanksgiving dinners is more than I can stomach, but I guess that is the price you pay for being the most eligible bachelor in town. I can only imagine what he will have to do for Christmas.

Regarding Christmas, I have put word out that we will be having an informal pot-luck Christmas dinner at the café a few days before Christmas Eve for all those that want to come. Everyone is to bring a dish and a dessert, and it will be an interesting event. George asked if we would be serving lutefisk to celebrate the holiday. Knowing how well things went this past summer, I told him no. And to my surprise, he saluted me. Sorry, Queen Crab, but your lutefisk recipe will have to wait until we build another utility shed out back.

The Finstunes, however, have always had lutefisk for Christmas, whether we liked it or not. Grandpa Finstune saw to it that we did. And for Thanksgiving, we had turkey. For Easter, we had baked ham. It was that simple—and to offer anything else on these holidays was sacrilegious, bucking the ancient traditions that had been forged by my great, great, great grandparents: Oscar and Fiona Finstune. There were other sacred traditions such as cutting off the end of the Easter ham before putting it in the roaster—a tradition that had been passed down from Fiona Finstune to my great, great grandmother, Fanny Mae Finstune, who had passed it down to my great grandmother, Florence

Finstune, who had passed it down to my grandmother, Freda Finstune, who had passed it down to my mother. When my mother finally asked why all the Finstune women had been cutting off the ends of the Easter ham, no one knew the answer, other than the fact that that it had always been done that way. Upon further investigation, it was discovered that great, great, great grandma Fiona Finstune's pan was too small and she had no choice but to cut off the end of the Easter ham in order to make it fit in the pot.

That's how traditions got started in the Finstune family. It was all related to practicality—nothing more and nothing less—except for lutefisk, of course. When great, great, great grandfather Thaddeus Finstune bought his model T Ford back in 1914, he always walked around the front of the car, a tradition he had learned from his father, who had always walked around the old gray mare before going anywhere to see if she could still see. He did this by waving his hat in front of her face—and if she whinnied, they were good to go. Just how long that tradition lasted is a mystery, but somewhere between World War I and World War II, the Finstunes no longer found it necessary to walk in front of their automobiles before starting out.

As I pulled into our old neighborhood and rounded the corner, I could see Karl's silver Audi parked in the driveway. His Massachusetts license plate seemed to foreshadow what I believed to be his life ahead. In an odd way it was like a statement, a pilgrimage from the old school of Minnesota to the brave new world of Harvard and beyond—a world of tort and corporate and tax law with a prestigious New York law firm. Harvard—it was where the world of law began. Others would argue that Stanford or Yale or Columbia or NYU were just as comparable, but inwardly—secretly—I believed they all knew that, when it came to law, Harvard was the standard and had always been so.

Even though I had already been accepted to the prestigious university, I suddenly felt like an outsider, and the thought surprised me. I had done all the grunt work. I had paid my dues and passed the necessary exams and filled out the necessary applications and whatnots that accompanied my portfolio. I had nothing left to prove, and yet I found myself wanting, like a lost, insolent child groping in the dark at night for a point of reference. Harvard—that subject and law itself would be the topics of conversation at dinner. And what role I was to play in the discussion presented a certain uneasiness—and even dread. How was I going to be received? I had not spoken to my father since his birthday. To him, I had become a disappointment ever since I had chosen to attend Bullpen University rather than Harvard. I had not come back within their timeframe and had stayed well beyond my estimated time at arrival, remaining at the

helm of the café, much to my parent's amazement—and disappointment—or
so I sensed. So where was I on their approval rating scale? A six out of a possible
10 and sliding, I presumed. But if the truth be told, my own self-worth was
hanging in the balance, and it was found wanting. I was wanting their approval
above all else. Perhaps that was the dread I was encountering. I wondered what
my father would be like after our last meeting on board the Delta Queen.
Perhaps he would be extra cordial with Karl's girlfriend in the house—or so I
hoped. I sensed that she, whoever she was, would buffer any tension between
us—at least for the moment.

And how had my mother been receiving my precocious ambivalence
toward Harvard University? It was hard to say. Perhaps she was beginning to
see Bullpen University as a pre-requisite that would somehow justify my future
standing among her fellow colleagues.

I wondered.

Over the years she had changed, becoming more calculated and more
calloused. I called it self-defense, and I believed it came as the result of the
natural selection in the survival-of-the-fittest, dog-eat-dog world of corporate
attorneys.

But it was only a guess.

As I looked at the Massachusetts license plate on the silver Audi, my
attention suddenly turned to Karl—the good boy—the elder brother who had
never strayed far from the family farm or the family business, as we called it. He
was no-nonsense Karl. Cause and affect Karl. And exactly when he had shifted
from a playful adolescent into an incorrigible legalist remained a mystery. And
just where was it that we lost sight of each other as brothers? Was it after Gerty
died? Was she the one who had kept us tender towards each other? Was she the
one who had kept two stubborn wills from drifting apart with nothing more
than her prayers and her own strong and stubborn will to keep us together?

I wondered.

I wondered what kind of girlfriend Karl had brought home. If opposites
attract, I would expect to find her on the wild side—but not too wild—spirited
maybe—but not too spirited. If nothing else came from my journey home for
Thanksgiving, I would meet this "girlfriend," and perhaps through her, I would
catch some insight into what my brother was really like—or was becoming.

I was met at the door by a warm reception from my own father, and it
surprised me. Next to him stood Karl and his girlfriend. It almost seemed as if

he had been waiting to show off his newly found prize. She was fairly pleasant and reminded me in a small way of Hillary Clinton—only prettier.

My mother then came out from the kitchen and greeted me with a hug that also surprised me. Suddenly, we all looked like one big, happy family—and who was I to disagree?

I was quiet during most of the meal. I guess I didn't have much to say—not that anyone was asking about Bullpen—not that Bullpen was necessarily worth asking about when there were more pressing issues at hand. So, I simply sat there at the end of the table, playing with my fork as I had done years ago when I had it used to catapult peas across the room. . . . Better not try it here.

Please pass the turkey.

I always liked dressing, the kind you stuff inside the cavity of the turkey and let it bake in the oven, absorbing all the fat-free juices of the big bird. Did someone say Big Bird? Did someone say Elmo?

Please pass the turkey.

Oops . . . a little too much potatoes. Have you ever made a gravy bowl out of mashed potatoes? You just stick your spoon into the mashed potatoes and make a crater, a great big reservoir, and then you fill it with gravy—and if the gravy spills out, oops, you have a flood down below, and your green peas had better evacuate before drowning in the hot lava that is spewing from Mount Mashed Potato. Look out green peas! Evacuate into the dressing dormitory. You will be safe there, at least for the moment, until we figure out a way to stop the hot lava flow.

Please pass the turkey.

Invisible man here . . . Please pass the turkey . . . Anyone home? . . .

Houston, do you copy?

Wow . . . invisible man has just drifted out of his body, like an out-of-body experience, and is drifting free in space without any gravitational constraints.

Houston?

Wow. What a great view from above the dining room table.

Houston, I see the Sea of Tranquility next to the gravy bowl, and the Great Turkey Divide and the crater of Mount Mashed Potatoes. Over?

And now I am doing jumping jacks—weightless in space—then cartwheels, followed by a few summersaults and wintersaults.

Please pass the turkey.

Houston, do you read me. Is anyone home?

302

Please pass the turkey.

I suddenly came back into my body as two different conversations swirled about me. My father and my brother were discussing various options after graduating—what firm to accept and where to live and what type of law was the most profitable and would advance his career the fastest. Mother, on the other hand, was deeply engrossed in a legal issue with Hillary, who seemed to hang on her every word, as a newly elected representative would take advice from an elder statesman. From time to time my mother would smile politely and then stare deep into Hillary's eyes, as if trying to gather all of the facts before making any recommendations or summary judgments. Then she would pat her hand as if she understood the plight of the novice attorney. It was evident that the two were in sync, and I could not help but notice the all-too-apparent pleasure on my mother's face as she continued to console and advise her new pupil.

Finished with dinner, I left the table and went downstairs into the den to watch football. As the Dallas Cowboys were about ready to take the field, I looked outside the glass sliding doors that led to the patio. Outside was cold and dreary. The surrounding trees that led up to the adjacent golf course were bare to the bone. And as I looked out over the golf course from the warmth of the den, I saw the tiny flakes of snow begin to float down upon the tiered landscaping and gazebo where I remembered my parents hosting summer parties years ago. It seemed so desolate now in the bleak autumn afternoon. As I glanced back at the big screen TV, the excitement of the game was just getting underway with a full house of football fans filling the massive Cowboy stadium. Alone in the den, I somehow wished I was among them. Soon, bigger flakes started coming down in abundance, making everything clean and crisp and white. I stepped outside and simply held out my hand and felt them—snowflakes. They had traveled miles from above, like little messengers from heaven, to where they came to rest and melt upon my palm.

Suddenly, a floodgate of memories opens up and I am hanging on to my red plastic sled for dear life. My uncle's truck pulls Karl and me through the streets covered with freshly fallen snow from a major storm. Both Karl and I are careening carelessly out of control and loving it as my uncle swerves to and fro along the carpeted streets, sending our little sled fishtailing into the curbs, which act like bumpers at the bowling alley. It is like waterskiing with a single, frayed tow rope that dangles, then stretches like a long umbilical cord attached to the mother ship, careening this way and that while sputtering up chunks of fluffy white powder—fresh and cold and clean. My brother and I struggle to hold on while wiping the snow from our faces, searching for the familiar red taillights before us. . . . Then suddenly there are red flashing lights and sirens behind us. We have been pulled over by the Mounties—the suburban police.

In my neighborhood it was a major felony to be pulled over by the police. Our neighbor, Mr. Angst, had spent no fewer than five years in prison, according to Karl, for a simple parking violation. Five years—count them on your hand—five full years in the big house, with no running water or TV or electricity, and they would slide you your food through the bottom of the cell door. You had to slide your empty plate back when you were done. And there were no seconds on prison food, but who wanted seconds when it was prison food anyway? And hungry rats would nibble on your feet at night. And there was no toilet and no toilet paper . . .

If by some minor miracle you *did* get out of your solitary cell, you would have to chop rocks like a chain gang or make license plates with funny names. Five full years. You do the math.

I could see it now, fingerprints and photos in every post office in the nation. Wanted dead or alive—my Uncle Roy, Karl, and myself. How was a young kid ever going to live that down? It would be on my record for the rest of my life. I would not be able to attend college, much less law school. And what would become of our uncle? Thrown into the big house forever? Horror of horrors. I remember that deep, sinking feeling, watching him talk to the officers . . . . Then there were two more squad cars that pulled up beside the first one, making a total of three police cars. Count them—three. The problem had intensified, requiring the need for backup. And what would become of us when we got out after five years—foster homes? Would I ever see Karl again?

I remember praying hard, as hard as I ever had before in my life. "God spare us. God have mercy," was all that came to me in that moment of desperation. "God have mercy," was all I could remember from my Sunday School class . . .

And then the miraculous happened. My uncle had gotten off scot-free. It was only a warning—just a warning. . . . There was a God.

But, it was not so much the warning my uncle received that afternoon from the police, but the tongue-lashing my mother gave him that evening when she arrived home from London. Yes, that's what I remember most about the incident. She was in full battle array with her black power suit, having rolled up the driveway in her new Cadillac. She was to school him in the hierarchy of power, and he was to find his rightful position beneath her. She went on for what seemed like a full five minutes, thrashing him with accusations, including the full weight of their legal ramifications, and then she started lecturing him about the evils of foolishness and its consequences and long-term ramifications—especially when it came to insurance and the uninsured—and then more definitive reasoning as to why it was a stupid, foolish idea to pull us kids behind his truck and that he was to never do it again—ever.

Even as a kid I could sense this incident was more than just about pulling kids behind a truck in the snow-covered streets of our neighborhood. No, there was something else going on beyond her words. There was an undercurrent of vengeance, and it was as if the incident itself was only a catalyst—an excuse that provided my mother her long-awaited opportunity to pounce on him with all her fury. I had never seen my mother like that before, and it scared me.

Where my father was, I don't remember. But it was as if she had timed her attack in his absence and then would validate her side of the story later when there were no witnesses.

But there were witnesses that afternoon. There were Karl and I, and it seemed as if she had made sure that we were both present to hear her bitter accusations.

It was uncomfortable to see her try to belittle my uncle, but try as she might, he kept standing and kept looking at her while taking every blow. It was as if he was an experienced shortstop, fielding every ground ball that came to him with ease. He deflected blow after blow, accusation after accusation, without as much as a word. Not once did he cower. He simply let my mother rage on for what seemed like an eternity, and when she was through, he simply asked her a question of his own:

"Is that all, Martha?"

Suddenly, there was an odd silence between them. My mother looked exhausted and ugly—like a spent boxer who had thrown every punch she could muster.

"Is that all, Martha?" he asked again, breaking the silence between them.

The words seemed to baffle my mother. Even as a kid, I knew intuitively that she had been beaten—like the wind had been taken out of her sails. The legal world that she was so accustomed to, with all of its familiarity and parliamentary procedures and proper courtroom proceedings and written and unwritten rules of engagement, had suddenly been thrown out—dismissed. My uncle had refused to be drawn into her world—the corporate world where predictability and certain expectations were to be met—the proper etiquette among armies.

Like a soldier in the Revolutionary War, my uncle had refused to wear red and shoot in straight lines. He would not conform to the conventional military tactics that the Europeans had been so accustomed to at the time. No, he would not be bullied or boxed into the corner. He would choose to fight on his own terms.

"Is that all, Martha?" he asked again.

As if now boxed into a corner of her own, my mother resorted to the only thing she could do to save face—an emotional outburst. A tirade of anger and vengeance filled the room as she rallied one last volley.

"You just don't get it, do you?" she cried. "You never do. When are you going to grow up, Roy Finstune? When are you going to grow up?"

She had attacked his character. It was a legal strategy to fall back upon when all else failed—when the truth of your own logic had been exposed and dismantled, you had no other choice than to resort to defamation of character. Lawyers did it. Politicians did it. And now my mother had done it.

She then left the room slamming the door behind her, as if to gain further advantage by having the last unrebutted word. But it was grade-school stuff, and I knew it—even then. I knew intuitively the irony of the situation. She had stormed off mad, like little girls at recess when they didn't get their own way. But even as a kid, I sensed that my mother—the lawyer—had some growing up of her own to do.

I don't know who won the football game that afternoon. They say that turkey has tryptophan, something that makes you sleepy. And that's just what I did. I slept. And when I awakened in the den hours later, there was a blanket of freshly fallen snow about three inches deep that had covered the patio. I love snow, and the first snow of the year is always a pretty sight, but driving back in it and on it was nothing short of exhausting.

It was after one o'clock in the morning when I arrived back in Bullpen. Even though it was late, I was welcomed by the one-and-only street light, illuminating the fluffy white flakes that continued to blanket the sleepy little town. Tufts of cold cotton clung to the tree limbs like clusters of white grapes, then fell softly to the ground from their own collective weight. When I looked across the street, I could see the light in Jerome's apartment was still on. I thought about stopping by, just to talk to someone . . . but I didn't.

December 4 . . . It's Too Good to Be True

It is a bitterly cold day in Bullpen with a wind-chill reaching ten degrees below zero. Winter is here and in full fury. For us in Minnesota, it takes a while for our blood to thin and get used to the colder temperatures. I was told that when Bud Grant, former head coach of the Minnesota Vikings, found out that the blood of Eskimos was the same as the blood of any other human being, he took away the space heaters along the sidelines in the old outdoor Met Stadium. His thinking, apparently, was that if Eskimos could take it, so could the Minnesota Vikings. It is funny about cold, however. When spring comes around and the temperatures reach 40 degrees, it is considered a heat wave. I guess Bud Grant's reasoning was right—it is all about what you become accustomed to. If only his reasoning had been more successful on the field. Despite having gone to the Super Bowl four times under his tutelage, the winless Vikings came up empty-handed all four times—a thorn in most Minnesotans' side and a topic that is still taboo among the faithful.

With winter upon us and Christmas just around the corner, Bullpen has settled into a more festive character, and there is a big to-do about the annual Christmas play at church. With only a few weeks before Christmas, Mrs. Sherburne is in desperate need of a Joseph and a Mary. Apparently, she has most of the wise men covered, along with the lambs, but they are still in need of an innkeeper, a few angelic hosts, and, of course, Mary and Joseph. I suggested Abby and Edgar, but she told me she needed someone older. Besides, Edgar was a shepherd, and Abby was part of the angelic hosts—namely Gabriel—or Gabriella in this case. Christmas plays had always intrigued me with various interpretations of that fateful night. It was, of course, a play most church goers knew by heart, and, therefore, the director was under careful scrutiny, unable to stray too far from the original text. And that was the problem for most directors—everyone knew the play and knew the outcome and the end of the story, and to mess it up or to tell it differently would be blasphemous, incurring the wrath of the church counsel, the pastor, and the elder board—and not necessarily in that order. It was a thankless job, and to my surprise, given my

English and Literature major, I was not asked to direct it.

It is too good to be true . . .

I have enough things to do of my own, including the organization of the "all-town-bring-a-dish-and-a-dessert potluck dinner" at the café. I am still not sure what the word "potluck" means, and I can't seem to find it in my Lutheran-to-English Dictionary.

Not only will there be a potluck dinner at the café, but the Mayor—not wanting to miss an opportunity to capitalize on any good publicity event—wants to hold an all-town Christmas celebration along with it. He has suggested sleigh rides down Main Street, along with a few carolers who will start at the café and then migrate door to door, depending on the weather. I was told that they will end up back at the café and to make sure the piano would be in tune.

So, like the children's story "Stone Soup," all the townsfolk seem excited about the notion and are offering to contribute something to the all-town potluck dinner. Slater has a book of Christmas poetry he wants to read, and Millie wants to do a Christmas skit with Maynard. According to Jerome, they will be doing an excerpt from the movie *Driving Miss Daisy*, and Maynard will be driving an imaginary car while talking with Millie in the back seat. What that skit will have to do with Christmas remains a secret, but Millie seems pretty excited about the idea. This is all scheduled for Saturday, December 19, at 6:00 pm at the café.

Fellow bloggers, feel free to join us—just bring a dish (hot dish preferably) and a dessert to share.

December 6 . . . It Was Too Good To Be True

Mrs. Sherburne slipped on the ice this past week and broke her leg in more than one place. She will be laid up in the hospital for at least a week. So, whom do you suppose she thought of while en route to surgery?

I'll give you three guesses.

I guess not being asked to direct this year's Christmas play *was* too good to be true. But at least I can now say that I am a proud member of the Christmas Play Directors Guild.

"But I'm not a director. I'm a writer," I kept telling Mrs. Sherburne over the phone.

Have you ever tried to reason with a woman who has just been given an anesthetic and is incognizant of her own surroundings, making no sense at all while still pleading her case?

"But I am not a director; I am a writer," I kept telling her.

But as many times as I tried to convey that simple but often misunderstood concept, she couldn't see the difference—or at least that is what she told me—and being drugged to the hilt might have had some bearing on her impaired judgment. But as she continued to plead with me over the phone while being wheeled in a gurney into surgery, I suddenly found myself saying okay—against my better judgment.

"Okay," I told her, "but under one condition—under one condition," I kept saying.

And that's when the phone cut out.

That crafty Mrs. Sherburne.

Afterwards, I kicked myself for being such a sucker. I was sold a bill of goods, and I was resenting it. Not being asked to direct this year's Christmas play in the first place *was* too good to be true.

The play is at the Bullpen Lutheran Church on Sunday, December 20th, fellow bloggers, not that I expect any of you to be there.

Right now, I have to find a Mary and a Joseph before D-Day.

Any ideas?

December 7 . . . In Search of Wise Men

Thank you for your input, fellow bloggers. Far Quart suggested Maynard and Millie for Mary and Joseph, and I thought it was a joke at first—after all, who would put a couple of adults in a traditional children's play? Someone that's desperate, that's who. But does it have to be a children's play? Why not adults and kids?

The more I thought about it, the more I agreed with Far Quart. To date, we have Millie and Maynard as Mary and Joseph with Homer as the innkeeper. I asked George and the Boys if they wanted to be wise men, but they declined the offer, abdicating the role to someone far wiser, someone—according to George— who was known for drinking a lot of beer.

"Beer?" I asked him.

"Beer," he replied.

"What does beer have to do with wise men?" I asked him.

"Beer makes a man smarter," he replied.

I should have known he was up to something when the Boys began to smile.

"How so?" I asked him.

"It made Budweiser, didn't it?" Then he and the Boys broke out laughing.

"Great, that's just great." I said sarcastically. "Here I am trying to find people for the play, and all you can do is joke around."

Director's notes: Never ask wise guys if they want to be wise men.

December 8 . . . It's a Dog-Eat-Dog World

It's a dog-eat-dog world out there. Never before have I encountered so much drama over a drama. There is news going around town that I have simply given the role of Mary and Joseph to Millie and Maynard without an audition (which is true), thus showing favoritism (which is not true). Apparently, others had been interested in the afore-mentioned roles of Mary and Joseph and wanted an audition.

Auditions for a Christmas play?

Who in their right mind auditions for a Christmas play, unless you are performing some mega church-sponsored Christmas program with real goats and sheep and cows and pigs and camels and whatnots? But Bullpen? Auditions for Mary and Joseph in Bullpen?

How was I to know that Mary and Joseph were such coveted roles? To date, there have been no fewer than seven other interested parties—four of whom were elderly—that have inquired about the roles of Mary and Joseph and why they were not informed about the audition in the first place.

Auditions for a Christmas play?

In all fairness to the community and the world at large, we are holding auditions tomorrow night at seven o'clock at the cafe—and far be it from me to show favoritism and leave any of you fellow bloggers out of the mix.

December 9 . . .
Getting on with the Business at Hand

Congratulations to Millie and Maynard—especially Maynard, who recited the whole Gettysburg address from memory during his audition. The Bullpen Rotary, with the mayor presiding, declared the couple unanimous winners. Be it also noted and confirmed by the Honorable Mayor that a couple from Kasson, Minnesota, received an Honorable Mention. With no more honorables to mention, I hope that we can now safely proceed with rehearsals and get on with the business at hand.

December 10 . . . The Road Not Taken

Tonight we had our first official rehearsal at the church—and to my surprise, Maynard had memorized all of his lines. The only problem was he came to the practice wearing a Roman toga. I told him it looked like a toga, and he assured me that it was an ancient Hebrew garment. I disagreed. He disagreed and was determined to wear it the night of the performance. I told him that, if he did, he had better start learning Latin, because that is what he was conveying to the audience—not a humble Hebrew carpenter. He disagreed. I disagreed more. He threatened to leave. I told him to go ahead and make my day—I wasn't getting paid for this directing thing, anyway. As he started to walk off the stage, Millie intervened. She told Maynard that I was the director and that he was being stubborn. I agreed. She told me that I was being arrogant. Maynard agreed. I told the two of them that I was the director and that the director is the boss and that sometimes the boss has to be bossy.

"Well, you don't have to be bossy about being bossy," Millie told me.

I disagreed. Then Millie got miffed and threatened to leave with Maynard. Maynard then told Millie that she was being belligerent, and I agreed. Millie told Maynard that he was being his bullheaded self, and I agreed, and then she threatened to leave the Bullpen Café and find another job. I told her to go ahead—make my day—just try and find another job in Bullpen and see if I will give you a good referral.

Meanwhile the kids—and all the angelic hosts—were watching us grownups sparring like prizefighters. Their heads would turn back and forth as if watching a tennis match—first to Maynard, then to Millie, then to me—then back to Maynard, then Millie, then me. When I was about ready to strike the final blow, Abby asked us, "What would Jesus do?"

"What?" I asked.

"What would Jesus do?" she asked again.

"What does any of this have to do with Jesus!" I yelled.

"Because Christmas is about...Jesus?" She half asked and half stated, in a sweet angelic voice that you could barely hear above the clanking boiler pipes in the basement furnace.

Christmas . . . yes, it was all coming back to me now.

"Good point, Abby," I said. "Good point."

When I apologized to Maynard and told him he could wear his toga, a big smile broke out across his face. He then reached out and shook my hand, and suddenly there was peace on earth.

As a director, I will chalk the toga thing up to artistic interpretation, but as a fellow human being, I will chalk up tonight's rehearsal to the road not taken. I was this close to throwing in the towel and content to let the play go because of a toga—a simple, stupid toga. Thank God for Abby. Thank God I didn't go down that road.

Millie will stay on as a waitress, Maynard will get to wear his toga—and I? I took the road less traveled, and tonight at least, that has made all the difference . . .

December 14 . . . Poor Man's Lobster

I received an email from Mother yesterday, inviting me for Christmas Eve dinner. I wrote her back to tell her that I would be there. Karl will be in New York visiting his girlfriend's family over the holidays, and the only other relative that will be among us will be Katie, my mother's one-and-only younger sibling, whose husband, Troy, died over 10 years ago from an apparent heart attack. Where Katie was for Thanksgiving, I don't' know. All I know is that I am to pick Katie up at her home in Richfield on my way up from Bullpen and then take her back home after supper. Katie is a seventh grade schoolteacher and was always a mystery to me. I always thought it strange why a woman of her disposition never had children. Perhaps she had seen enough kids in her day to discourage her from having any of her own. At any rate, it will be a quiet Christmas Eve night at the Finstunes'.

Jerome, on the other hand, has informed me that all four of his kids will be coming to join him for Christmas on Christmas Eve—and he is bedside himself with joy. I, too, am happy for him and looking forward to meeting his kids. So, in preparation for their arrival, our weekly supply trip into Rochester included more than the usual staples that we get each week. He has a whole Cajun menu in store for his kids—and trying to find Cajun ingredients in Minnesota is like trying to find Polish sausage in Ireland or Holy Mackerel on Devil's Island. Imagine trying to find catfish or crawfish at your local grocery store in the middle of winter. Or how about okra or gumbo or smoked andouille or spicy Cajun sausage? Nice try, Bubba. Keep looking a little further down the aisle—like 1,500 miles south down the aisle, to be exact. And what about lobster and lobster sauce? Have any of you bloggers priced lobster lately? Yeah, it's like 20 times more expensive than codfish—a lobster substitute. So, I suggested that he get some "poor man's lobster" (cod soaked in butter) and just call it lobster.

But he just gave me the old trout eye—as if I had blasphemed the very essence of Cajun culinary art.

Hey, if poor man's lobster was okay for the Scandinavians, why wasn't it good enough for his Cajun kids? Were they too highfalutin?

I asked him that using that very word, "highfalutin." He gave me another trout eye, and I decided to hold my peace since it was, after all, the Christmas season.

For those of you who don't know the story behind "poor man's lobster," it all started with the Scandinavians hundreds of years ago who ate codfish with lots of butter and pretended that they were eating real lobster—high-off the-hog lobster. And for all practical purposes, they were—or at least thought they were. And all was right with the world for generations until Sven and Ole ruined everything by going and calling it "poor man's lobster." Until that point in time, Scandinavians everywhere thought that they were somebody special eating all that "lobster." And we were. We were more special than the Germans, the Irish, and the Polish because we were eating what we thought was the real thing. After all, nobody could remember what real lobster looked like after all those generations—until Sven and Ole met some real lobster fishermen who told them the truth of the matter. Being respectable Scandinavians, they decided to take it upon themselves to inform the rest of the Scandinavians of the lie that we had all been living for generations. And—horror of horrors—we discovered that not only were we not better than the Germans, the Irish, and the Polish, but we had to take a back seat to every other culture because we realized that we had been eating "poor man's lobster" all along—a term that defined your status in life. Doggone Ole and Sven (and Lena for that matter) for naming it "poor man's lobster" and giving all of the Scandinavians a "poor man's" complex.

You would have thought that somebody somewhere would have thought things through and left well enough alone, knowing full well the effects it would have on future generations.

But nobody did . . .

And so, the generational curse filtered down from father after father to son after son until someone had the audacity to call it what it was—codfish with a lot of butter. And suddenly, like Luther's Reformation, there was a great awakening in Norway and Sweden and even parts of Finland. Scandinavians everywhere began to think differently about themselves. Suddenly we were no less than the Germans or the Irish or even the Poles. No, we were not beneath any other culture. We were regular human beings, and, by golly, we were going to show the world just that.

315

It was that revelation, fellow bloggers, which changed the world, giving impetus to Leif Erickson and the Vikings, who now had the courage to venture into faraway lands where no Scandinavians had gone before—a little known fact that is suspiciously absent from most history books. I told Jerome that while in the freezer section of the grocery store. But to my surprise, he just shook his head and gave me another trout eye.

. . . At the end of the day, we never did find real lobster or real crawfish or real catfish or real poor man's lobster—but the one thing Jerome did find was smoked andouille, and you would have thought he had just won the lottery, whooping and hollering up and down aisle six after he found it.

But after paying for the expensive smoked andouille, Jerome had become, in fact, a "poor man."

And far be it from me to tell him that he was.

December 17 . . .
Remain Calm and Carry On

Tonight during rehearsal, we had a fire in the boys' bathroom. Apparently, one of the 13-year-old Ferguson brothers—Tommy to be exact—extinguished his Swisher Sweet cigar in the garbage can. About halfway through rehearsal, just when the heavenly host was about to come upon Mary, the trash can in the boys' bathroom burst into flames. Had it not been for Terry, Tommy's younger brother (who had found it while trying to find a quiet place to smoke his own cigar—or so the rumors have it), the church might have gone up in smoke—not to mention the play. Terry, like any normal ten-year-old, got scared when he saw the flames and ran out into the hallway screaming "fire" and yelling that we that were all going to "burn alive"—a rather disturbing thought for most kids. Since Bullpen has no fire department, Millie called the Bullpen volunteer fire and rescue workers—the First Responders. With kids screaming and wailing and running around in fear, Maynard and I did the best we could to herd them out into the bitter cold cemetery—which, I had to admit, was not the best place to go after being told we were all going to die. But hindsight is always 20/20. During the whole chaotic procession, all I could think about was Queen Elizabeth and her royal disposition: Remain calm and carry on—at least until the First Responders arrived. To calm the little kids, Maynard suggested we start singing "Kumbaya," and, sure enough, the singing seemed to calm their fears.

Lenny was the first to make it on the scene, dressed in his dirty dungarees. The rest of the volunteers arrived shortly thereafter with pick axes and shovels—including the mayor. But by that time, Lenny had doused the fire with water. Then—except for the shivers, the smoke smell, the partially charred wall next to the trashcan, and the skittish kids crying out for their parents and hoping they wouldn't die—all was back to normal.

I told Tommy that, if I ever caught him smoking again, I would stuff a Swisher Sweet up his nose and smoke it myself—and I meant it. Needless to say, I cut rehearsal short to allow the bathroom fans to air out the basement and the sanctuary and the kitchen and the hallway and the classrooms and the . . .

December 18 . . .
Captain Morgan's Puerto Rican Rum Wings

It's Friday night here at the church, and although most of the smoke smell from last night's episode is gone, the aftermath still lingers on. Tonight I don't know if we will have enough props for Sunday's performance. Not that it really matters. Not that we are going to have anything authentically Hebrew around here anyway now that Maynard has set the new standard in Christmas play attire with his Roman toga.

Hail citizen! Can you render me a room at the inn?

Tonight's rehearsal was long. The kids didn't have their lines down, and they were giggly, silly, tired, and out of control. With ten other things to deal with, I assigned Maynard to crowd control, which only made matters worse. Just picture for a moment an ancient Roman senator orating to his fellow Romans about the effects of bad behavior, reciting an obscure postal code regulation while pleasure-seeking plebeians are making a mad dash for the Coliseum.

Welcome to my world.

Places everybody . . .

Then picture five-year-old Angela Fleming fluttering about in her angel wings that were cut out of an old Captain Morgan's Puerto Rican rum box. What Christmas play would be complete without Puerto Rican rum wings, anyway?

And to think I didn't think we had enough props . . .

December 19 . . . Make it a Good One

The final rehearsal was another disaster, and I'm feeling as if we really need to cancel this whole Christmas play thing. Whose idea was this, anyway? Not mine. Mrs. Sherburne assured me that all would go well, which was easy for her to say, sitting on the sideline in her wheelchair. I glanced over at her from time to time and could tell she was doing everything in her power not to make any suggestions for fear that she might be called upon to actually help out . . . that crafty Mrs. Sherburne.

She did, however, suggest we pray at the end of our rehearsal, and it seemed like a good idea because God knows we needed it and will need it tomorrow. She asked that we all hold hands with the person next to us, and we did. I reached out for Tommy Ferguson's hand—I thought I smelled cigar smoke. On the other side of me was Angela Fleming, standing there as angelic as possible with her Captain Morgan Puerto Rican rum wings that I had forgotten to paint before tomorrow's performance (note to self not to forget to bring white spray paint). And there I was, standing in the middle, between the sinner—Tommy Ferguson, the lowly shepherd boy—and the saint—Angela, one of the angelic hosts.

As Mrs. Sherburne started praying for us, Tommy was looking about for anyone else who was looking about, and he caught his brother Terry's eyes. He snickered at his brother, and his brother snickered back, as if mocking the whole event. When he saw that I saw him, he ducked his head down, looking as devout as possible. Angela, on the other hand, was squeezing my hand and squinting hard, as if praying in earnest.

I don't remember much of what Mrs. Sherburne said that afternoon in her prayers. All I could remember was the line from the movie *Hoosiers* when coach Norman Dale, played by Gene Hackman, tells one of his players by the name of Buddy to pray for the team before one of their biggest games of the season—and just before Buddy starts, Coach Dale tells him to "make it a good one."

"Make it a good one, Mrs. Sherburne," I kept thinking to myself . . . "Make it a good one . . ."

Later That Night . . . Bullpen's First Annual Christmas Dinner

It was the all-town pot-luck Christmas Dinner at the café tonight.

I had almost forgotten about it. Since working on the play, I had devoted little time to the event, leaving it up to Melissa and Jerome to do the organizing and decorating. After a long day of rehearsal, I came home "plum tuckered out and a little discouraged," but after seeing all of the Christmas decorations, I was revived and feeling all Christmassy again. Every corner was covered with quaintly decorated tables and accompanying chairs. In the center of each table was a simple white candle placed in a brown paper lunch bag and weighted down by sand. In spite of their tacky simplicity, the brown-bag lights gave off an aura of warmth on such a bitterly cold evening. A flocked tree stood at attention beside the cash register, with an angel perched from the highest branch, blinking effortlessly like a warning light on top of a tall corporate building. I later heard Jerome affectionately refer to her as "Our Lady of Blink." Tinsel was draped across the smiling moose, while the flirtatious little lure that hung from the mounted muskie's mouth twinkled from the lights of the paper bag candles. On top of the old upright piano lay a velvet red runner and a catechism of large pine-scented candles that cast mesmerizing shadows in their own reflective pools of melted wax. Even the toy train that ran around the room above the door was dressed for the special occasion, carrying little sprigs of holly and ivy.

Suddenly Bing Crosby's "White Christmas" began to play on the nearby CD—and I was missing Karen. We had watched the movie *White Christmas* together no fewer than ten times over the years at the university, and we had watched *It's a Wonderful Life* with Jimmy Stewart and Donna Reed no fewer than five. I found myself suddenly feeling melancholy when Jerome came out of the kitchen wearing a red and white Santa's hat. I told him that he did a great job decorating the café, and he told me he had help from his elves.

As people arrived in their festive Christmas attire, they brought a plethora of different Scandinavian, German, and Polish foods: krumkake, rosettes, lefse, flatbread, julekake, pickled herring, lutefisk, and Swedish meatballs. And, yes, Weiner schnitzel, sauerkraut, polish sausage, and a honey-baked ham. Oh, and potato dumplings, mashed potatoes, au gratin potatoes, green beans, salads, baked beans, corn muffins, casseroles with French-fried onions and mushroom soup, corn, and more lefse, and flatbread and chocolate bars and cherry cheese cakes and more lefse, and on and on they came, each member of the town carrying his or her own prized possession to add to the endless serving tables of food. It was like the first Thanksgiving at Plymouth Rock, with a line that stretched out beyond the door. Townsfolk waited patiently in the cold, holding their cherished possessions tightly to their chests, inching ever forward while others made room in the crowded café. Little girls in Norwegian sweaters huddled in the corner by the piano, while little boys in bib overalls congregated on the other end, just out of eyesight of their parents.

There was electricity in the air as the well-anticipated evening was about to begin. Voices were rising higher and higher, trying to be heard above the festive air that was now growing to a crescendo, but no one seemed to care. They only talked louder, laughed louder, and greeted each other louder.

As the clock struck seven, Slater Gray, dressed in a blue cardigan sweater and red "uffda" socks, looked my way as if asking me to start the event. And I was lost in thought, seeing all of the familiar faces dressed for such a special occasion. I yelled across the room to get everyone's attention, but to no avail. Then Jerome, seizing the moment, let out a shrieking whistle—the same shrieking whistle he had used at Halloween during his theatrical rendition of the song "When Crawdad Daddy Met Polecat Momma." Soon the room became so still that you could hear the sound of the hot water heater downstairs. Everyone stood there in amazement, baffled by how the human body could defy the physics of anatomy and produce such a shrill.

Then Jerome, puffing his chest out like a proud seafaring captain, announced that the Reverend would be saying grace and asked for everyone to take off their hats and bow their heads. The pastor seemed surprised and caught off guard by Jerome's announcement, but he quickly rose to the occasion, nodding definitively. He then bowed his head and began to pray:

Dear Lord:

We have gathered here on this bitter cold night to enjoy each other's company as we celebrate the reason for this Christmas season: the birth of your Son Jesus Christ, who was born in a manger to save the world from our sins. We thank you for coming to earth and showing us the way. We thank you for dying on a cross for us that we may know heaven and not hell. To the one who was and is and is to come, bless our food and fellowship this night. In Jesus' name we pray. Amen

As if on cue, we all said, "Amen," and like the end of the national anthem sung at a major sporting event, Jerome—still beaming like a proud seafaring captain—took off his Santa hat, twirled it high in the air, and yelled, "Let's eat!"

And eat we did, with two lines forming on both sides of the serving table. Both young and old took their own plates and served themselves, eyeing each dish and trying as best they could to take a little of everything. Young and old, rich and poor, male and female all moved about together through the lines as one disseminating mass of humanity. One toothless old man I had never seen before came wearing an old, beat up trench coat, barely warm enough for the early autumn in Minnesota, much less the bitterness of winter. He reminded me of Clarence Oddbody, the angel in the movie *It's a Wonderful Life*, only more beaten down by what appeared to be the bitter cold and struggles of life. He shuffled along the table and ate as he went along, stuffing food into his mouth like a starved man. As I made my way to introduce myself, I was interrupted by Miss Maddie, who had come with Lenny and his wife. We talked briefly, and then the mayor cut in with a Christmas greeting of his own. By the time I finished talking, I went to look for the old man again, who had now moved closer to the dessert table. As I began to move towards him, I was again interrupted.

And before I knew it, I was standing in the food line with Miss Maddie and Lenny and his wife. Lenny began to share the story of my driving a stick shift for the first time around his barn and then coasting into town in my uncle's truck the first day he met me.

It was that way the rest of the night as I heard story after story about my uncle and the café and the stories behind all of the knickknacks and behind the walls themselves. If only walls could talk, Lenny would say again and again . . . if only walls could talk.

When all were finished, Slater Gray read from his book of homemade poetry. The Boys and George politely refrained from their sarcastic comments, under the careful scrutiny of George's wife. It was as if George had been briefed at home not to ruin Slater's poetic moment—and it was all he and the Boys could do not to giggle their way through the "thee's" and the "thou's" of Slater's artistic rhetoric of "twinkling lights and starry, starry nights."

I am not sure what Slater meant to say in all his poetic rhetoric, but it sounded cool, and when he was done, the people applauded even if they didn't understand a word he was saying. Then Millie and Jerome did their *Driving Miss Daisy* skit, and everyone laughed—especially Jerome—even though the skit made no sense at all and had nothing to do with Christmas or the movie itself.

Then there were songs—lots of Christmas songs hammered out of the old piano by the church organist who did the best she could with the untuned, toothless piano. Except for the fact that we were all singing the well-known carols and drowned out the dissonant sounds of the missing ivory keys, all would have been lost. After "Joy to the World" and "Hark the Harold Angles Sing," we ended with "Silent Night"—but the café was anything but silent that night.

It was after midnight by the time the last of the patrons had left. The last to leave were Homer, Millie, and Maynard, who drove Homer home in the cold. As I stood by the piano where, only an hour before, people had pressed up against it singing Christmas carols, I thought of the old man who looked like Clarence Oddbody. Was he an angel?

Years ago, I had heard our minister talk about a passage of scripture in the Bible that speaks of entertaining angels unaware and I always remembered it. Maybe he was an angel, or maybe he was someone who had nowhere else to spend the night and simply wanted to get out of the cold. I don't know. But afterwards, I couldn't help thinking about George Bailey and his guardian angel, Clarence Oddbody, who jumped in the river to save George from taking his own life. It was an odd paradox of sorts—George Bailey saved his own life by saving another man's life. I guess life is like that at times. At a time when we expect it the least—and need it the most—heaven sends an angel, and by the grace of God we jump in to save him or her—and in the process, we save ourselves.

As I sat beside the piano watching the last of the large pine-scented candles cast their mesmerizing shadows in the reflective pools of melted wax, I thought about the classic Christmas movie *It's a Wonderful Life*. I thought about George Bailey, who had been given a chance to see what life in Bedford Falls would have been like had he never been born. And suddenly I thought of my Uncle Roy and wondered what Bullpen would have been like had he decided not to stay.

December 21 . . .
The Christmas Play from Hell

We performed the annual Christmas play at the church tonight, and if there were any theater critics among the congregation, they would have had a field day. George called it a "Toga Party with a Christmas Twist," referring, of course, to Maynard's Latin attire. My first clue that things were heading south for the evening was when the white spray paint—which was supposed to cover Angela's Captain Morgan's rum wings—did nothing more than highlight the Captain with a milk-white, angelic aura with the first coat of paint. In the hubbub of trying to get everything ready for the performance, I forgot to apply the much-needed second coat (and third and fourth) to completely cover the Captain. When Angela went out to proclaim the glory of the Lord to the Virgin Mary and to announce how the Holy Spirit was to come upon her so that she would soon be with child, Captain Morgan was right there with her to celebrate the good news.

Then Maynard forgot his lines—which wasn't so bad in and of itself, because anyone can forget a line or two, but when Maynard gets nervous, he resorts to citing US postal regulations, whether they are applicable or not. I don't believe that any innkeeper has ever heard either the directions to correctly apply for a change of address with what would have been the Roman government at that time or the words of Section 508 of the Recipient Services, found in the USPS Regulation handbook.

And the hand bell choir? Did I tell you we had a hand bell choir? Yes, Thelma Torgelson and her hand bell choir accompanied the shepherds to the stable by playing "Hark the Herald Angles Sing." The only problem was that one of the bell ringers, by the name of Rose Clifford, was out ill, and so every fifth note was missing. In lieu of the butchered song, the shepherds tried as best they could to keep in step with the clanging discourse, jerking back and forth like a bevy of student drivers learning how to drive a stick shift.

And then there was Oscar Flomm, who decided to get up in the middle of the play to take a smoke. That wasn't so bad, but the fact that he asked all those around him if they had seen where he had dropped his cigarettes was just a little distracting. Didn't Oscar get the "all-church-no-smoking-at-least-not-during-the-Christmas-play" memo? Apparently not.

And last, but not least, were the Christmas cows—played by little toddlers from the nursery. After their cow song, they were herded off stage. But one of the misguided cows decided to exit in the other direction and tripped over the extension cord that lit the Christmas tree. Had the cow stopped, all would have been okay, but like a stubborn mule in search of greener pastures, this cow kept moving, taking the tree and all of its bulbs with him. Before the toddler police could stop him, the tree and all of its lights came crashing down, blowing the main circuit. When the little kids began screaming, Maynard quickly led us in another rendition of "Kumbaya," as he had done in the cemetery only days before—only this time it seemed to have an adverse effect upon the kids and only made them cry harder. After the same verse of "Kumbaya" had been sung for the ninth time in the midst of all the screaming pandemonium, the janitor finally located the fuse box and flipped on the lights, and suddenly—suddenly—there was peace on earth.

When it was all over, the pastor came over and told me it was the most unusual Christmas play he had ever attended. I quickly reached out and shook his hand as a preemptive strike to let him know that I took his comment as a compliment in spite of his surprised demeanor. And while shaking it hard, I overheard a couple of the ladies telling each other that I had done the best I could. Yes, Charles "did-the-best-he-could" Finstune had directed an amazing performance: unparalleled, unprecedented, and, yes—"unusual."

December 22 . . .

The Trucker from New Hampshire

Thanks for all your comments about our "unusual" Christmas play, fellow bloggers. One of you, by the name of Cora, was a former school teacher in a small town in Iowa and had put on numerous Christmas plays at her local church, one of which was more unusual than mine. As a director, she once made the mistake of using real sheep and cows and a stubborn mule. Enough said.

I am spending Christmas Eve with my parents and then coming back to Bullpen after dinner. I would have stayed the night, but they were leaving for Hawaii on Christmas day. I am guessing they booked the flight when they heard that Karl would not be coming home. He will be spending Christmas with his girlfriend, and when my mother told me so, you could tell there was a little disappointment in her voice. I will be picking up my aunt that afternoon and then driving her back home that evening. It will be a little awkward being the only sibling there, but my aunt will be a welcome addition.

Jerome's kids are coming on Christmas Day and will stay for a week. He is more excited each day. He marks off their expected date of arrival with a pencil on a homemade calendar above the grill and has it all planned out with each day's events scheduled down to the last detail. He is a new man, Jerome. He is *"the man,"* I tell him. He is Dad personified and proud of it all. Now, I don't know what all he has planned for food, but the one thing I do know is that lutefisk will not be part of it.

This afternoon, however, we had a Christmas tree hauler by the name of Pete Stottert join us for lunch. He is a trucker for a company out in New Hampshire that hauls Christmas trees all over the country. He reads *News from the Bullpen Café* on a regular basis and was dropping trees off in Rochester, so he decided to pay us a visit. He is a spirited trucker with a sense of humor and a slight Canadian accent, aye? And now he has a few of his trucking buddies hooked on the site, as well as his wife. He arrived late in the afternoon—

just before we were getting ready to close up. Homer was the only one there besides Jerome and me, and he shook our hands like a true lumberjack. Then he asked Homer if he could play a game of Crokinole—apparently a big game in Canada, where he had grown up.

It's funny, but as he sat at the table, he talked as if he knew everyone in town. He asked if George and the Boys were around. I told him that they had left about an hour earlier, along with Millie. Then he went on to talk about *News from the Bullpen Café*, much to the surprise of Homer, who has no computer and no Internet and had no idea what he was talking about. I did not elaborate or expound on the subject, thinking that, if the town ever did find out, they might deem themselves to be famous and act accordingly.

We had a great visit that afternoon. And when he was ready to leave, Jerome slipped out and then came back and gave Pete a jar of Stinky Bait with a red Christmas ribbon wrapped around it. He told Pete that it would keep for months in a sealed jar—as if it could get any worse. Pete thanked him and told him he would try it out next spring. Then just before he left, he asked Jerome if he would sing "When Crawdad Daddy Met Polecat Momma."

And Jerome did.

As I watched Pete's flatbed semi pull away late that afternoon, hauling the remainder of his Christmas trees, I wondered how many others of you are out there like Pete. I wondered about those of you from New Hampshire and California and Texas and Alaska and Florida and Louisiana and Washington and Canada and New York. And suddenly I wondered about Mary from New York. Hope you are doing well, Mary. I haven't heard from you since this summer.

And a Merry Christmas to all of you, fellow bloggers. If you are ever in the vicinity of Bullpen, please stop by for a free cup of coffee and a complimentary jar of Stinky Bait. It makes a great stocking stuffer.

December 24 . . . Aunt Katie

I picked up my aunt this afternoon in Richfield, a southern suburb of Minneapolis, and took her with me to celebrate Christmas with my parents—a tradition we had done ever since her husband had died over 10 years ago. When I met her at the door, she was holding a large paper bag full of Christmas gifts and smiled politely when I offered to carry them. Aunt Katie had always been polite, but distant.

I drove the Toyota, and it still had a faint smell of tequila from the heater. I had thought of driving my uncle's truck but felt it might be a little presumptuous knowing that my uncle had been a taboo subject while I was growing up.

Our trip was a fairly short ride, and getting my aunt to talk was a little more than challenging. At first we talked about the cold weather and how the school year was going. Knowing she was a schoolteacher, I asked her if she had any students in particular that she remembered. She smiled politely but never responded, as if I asked the wrong question. When I asked her about my Uncle Roy, she seemed hesitant and redirected the subject, beginning with the weather. When I glanced over and saw her, it looked as if she was wanting to say something about him but decided not to for reasons that were a mystery to me.

Seeing her sitting there in the front seat holding the gift bag on her lap, I thought that she suddenly looked older than I remembered. And although she was three years younger than my mother, she looked worn and tired, as if dealing with unruly seventh graders had finally taken its toll.

When we arrived at home, my mother was the first to greet us at the front door. She hugged her sister cordially, but with a slightly condescending air, which I had never noticed before. It was as if my aunt seemed to cower in her presence, the way a pack dog would acknowledge the alpha dog. It was then I was hit by the recognition of a hierarchy of power and position that I had never noticed before. My aunt lived in a simple rambler in a nondescript neighborhood. We lived right on a golf course in a large, tutor-style home.

My mother was an attorney. My aunt was a simple schoolteacher. And as my mother hugged her from a politically correct position, it was almost as if I could sense my mother pity her sister and her lot in life.

"Oh, so good to see you, Katie," she cried.

She then gave me a hug and asked me how the road conditions were coming up from the south, carefully avoiding the word "Bullpen."

"Fine," I told her. "The roads were fine."

My father then came to greet us, wearing his traditional red Christmas sweater, and, like my mother, he too carefully avoided the word "Bullpen."

It was shortly afterwards that all four of us sat down at the dining room table for our traditional Christmas Eve dinner. As we passed our food, the conversation was stilted and forced. Like a good hostess, however, my mother tried to establish some kind of topic in which we would all be engaged—and having failed in her attempts, she simply smiled politely while my father then took his turn, getting my aunt to finally open up about the politics within her school district. Having exhausted all of the school politics, he then turned to me, and like my mother, he was careful to avoid saying the "Bullpen" word. A skilled attorney, my father smoothly steered far away from the topic of controversy, and I was careful not to bring it up. When an uncomfortable silence filled the room, I suddenly sensed that the inevitable was coming. It was the elephant in the room that no one had been willing to address.

'So, have you contacted Harvard admissions to let them know you are coming next fall?' my mother finally asked.

"Not yet," I said.

"Well, don't you think you need to?" she replied.

My mother pretended as if the question was of no significance, then asked my aunt if she wanted more potatoes. But her senses were acutely tuned to my reply.

"Yes," I found myself saying, and suddenly it was as if the tension in the room had lifted.

We opened gifts after supper, as was our usual Christmas tradition. I gave my father a golf shirt for Hawaii and a blue cardigan sweater. I gave my mother a new set of Titleist golf balls, a pair of leather gloves, and scarf with matching hat. I gave my aunt a bracelet. I received my usual gift certificate to Borders bookstore.

I don't remember what my aunt gave them or received from them, but when our Christmas obligations had been mutually fulfilled, my aunt politely thanked us for our gifts and then placed them carefully in the same bag that she had used to bring hers; shortly thereafter, we said our good-byes and left.

The drive to my aunt's home that night was as uneventful as the trip to my parent's home earlier that afternoon. There was the same emptiness, but for the first time I suddenly saw a brokenness—a certain sadness—in my aunt, something that I had never seen growing up. As we turned down the street towards her home, she suddenly thanked me for picking her up and making her feel special.

I was taken aback by the word "special," for I didn't think I had done anything to warrant such a response. Then she continued.

"You asked me earlier about your Uncle Roy."

"Yes," I replied.

She seemed to hesitate, and I sensed that she was trying to convey something of greater importance.

"I know you've have taken over his café in Bullpen, but—"

Her voice suddenly stopped and she began rubbing the backs of her hands as if deliberating about what to say next.

"But I think there is something you need to know about your uncle," she said at last.

"What?" I asked.

"Your mother loved him."

Later that Night . . . The Drive Home

As I drove back to Bullpen that night, my mind was racing about thoughts of my mother and my uncle. I had always thought of Aunt Katie as a discrete woman, so it struck me odd that she would tell me such a thing. But she did.

My mother and Uncle Roy had actually been dating when my uncle was attending Harvard Law School. According to my aunt, my mother had started to make wedding plans, believing there would be a day when he would ask her to marry him.

But he never did.

330

Instead, he found himself on a blue highway in the middle of nowhere, in a town so small that it wasn't even found on most state maps. Yes, he had found his wife in Bullpen, and in doing so, he had crushed all of my mother's hopes of any kind of life together. She was devastated when she heard the news, and according to my aunt, she talked to no one for weeks, harboring resentment and hatred and sorrow deep within her heart, often crying late into the night—refusing anyone's comfort, especially that of her own sister. No one could get through to her, she told me. Suddenly, I thought of Miss Havisham in the book *Great Expectations,* by Charles Dickens—and for the first time in my life, I began to see my mother in a light that I had never imagined nor understood. It was as if I was beginning to feel a certain sense of sympathy for her—something I believe she would have interpreted as pity. My mother hated pity. Pity was for the weak, and my mother was always so strong—or had tried so hard to be. Perhaps it was the veneer she had come to fabricate to protect herself from the vulnerability of having lost at love.

"But where did my father come in?" I asked my aunt.

She told me in her own words that she thought my mother married my father "on the rebound," as if trying to get even with Uncle Roy. It was a quick wedding, and, according to my aunt, my father had always loved her and had agreed to marry her on the spot. Nine months later Karl was born—as if she needed a child to solidify her determination to break free from my uncle. According to my aunt, my mother married my father for all the wrong reasons, and when Uncle Roy moved to Bullpen, the pain of his memory only worsened.

"Was my father aware of all of this?" I asked

"Yes," she said. "But your father had always loved your mother and tried hard to prove it by becoming one of the best lawyers in the Twin Cities. Performance was what he thought would win her over. And performance was what he pursued, my aunt went on to say—spending long nights studying for the bar exam and then spending even longer nights at the firm, until he rose to the top of his profession—as did my mother.

As I drove down the highway that night, I began to see the issues surrounding our family more clearly now. I was beginning to understand all of the few, awkward times Uncle Roy would come to visit us during the holidays.

As I watched the mesmerizing white lines pass along the highway, heading towards home, I felt a deep sorrow for my mother—and, for the first time in my life, I felt an even deeper sorrow for my father.

December 25 . . . Christmas Day

I over slept this morning, right past the Christmas morning service. In a way, I was disappointed, but in a way, I felt relieved. I had been up most of the night going through my uncle's notes and files, but I had found nothing that indicated any kind of affection toward my mother. What my aunt had said last night, however, made sense. It was as if the last piece of the puzzle had been put into place and the big picture was suddenly all too apparent.

The café had been closed for the holidays, and I went downstairs to make myself a cup of coffee. As I sat drinking it, Jerome came bursting through the door and asked if he could take my Toyota to pick up his kids at the airport. He looked desperate and I told him to go ahead and take it. He told me that his oldest son was supposed to arrive on an earlier flight, wait until the rest of his siblings arrived at the airport, rent a car, and then take them all to Bullpen. That was the plan, until he found out that the car rental would not take his credit card. When his kids did not show up early this morning as planned, Jerome began making some calls from the café. He finally reached his oldest daughter on her cell phone, and she explained the situation.

He shot straight into the kitchen, asking me what he should bring along in the car, knowing that his kids would be hungry from their long flights. I told him to take the rest of the day-old donuts and whatever else he could find.

As he scurried about gathering various food items and stuffing them into a paper grocery bag, I began to see Jerome in a different light—one that I had never seen before: the role of a father. It was as if he was proud of the fact that he was being called upon to help in a time of need. I sensed that there had been few occasions which had allowed him to do so before—perhaps it was because he was the one, more often than not, who needed help. It was as if he was trying to prove to himself, his kids, and the rest of the world that he was the one his kids could count on in the clutch—like a backstop in baseball that keeps the ball in play despite foul balls, wild pitches, and other unforeseen events. Parents were supposed to be like that—backstops—especially dads. Dads were the ones kids were supposed to count on when the ball got loose and out of play. It was a God-given unction and one that had suddenly been awakened deep within the recesses of his very being—and he was proud of it. And so was I.

"Do you think that is enough?" he said, showing me a grocery bag stuffed to the gills with food while looking at me like a kid at a candy store, desperate for some kind of affirmation.

"Yeah," I found myself saying. "That ought to do it."

He nodded and was out the door.

He arrived later that afternoon with his kids and the same grocery bag stuffed to the gills with food. They hadn't eaten anything. I was to find out later they didn't have to. Jerome took them to Denny's for lunch.

When he introduced me to his children, he was beaming with delight, and his hands could not stop patting or rubbing each one on the back or on their heads. They were cute kids, all of them. Starting with the oldest, he introduced his eighteen-year-old son, his sixteen-year-old daughter, his ten-year-old daughter, and the mischievous one—his seven-year-old son—a spitting image of Jerome himself. On his command, they all politely shook my hand, as if it had been rehearsed, and I told them what a good man their father was and the best cook in the county. They all smiled—especially Jerome. I told them that I was looking forward to their time with us this week.

And with the greetings out of the way, Jerome pushed me aside and went straight to the kitchen, with his kids following him like the Pied Piper. It was there he began to show them all of the cupboards, pots and pans, spoons, ladles, spatulas, and strainers—describing them all with great detail and explaining how important each of them was to the café. And when he was done, they nodded, as if impressed, except for the seven-year-old, who grabbed the spatula and started beating his older sister on her buttocks.

When Jerome started shelling out disciplinary actions, I felt it best to leave family matters well enough alone and went upstairs to my uncle's apartment.

I practiced the fiddle for a while, since I had not done so since our group had disbanded for the holidays. Then I grabbed one of my uncle's novels and started reading it on the sofa but soon fell asleep.

When I awakened, it was after eight pm. There was a knock on the door, and when I opened it, I found Jerome standing there in his dirty apron telling me supper was ready.

Surprised, I went downstairs to a candle light dinner. His oldest son stood by my chair as if I was the guest of honor. It was a feast, and it was served on the ordinary plates that sparkled in the candlelight, giving the room a strange elegance. There were laughter and teasing and stories that only family members knew.

It was late by the time all the dishes were done and Jerome and his family had gone. As I walked up the stairway that led into my uncle's apartment, I noticed a gift wrapped in newspaper and a pretty red ribbon sitting on one of the steps. I took it and went inside my apartment, grabbed my winter coat, and stepped out onto the balcony overlooking Main Street. I looked out at the sleepy little town and then across the street to Jerome's apartment. Through the window, I could see his family moving about with pillows and sleeping bags and makeshift beds, getting ready for the night. Suddenly the mischievous one started hitting his sister with a pillow. She retaliated. Soon mayhem erupted and all of Jerome's kids were smacking each other with pillows. Jerome finally restored order, then drew the shades, and moments later the lights went out.

I then opened the gift. It was tree ornament—car dice—with a note that read: "Thanks Charlie, for not giving up on me and giving me a chance. God Bless you and Merry Christmas . . . your friend, Jerome Boatman."

I don't know why I got all teary eyed that night holding a simple two-dollar-and-twenty-nine-cent tree ornament with the price tag still on the bottom—but I did. Car dice. It was a symbolic reminder of the humble beginnings that he had come from when we first met at the restaurant in Zumbrota, Minnesota. From that time until today, he had gone from living alone in a 1983 Chevy Impala to living in his own apartment with his own family.

As I held the string that held the dice, I wondered how many other Jeromes were out there out there that were misunderstood and needed another chance in life—or guidance or direction or affirmation or just forgiveness.

I then wondered what it was that had kept me from driving away after our interview at the restaurant that day in June. And the thought of almost not coming back to hire him scared me. What if I hadn't come back to hire him? What if I hadn't given him a chance? Was it simply the roll of the dice, or was it the hand of God that made me go back that day? As I found my perspective on life beginning to change, I thought about the blog I had written in August and how hard I was on Jesse Jackson. Perhaps we don't have the right to judge a man until we have walked a mile in his shoes or slept a night in his car.

Houston, do you copy?

Then it started to snow. Gentle, velvety flakes began to carpet the dirty street below with a milk white aura, as if covering the shame of a broken world. It was like grace falling from heaven that made all things clean and new. It was Christmas. It was Emanuel. It was God with us.

I had never really thought much about the meaning of Christmas or Jesus' birth. It had come with presents and decorated trees and time off from school. I had listened to the Christmas Eve sermons year after year and had lit my candle along with all the other members of our congregation. I had sung "Silent Night" along with everyone else as we slowly walked out of the sanctuary. But it had never gone any deeper than that. Its significance was nothing more than a tradition with its origin understood but never felt—never experienced. But standing there on the balcony, looking upwards and feeling the cold, melting flakes across my face—I felt as if something inside me began to awaken.

I don't know why, but I found myself saying, "Thank you, Lord. Thank you for not giving up on me as well."

December 31 . . .
New Year's Eve at Miss Maddie's

Miss Maddie had invited me, along with Jerome and his kids, to a New Year's Eve dinner. It was complete with mashed potatoes, an eighteen-pound roasted turkey, gravy, green beans with bacon, corn bread, sweet potatoes, and a strawberry Jell-O salad. For dessert, she brought out two blueberry pies that we had made last summer and one apple pie. We ate them all—unashamedly. Jerome's oldest son, J.R., ate most of the apple pie himself. And since we all had at least one slice of blueberry pie, we had a "whose-tongue-looks-the-bluest" contest—and Jerome won. What was funny was that we were all sticking out our tongues, including Miss Maddie, who was right there in the thick of the competition, wagging her tongue from side to side to show us all that she deserved to be the winner. In doing so, she found a new friend—the mischievous seven-year-old Emit, who was attracted to the silly old woman. Eventually, he would grab her hand and would not let go—clinging to her through the night, like some kids cling to blankies. When we played Southern-style Scrabble, Emit sat on her lap and would quietly gaze up at her silver hair, occasionally stroking it as though to find out if it was real. Miss Maddie only smiled, as if enjoying the company of her young admirer. Whatever it was that had soothed the savage beast in Emit, it didn't matter. All I knew was that the little boy from hell had been soothed by the Pied Piper from Bullpen, who would occasionally sneak him bits of candy when his father wasn't looking.

Jerome's youngest daughter, Elsa, is a quiet, cautious girl. I sensed brokenness in her, as if she had been scarred from all the circumstances of life. I could only imagine what her life had been like—jockeyed from place to place, sometimes in the middle of the night to avoid landlords or drug dealers or police—never knowing whom to trust. According to Jerome, their mother was a drug addict and had taken them all hostage across state lines, carrying her contraband kids and her contraband drugs by her side. His oldest daughter, Tamara, was a walking example of responsibility in action. If she had been scarred by life's ugly hand, it didn't show. She acted well beyond her age of sixteen years, herding and guiding her younger siblings like a mother hen. J.R. was a tenderhearted kid who was looking to enlist in the military. He struck me as too kind to be a soldier, and I wondered what the military would do to him. He was awkward in many respects, and even though he was a young man, you had the notion that he was still dependent upon the affirmation of his father.

Little Emit was as much of an angel that night as he had been a monster for the last few days, and he reminded me of Ivan the Terrible . . . and suddenly I missed Ivan.

Although easily angered, Jerome would catch himself at times, as if he knew he had been too hard on his children. He would waver between father and friend, as if knowing how little time he had before they were to leave. If I was to describe Jerome in a nutshell during that week, it was "intentional." He was intentional about everything it seemed, from making sure the kids were polite and kind to seeing to it that they addressed the café patrons by their names. And those whom they did not know, they were to address by "yes, sir" and "no, sir" and "yes, maam" and "no, maam"—phrases that Emit seemed to forget from time to time. Jerome was intentional about teaching his children the importance of responsibility and hard work and pursuing their dreams. When he showed them his Stinky Bait factory and canning jars, J.R. and Elsa seemed to snicker behind his back. When he sensed their sarcasm, he rebuked them and then trumped them with the age-old adage, "just wait and see." And while he continued to describe the details surrounding the art and science of fishing and bait—Tamara, like a young woman wise beyond her years, simply smiled admiringly at her father as he continued to ramble with great enthusiasm about a topic she knew nothing about. I sensed that she had seen these kinds of dreams before but still believed in him. They were the kinds of dreams that had probably come and gone without any attachment or any results—like computer viruses—cruel glitches that allowed you to see only the main screen over and over again, without any functionality behind it. Tamara was Jerome's pride and joy; she was Daddy's girl, and you knew it. But like a good father, he tried to reach out to Elsa, seemingly without any apparent success. As if frustrated by his own lack of results, he would confide in Tamara, coaching her as if she were his ambassador to her younger sister.

As the New Year's Eve began to wane, we all gathered by Miss Maddie's clock and then celebrated the New Year when it struck midnight. But the celebration was short-lived.

The next day we took Jerome's kids to the airport in Maynard's Cadillac that Millie had volunteered—much to Maynard's displeasure. I drove since Jerome wanted me to come along. When I dropped them off at the ticket counter outside the airport, they all got out and gathered around their father, who hugged them and would not let go.

Fighting back tears, he finally said to J.R., "You're a man now." And J.R. nodded, fighting back tears of his own. Then he kissed the foreheads of all his children as the airline police gave him a warning before they would ticket Maynard's car.

J.R. then herded all of his younger siblings away toward the entrance, the last of whom was Emit, who refused to let go of his father's leg. When he did, he and his siblings disappeared into the crowd like the fin of a fish sinking back into deep, dark waters.

As Jerome stood there with tears running down the sides of his face, the airport police gave him one more warning. But he never acknowledged their presence. He simply continued to stare in the direction of where he had last seen his kids.

I then got out and reassured the officer we would be leaving. I opened the passenger door, and Jerome got in.

He never said a word on the way home.

January 10 . . . Orion's Belt/Slater's Buckle

It is a cold but clear night up on the hill, and the three stars of the constellation Orion's Belt are in full view: Alnitak, 800 light years away; Alnilam, a full 1300 light years away; and Mintaka, over 900 light years away. What amazes me, however, is that the light we see from these stars is light that started on its journey over 800, 900, and 1300 years ago. A light year is distance that light travels in one year. In other words, if light travels over 186,000 miles per second and there are over 32 million seconds in one year, then light will have traveled over 5.8 trillion miles in one year. And if the stars of Orion's Belt are between 800 and 1300 light years away, then what we are seeing now is light that began its journey to earth in 700 AD from Alnilam and 1100 AD from Mintaka and 1200 AD from Alnitak, according to Slater, who got his information from *National Geographic*.

That was the topic of discussion this morning at the café, and it was Slater who had started it all with Orion's Belt. He then went on to explain (as only Slater could) about Einstein's Theory of Relativity—information that he also had gotten from *National Geographic*. George, skeptical of the whole matter, chimed in with information about aliens that looked like politicians, with information he had gotten from the *National Enquirer*.

"So what is time?" Slater asked all of us.

"Ticks on a clock?" said Millie.

Others chimed in with answers of their own, but Slater, playing the audience like an insidious professor, suddenly cut us all off by his own definitive answer.

"Time," he stated proudly, "is only relative to distance and speed, and it starts with a formula like the speedometer in your car that tells you how fast you are going."

Then, writing on the place mat for all to see, he began to diagram the formula: Speed=Miles/Hour.

We all nodded like school kids.

"Now, if we substitute Distance for Miles and Time for Hour," he continued, "then the same equation can be written as Speed=Distance/Time."

We continued to nod like school kids.

Then Slater performed what he called a simple algebraic equivalent of this formula by setting everything equal to time. It read: Time=Distance/Speed.

"So what does this tell us?" he asked everyone excitedly.

No one said a word.

"Distance and Speed are relative to Time," he began. "In other words, time can only be measured by the speed at which an object covers a certain distance, and that distance is called space. Think about that for a moment," he said, getting all excited. "If time is measured by the speed of an object going through a certain distance of space, then speed and space are relative to time. In other words, without an object moving through space, there would be no time. Time is only measured by motion: an object moving through space. If all objects were frozen in space, there would be no time, correct?"

No one answered.

"So time has to be relative," he continued.

Still no one answered. But that didn't stop Slater. He then began his flamboyant dissertation on Einstein's theory of relativity, stating in essence that, if we were all moving in slow motion (as he demonstrated and George and the Boys imitated), then that would be our basis of comparison to other speeds of time. And the same would be true if we were all moving at a faster pace in time. We judge time based on our perception of speed, and we measure everything in relation to it as either faster or slower than the time frame we are accustomed to. Then he paused as if considering his next line of reasoning.

"But who is to say our time frame is slower or faster than, say, another universe's time frame?" he asked.

Still no one answered.

"And what if we could see into another universe with creatures on its planets, like ours, and they were all moving four times faster than we were—would we not say that their time frame is faster than ours?" he said with an artistic flare.

Still no one answered.

"Of course we would!" he shouted triumphantly. "And if speed is relative, then isn't time relative as well?!" he continued, waving his pencil in the air as if brandishing a sword. "But relative to what? . . . Relative to other objects in motion. So, if one object is moving faster than another, how can we compare that speed to the other's speed? In other words, is there a constant speed in which to compare those objects in motion? Yes, according to Einstein. It is the speed of light. The speed of light is the same speed in any universe at any point in time. The amazing thing about the speed of light is that the closer we get to the speed of light, the slower time becomes—an inverse phenomenon. And if we go faster than the speed of light, time can actually be reversed. And if you are not traveling at the speed of light, then for you time continues on in your normal frame of time—but for the person traveling at the speed of light: ho-ho-ho," he added with bravado. "For them . . . for them," he touted like an ancient Greek orator, "time stands still, and they age not, according to Einstein."

He suddenly ended his lecture with an enthusiastic crescendo, expecting at least someone to applaud the depth of his understating.

But no one did.

"The Theory of Relativity, class" he cried out, "is the premise upon which our universe functions! It is the belt buckle in the cosmic realm of scientific investigation that holds all things together."

He then stopped and stared hard at the confused café patrons, as if he himself had lost sight of reality and had been taken back in time to a classroom far, far away.

"Don't you see it?" he chided his pupils.

But no one did.

And as puzzled looks stared up at the professor at large, frustration began to build in Slater's vibrato. Desperate now for something to prove his point—an object that could replicate his own predisposition—he glanced about the café like a madman. Then his eyes lit up as he glanced down at his own belt, and suddenly he removed it with one dramatic yank.

"Don't you see it?" he shouted, pointing to his own belt buckle. "Einstein's Theory is like the buckle that holds the universe in place! . . . If you remove the buckle, then the entire universe stands to collapse!"

I don't remember ever seeing Slater's shorts before, but there they were, bigger than life, as his slightly bigger than normal pants dropped to the floor without the support of his belt—and buckle.

"I see it now!" cried George as he and the Boys began laughing. "I see it now!"

Houston, did you follow that?

341

January 31 . . . SEO Stuff

Tim Belcher, a friend from the old neighborhood, called out of the blue today. I hadn't seen him in years, and we must have talked a good thirty minutes on the phone, recalling our childhood days in the neighborhood. He had found my blog, *News from the Bullpen Café,* on the Internet. Tim is in the web design and search engine optimization (SEO) business that promotes websites on the Internet through key word searches, links, and pay per clicks (PPC).

He has an appointment with a company in Lacrosse, Wisconsin, next week and thought he would stop by Bullpen and pay me a visit on his way home to Minneapolis. Being in the web development business, he asked me if he could run some numbers for me to see what kind of hits I was getting on the site by using a tool he called Google Analytics. I told him to go ahead and then I gave him the URL address that I had gotten for the blog and everything else he needed do his research. His initial impression was that the site was generating some significant numbers, and he will have those figures for me when he comes next week, along with some steps that I could take to drive more traffic to my site. The notion of promoting *News from the Bullpen Café* seemed appealing at first, but I am not sure what the additional publicity will mean for me or for the people of Bullpen. Most people in town have no idea that their lives are being displayed on the World Wide Web. And if they did, would they be as apt to be themselves, knowing they were on display? I don't know, but I look forward to seeing Tim and his results.

Apart from that, things are pretty quiet in town. The Bullpen Rotary continues to meet on a semi-regular basis, and we have started to plan next year's Bullpen Days. We're seeking to get former Governor Jesse (The Body) Ventura to come. Regarding Rocket Man, there was a heated debate about asking him to come back. Apart from his questionable lifestyle, there are serious questions about insurance. What if he were to overshoot the canopy and land in the parking lot? Hmmm . . . good point, Mr. Mayor.

The bluegrass band is up and in full swing. Gary has us all on a strict practice schedule and plans to take us touring this summer to the local festivals around southern Minnesota.

He keeps looking at me when he talks of practicing—and I'm beginning to get the message. I get the impression that he thinks of me as a type of Jack Benny—the old TV comedian who couldn't hit a note on the violin.

Am I really that bad?

I'm having second thoughts about Harvard. They called me this week to see if I am coming next fall. I asked them how long I have to decide, and they told me a few weeks. Amazingly enough, my mother called shortly afterwards and asked me if I had been in contact with the school. Why do I get the feeling that she is coordinating this whole affair? My father seems suspiciously silent on the matter and will probably only get involved if my mother needs some backup. In a way, it reminds me of the "good guy/bad guy" cops who work in tandem to get the results they want.

February 10 . . . The Discovery

It was after business hours when Tim Belcher stopped in with the news about the blog site *News from the Bullpen Café*. He had just come back from La Crosse and seemed excited about his findings. He was going to jump right in with the statistics, but since neither of us had had lunch yet, I put on a pot of coffee, and we had a sandwich together.

"So, what's up with *News from the Bullpen Café*?" I asked him.

"Do you mean the *good* news about *News from the Bullpen Café*?" he asked me.

"Yeah," I said smiling.

He told me that I have an average following of over 10,000 hits a week, and it was growing. Then he asked me if I knew what that meant.

"No," I replied.

"It means that you should upgrade your site," he replied. "This is huge, Charlie. You have over 10,000 hits a week, and when I researched your blog since you started in June, you have grown at an average rate of 23 percent, starting with the second week in July. You have readers out there, Charlie, and that means that you are doubling your following almost every month. If you add Internet marketing into the mix, you could reach close to a million followers by August. Do you know what that means?"

"No," I replied.

"It means you'll be famous."

"Really," I said.

"So, what you need to do is to implement some sort of Internet marketing plan."

"How so?" I asked.

"Content never makes money, but followers do—and your content drives your followers. There is something about your content that has struck a chord with your readers, Charlie. They like what you write or you wouldn't have that many hits. My suggestion is that you develop your own website with the same

URL address. Just beef it up and then put links out there to other websites so you can drive even more traffic to your site and vice versa. Then find an advertiser . . . or sell stuff like Bullpen coffee cups or Stinky Bait."

He laughed.

"How do you suppose the owners of *Life Is Good* got started? You ever see those shirts and cups? Their following grew, and they capitalized on their own merchandise. So why can't you do the same?"

"I don't know," I said. "I just don't know. It would seem as though I'm proselytizing my position here."

"But you're not. Whatever you have to offer, Charlie, people seem to like. Maybe it's the down-to-earth lifestyle that people are craving in today's hectic world. Our world is falling apart at the seams, Charlie. We are on a cultural crash course and have lost our innocence. Maybe that's why your stories are hitting home. Would it be so bad if people wanted a part of that for themselves?"

He stopped and drank his coffee, and I drank mine; my head was spinning with ideas.

"Hey, I am a marketer, Charlie," he began. "That's what I do. Look at Thomas Kinkade. Not everyone can buy the real thing, but they can buy a coffee mug or a post card—something that reminds them of a simpler time. I think in the long run you can reach more people and affect more lives— and perhaps even give them a sense of hope by driving more traffic to your site through an SEO program. Hey, Charles Dickens changed a nation's social conscience through his stories. Why not you? Why not at least get your stuff out there on a greater scale and let the readers decide?"

I wasn't sure what to say after that; it was all so new. Would publicity change Bullpen? That was the real question. Would people come to Bullpen as a tourist site? And would that change the nature of the town? It would be as if we were all on display like actors or actresses when tourists came to visit. It was like having company as a kid and being told by your mother to be on your best behavior. Could Bullpen survive that prestigious position, or would its citizens succumb to an artificial facade, pretending to be something other than what they really were? It was escape from that very notion that had driven me here to begin with. The suburb I grew up in was full of artificial facades with people chasing nebulous, mechanical rabbits that could never be caught around a never-ending track, bent on getting ahead—and looking good while doing it.

We were all on display whether we knew it or not. The notion was, after all, an illusion, the same illusion and the same race that my Uncle Roy had been running for years—until by chance or fate or destiny or the divine intervention of God, he had stumbled upon a little, unknown town, a back eddy from the fast-paced life around him. And now the potential irony was that the very town he knew to be authentic and real would be in jeopardy of becoming something artificial—constantly on display, coming to portray ourselves to the world in ways we wanted to be perceived. In the end, Bullpen could become the very image of what people thought we should be—and that would be the irony of ironies. Our town, our way of life, would become nothing but a brand, no different from corporate products like Coke or Pepsi or McDonalds. In the corporate arena, branding was everything—and perception was god. It mattered not if the truth be told, because it was all about numbers . . . hitting numbers—and the commercialism that goes with it.

Once upon a time commercialism had been properly confined to the corporate marketplace, but not today. Today the hyper reality of its tentacles has pierced the corporate veil and now reaches down into our own personal lives, so we too, can advertise and sell ourselves to the world on an altogether new level of commercialism through Facebook, Twitter, and other sites.

"Aren't I pretty? Aren't I cool? See my face on the World Wide Web."

"Aren't I fast? Aren't I swift? See me getting ahead of my neighbor . . ."

The notion of exposing Bullpen on a more grandiose scale could result in the very demise of its authenticity—and that was my greatest fear. How would Bullpen cope under a magnifying glass for the entire world to see? When I first started writing, I never thought about that concept or the consequences thereof. I wrote because I am a writer and wanted to share my experiences and observations and values and predispositions and presuppositions about life: good, bad, or ugly. Was I right? Was I wrong? Was sharing my life in Bullpen a violation of privacy? And if so, was anything in life really private?

There were more questions than I had answers. Would commercializing Bullpen be any different? Was I self-absorbed by the very nature of writing *News from the Bullpen Café*? The readers had chosen its destiny so far by the mere act of their own participation. But would they continue to do so without the help of marketing?

I wondered.

"I'm not sure about stuff right now, Tim," I said. "I'm not sure what publicity will do to me or this town. I guess I need to think about it."

"If you continue at the rate you're at, Charlie, your readers just may decide your fate for you."

I nodded, trying to get my mind around the concept of publicity in the midst of innocence. Suddenly everything was on display, and I saw it as both a blessing and a curse.

Houston, do you copy?

My mind continued to spin as we talked about other things. I could see his lips moving, but I didn't hear a word, wondering what might become of Bullpen if it were exposed to multitudes of readers. I had never thought about that.

He suddenly asked me if I had been in touch with anyone from North Cedar.

The question jarred me back to reality. I told him no, not anyone in particular since I had been in college.

I then asked him if he had been in contact with anyone.

"Just Mary Jenkins," he said candidly.

"Oh?" I asked him. "Didn't she move away or something back in grade school?"

"Yeah," he said. "It was at the end of fourth grade."

"Yeah, it seemed like she just disappeared," I commented.

"Her parents died in a car crash," Tim said, "and she and her younger brother moved to New York to live with her grandparents."

"Really," I said. "So she had a younger brother?"

"Yeah, he is in the military now—stationed in Afghanistan."

"So, what's up with Mary?" I inquired.

"She writes for a local paper in Seneca Falls, New York."

"Really?" I asked stupidly.

"Really," Tim said. "We write to each other every now and then. She even has her own blog."

"Really?" I asked again.

"Really," said Tim.

"So, what does she call herself?" I asked him.

"I don't know. I just know that—"

Then his head jerked forward and he eyed me quizzically. A grin came over his face, as if he had just stumbled upon something significant for the first time.

"Why of course!" he stated emphatically. "Why, that's Mary from New York."

Later That Night . . . Cinderella's Slipper

Hi, Mary from New York:

I'm not sure why you have not written back all these months. Perhaps it was a fear of being discovered, as you had been at recess years ago. When you approached me on the street during Bullpen Days, you wanted to know if what we had here was real—and from a distance, you found out it was while pretending to be something other than who you really were. That's the way I see it, anyway. Perhaps it was better that way. Perhaps our own past can cloud other's perceptions of us or stand in the way of what or who we really are—or have become.

As I sit here typing in my uncle's truck, I can still see Mary Jenkins at recess that afternoon in fourth grade. She is blushing behind her own hands—exposed and embarrassed as she was only months ago when I asked you if I knew you. It's funny, but I didn't know what to think of your suspicious absence the next year in fifth grade, nor did I this summer on the streets of Bullpen after you turned and walked away. Like Cinderella, you left the ball in haste, blending indiscriminately back into the kaleidoscope of colors and patterns and anonymity.

How was I to know who you really were?

February 14. . . Valentine's Day

Dear Charles:

You asked me a simple question that I had never anticipated that afternoon on the streets of Bullpen—and the answer is yes. Yes, Charles, you know me—or at least you know of me. And as you bare your heart and soul without any apparent fear of doing so, I feel as though I know you and a small town that has come to take its own place within my heart.

Like Cinderella, I was afraid. That has always been my nemesis when it comes to relationships. Even now as I write, I tremble with the fear of being discovered—or asked to dance.

Mary Jenkins

February 15 . . . The Day after Valentine's Day

I don't know what to say, Mary Jenkins. I am sitting on top of Thomforde Hill at a loss for words.

Will you come to Bullpen?

Charles Finstune

February 16 . . . Two Days after Valentine's Day

Yes.

Mary Jenkins

February 17..... Three Days after Valentine's Day

When?
Charles

February 18 . . . Four Days after Valentine's Day

As soon as I am able.
Mary

February 19 . . . Five Days after Valentine's Day

I'll be waiting . . .
Charlie

February 20 . . . Six Days after Valentine's Day

I'm not sure why I'm happy, but I am. I don't even know Mary that well, but the thought of her coming tweaks my heart more than I imagined it would. I thought I was able to hide it, but Jerome, like a bloodhound, is wondering what's up.

"I'm just happy," I told him. "Can't a guy be happy once in a while?"

But Jerome is smarter than that and has been poking around, asking questions as to the nature of my nature.

"It must be a woman," he finally told me in the kitchen. "I know 'bout these things. I bet that Italian woman's come to her senses."

"No," I told him. "The Italian woman is still in Italy and probably will be the rest of her life."

350

"Oh," he said with a puzzled look upon his face. "Well, she ain't the one for you, anyway, Charlie. No sirree, she ain't the one for you . . . So who is it?"

I didn't say anything, and I could tell he was getting upset. He finally blurted out, "Well, doggone it, Charlie, if you can't tell Jerome, who can you tell?"

"So, you will keep this thing between us?"

"Cross my heart and hope to die," he replied.

"Okay," I said. "There was a woman who was here during Bullpen Days, and she and I went to grade school together."

"Hmmm . . . ," he said. "This could be serious. Grade school, huh?"

"Yeah," I said.

"Second grade?" he asked.

"No, fourth grade."

"Oh, yeah," he said as if he knew something I didn't. "This could be serious."

I thought he was joking, but he just kept hmmmming to himself, rubbing his chin and staring up at the ceiling, as if deep in thought.

"Oh, yeah," he finally said after a long pause. "Hmmmm . . . fourth grade . . . yeah, this could be serious."

"Like you would know," I said sarcastically.

"Oh, yeah," he replied earnestly. "I know all about that stuff."

"Well, just keep this between us—you got that?" I told him, breaking the low drones of his hmmmming.

"Oh, yeah . . . oh, yeah . . . just between you and me," he said.

"Good. I expect it to stay that way," I replied.

I turned and began to walk away when Jerome suddenly asked me what her name was.

"Mary. Why do you want to know?"

"Oh, just askin'," he said. "Hmmmmm . . . why, that's a nice name, Mary. Yeah, Mary . . . I likes that—yes sirree—yeah, that there is a nice name . . . and you said this all happened in the fourth grade, huh?

"Yeah," I said defensively.

"Hmmmm . . . the fourth grade . . . Hmmmmmm . . . Well, Charlie— your secret is safe with me. You can trust Jerome."

351

February 21 . . . Spilling the Beans

I walked into the café late this morning, and when I did there was a bigger-than-life banner stretched across the smiling moose that read "*Welcome Back to Bullpen, Mary.*" Millie, Maynard, and Melissa were hanging it up—and Jerome was standing back orchestrating the whole thing.

Miffed, I asked if I could have a word with him back in the kitchen, and he excused himself like a whipped dog.

"Oops" was the first thing that came out of his mouth. And then he began to backpedal as I approached him with a bread knife in my hand—the first thing I found on the counter.

"So, who let the cat out of the bag?" I demanded.

"Now, just wait a minute there, Charlie," he kept saying. "Now just—just—just-- wait a doggone minute. Let's not do anything we is gonna regret later, huh?"

"No," I shouted. "Let's not do anything 'we' are going to regret later."

"Now, Charlie, let's just put that knife away and ah—let's just talk about this—this thing here a—this thing for a moment, huh? I mean, how do you really know it was me that let the cat out of the bag?"

"Because you were the only one holding the bag!" I shouted, coming closer.

He nodded regretfully, and then suddenly an angry look broke across his face.

"Well, doggone it, people gots to know 'bout it if we's gonna give her a proper welcome."

"You don't even know when she's coming!" I yelled. "I don't even know when she's coming!"

"Well, that's just it," he said. "We don't know, so we better gets prepared."

I don't know how long Jerome and I were in the kitchen shouting at each other, but it must have been long enough, because George and the Boys and Slater and Maynard and Millie and Melissa and Homer and Lenny and Gary and others came in asking about Mary.

We are waiting for you, Mary—me and the rest of the town.

February 22 . . . Celebrity Status

You are now a celebrity around here, Mary Jenkins. Rumors are starting to surface as to your true identity. Maynard calls you "The Cat Woman," because—as rumor has it—you are an actress who starred in the Broadway musical *Cats*. As recently as this morning, Maynard took me aside and asked if you wouldn't mind getting him some tickets for the show—if *Cats* is still playing, that is. Even though he is allergic to the little animals, he wanted to surprise Millie with some tickets. Front row seats would be great.

Another rumor circulating around town is that you own your own clothing line that features only the latest in fashion. To date, you have designed multiple hats, a few dresses, a couple of purses, and of course a swimsuit. The Ladies Auxiliary is now eagerly waiting to see your latest design.

On a more personal note, Slater claims that he knew all about you the minute you stepped into the cafe this summer—he just can't remember what you look like (a picture would help). And Homer distinctly remembers playing Crokinole with you during Bullpen Days and claims that he won all three games (please verify—his reputation is on the line).

I (we) look forward to your coming. You are the mystery woman from New York, and the suspense of your arrival supersedes anything George, Slater, and the rest of Bullpen have been reading about in *The Tri-Town Beacon*—your reputation precedes you.

February 23 . . . Confirmation

Mary's arrival has been confirmed. She is scheduled to touch down the middle of April. I told members of the Rotary the news this afternoon, as well as the Bullpen local patrons. Even Jared—who occasionally works Saturdays—is looking forward to your coming.

I hope you like Cajun food, Mary. Jerome has gone so far as to write to some of his "long" and "lost" relatives back in Louisiana—asking them for some of their "long" and "lost" recipes.

He is actually willing to prepare anything—as long as it is not lutefisk.

March 1 . . . The Alberta Clipper's Last Hurrah

It was a cold and blistery winter day here in Bullpen, with the wind-chill exceeding 15 degrees below zero, fellow bloggers. Very unusual for March. The weather forecasters, however, are predicting that it will be the last Alberta Clipper of the season—much to their own chagrin. If their predictions are correct, then they won't be able to use the highly popular and somewhat controversial phrase "Alberta Clipper" for another seven to eight months. What that means is that their Nielson Ratings will suffer because of it. To offset their seasonal "dip" in the ratings, I suspect that they will resort to other seasonal phrases to try to bolster their viewership and advertising sponsors. Whatever phrases they concoct or invent during the winter's "off season" will be mild, if not miniscule, in comparison to the phrase "Alberta Clipper."

The absence of such a phrase, however, means only one thing to Minnesotans. Like Ground Hog Day, it is time for the good, honest, and law abiding (did I mention hard working?) citizens of Minnesota to get out of their homes and into their snow-shoveled driveways and see, once again, their long-lost neighbors for the first time since November, when they had first sought shelter for the impending doom of the "Alberta Clipper."

Spring is in the air, fellow bloggers, and warmer days lie ahead—at least, that is what the weather forecasters tell us.

March 4 . . . Ivan's Prayer Card

As I sit blogging on top of Thomforde Hill, I'm amazed at the turn of events that have happened within the last few hours. Earlier today, I received a phone call from a farmer in Nebraska who found Ivan's three-by-five prayer card on a branch of an old oak tree that borders on one of his cornfields. He told me he found it this morning while he was out cultivating one of his fields. He said the three-by-five note card—that was still miraculously attached to the string by nothing more than a staple—was fluttering in the wind and appeared as though it was waving at him to stop.

He did.

And when he read Ivan's prayer request, he and his wife called my cell phone number on the back, inquiring about the circumstances surrounding Ivan. So I told them about our Sunday school class back in August. I had never read Ivan's prayer request that Sunday morning—I never knew that he had asked God to help his little brother's heart get better. So, when they asked me what they could do to help, I told them that I thought that maybe surgery would be an option. After a few minutes of conversing with his wife offline, he told me that they would be willing to pay for everything.

I sat there dumbfounded . . . A perfect stranger willing to pay thousands of dollars to help someone he didn't even know.

Ivan . . . your prayer has been answered. We just need to find you—and your brother—and your mother.

Fellow bloggers, can you help me find the whereabouts of Ivan Schmidt? I believe his mother's name is Linda, and his father's name is Jake, according to Millie. I believe he has family in Brainerd, Minnesota, but Googling them today, I found nothing. Please let me know if any of you know where he might be.

There is a farmer and his wife in Nebraska who want to help.

March 6 . . . The Search Continues

One of you fellow bloggers (by the name of Sand Trap) contacted a friend of yours who is a private investigator and wanted to let me know that private investigator has taken it upon himself to find the whereabouts of Ivan and his brother and will get back to us with any results.

Thanks

March 8 . . . Where Are You Ivan?

It has been two days, and there is still no word of anything about Ivan or his brother. I have told the farmer and his wife about the situation and referred them to our blog.

Where are you Ivan?

March 9 . . . The Flood of Inquiries

As I sit writing on top of Thomforde Hill tonight, I am overwhelmed by the number of inquiries by many of you with possible leads or suggestions for finding Ivan. It is as if an all-points bulletin has been posted worldwide, and there is an influx of suggestions, donations, and prayers that are coming in from all parts of the country and all parts of the world: California, Texas, Wisconsin, Missouri, Florida, Tennessee, New York, Arkansas, Canada, Mexico, Europe, and Asia. The mayor, too, is astonished and has set up a bank account for Ivan's mother. He is now depositing the money some of you are sending anonymously to "Ivan" in Bullpen, Minnesota.

Wow . . . thank you for your generosity and your help.

March 13 . . . The Good News

I received a call today from a nonprofit organization that wishes to remain anonymous. Through a series of events, the lady told me, her organization had found Ivan and his brother living in a downtown Minneapolis shelter for the homeless. I am taking the day off tomorrow to tell Ivan's mother the good news and get Ivan's brother enrolled at the Children's Hospital in St. Paul.

Thank you all for your help, fellow bloggers.

In a world where evil and greed and oppression often take center stage, it is great to know that there are those like you: the unsung heroes—that still pitch in—that still help out—that still try to do what is good.

Thank you.

March 14 . . . Who Knew?

Ivan is alive and well, and his brother is in good hands. I arrived this morning and found his mother at the homeless shelter, just as the lady on the phone had told me. When I told Ivan's mom about the farmer and his wife in Nebraska who had found the note Ivan had written last summer and how they wanted to pay for his surgery, she broke down and wept. Then I told her about all of the bloggers who want to help her get set up in her own place, and she just kept sobbing, as if the weight of the world had suddenly been lifted from her shoulders. Not knowing what to do, I simply stood there and tried to imagine where she had been and what they all had been through these last few months. Ivan's brother was sleeping on a towel in the corner of a room that had but one bed. And I could only guess what their lives had been like up to that point. When Ivan came in and saw me, he simply stared at me as if he didn't know me. His mother then told him about the prayer he had written for his brother last summer and the balloon that had carried it away. As she told him, he just stood there listening as if he had no idea what she was talking about.

And then, as calm and as matter-of-fact as he could possibly be, he said, "I knew God would do it."

Then he asked me if I had any donuts.

"No," I replied, but then I told him that I wanted to take them all to lunch, and he could order as many donuts as he wanted.

It was then that a big smile broke across his face.

After lunch we checked his brother in at the Children's Hospital. I sat out in the lobby with Ivan while his mother sat at the information desk with his little brother still sleeping in her arms. There were still tears in her eyes as she answered questions while the attendant filled out the necessary paperwork. When it was all done, the attendant, a young woman in her early twenties, reached across and gave Ivan's mother a hug, and more weight seemed to lift from her shoulders.

Ivan then had to go to the bathroom, so I walked him down the hall and gave him to a nurse who helped him find the boys room. Suddenly, I had visions of him plugging the toilet and I yelled back at the nurse to that effect.

"Be careful, I told her—he has a way of plugging toilets!"

She looked confused and ignored me, as if I had gone mad. But when Ivan reappeared and I could see that there was no water on the hallway floor, I breathed a sigh of relief.

Two minutes later, however, Ivan spilled his can of Dr. Pepper all over the magazine rack. Good luck trying to read *Better Homes and Gardens* with Dr. Pepper all over the pages. A can of clear Sprite would have been a much better choice.

The hospital checked Ivan's little brother in that afternoon. I then took Ivan and his mother to a local hotel within walking distance from the hospital and paid for the room. I gave her some extra money for the next few days while Ivan's brother awaits surgery.

Ivan's mother could not thank me enough.

But it wasn't me.

It was all of you and your generosity. Thanks to you, Ivan's mother now has her own apartment in Bullpen, along with over nine months of reserve funds to give her a fresh start in life.

And to think it started with a three-by-five note card attached to a string and a helium balloon?

Who knew?

Who knew that we would have extra helium balloons from Bullpen Days that would provide the vehicle to jettison those requests into space that morning?

Who knew that an observant little 12-year-old girl by the name of Maria would be sent to help me that Sunday morning and suggested that I put my phone number on the back—just in case someone actually found the card?

Who knew that the prayer card would travel hundreds of miles before landing in a tree on the edge of a cornfield, surviving the long winter months with a single staple holding the string and the card together until they flagged down a generous farmer in Nebraska who was out cultivating his field?

And who knew it would start a worldwide search for a boy named Ivan who simply wanted to see his little brother get better?

Who knew?

As I sit and blog from the top of Thomforde Hill in my uncle's truck, I begin to recall all of the events that led up to what has happened these past few days. I'm amazed by one simple object lesson and the power of prayer. As I look up through the windshield at the stars above, I think about the single staple that held on to that request for months and would not let go, in spite of the harsh winter winds that blew across the desolate and deserted Nebraska cornfields. It was like Horton the elephant who would not relinquish his post or duty in Dr. Seuss' book *Horton Hatches the Egg*.

It was a single staple that faced all odds.

And as I continue to look at the endless stars above, I suddenly think of the countless single parents—especially the moms—who, like the staple, try to hold their families together as best they can in the midst of the harsh and desolate winter winds . . . and by the grace of God—they do.

March 18 . . . The Chastening Hand of God

The surgery for Ivan's little brother went better than the doctors had anticipated, and he is recovering nicely at the hospital. There is word from his mom that they will be coming back to Bullpen to live in the apartment next to Jerome in less than a week. When I told my first and second grade Sunday School class the news this morning, they were alive with questions. I told them everything—and we spent what seemed like an hour talking about God and prayer and the universe and all that it contains. Just when I thought we were making great spiritual inroads, Edgar Willis suddenly blurted out that he got a new muskrat trap. I guess it was a fair trade: twenty minutes of Sunday School and fifteen minutes of muskrat and mousetraps and mayhem. We spent the last fifteen minutes of class drawing anything they wanted, since I had nothing else prepared for them that morning. Then I asked them for their assignments at the end of the class period. They all gave them to me and then exited the room in single file. Edgar, however, was the last one to leave—as if he had planned it that way.

"Do you know what I'm believing God for?" he asked me, handing me his picture.

"Tell me," I told him.

"Muskrats," he said.

Sure enough, he had drawn a muskrat trap, dangling on the end of the string that was tied to a balloon that was heading towards what looked like a mountain.

"So, this is a mountain?" I asked him.

"Yep," he replied, pointing to the picture. "That's Muskrat Mountain, and that's where I'm going to trap 'em."

"I believe you will," I told him. Edgar smiled, then left, confident of his request. After he was gone, I glanced at his little kid picture and started to laugh at the little kid notion of trapping muskrats on some little kid mountain. But as I flipped off the light switch and stepped out into the hallway, I had this sinking feeling that I was wrong about the matter. And as strange as it seemed, I felt as though a hand bigger than mine was chastising me.

It's funny, but I found myself repenting right there in the basement of the church that morning, knowing that someday Edgar just might be bringing his muskrat pelts to Sunday school for show and tell—and wouldn't that beat all odds.

Houston, do you copy?

March 21 . . . The Best Is Yet to Come

Miss Maddie invited Jerome and me, along with the pastor, Lenny, LuAnn, Mrs. Sherburne and her husband, and the mayor and his wife, in addition to Millie and Maynard, over to her house after church on Sunday for dinner. Although it was sunny, there was still a cold nip in the air. Trying to defy the Minnesota weather, I wore only a long-sleeved shirt because this morning I had heard what I thought was the first robin of the year outside my window—supposedly a sure sign of spring—or so I thought.

Jerome, on the other hand, was wearing about five layers of clothing. When he got out of the truck, he resembled Ralphie's younger brother Randy when he got all bundled up in the movie *The Christmas Story*. I asked Jerome if he was going on an arctic expedition to one of the poles, but he didn't say anything and only continued to shiver. Jerome has never liked the cold, and he alone is the reason why the heating bill at the café is as high as it is. The worst thing about spring in Minnesota, however, is that, until spring finally decides to arrive, old man winter continues to wreak havoc, with frigid temperatures and freezing rain that chills you right to the bone.

Last week I read to Jerome and others in the café one of my favorite poems by Robert Service called "The Cremation of Sam McGee." During the bitter winter in the Canadian Yukon during the 1800s, a fellow musher agrees to cremate Sam if he dies from the cold. When Sam does die, the fellow musher stokes up a big fire in the furnace and stuffs him in. When he decides to take a peek at the burning body, he opens the furnace door, and to his surprise, Sam McGee is alive, telling him to shut the door so he doesn't get cold. Jerome told me afterwards that was the only poem that has ever made sense to him.

Being from Minnesota, I agreed.

For dinner, Miss Maddie had outdone herself—again. We had acorn squash, crescent rolls, cheesy potatoes, sweet corn, honey-baked ham, and a broccoli and bacon salad with a poppy seed dressing. And then to top it all off, she had made two chocolate French silk pies. I could only imagine how hard it must have been for her husband to keep from gaining weight all those years of marriage. When we were finished, we all retired to the living room where I saw her husband in one of her photographs on top of her upright piano. And I was surprised at how thin a man he actually was.

There were many pictures on top of the piano that I looked at that afternoon. There were pictures of her boys at an early age, one of her parents, another that looked like her husband's parents, and other black-and-white photos of what I assumed to be family. Then it hit me that it must be hard to grow old and look back upon those photos, especially those that have died before you. What was it like to get old and be the last surviving member of your family and to have outlived your own children?

I wondered.

When we all sat down, Mrs. Sherburne's husband told us all that Mrs. Sherburne was an excellent piano player, to which both the mayor and the pastor agreed. He tried to coax her into playing, but she wouldn't—until the pastor's wife asked her. Then she reluctantly asked Miss Maddie for some sheet music—and soon we were off and running, singing many of the old hymns I had sung in church as a kid. Jerome was in his element, belting out song after song, without any regard to his tone-deaf ear.

We then sang "How Great Thou Art." When we were done, Miss Maddie said that that was the song she wanted us to play at her funeral.

A sudden quiet came over us all, and she smiled.

"Well," she said defiantly, "we all have to go sometime, unless we're raptured."

The pastor laughed, and so did everyone else.

"And when I'm lying there in my coffin," she continued, "you make sure there is a fork in my hand, Pastor."

"Why is that?" he replied.

"As a little girl, I was always told to save my fork for dessert," she said. "And I did—because the best was yet to come."

We all laughed, but I sensed there was more to Miss Maddie's comment than met the ear.

When we had dessert for the second time that evening, I could not help but notice that she served us but had none herself.

It was late in the evening before we left Miss Maddie's house. We had all stayed longer than we had expected, eating both dinner and supper at her dining room table. Jerome and I were the last to leave, and as we turned and departed down the driveway, reflected in my rear view mirror, I saw her waving to us. It was then I had a strange notion of time, like déjà vu—driving forward, while looking back. I don't know why, but the memory of her standing on the porch waving to us as we drove away stuck in my mind—almost as if I had seen the picture somewhere before.

March 25 . . . Scaredy Cat Finstune

Dear Abby and Dr. Phil:

My mother called today to tell me that she enrolled me next fall at Harvard because apparently I had not done so. It was an unusual conversation, and the fact that she had taken it upon herself to decide the direction for my life was a little disconcerting. I apparently had not moved fast enough, according to her time line, and she thought it in the best interest of everyone involved that I start in that direction—including mine.

So, what do you tell your own mother? And how do you say no to your own mother? Can you say "no" to your own mother? Of course you can. Simply open your mouth and say the word "no": "No thanks, Mom. I would like to make that decision for myself, thank you." But did I put on my big boy pants?

No.

For some reason, I simply nodded on the phone and agreed to all of the terms and conditions of the agreement. Did someone say agreement?

I did not take the high and noble road. I defaulted and took the low road—the under-the-radar road, the "don't-rock-the-boat" road, and the "go-along-to-get-along" road.

Houston, do you copy?

Okay, so I was afraid of standing up for myself. Maybe I was a little intimidated. Okay, so I was a little more than intimidated. In my own defense (to continue on with legal terminology), however, I was caught off guard. I had not prepared for my defense, and when I was suddenly served papers, I buckled under the weight. Yes, Charles Robert Finstune buckled under pressure.

On the flip side, however, there is a portion of me that sides with Harvard. It is, after all, a good—no, a great—school, and I am fortunate to have been accepted. After all, how many other legally minded opportunists have actually been accepted into Harvard? Not as many as apply, and that

364

thought alone is worthy of consideration. After all, legal life is not all that bad. You study hard, you get good grades, you intern with the right firm and—voila!—you are in for the rest of your life—an official member of the prestigious bar club with fellow white-collar companions.

There is something enticing about law, and there is something enticing about Harvard. It is, after all, life in the fast lane—warp speed compared to life in Bullpen.

So, why am I feeling like a whipped dog tonight as I wrestle with my future, my reputation, my self-esteem, and of course—my mother? Is there really a future in Bullpen?

Apparently, not. According to my mother, it has been a nice internship, but that is where the story ends.

"Really, Charles . . . a café owner in Bullpen? You have been accepted at the finest law school in the country, and you are thinking about Bullpen? Is that what you want your life to amount to—a café owner in Bullpen? Think of your future, Charles . . . Stop for a moment and think of your future. [I am trying.] Will you ever look back and wonder if you made the right choice? Will you ever look back and regret your decision?"

Like a boxer in a ring, I found myself retreating to my corner before the bell had rung.

Houston?

What I did not tell her was that I was wrestling about the after-shock of choosing not to run with the big boys. How would I ever be able to show myself in public? . . . You do what? You own a what? In where? . . . Yes, I am the proud owner of a small-town café in Bullpen—no bull . . . No bull? . . . Yes, no bull.

Can an owner of a small town café really hold his head up in Suburbia?

Does he need to?

Sincerely,

Scaredy Cat Finstune

March 26 . . . Dysfunctional Families

Thanks to all of you Dear Abbys and Dr. Phils out there in blog land. Your comments on what to do and where to tell my mother to get off were informative, descriptive, and very insightful. I would have to say that most—if not all of you readers—favor Bullpen over Harvard, simply because the majority of you are not attorneys, which has skewed the bell curve in favor of Bullpen. What I did not anticipate, however, were the passionate responses towards my mother—and I'm sorry to say that I have hit a nerve with many of you fellow bloggers—and in the process of describing my own personal life on the home front, I have opened up a can of worms. As an addendum, the blog site was supposed to be about the events of Bullpen and the café, but as with all stories, it is hard to separate the author from his personal life. My apologies.

Having said that, I want to thank all of you who took the time to vent about your own "dysfunctional families" (to paraphrase one reader) in ways that we could have only imagined before.

Ax Man, I would strongly encourage you to lock up your knives so that, when you do get upset, you stop throwing them against the wall. Pastor X from Oregon, I would encourage you to stop making Popsicle stick churches in your spare time and then smashing them out of anger after your quarterly steering committee meetings that are dominated by a few controlling women. Jerry from Rhode Island, I would suggest a more subtle approach in talking to your father. At 45 years of age, I think you can make your own decisions now. As far as Sarah and trying to tell your dead mother where to get off (and on) via a séance—this is not something I would recommend. And George, I understand your Dad was pretty controlling growing up . . . I would take down that dartboard with his picture on it if I were you, as soon as you can.

In conclusion, I would strongly encourage all of us to grow up and stop the blame game. We all know people who play that game and have become the victims of their own demise. And aren't they just fun to be around?

I don't think so.

As Eleanor Roosevelt once said, "We teach people how we want them to treat us." (I think she was the one who said that, anyway.)

I believe the psychologist from Maine (who wishes to remain anonymous) said it best regarding the topic of unforgiveness—apparently a common theme among "dysfunctional families" that have been subject to a controlling, legalistic (no pun intended for all of you attorneys) nature themselves. I have paraphrased his insightful dissertation on its neurological, psychological, and spiritual effects below.

There are neurons and synapses in our brain and nervous system that act as tiny electrical impulses or arcs, like those that come from a spark plug. These neurons are transmitted over certain nerve endings with electrical impulses. These channels or avenues—when repeated—become like an insulated wire and it is hard to break that channel—like a gutter ball in bowling. In other words, everything defaults to the gutter or the insulated pathway through continued use or thought. When we choose to forgive someone, that pathway is altered or rewired from hurt to healing, but it takes time to feel its effects because the electric arcs of unforgiveness want to jump back into their familiar gutter (insulated pathway), and it takes effort to break that route. But over time—with intentional application, forgiveness does manifest itself to where we do not feel angry with the person who has influenced us the wrong way or done us harm. Having said all that, forgiveness, however, is more of a spiritual issue than it is a physiological or neurological issue. Man is comprised of three parts: sprit, soul, and body. If our soul is healed but our spirit is not, remaining wounded from an act of injustice, then the root of the matter will continue to fester like latent cancer. True forgiveness can only come from a spirit to bring about healing in our own spirit. In other words, it takes a spirit to heal a spirit—and that is something that can only come from a spiritual force greater than ourselves. It is, in fact, a spirit of forgiveness that, through divine intervention, empowers us to let go of any injustice we might claim to have upon our assailant or agitant. That act alone transcends our own definition of righteousness. In other words, it would not be just or right to forgive someone who has done something unjustly to us. But, true forgiveness yields our desire and will to the will of God, who in turn forgives us our injustices or trespasses. At its premise, forgiveness is a divinely ordained act in which the neurological, psychological, and spiritual dimensions all miraculously work together to bring about the healing process as the nerve endings of hate are rewired or redirected with the nerve endings of forgiveness. And although we will never forget the incident or series of incidents, the sting of the memories will diminish as we intentionally choose to forgive, thus allowing God's hand to intervene on our own behalf because we no longer lay claim to our own justice. With God's help, we can get there. We can get to that place called forgiveness.

God help us all get to that place, wherever that forgiveness place is . . .

March 30 ... The Sinking of the USS Chevy

George received a notice late last week in the mail regarding his ice fishing house that was supposed to have been removed three weeks ago and now sits on Lake Shetek by its lonesome self.

He was given one ultimatum: remove the fish house or pay the consequences of a stiffer fine. The problem is that since the advent of spring and some warmer weather, the ice was now less than two inches thick—and even less in some spots. So who wants to help pull a 400-pound ice fishing house off the ice?

Not I, said Chicken Little. Not I, said Porky Pig. Not I, said the Big Bad Wolf.

"No volunteers?" George asked everyone in the café.

No responses. . . . Even the Boys were silent.

As he threw up his hands at the injustice of it all, Jerome came out of the kitchen and volunteered to help. Not willing to let Jerome get all the credit of possibly falling through the thin ice himself, I agreed to help out as well.

Later that afternoon, we had a game plan that was orchestrated by the field general himself. Jerome and I were to venture out to the ice fishing house, pushing one of George's old fishing boats ahead of us in case the ice broke, then wrap a long steel chain around the fishing house so that George could pull it off the frozen lake with his 1982 Chevy pickup.

Sounded good to me.

The only problem was that by the time we wrapped the chain around the fish house, we didn't have enough length of chain left to reach his pickup truck on shore. That meant that George would have to back his truck onto the ice itself, which was not a problem as long as the ice held beneath it—which it did. Once the chain was attached to the truck, George put it in gear, but the fishing house wouldn't budge—having been stuck to the ice all winter.

But that didn't stop George. Like any good military man, he came up with a contingency plan to "yank" the fish house free and clear from Lake Shetek's icy hold by creating slack in the chain, then accelerating and yanking it free.

Sounded good to us.

So George backed up his pickup further onto the ice to give us more slack in the chain. Then he revved up the motor and slammed the Chevy into gear and shot across the icy pathway back to shore. When the chain pulled tight, it yanked the fish house free from the lake's icy grip that had held it all winter. The only problem, however, was that the shock to George's transmission was greater than anyone had anticipated. It was there—30 feet from shore—that George dropped the Chevy's transmission. Pounding his fist against the driver's door of the idling truck, George let loose a volley of expletives that could make a sailor blush. Just as he was about to let go another round of descriptive adjectives, the ice around him began to crack.

Jerome and I stood and watched in horror as the truck began to sink. Then George let out a cry for help. Quickly Jerome and I scooted the wooden boat over to the sinking truck. And just before the unforgiving waters of Lake Shetek began to swallow up his Chevy, all three of us hopped in the boat.

"My truck!" cried George, sobbing like a mad man as we all saw the last of the taillights slip beneath the surface of the frigid waters. . . . "My truck!"

Then, adding insult to injury, we all sat and helplessly watched the chain drag the ice fishing house with it into the deep waters below.

"My fish house!" George cried as he continued to sob like a mad man. . . . "My fish house!"

As luck would have it, a teenager just happened to be nearby talking on his cell phone, and he snapped a photo of the three of us in the boat, watching the truck and the ice fishing house slip down to the bottom of Lake Shetek. It was the same photo that miraculously found its way onto the front page of *The Tri-Town Beacon*: "Local Man Loses Truck to Lake Shetek."

Slater's ode to the USS Chevy is now taped to the Beacon's article and hangs proudly on the wall next to my article on deer hunting. Both articles are displayed just to the left of the coffee cup hall of fame—just in case you decide to frequent the café, fellow bloggers, and want to know where to find them.

April 6 . . . Awaiting Your Arrival on the 28th

Dear Mary,

I received your message earlier about coming the 28th of April, and I and the town are awaiting your presence.

Charlie

April 8 . . . What Am I Missing?

Ivan and his family are now settled and living down the hall from Jerome. Ivan visits him relentlessly—before, during, and after work. Jerome is wondering if it was a Godsend or a curse that the balloon was found in Nebraska. I prefer the former, but then I don't live one door down the hall from Ivan and his brother. His brother is doing great, and so is his mother. Ivan has made himself at home and now makes daily visits to the café with pennies in his pocket, which is sufficient to buy the day-old donuts. Needless to say, however, he and George now compete over these coveted pastries. And George, like a little kid himself, had managed continually to beat Ivan to the front door for the goods until Ivan figured out a way to counter the wily old veteran's tactics. He began camping in front of the café early in the morning, knowing that George (being the adult that he supposedly is) would not stoop to the same "little kid" level. Ivan must have figured that even George has a certain dignity—a threshold that he himself cannot cross. The irony, however, is that little Ivan has George in a tizzy, and even the Boys have started to rib the old veteran about it.

As the proprietor, however, I have to find a way to appease even the most stubborn of patrons, and just yesterday I made a secret arrangement with George. I have agreed to set aside—just for him—any day-old pastries with chocolate. In doing so, I felt like President Kennedy during the Cuban Missile Crisis, when he negotiated secret deals with Khrushchev behind closed doors. Fellow bloggers, I think we have finally negotiated détente.

The bottom line is that George is now happy—and when George is happy, everyone is happy.

With less than two weeks before Easter, my mother called to tell me that she and my father are flying out to visit Karl in Boston. I was invited by Karl as well but decided not to accept his invitation. I will be seeing him at his graduation ceremony at Harvard in early June, and I could not justify spending money on another plane ticket to visit him for Easter when I will be seeing him in less than two months. He seemed okay with that.

I think I did the right thing.

Only a year ago, my parents would have paid for the entire trip, but now that I have joined the working world, they felt that I was able to pay for it myself. So, does that mean I can decide my own future as well?

I was about ready to ask my mother that question, but I knew that it would only lead to something less than détente. In summary, I can pay for my own flight, but I cannot decide my own future? What am I missing here?

No need to comment fellow, bloggers—I don't want to open up another can of worms—Okay, Ax Man?

April 12 . . . Easter

It was a full house at Millie and Maynard's on Easter for dinner. Millie invited Jared, his mother, Miss Maddie, Ivan and his brother and mother, Jerome, Melissa, and her husband. She had invited Homer, but apparently he had four other engagements that afternoon and was coy about all of them. It is no secret around town that Homer is the cat's meow for the eligible women in Bullpen over the age of 75. It is also no secret that he caters to all of them—being sure he offends none of them. He is both suitor and pursued in the never-ending game of courtship, and he delicately jostles between his debutants with the most gracious of diplomacy. As the ambassador of love, Homer plays his cards tight to the chest, knowing full well that any flagrant display of affection to any one particular lady could, and would, ignite the most cataclysmic of events, which could lead to nothing less than a third world war.

I have admired his art of diplomacy from a distance and often thought of writing a book on the matter, about his expertise, and then sending it to Washington D.C. The idea is that all "would-be" foreign ambassador "applicants" would have to play and then pass the "multiple courtship" exam. If such an applicant were to succeed at keeping multiple suitors (at least four) content and at bay for a predetermined period of time, then—depending on how well the applicant had performed—such an applicant would be given the role of ambassador to any nation of his or her choice. Training would include testimonials and videos from the professor of love himself as well as a toll-free number that any one of the students could call about any sticky situations, inconveniences, encumbrances, or any combinations thereof that they could encounter during their "exam." I would call the book and corresponding coursework *Diplomacy 101: The Complete Guide to Becoming an Ambassador at Home and Abroad* . . . or simply, *L'amour et l'amitié* (French for something that has to do with love).

And speaking of love, I was interrogated at the dinner table about you, Mary. Millie, then Maynard and others drilled me about who you are and how we met. Do I tell them we met in fourth grade? Actually, I thought you could

372

tell them yourself when you get here. Millie has gone out of her way to make sure that the room you stayed in during Bullpen Days has a new coat of paint, a new bed and pillows, and a new night stand. Maynard has been working overtime and has paint on his fingers to prove it. I am assuming that you are still coming on April 28?

The Easter dinner was great. Maynard had deep-fried a turkey in his new propane cooker. Melissa and her husband brought desserts, and Jerome made some kind of Cajun rice thing that was too hot to swallow. Millie made her famous glorified rice, and I brought rolls.

Ivan was on his best behavior and didn't spill a thing. His little brother is progressing ahead of schedule and has affectionately attached himself to his neighbor down the hall—Jerome. You can tell Jerome is a little embarrassed at the partiality of the little guy's affection, but inwardly he is glowing like a surrogate father playing wink-em (Jerome's name for some kind of wink game) and then peek-a-boo. When the little guy fell asleep, it was Jerome that picked him up and held him. Ivan, too, is constantly by Jerome's side, and it seems to annoy Jerome at times, but only for a moment. It seems that he, too, has grown on Jerome.

I asked Jerome later if had changed his mind about their moving down the hall. He simply shook his head as if he didn't know what I was talking about.

After dinner, we sat around the living room, and Maynard lit a fire in the fireplace while we talked for hours. Jared is doing well at his vo-tech class and hopes to be done by the end of May.

In the back of the living room, Miss Maddie was reading the book *Green Eggs and Ham,* by Dr. Seuss, to Ivan. It seemed to be Ivan's favorite. Miss Maddie was quiet but expressive as she continued to read to Ivan, who sat on the floor beneath her feet, hanging on her every word. Her inquisitive looks and various voices brought the story to life. Every now and then, she would stop, pause, and look at Ivan, asking him what he thought of the story. You could hear them converse like little adults, with Ivan sharing his thoughts and ideas as Miss Maddie would nod her head in approval. Then she would continue. And when she reached that part where Sam actually tried the green eggs and ham and liked them, she stopped and stared at Ivan like a statue with a comical inquisitive look about her face. When Ivan started to laugh, so did Miss Maddie—and it was as if the two of them seemed to share in the ageless intimacy of a teacher and pupil discovery.

As I looked at the two of them that night, carrying on in their own little world, with Ivan sitting at the feet of the master and eyeing her ever so intently, it struck me what a wonderful teacher she was—ever guiding and sharing and conveying to her pupil in the most subtle of ways direction or thoughts he had never considered. But what made her great was that her teachings seemed not to come from her head—but from her heart.

It was late that evening when we left Millie and Maynard's house. Maynard drove Miss Maddie home. As the rest of us left and started walking down the driveway, we saw Homer, the ambassador of love, walking home from what I guessed was his last appearance of the night. When he saw us, he waived and then turned the corner and disappeared just as he had done the first time I met him so many months ago.

L'amour et l'amitié was all I could think of . . . *L'amour et l'amitié.*

April 17 . . . News about Mary

Tonight Mary wrote back and told me she is not coming to Bullpen.

I guess I really don't need to know why. Her words were brief—almost apologetic in nature—and I am not sure what to say . . . Perhaps the buildup to her coming had scared her off . . . Perhaps it was something else.

I don't really know Mary, but tonight I suddenly feel as if I did or do—and it is a lonely feeling—a romantic notion that there might have been someone out there that you'd like to meet again.

I will break the news to the others tomorrow, but tonight . . . tonight I'm sorry that Mary won't be coming—and if I admit it, I am feeling empty.

April 23 . . . Miss Maddie

I received note from Miss Maddie today. It was an invitation to her house for lemonade.

"Just wanting to see you again," it said, and that was it.

I wasn't sure what to think of the note, but when I arrived later that afternoon—after the café had closed—I saw that she was dressed in her Sunday best and wearing her Audrey Hepburn bonnet. She looked comical—a paradox of fashion—with her gardening hat and long, formal dress. I wasn't sure what to think of her appearance. The first thought I had was that I had misread her invitation and that this was to be a formal affair, like a British high tea, but she quickly dismissed the notion when she told me I looked comfortable in my own jeans.

It was a warm spring day and the smell of thawing fields was in the air. We went out onto her porch that overlooked the Zumbro Valley. Flint sat beside us as she tenderly stroked the back of his neck. When I had finished drinking my lemonade, she tapped my hand as she had done so many times before, then suddenly took it in hers and squeezed it hard.

"After your aunt died, your uncle and I used to sit here often and look out over the valley. I would sometimes hold his hand as I am holding yours. He was a good man, your uncle," she said.

"How so?" I asked.

"He cared more about people than his own career," she replied. "He had a brilliant mind and had numerous offers from firms across the country. I don't know how they got his name. I am guessing that they were recommendations from his professors at Harvard. One of the top law firms in New York offered him an internship shortly after Suzanne died, and I encouraged him to take it. 'But who would run the café?' he asked me. 'What would become of Bullpen without the café?' Your uncle was like that, Charlie. He was like George Bailey that way."

She squeezed my hand again and looked out into the Zumbro Valley.

"He often spoke of you and your brother Karl and prayed for your family often. You were all he had left."

I didn't say anything to Miss Maddie. I just sat there as she held my hand. I didn't tell her that I really didn't know him. I didn't tell her that I had always thought he was a failure, a recluse, and an outcast from the Finstune family tree. I didn't tell her that my mother never approved of him and told me on more than one occasion that he had wasted his life in such a small town. I didn't tell her that she had once loved him and then hated him for leaving her for a small-town waitress. I didn't tell her that he was a taboo subject around our house. I didn't tell her that I never knew I had a cousin who died in childbirth. I didn't tell her anything—but it was as if I didn't have to—it was as if she already knew.

I really can't describe what else happened that afternoon, sitting there on her porch as she continued to hold my hand. The light of the setting sun began to cast long deep shadows across the valley. It was peaceful as we sat there in silence. But when the numbness that comes with holding your hand in one place for so long began to creep its way up my arm, I tried to pull away—but she would not let go.

And when she did . . . it was for the last time.

Later That Night . . . Houston, I Am Undone

Tonight I sit alone at the top of Thomforde Hill where I have sat so many times before. I am listening to Paul Potts sing "*Nessun Dorma*" on the Internet. The simple, broken-toothed mobile-phone salesman from Wales opens his mouth and astounds the audience with his simple and transparent passion that resonates throughout the concert hall—and throughout the world—on the show *Britain's Got Talent*. When he finally hits and sustains the highest tenor note in the apex of the opera song, I weep out loud. And as the people stand and cheer this humble man—I see you, Miss Maddie. I see you.

You will never stand on stage and share in the limelight of a triumphant encore—and few will ever know the legend you leave behind.

But those of us who knew you will.

Tonight I am undone, Houston . . . tonight I have lost my friend, and I am undone.

April 26 . . . Miss Maddie's Wake

It has been difficult to write these last few days. Miss Maddie's wake was tonight, and I am exhausted and spent. Although the funeral director did the best he could, the person lying in the casket did not look at all like the Miss Maddie we knew. Although Millie had chosen her dress, earrings, and jewelry, it was Miss Maddie—according to the funeral director and pastor—who had chosen the fork that rested in her folded hands.

Perhaps there is hope after death, Miss Maddie. Perhaps the best is yet to come.

The funeral is tomorrow morning at 11:00, and all of the preparations have been made. She will be buried next to her husband and two sons, beside the church. The pastor will perform the service, and a luncheon in the church basement will follow. You are all welcome to come.

Flint is now in my custody, and he knows intuitively what has happened, as do most animals. He simply sits quietly by himself in the corner near the pool table in my uncle's apartment. Although he will lick my hand, he will not lick out of his bowl, nor will he eat—and I am concerned about him. I hope a dog cannot die from a broken heart—I know people can.

In closing, I want to thank all you fellow bloggers for your kind comments and prayers.

Charlie

April 27 . . . An Unexpected Guest

It was standing room only that morning in the Bullpen Lutheran church sanctuary. People had come from miles to pay their respects. Since Miss Maddie had no immediate family, a few of us were chosen by the pastor to sit up in the front pews that were traditionally reserved for members of the family: Jerome, Lenny and LuAnne, Mrs. Sherburne and her husband, the mayor and his wife, along with Millie, Maynard and me.

As the sanctuary filled beyond its capacity, we waited in the back to enter. As the soloist began her prelude, Jared came in the back door. He had taken the day off from his Vo Tech classes to attend the funeral and was dressed in a suit. I did not recognize him at first when I saw him before we were ushered in, I told him he looked good in a suit and that he might want to consider a desk job.

He smiled, shook his head, and told me, "No, thanks."

I told him how much it meant to see him take the day off and attend Miss Maddie's funeral. He nodded and then just stood there. Words were never easy for Jared, and I sensed he was struggling to find something to say. When the prelude ended, the pastor signaled for us to enter, but before I did, I tapped Jared on the back and told him how much it meant to have him there. He smiled a boyish grin, and I turned and entered the sanctuary with the others.

We were ushered to the front and then sat down. I simply stared at the closed wooden casket that stood before the altar.

It was a simple service—the kind I believe Miss Maddie would have liked. There was music and the reading of scriptures and a short message from the pastor. When he was finished, he asked if anyone had any testimonies or stories about Miss Maddie that they wanted to share. It seemed as if half the congregation came forward to share their own stories about a woman who had helped them in ways that no one would have imagined.

When all were done, the pastor asked if anyone else had anything to say. It was then that George stepped forward in his full military uniform covered with medals. He stopped and took the microphone from the pastor. It was obvious that he was having trouble finding words, as he cleared his throat again and again.

"She was a damn good woman," he finally stammered, "with two good sons who died fighting the same war I did."

Moved with compassion, he told the congregation that when he was diagnosed with colon cancer, it was Miss Maddie that came to the hospital to pray for him and was determined that he was going to live, whether he wanted to or not.

The congregation laughed.

He continued to tell us that, although he was sedated with medication, he could hear her cry out to God for his life.

"I had to live," he finally said. "She scared the hell out of me . . . Why, I was more afraid of disappointing her than I was about dying."

The congregation laughed again.

"She was a damn good woman," he continued. "She was a damn good woman and a saint, if I ever saw one."

He then turned to the casket and took off one of his medals and laid it on top. Then he snapped a sharp salute and held it while tears streamed down the sides of his face. Finished, his arm slowly dropped down to his side, and he did an about-face and walked back to his seat and sat down beside his wife.

After a long moment of silence, the pastor rose up and thanked George and all of the others who had given their testimonies. Then he blessed us.

"The Lord bless you," he began, "and keep you. The Lord make his face to shine upon you and be gracious unto you. The Lord lift up his countenance upon you and give you peace. In the name of Jesus Christ, our Lord and Savior. Amen."

It was then that a woman began to sing the age-old hymn "How Great Thou Art."

When she was done, those of us in front were ushered out of the sanctuary down the center aisle. And as I neared the end of the row of pews, I saw her . . .

It was Mary from New York.

Later That Morning . . . Meeting Anders

After all of the people were ushered out of the sanctuary and down into the basement for lunch, I found her in the back of the church. She stood there smiling awkwardly, holding the hand of a little child.

"Mary from New York?" I asked.

"Yes," she said, extending her hand.

I shook it and then stared down at the child.

"And who is this?" I asked.

"This is my son, Anders."

I extended my hand, and the little boy, who looked about three years of age, reached out and politely shook it.

"Good to meet you, Anders," I said.

The boy smiled shyly, then retreated back to his mother's side without a word.

"I didn't know you had a son," I said.

"I do," she replied.

"Is his father around?"

"No," she said. "He never was."

I shook my head as if to tell her I understood.

"Well, I bet you're hungry. Would you care to join us for the lunch downstairs?"

Looking uncomfortable, she hesitated. Suddenly, I could imagine her slipping away into the crowd as she had done before, to catch some imaginary plane for some imaginary reason. I braced myself for her reply.

"We would," she said at last.

Her answer startled me, and suddenly I saw her beauty as I had seen it months ago. There was something simple and unpretentious about her facial features and her hair that barely covered the nape of her neck.

"Well, let's eat then," I found myself saying as I reached out and took Anders hand.

When we stepped down together into the church basement, Millie, Melissa, Maynard, and others were busy serving food behind the rows of tables. When Millie saw me standing there with Mary and Anders, she motioned for me, as if asking me to help, but when she recognized Mary, she dropped everything and came over to give her a hug.

"Why Mary from New York," she cried out. "We thought you weren't coming."

As if on cue, others began to crowd around her, including the mayor.

"Why, welcome to Bullpen, Mary from New York. We have heard so much about you," he said, shaking her hand.

And then Jerome came over, as well as Homer, Lenny and his wife, LuAnn, George, Slater, and others—all eager to see this mystery woman and shake her hand.

Mary smiled politely and appeared somewhat uncomfortable about all the sudden attention in the crowded basement.

Startled, Anders began to cling more tightly to his mother's side, but she simply stroked his hair as if to reassure him it was all okay.

And it was.

Later That Night . . . The Press Conference

By the time we had buried Miss Maddie, it was after five o'clock. It had been a warm, sunny afternoon—a perfect spring day, according to Maynard. It was then that Millie told us all to come over to their house for supper and insisted that Mary and her son stay with her for the night, in the same room that she had stayed in during Bullpen Days.

When Mary agreed, I was surprised even more. I didn't know Mary's schedule. I didn't know how many days she would be staying or if she had driven or flown. I knew nothing of her son or her life in New York. I had little opportunity to ask her any questions with the social entourage that accompanied us everywhere, like the Italian family in the movie *The Godfather*, with Marlin Brando and Al Pacino.

When we arrived at Millie and Maynard's home, we were seated around their big dining room table for supper. As the food was being passed, the barrage of questions began. It was like a small press conference, and Mary handled herself with a quiet poise as she continued to comfort her son, who still seemed apprehensive about all of the sudden attention. It was during the press conference that Maynard's preconceived notions about her debut on Broadway in the musical *Cats* were finally put to rest. Slater too had most of his questions answered, and he seemed a little disappointed in her ordinary lifestyle.

I sat quietly at the other end of the table during the inquiry, simply watching her while she began to field all the various questions with a certain grace and transparency. I wondered about her son. I wondered about his father. I wondered about her previous life and her present life in New York. I wondered what her junior high days were like, and her high school days. And what was it like to have lost both your parents at an early age?

Our eyes suddenly met, and a certain shyness came upon her—a certain embarrassment that comes with having eavesdropped on someone. She quickly looked away and smiled politely as she continued to answer each question with a thoughtful response.

I then saw Millie looking at me. She smiled at me as if she had been eavesdropping in on my own personal thoughts about Mary—as if she knew what I knew.

I smiled back.

Still Later That Night . . . The Reason

Later that night, Anders fell asleep, and Millie put him down in an inflatable mattress next to Mary's bed.

After the others had left and Maynard and Millie had gone to bed, Mary and I talked in their living room for what seemed like hours.

We talked about the death of her parents, her grandparents, and her brother in Afghanistan. Finally, we talked about her son.

She was hesitant to talk about her short-lived relationship with Anders' father—an athlete who loved hockey more than anyone or anything else. They were never married, nor would they ever be, and yet she told me that she would always be grateful to him for her son.

Anders was her life, and you knew it.

When I asked her how she found my blog, she told me that she was curious one day about what had become of me. She had found *News from the Bullpen Café* on Google back in July and decided to come to Bullpen to see for herself if it was real.

When I asked her why she decided to come back after she told me she couldn't, she got quiet.

"I got to thinking about Anders and how much he means to me," she said at last. "I couldn't think of a life without him—and then I began to think of how I had kept him a secret all this time as a single mom. And suddenly I got scared and thought that maybe . . . maybe I might lose you because of him . . . I don't know why, but I decided to make your decision easier by not coming."

There were tears in her eyes.

"But when Miss Maddie died," she continued, "I just knew I had to come."

It was then she began to cry. Not knowing what to do, I reached out and touched the back of her shoulder.

"I'm glad you came, Mary." I said at last . . . "I'm glad you came."

April 28 . . . The Picnic

It was another warm and sunny day when I came into work this morning. As usual, I met Millie and Jerome in the kitchen. They were busy packing a picnic basket full of food, while Flint was eating scraps off the floor, which had been intentionally dropped there by Jerome. As upset as I was about having the dog in the kitchen, Flint was eating again and was looking better than he had in days—and that was a good thing.

When I asked her who was going on a picnic, Millie told me it was me.

"Me?" I said stupidly.

"Why, you gots to get to know her before she leaves on that flight back to New York," Jerome said, wrapping up a piece of Millie's lemon cake and licking his fingers.

"Well, who said we were going on a picnic?"

"Why, you'd be a blind fool not to take a woman like that out on a picnic on a nice day like today," he continued, sampling another piece of the cake from the picnic basket and licking more of his fingers. "And if you just gonna sit around and dilly dally, like some one-eyed dog waiting to tree a three-legged coon, then you'd be waitin' till hell froze over. A man gots to act now or there may not be a tomorrow."

"What do you mean, there may not be a tomorrow?" I asked stupidly.

"Why, that woman is gonna get on a plane and who knows what the future may hold if you don't act," he said.

"She has a job offer in London," Millie chimed in, handing a sandwich to Jerome, who sampled that as well.

"A job offer in London—England?" I asked.

"Oh, yeah," Jerome said, sampling another piece of the sandwich Millie had just handed to him. "One a them Brit companies is askin' her to come over for a job interview and—and God only knows what that will lead to. You know how them Brits are."

"No, how are they?" I asked.

"Well, they's all prim and proper with the queen and all that, but when they see talent, they don't mess around makin' decisions. No sirree! They see someone they like and they snatch 'em up. Oh yeah, them Brits are quick to jump all over talent."

"How do you know all that?" I asked him.

"Ain't you never seen the show, *Brits Got Talent?*"

Jerome laughed, but Millie was more serious.

"Well, what about Anders?" I asked.

"Maynard is taking care of Anders," she replied.

"Maynard!? Maynard is taking care of Anders?" I asked.

"Maynard," said Jerome. "Oh, he's good with kids."

I could suddenly hear Maynard singing "Kumbaya" in a sanctuary full of screaming kids after the lights had gone out during our Christmas play. It didn't work then, and I imagined that it wouldn't work now. So what would Maynard do if he was in real trouble?

I didn't have long to think about the matter as Millie was giving me last minute instructions on what to do and where to go before Mary had to leave for New York on her five o'clock flight.

"You don't have much time to get to know her," she said, handing me the picnic basket, while escorting me towards the door. "A fine girl like Mary doesn't come along every day, you know . . ."

"Well, what about me?"

"What about you?" said Jerome.

"Don't I have a say in the matter?"

"Not today," said Millie, opening the front door and pushing me outside.

So, I got in the pickup truck at 7:45 in the morning and started heading to Millie and Maynard's home down the street.

As I drove up their driveway, Maynard came rushing out whispering about as loud as any normal person would talk, telling me not to slam the door and wake up Anders. He then tiptoed back to the front door, motioning for me to do the same.

I refused his offer.

By the time Maynard made it back to the front door, Mary was standing there waiting for him dressed in a pink floral dress. When she stepped out, Maynard caught the door and then closed it gently. Then Mary began to whisper what I thought were some last minute instructions, and then showed him her cell phone. He nodded intently, staring down at the cement walkway as if taking mental notes. Then she turned and walked to the truck. Maynard was quick to follow, opening the door for her like a true gentleman and then shutting it without so much as a sound. As we backed out of the driveway, he stood there waving to us like a little kid. Mary waved back and then turned to me, smiling.

It was as if I was seeing her for the first time—and she was beautiful.

"Good morning," I said.

"Good morning," she replied.

She was very beautiful.

"Did you sleep well?" I asked.

"Yes, and you?"

She didn't look this good in fourth grade. I was trying to remember what she looked like in fourth grade.

"Good."

Did she have a ponytail in fourth grade? . . . No, that was Jenny Evert—I remember pulling it and getting in trouble . . .

"So, where are we going?" she asked.

And where was I standing when I found out (along with the rest of the fourth grade class) that she loved me? . . . Ah yes, I remember now—it was near the swing set.

"The swing set," I said out loud.

"The swing set?" she asked.

"No," I said…"I…I meant that we are going on a picnic near some park with a swing set."

So what do you do when you when you are in fourth grade and find out a girl loves you and will till the day she dies?

"I see you brought Flint along," she said, peering through the back window.

You run and hide . . . that's what you do . . . Love is a scary and serious proposition in fourth grade . . . It may lead to marriage . . . so who wants to get married in fourth grade?

"Not me," I said out loud.

I've got places to go and people to see. I have a whole life ahead of me. Besides, they say fifth grade is better than fourth, and how can a guy enjoy fifth grade if he is married?

"So then how did he get back there?" she asked.

"How did who get back where?" I asked.

"How did Flint get back there?" she said, pointing to the truck bed.

"Flint?" I asked.

"Yes," she said. "That's Flint, isn't it?"

Sure enough, when I looked back, there was Flint with his nose sticking outside the truck bed, smelling everything in sight as if it was some kind of dog-infested smorgasbord, while we drove down the road.

"Yep," I said, "that's Flint."

"So, you didn't put him in?" she asked me.

"No, he must have hopped in the back when I was backing out."

"Are you feeling okay?" she asked me.

"I'm feeling fine," I said.

She nodded.

"Still waking up?" she asked me.

"Yeah, yeah, I feel like I'm still waking up."

"Me too," she said.

As we gathered speed up Thomforde's Hill, I tried not to stare at her as the wind coming through the open window brushed through her hair. She sat quietly looking about the cab in what appeared to be a silent admiration.

"So, this was your uncle's truck?" she asked, touching the dashboard.

"Yeah," I replied.

"The same one that took you snow tubing on the streets of North Cedar?"

I smiled.

"Yeah."

"I would have liked to have met your uncle," she said at last.

I nodded.

As we approached the church cemetery, she asked if we could stop.

We did.

Without so much as a word, Mary got out and started walking among the tombstones. When she found my uncle's gravesite, she knelt down and touched the tombstone, then Suzanne's. She then simply stared at the little cross that marked my niece's gravesite.

There were tears in her eyes when she got up. She seemed embarrassed when our eyes met. She tried to smile but couldn't. She wiped her tears and then regained her composure.

"I'm sorry. I must look like a mess," she said.

"It's okay," I replied.

"I have often read his letters from the blog that you wrote about him months ago."

I nodded.

She forced another smile, got up and walked a little further down. Suddenly, she began to laugh, pointing to a marker.

"So this is Ole Gunderson's grave?" she asked.

"Looks like it," I said.

"And that must be Lillie's," she said, pointing to a marker beside it.

"I think so," I replied.

She stood there laughing.

"So, they actually lost the baseball in Ole Gunderson's field?"

"That's how the story goes around here," I replied.

She started laughing again, cupping her hands in her face.

"Bullpen," she blurted out. "Who would ever name a town Bullpen?"

"Immigrant Norwegian farmers," I answered.

She started laughing.

"What's so funny?" I questioned.

"Jerome," she replied. "I can still imagine Jerome running out of the smokehouse with his hands full of lutefisk."

I started to laugh.

"Yep," I replied.

"And then the news reporter asked for your recipe . . . "

She was laughing hysterically now, with her voice making honking-type sounds. And suddenly I was laughing, too.

"Yeah, it was another red-letter day for the Bullpen café," I said as we both continued to laugh.

"My grandmother tried to make lutefisk once—and once was enough, according to my grandpa."

She then got quiet.

"Are they still alive?" I asked her.

"No. They are both gone now," she said. "My brother is all I have left."
She got quiet after that, and so did I.

I had visions that morning of having our picnic at the park in Cannon Falls, watching the Cannon River flow by. Cannon Falls had a pretty park, but we never made it that far. Instead, we found a spot next to the cemetery, not too far from Ole Gunderson's gravesite. We rolled out a blanket and just talked as Flint scurried about watering every tombstone he could find.

We talked about the sudden death of her parents in a car crash at the end of fourth grade and how she had to move in with her grandparents in New York. She talked about how good they were to her and her brother. She talked about how hard it was to leave their home that day and how much she missed her friends in North Cedar. She talked about where she attended college and how she met Anders' father—and how he wanted nothing to do with his own son.

And it amazed me.

How could any man not want to know his own children? I thought of the prima donna athletes and others who had brought children into the world but had abandoned them. How selfish and cruel . . . heroes on the field or on the court or on the ice, but cowards off it. It made me angry. It made me want to grab the man and shake some sense into him.

As she continued to share more of her life with me that morning, I had a sudden notion of wanting to share more of my life with her.

When I looked at my watch, it was close to one o'clock, and we had not even opened the picnic basket.

When I told her the time, she was surprised and asked if we could make a quick trip out to Miss Maddie's home, and I told her yes.

When we drove up to the empty estate, Flint hopped out of the back of the truck, as if glad to be home. The house was open as it had always been—and I took Mary for a tour.

Every now and then, she would stop and stare at various items along the wall. The little knickknacks that seemed of small significance to me were of greater significance to her. She would hold them thoughtfully and then carefully place them back where they had been. She touched the staircase and furniture and walls as if lost in memories all her own. Finally, we went and stood outside on the porch overlooking the apple orchard and the Zumbro Valley that lay beyond it. You could smell the cherry tree blooms and see their pink flowers sway in the gentle wind. As we stood there in silence, Flint came up and licked my hand, and I reached down and began to pet his thick, soft coat.

"She won't be coming home anymore," I told him—and then I began to cry. And as I stood there with tears streaming down the sides of my face, Mary reached out and took my hand, as Miss Maddie had done so many times before. And without so much as a word, she simply held it.

When I had regained my composure, I wiped the tears from my eyes and saw that she too had been crying.

"I wish you had gotten a chance to know her," I said at last.

"I did, Charlie," she replied. "You were the one that told me about her."

We arrived back in Bullpen later than what we had expected, and there were people in the café, peering out the window at us when I pulled up. Since we were running late, she had phoned Maynard and had him bring her rented car from the airport. It was ready to go, and when Anders saw his mother, he ran to her and hugged her leg. She affectionately stroked his face and kissed him on the head. It was a tender moment, and all I did was watch. Then she turned to me and extended her hand. I shook it and she smiled politely.

"I had a great time, Charles Finstune," she said. "Thank you for everything."

Then she turned and walked towards her car, and I suddenly saw her as I had before, slipping back into a crowd like the fin of a fish sinking back into deeper waters—like London or Britain or wherever that job offer was that Jerome and Millie had told me about earlier that morning.

And would I ever see her again?

Suddenly, my heart began to pound, and I found myself moving toward her car.

"Mary," I said.

She stopped and turned around.

"Once upon a time, I lost you in a crowd, right here in the middle of Main Street. I don't want to lose you again." I said.

It's funny, and I don't remember rehearsing any of this, but I got right down on my knees (like those guys in those cheesy chick flicks, which I promised I would never do)—right there in the middle of Main Street—in front of God and everybody.

"Will you marry me?" I asked.

And suddenly she burst into tears, knelt down beside me, and buried her head on my shoulder.

April 30 . . . The Job Offer from London

The café was abuzz with people this afternoon, people I hardly remember around town, patting me on the back and congratulating me. I had visions of a picture being taken of us in the middle of Main Street, with a caption in *The Tri-Town Beacon* that read: "Local café owner to marry Broadway Star."

I could see Slater behind it all and braced myself for the news. But it never came.

It was a busy day at the Bullpen Café, an actual red-letter day for the Finstunes. When things did quiet down, I asked Jerome how he knew Mary was going to London for a job offer.

He looked at me like a dog at a new pan.

"What job offer?" he asked.

"The job offer you and Millie told me about yesterday morning," I replied.

"Oh, that job offer," he said. "Oh, yeah, I remember now . . . let's . . . ah . . . it . . . Well, I'm guessing that it fell through."

There was something awkward about his mannerism. I grabbed Millie just as she was going out the door.

"Millie? How did you know about the job offer in London?"

"You tell him, Jerome," she said. "Maynard and I have to get going."

"So, it was a set up!" I shouted.

Jerome suddenly got mad.

"Well, doggone it, Charlie. Somebody's got to get your sorry butt off center to pull the trigger. Why, if we hadn't a pushed you, you'd be still dilly-dallying about like a one-eyed dog looking to tree a three-legged coon."

"So, you messed with me!" I said to the two of them. "You're like two little matchmakers—so, who thought up that little scheme, anyway?"

"It was both of our ideas," Millie confessed.

Jerome shook his head.

"Hey, you see us makin' that decision for you? You see us tellin' you to get down on your knees in front of God and everybody and proposin' like that? No sirree. We just helped you see somethin' a little bit faster than you would a—"

"Eventually seen on your own," Millie jumped in, finishing Jerome's sentence.

"The bottom line," began Jerome, "is . . . is you or is you not happy 'bout gettin' married?"

I stared at the two of them. They were staring back at me

"Well?" Jerome finally said, "What's it gonna be—happy or not happy—which one? 'Cause you can't have both."

"I'm happy," I said at last. "There, I said it . . . so, are you happy now?"

"Oh, everybody's happy now," stated Jerome, breaking into a big smile. "And there it is. Yep, there's your proof—you said so yourself. So don't you go blamin' us for what you already knew was in your own heart. Why, if anything, you ought a be thankin' us for what we done."

I stood there for a moment thinking how the tables had suddenly been turned on me. I could see Jerome as an attorney—the kind my own father would have been proud of.

"Okay," I finally said . . . "Thanks."

"You are most entirely welcome," said Jerome, beaming with pride.

May 3 . . . Some Possible Guests

Mr. Tennessee Tuxedo was bombarded with questions this morning in my Sunday School class—about marriage. It all started with Ivan, and then Abby chimed in.

They are wondering when they get to see the bride . . . Do you want to answer that one, Mary?

We have set the date, fellow bloggers, for Saturday, June 12, one week after my brother graduates from Harvard Law School. Already Millie and Melissa are making preparations and have been on a few calls with Mary about food. I have chosen to stay out of the matter—too many cooks spoil the broth. We will be married in the Bullpen Lutheran Church and will have the reception at the café, as opposed to the church basement. Jerome is thinking that we will need to set up tables and chairs out on the sidewalk in front of the café—and Millie agrees.

Some of you have inquired about coming, and I'm honored that you would even consider doing so. Queen Crab from Alaska has already booked a flight into Minneapolis. She is coming with her bowling friends that have taken an interest in these blogs. One of her elderly friends wants to meet Homer. As the ambassador of love, I am sure that he will find a discrete way to work her into his dance card. Please let me know ahead of time, and, like Bullpen Days, I'm sure that we can find some kind of accommodations. Some of you can even stay at Miss Maddie's house. It is always open.

Speaking of Miss Maddie's house, I was told by the estate attorney yesterday that she had left it to me in her will—the house and all of her land.

I'm beside myself.

Then Lenny and his wife invited me to their house last night for supper and gave me the balance of what my uncle had loaned them: $14,000. There was nothing in writing, and who would have known if they had not paid it back? That is what I asked them, but Lenny said he would have known, and I guess that was enough. And as Lenny and his wife told me more than once, they never intended for my uncle to help them out when they were in the midst of foreclosure, because paying back friends can be a sticky situation—especially if the borrower defaults on his loan for reasons beyond his control. Lenny told me that my uncle never intended to be paid back. It was a gift, he had told them. He didn't want money to create what Lenny called a vertical friendship, whereby the lendee was servant to the lender. It would have ruined their friendship, something that my uncle valued more than money, according to Lenny.

I have not written much about Lenny. He is a "behind-the-scenes" kind of guy, a pillar in the community and willing to help out whenever possible. As I write, I see him leading the pack of combines, like a tank commander, to help Felix Manion with his harvest since he had had his accident on the farm last fall. Lenny is the kind of man that flies just under the radar until needed, and then he takes charge.

As I sat there at the dinner table, I thought about $21,500. It was a lot of money, and yet it was nothing compared to what might have been financial ruin for Lenny and his family. And had he folded and lost his farm, what effect would that have had on Bullpen? It's as if each man's life is an integral part of the whole. I wondered if I would have given him $21,500 with no strings attached because he needed it more than I did. And would I have simply given it to him without a contract or legal advice or strings that are so common in our litigious society?

I wondered.

When I was about to leave, his wife handed me a card. In it was a note that told me how much they appreciated my coming to Bullpen. On the bottom was another check for $2,500 to cover expenses for our wedding and our honeymoon.

I simply stared at the money and didn't know what to say . . .

May 8 . . . The Elephant in the Room

My mother called yesterday to remind me about Karl's graduation from Harvard Law School. She and my father have now bought me a plane ticket, and I will be accompanying them to Boston and staying in a double room with them at the Charles Hotel. So why did they decide to buy me a ticket to Boston for his graduation but not for Easter? To provide motivation? Hmmm . . . Do you think that standing on the campus grounds might provide a little more of an incentive to help push me over the edge? Hmmm . . . and a free plane ticket to boot. She also reminded me what paperwork needs to be filed for my own admission next fall. Since my mother already registered me, I am looking forward to meeting my new roommate.

Yes, fellow bloggers, I have not told any of my family about Mary, or Anders, or our wedding.

Why not?

Okay, so I am chicken.

It is a huge weight that hangs over me, and I feel as though I'm leading a pretentious life. One life wants to appease my parents while the other life wants to be left alone to decide my own destiny. I continue to hedge like a gambler. I am afraid to make a choice and go "all-in."

Yes, fellow bloggers, I am caught between two worlds, and that moment of decision is coming to a head, like a huge prevailing storm, and I don't like it. I do not like conflict. I dread conflict—personal conflict. I don't like to rock the boat. I like status quo, as uncomfortable as that may be at times.

So how in the world did I possess the courage to come to Bullpen in the first place? Perhaps it was easier last summer. I had graduated from college, had already been accepted to Harvard, and my options were still open. I like options . . . it keeps decision making at bay. Life was good with options. After all, I was simply taking a sabbatical from life, and that is always less threatening than a permanent decision.

It is that decision, that elephant in the room, which nobody wants to address (okay, I don't want to address) that is coming over to my side of the table. He is sniffing me now with his trunk and asking to be fed—and I am running out of peanuts.

May 10 . . . Take, for Example, Parents

Mary and I have been talking on the phone every night, and I love to hear her voice. It is as if I am beginning to know her in ways that keep unfolding, like peeling back the layers of an onion—without the smell. We talked for hours last night, and I updated her, as I do you, about the events of Bullpen. I have grown quite fond of her laugh. I remember the first time I heard it in the cemetery. They say laughter is the shortest distance between two people. If that is true, then the distance between us has grown dramatically shorter. She laughs at my jokes, and I don't know if that is because there is newness about us or if I am really that funny. I prefer the latter.

I wondered if she would laugh at my jokes two years from now or five years from now—or 50 years from now. Where is the point that married couples become so familiar with each other that they lose that sense of newness and wonder? Will I be the type of husband that grows indifferent? That is my biggest concern. What will I be like over time? What will make her upset? What will push her buttons, and what will push mine?

Relationships are complex. Women are such a mystery to me and always have been. They are different than men, and viva la difference. I have been reading the book *Men Are from Mars, Women Are from Venus*, and I am being enlightened on the nature of women.

I have always thought a lot about women. It takes a woman to define a man, as it takes a man to define a woman. I know some of you would argue, but those are my thoughts. How can you know what salt is if all you know is sugar? It takes the opposite of what you are to define you. If God didn't make a woman, how would Adam know he was a man? There are tremendous notions of value that each bring to the table, in which both sides help define each other through their different predispositions in life, and the attraction between a man and a woman has always been a mystery to me—a powerful mystery.

So what is love? What is it that attracts a man to a woman and vice versa? For most women it is beauty that attracts, and for most men it is strength or power. But not in all cases. So what makes a man attracted to a woman? And what makes a woman attracted to a man?

I really don't know.

It is as if each man and each woman has a tank inside that needs to be filled. Perhaps it is a longing or a desire to belong—and if unfulfilled, it manifests itself in the most unusual and often destructive ways.

This much I do know: affirmation is crucial. Am I valuable? Do I matter? Somewhere in this strange and powerful notion of love is the concept of being affirmed and belonging—and when we are not affirmed, when we do not feel we belong, we search for affirmation and belonging in ways that even we do not realize. It is as if a deep, inherent need is searching—continually searching to be filled. Those feelings may manifest themselves more intensely at certain times than others, but they never go away. Like a latent disease (dis-"ease"), the need for affirmation and love always surfaces, like a fishing bobber that will not stay below the surface of the water.

I suddenly thought of my own mother and wondered if she had ever been affirmed, and if so, by whom. Her children? Her husband? Her career? Was she really happy as an attorney and did her success there fulfill the affirmation she desired? Or was it simply a placebo that had been brought about by an inordinate exchange that replaced her own inherent values with that of the corporation or partnership....yes, she could be anything and everything she wanted to be and more because it was all about her: her own career, her own independence, her own happiness, her own identity. Yes, identity.... Why had she refused to take my fathers last name as her own when she married, choosing instead to hyphenate it? Was it to preserve her own sense of independence? Her last name (Finstune-Sathre) was really no different than the corporate name of the law firm in which she was a partner: Ogerley-Fergeson-Finstune-Sathre. She had wanted it that way and had signed a prenuptial agreement knowing all too well that such an agreement contained within itself the seeds of separation: separate bank accounts, separate careers, and yes—a separate name. She had chosen her own identity as she had chosen her own career. And she blossomed in it. She blossomed in corporate America with all of its perks and benefits and independence. There were those, of course, who had no choice but to work outside the home because they had to out of necessity. But not my mother. She chose that road not because she had to, but because she wanted to. Then she abdicated the rearing of her own children to a third party nanny.

But what had driven her to do so? Had she been the victim of a trend? For years, it was fathers who had been guilty of pursuing their own careers at the expense of their families and had brought and wrought more pain to the future generations than anyone else. But now it seemed as though mothers were also opting for careers over family, and in doing so, the last bastion of family strength and stability was leaving home—and applauded for doing so. And what about the "stay at home" moms? What had become of them according to the trend? Were they now considered archaic, second-class citizens? Were they women who suddenly found themselves out of sync and out of step with the rest of society? I wondered. I wondered about women who were opting for careers over family and I wondered what message that conveyed to the self-worth of their children as individuals. I wondered what affect that had on Karl and I while growing up. I wondered if we both harbored a certain resentment towards our mother knowing we were not as important as her own career.

I thought of the book *One Thousand White Women* by May Dodd. Although fictitious in nature, it touched upon a profound theme: it is women that help define culture by raising the next generation. Irony of ironies. Yes, it was women: soft skinned, nurturing, and morally courageous women who were more instrumental and influential in defining the culture of the next generation than armies and laws and corporations.

Yes, the power of a woman…they are different than men. You knew it as a kid. You knew it on the playground and in the lunchroom and on the bus. Girls were different than boys. They were more compassionate, more relational. They huddled together in bathrooms and cooed around babies. Was that a weakness or a strength?

I wondered if my mother would ever regret looking back at what she could have had and could have been. Would she ever regret not having been there at the time when she was needed most? Would she ever regret not having seen our first steps as toddlers? And . . . in the end, would she regret her time in the nursing home wishing she had spent more time at the office, eaten more power lunches among colleagues, or acquired more clients?

Take, for example, parents—the precious guardians of little, innocent people who too will inherit the earth.

It was then I realized that I didn't want a corporation.

I wanted a family.

May 15 . . . Cows and Global Warming

It all started Wednesday morning at the café when Slater was reading about thermal topography and global warming in one of his science magazines.

George thought global warming was a bunch of hogwash invented by Al Gore to impose more regulations on business, making him wealthy off of carbon credits, which would tax farmers just as much as some manufacturing plants. The reason—because when their cows farted and released CO_2 and other deadly gases, it would affect the delicate eco-structure, leading to more global warming.

Slater, however, thought global warming was the real deal.

The two argued about farting cows for over 15 minutes, until George proposed that Slater go out and see for himself. With an infrared camera, George argued, Slater would be able to see which field actually emitted the most carbon credits: the Henderson's dairy farm, full of farting cows, or the adjacent land across county road 30 that lay fallow.

George was kidding.

Slater was not.

So how was Slater to see for himself the difference between the two fields, apart from a higher altitude?

That was the question and the problem of the day—how to get Slater up in the air to compare the two fields. A helicopter was suggested, but it would be too expensive. When the mayor came in that afternoon for lunch and the question was put before him, he jokingly suggested helium balloons and a lawn chair—like the kind he had seen on TV that a fledgling pilot had used years ago.

The mayor was kidding.

Slater was not.

For the next few days, Slater was not to be seen. When he came into the café this morning, he was beaming with pride. He had bought himself a rope, helium tanks, large helium balloons, and an infrared camera, and a lawn chair.

Things were looking serious.

That night, no fewer than 50 people stood on County Road 30—in the dark—watching Slater blow up his helium balloons and attach them to his lawn chair under the cover of a few car lights. He wore aviation goggles and resembled a World War I flying ace. And when he had filled up enough balloons for liftoff, he asked his ground crew to make certain that his rope was tied securely to the chair so that he would not drift off into space.

Do you copy that, Houston?

By the time Slater and his ground crew had blown up the eighty-fifth balloon, Slater and all his gear began to rise.

We actually clapped as he started drifting upward into the wild black yonder. He waved and then began fumbling with his camera, night light, and other gear as he ascended into space. Meanwhile, the ground crew continued to let out rope—100 feet of rope to be exact, enough for Slater to take his pictures. While he was clicking away, no one noticed that the rope that had been tied to the lawn chair had loosened—that is until it dropped to the ground.

Suddenly Slater began to drift into space.

Realizing his situation, he began to panic. He started popping balloons left and right with a rabid fervency.

The only problem was that he popped too many balloons too soon and started to descend more rapidly than he or anyone else expected. He drifted across County Road 30 and into Henderson's dairy farm, while the ground crew, and everyone else, ran after him. The mayor shouted for him to throw out any extra weight. Desperate, Slater began throwing anything he could get his hands on, including his camera, which smashed on the ground.

Slater's craft landed in a tree just south of where County Road 30 intersects County Road 14. It took Jeremy Henderson and all of his thirty-foot ladder, as well as the forklift, to reach the startled balloonist.

Slater came down unharmed, but his camera was in shambles. There were no photographs that night of any thermal topography, nor would there be any time soon.

The debate still rages . . .

May 21 . . . Breaking the News

I broke the news to my mother and father tonight.

"Just wanted you to know that I'm getting married the second week in June," I said on the phone.

There was silence on the other end of the line when I told them. I thought that we had gotten disconnected, so I hung up and redialed. It was five rings later before my father answered. I can only imagine what they were thinking or talking about during that time between calls. After the fourth ring, I imagined my mother handing my father the phone to talk some sense into his youngest son, but it never happened.

"Hi, Dad . . ."

Dad always started out with the facts of the case: the what, the who, the where, the when, and the how. As he was gathering the basics, I imagined my mother on the other end of the line, coaching him with pad and paper on what to ask for fear of being too nosy herself.

"So, how long have you known her?" he asked.

"Well, I guess since fourth grade," I said.

Oops . . . I said the "guess" word. I knew the minute it left my mouth that he would hone in on it. My father was always a stickler for details, and with years of cross examinations, the vague word "guess" was a red light flashing in the dark.

"Ah . . . well, actually, I've kind of known her since fourth grade—if that helps . . ."

Oops, another vague term . . . I was beginning to sound fishy, as if I was hiding something.

"Well, I knew her in fourth grade," I told him over the phone. "But she moved away, and then we started to get to know each other again . . . and well . . . No, no it's not that girl from the university, Dad. . . . No, she ah . . . she got married to this Italian guy last summer. . . . This girl I'm marrying? . . . No, she is not Italian. . . . I'm not sure what she is—Lutheran, I guess? . . . I don't know…maybe Baptist? . . . She lives in New York. . . . Yeah, yeah, the second week in June—hope you can make it. . . . Yeah, right here in Bullpen."

There was a long pause on the other end of the line. I had said the "Bullpen" word, which meant that I was not getting married in the church I had grown up in as a kid. "Bullpen" smacked of permanency, something that would compete against my future as an attorney. But what else was I to say?

"Is mother there? . . . No? . . . She had to step out for a moment? Well, you tell her the news. . . . Hope you can make it, Dad. . . . Yeah, good night . . ."

It wasn't so bad after all. I had conveyed the message, and now the ball was in their court . . . or was it lost in the tall grass, like the one in Ole Gunderson's Bullpen?

I choose to believe the former.

May 25 . . . The Suspension of the Ethical

Mary sent out the last of the wedding invitations today. I had given her a list of my frat buddies and some friends from high school as well as every family member I could think of, including my distant great uncle, Oscar Finstune, in Orlando. I hadn't thought of Oscar in years. He made his money as a professional poker player and then bought real estate in Florida. He is somewhere north of 80 years old, I'm guessing, and has never been married. The last I heard about him, he was courting a woman half his age, and my mother thought she was in it just for his money. Maybe this time around he is serious about making a commitment and putting all his chips on the table . . .

Mary's brother is looking to get time off from the military, and hopefully he can make it.

The thought of marriage is still sinking in, fellow bloggers. It is like Kierkegaard's suspension of the ethical and Abraham's leap of faith. No one can tell you what it will be like until after you jump.

Faith is like that.

I remember reading about the Danish philosopher Soren Kierkegaard in one of my philosophy classes at the university. He described Abraham as the father of faith. It was a radical notion and completely unethical to ask a man to sacrifice his own son, which God had asked Abraham to do with his son, Isaac. It was a matter of obedience for Abraham, and it ran counter to everything he had come to believe and know to be true. Killing your son just because God said so? . . . Hmmm . . . let me think about that.

According to what I remember Kierkegaard saying, that moment in which Abraham raised the knife to sacrifice his son was the moment Kierkegaard called "the suspension of the ethical." It was the moment in which the ethical was suspended in obedience to the most ethical and most just of all beings— God. I had often thought, "Why would God require Abraham to sacrifice his son after he had waited 25 years to have him?" The question bothered me, so I asked my professor.

He replied something that I had never considered. In Genesis, he told me, God made a covenant with Abraham. It was initiated and fulfilled by God because man—any man—was incapable of fulfilling his end of the deal. So

God had to fulfill man's part of the agreement for him. And he did it by putting Abraham to sleep and then swearing to fulfill man's part of the agreement himself. In other words, God would fulfill both sides of the covenant as only he could—and he swore by himself, because he could swear by no greater being, thus fulfilling both sides of the covenant.

Then according to the nature of the blood covenant, both parties entered into a mutual and binding agreement that in essence stated that what was mine was yours, and what was yours was mine. Your possessions were my possessions, and my possessions were your possessions. Your enemies were my enemies, and my enemies were your enemies. It was eternal and orchestrated by God Himself to get his covenant back into the earth so that he could bring forth a savior to save the world after Adam had subleased the world to Satan through sin (correct me if I am wrong, fellow theologians). In other words, as my professor explained, in order to save mankind from their sins, God had to send a savior into the world. But first and foremost, he had to have an agreement with man—a covenant with man that He could do so since God had given man dominion over the earth to begin with.

That covenant with Abraham began the moment Abraham raised his knife in obedience. Abraham probably didn't know what he was doing, but God did. He was proving man's end of the covenant by his willingness to give his son to God so that, by the mutual definition of the covenant, God could give his son to man.

I remember now. There was fire and passion in my professor's eyes as he stood there trying to explain the significance of Abraham's act of raising the knife to sacrifice his son, Isaac.

"Abraham believed the Lord, and it was accounted unto him as righteousness," he kept saying over and over. It took God twenty-five years to get Abraham to the point in his faith where he would obey him without reason, without understanding, and without ethics. To Abraham, it made no sense to be asked by the most just and most ethical and most holy being to sacrifice his son. But to God—the very act of Abraham's willingness to offer up his son as a sacrifice meant that, according to the covenant and its mutual duplicity, God could now offer his son as a sacrifice for the sin of the world. In other words, it opened the door for God to legally act by means of the covenant (as a Finstune, I knew that there had to be a legal aspect of God in all this).

All eyes in the spirit realm were on Abraham that day as he raised the knife to sacrifice his son, Isaac, my professor told me. Abraham was on center stage, and all spirit beings witnessed his willingness to sacrifice his son by raising the knife. And when God saw it, he must have smiled, knowing that now, by definition of the covenant, God could offer his own son to redeem a lost and sinful world. Abraham never killed Isaac. The act of raising the knife was enough, and then God instead provided a ram that was stuck in the bushes for the sacrifice.

But imagine Jesus, he said. Jesus was the son to be sacrificed on a cross for the sin of the world. In our own minds we can only imagine the trauma of the cross, that he was chosen to die in order to redeem mankind from their sin. It was the epitome of self-sacrifice, and it all began by faith.

I'm not sure how I got on this topic, fellow bloggers.

I was talking about marriage and the leap of faith, and I guess that led to Kierkegaard, to Abraham, and to the cross.

Apart from the rabbit trail, all I really know is that marriage is a leap of faith. Would you agree, Mr. Kierkegaard?

May 30 . . . "Cat's in the Cradle"

I am leaving at the end of the week to meet my parents at home. We will then take a taxi to the airport and fly out to Boston. My brother called to say that he is sorry but he will not be attending my wedding. He has a job interview in London. I'm impressed. It's okay, Karl, I told him. Interviews like that don't come along every day. I was going to tell him that the wedding of his own brother doesn't come along every day, either, but I didn't.

I guess if you were to ask me, I am a little disappointed that he would put an interview above a family event of this magnitude.

As I was talking on the phone, I asked him about his girlfriend, and he seemed somewhat guarded. I don't really know Karl anymore. We had fun as brothers, but things are different now. I then told him about Anders and Mary. I told him about our history, and he seemed to understand. I was going to go into more details, but I could sense that he was busy and needed to get going. My time was up, I guess. I was sad after I hung up, and all I could think of was the classic 1974 song "Cat's in the Cradle," by Harry Chapin.

"When you coming home son? I don't know when, but we'll get together then, son—you know we'll have a good time then . . ."

June 2 . . . Where Are We Going?

Tonight I am blogging from the top of Thomforde Hill, looking up at all the millions and billions of stars—whose light, according to Slater, is just reaching earth now after millions of years of travel. In a couple days I will be traveling to Boston for my brother's graduation ceremony at Harvard Law School, and that time seems but a speck in the eternity of things.

It is hard to grasp the concept of eternity; it is something that never ends and never begins.

So, what is time? It all seems so long ago when I first started blogging. I think about my life and what has happened (or not happened) in the last twelve months. I see myself like a small twig caught in the back eddy of a fast flowing current—a strong current that passes all too quickly. Bullpen seems so insulated from the notion of change. When I think of our world today, I see a world that is spinning faster and faster—constantly accelerating into the future. It is as if we are trying so hard to get somewhere faster—and I'm not sure where that somewhere is.

I think about Ole and Sven and their trip to the Chicago's World Fair back in the 1890s. I wonder if life back then was any less fulfilling than life today. Does technology make life more fulfilling? Would I have gotten to know Mary and all of you other bloggers apart from it?

Obviously not.

The Internet is a great thing, and so are blogs, computers, and cell phones, but they all come with a price. And the great irony is that the very things that we have invented to serve us are the very things that we now serve. Just ask yourself where you would be without your computer—or your cell phone.

So where *are* we heading, fellow bloggers? And are we really any better off today than we were over a hundred years ago?

I wonder.

June 5 . . . Boston

We arrived at Logan International Airport in Boston the morning of June 5, rented a car, and checked into the Charles Hotel later that morning. My mother had reserved connecting rooms at the hotel months ago. I had my own room with a double bed.

Class Day ceremonies started at 2:30 on Holmes in front of Langdell Library, with the reception following at Jarvis Field, behind Hauser Hall, at 4:00 pm. We were to meet Karl at noon in front of the Langdell Law Library prior to the Class Day program. Since it was a nice day and the Charles Hotel was only a few blocks away, my father wanted to walk. My mother disagreed, so we drove the car and parked a few blocks from the Langdell Law Library.

Shortly thereafter, we met Karl. My mother rushed to greet him. She was beaming with delight as she continued to hug her oldest son.

"My god, Karl," she kept saying, "how proud I am of you."

My father also seemed to beam with a quiet dignity as he embraced him, then pushed him back with outstretched arms, as if trying to get a better perspective of his own son. I, too, reached out and shook Karl's hand. I sensed a change in Karl. It was a self-assuredness that bordered on arrogance. I could see it in his eyes. It was more than a quiet confidence that projected from his demeanor that afternoon, and it startled me. As we stood there on the open field before the podium, a few of his classmates came and went, with each one patting him on the back.

Suddenly, Hillary came. When my mother saw her, she could not withhold her affection, hugging her as she would her own daughter. Hillary, too, enjoyed the long embrace, and then my father came and gave her a hug as well. When he was finished, I reached out to shake her hand.

It was then Karl took Hillary into his arms and the two of them turned to face my parents.

406

"We have something to tell you," he said.

My mother's face began to glow in anticipation of what would come next.

"We are getting married," announced Karl.

My mother let out a shout of joy as she rushed to Hillary and hugged her as tears began to stream down the sides of her face.

"Congratulations!" she said over and over again. "I am so proud of you."

My father also reached out and hugged Hillary and then hugged my brother. Suddenly, I felt like a fifth wheel—an outsider—as I watched the four of them lost in the celebration of their engagement. When the wave of congratulatory accolades had passed, I stepped in to congratulate my brother and his fiancé. I hugged Hilary and shook my brother's hand.

"I was going to wait to tell you later," my brother continued, "but I wanted to break the news to you before the program."

My mother nodded, wiping away the tears on her face as my father reached out to shake Karl's hand again.

"We're so proud of the two of you," my mother said, standing back and looking at the two of them as if for the first time.

Then my father began with a few accolades of his own. When he was finished, my mother got out her camera and started taking photos of the two of them. Then she asked if I could take a picture of the four of them, and I did. I was about ready to put the camera away when Hillary asked that I join them.

Karl then flagged down one of his classmates, and the five of us stood there for a photograph. It was an awkward moment when the camera clicked. The photo showed me standing off to the side and looking like an after-thought—which I was—but the good news is that I was smiling.

Thank God I was smiling.

I don't remember much about the rest of the day. My mind began a panoramic view of the school I might be destined to be a part of.

What was life like here at Harvard? I had never been on campus before. I had only seen it from the photos, and it was the only school I had ever considered. I had never set foot on campus, and yet it was to be one of the most important and pivotal experiences in my life. It would propel me into my own future, faster than anything I could ever do (or even think of doing) on my own. It was the launching pad for countless graduates who were to ascend the final frontiers of law and order. And I wondered what life would be like here . . .

At the reception at Jarvis Field after the ceremony, my mother was in her element. Like a social butterfly, she began to move about from table to table, hobnobbing with faculty, politicians, and what I presumed to be other notable people. My father was doing the same in a more reserved fashion. I sat at the round table enjoying the view and the warm summer sun when suddenly I felt as though I had been transported back to the Delta Queen last summer during my father's fiftieth birthday party.

Only this time I had not drunk any champagne, made a spectacle of myself, or disgraced my family . . . Life was good.

That night we celebrated my brother's wedding engagement with Hillary's parents at the classy Moo Restaurant in Boston. Like my own parents, they too were in their fifties and had been successful with their own careers. Her father was a vice president at one of the local banks in Albany. Her mother was a doctor at one of the clinics. The table conversation centered on each other's careers, achievements, and future opportunities—and of course, the wedding. I was content to watch the tennis ball of polite conversation as it was being lobbed back and forth in the discovery process. I preferred to sit on the sidelines and watch the various serves and volleys, but then the ball drifted into the stands, and I was forced to throw it back onto the court.

"So, Charles," Hillary's mother began, "what do you do?"

All eyes suddenly shifted in my direction. I was under a magnifying glass, and I had better answer thoughtfully.

"I run a local café in the small town of Bullpen, Minnesota," I replied.

"But he will be attending law school this fall," my mother quickly interjected.

"Oh!" came the reply of Hillary's mother. "That's wonderful."

"Yes, it is," agreed my mother, gently guiding the conversation away from her renegade son, hoping this loose cannon would not go off. No . . . far be it from me to say anything stupid. Just keep your mouth shut and smile politely. Let them think you are a delightful young man. Yes, Charles is such a nice young man. Very intelligent and very thoughtful.

I kept smiling like a blinking idiot, nodding politely as the conversation swirled about me for the remainder of the dinner. It was when dessert was being served that Hillary's mother turned to me and asked me how life was in Bullpen.

We conversed at length about Small Town USA. It was polite conversation until she asked me what my plans were for the summer—and just like that, it came out.

"I'm getting married in a couple of weeks," I said.

"Really?" she asked.

"Really," I replied.

I had touched upon the taboo subject of the day that we had all carefully avoided on the plane ride from Minneapolis. It was, after all, Karl's day and Karl's moment. Who was I to ruin it? Suddenly all eyes were on me.

"Well, tell me about your fiancée," replied Hillary's mother.

"Well," I started, "she is from New York."

"What part?" she asked.

"Seneca Falls," I answered.

"Oh, yes—that is such a quaint town. The movie *It's a Wonderful Life* was modeled after that town. So what does she do there?"

"She writes for a local paper and does some free lance writing as well," I replied.

"That's wonderful," she continued. "So does she come from a big family?"

"No, her parents died when she was in fourth grade, and she and her brother moved to New York to live with their grandparents."

"Oh, how tragic," she replied.

"Yes," I said.

"So are her grandparents still alive?" she asked.

"No, they both died a few years ago."

"So, it's just she and her brother?" she asked.

"No, she has a three-year-old son."

It was as if a bomb had gone off, and now the repercussions of the blast permeated even the thickest of walls and conversations. As the rubble and dust began to settle, I tried to look through the clearing and assess the collateral damage. It was extensive. Everything got suddenly quiet, and I could see the contortions on my mother's face begin to swell. She had not known about Anders, and I had not told her. It was bad enough that the news came on the heels of Karl's engagement, but it was worse that it came out via a third party conversation that my mother was privy to only by proximity. There was an awkward, uncomfortable moment that followed, and I could sense her anger. As usual, I seemed to have ruined everything.

"Oh," replied Hillary's mother, as if trying to placate the awkward moment as best she could through an act of social etiquette.

I suddenly found myself getting up from the table, and what came out next startled even me: "I'm sorry, but I need to go," I said to her. "I don't belong here."

I then turned to Karl and Hillary.

"Congratulations," I told them.

I then turned and walked away—past the hostess and the maître d' and out the front door to the busy sidewalk that lay beyond it.

A few steps down the block I heard my name.

"Charles!" my father yelled.

I turned around.

"Charles!"

I stopped and stared him in the face. I was expecting him to be angry, but he wasn't—and it surprised me.

"Charles," he said at last, "don't go."

"I don't belong here, Dad," I said.

"What do you mean, you don't belong here?"

"I don't belong at Harvard, and I am not sure I belong to my own family."

"Why, that's ridiculous," he said. "You will always be family."

"Will I, Dad?" I asked him. "Will Anders be part of that family, too?"

He simply stood there like a deer caught in the headlights. It seemed as if I had confronted him with the question his legal mind refused to comprehend. He was caught between two answers, and I could see the wheels spinning in his mind. If he said yes, that would incur the wrath of my mother; and if he said no, he would risk losing his son.

He chose the politically correct route and refused to answer.

"That's what I thought, Dad," I said at last.

I turned and walked away.

"Charles!" he cried out again.

I turned around and stared at him.

He was shaking now, looking bewildered. I was waiting for a reply, but there was none, so I turned to walk away again.

"Son, don't go . . . don't . . ."

"What is it that you want, Dad?" I said, turning around.

He didn't answer.

"Your brother found love in Bullpen, Dad . . . and so did I," I finally said.

"Don't be ridiculous, son."

"You never knew your own brother, Dad. He wasn't the crazy uncle you and Mom always made him out to be. Because he chose to run a different race than you, doesn't make him any less. The irony is that he still loved you. I found a whole file drawer of pictures that he had saved, pictures of you and him when you were younger: trick or treating, Sunday School, summer camps, family vacations—they are all there, Dad, in a file he called "My Brother."

People were passing now on both sides of us, but my father simply stared at the sidewalk. There was no rebuttal. There were no more arguments from the counsel and no objections from the bench. It is as though the words have penetrated deep, beyond the veneer of my father's plaintiff-minded heart.

"I hope you can make it to our wedding, Dad."

Then I turned and walked away.

He didn't follow me after that, and I never looked back. I just kept walking and walking and walking. I found my way to the Charles River that night and simply stared at the lazy current as it shimmered in the various streetlights, dancing across the tiny ripples. I wondered where the water had come from and where it was heading. Water was always coming from somewhere, as it was always heading somewhere with more water to fill its place, like soldiers filling the ranks of others. It kept pushing its way eastward toward the Boston Harbor where the first insurrection against the tyranny of England had taken place over 230 years ago. I thought about the Boston Tea Party. It was the first demonstration of freedom against an oppressive world power that sought to control and manipulate its colonists for its own personal gain. What would have happened had those men decided not to dump the tea into the Boston Harbor in 1773? Would we still be living under the oppression of another man's tyrannical whims? It was all about control and power and captivity and freedom. Freedom had always come first with a desire—then a declaration, and then a price. It would be eight long years before the colonists would defeat the world's most powerful army—a miracle by anyone's standard. After all, how could a ragtag corps of common, ordinary settlers defeat the largest and most powerful army in the world—apart from divine intervention?

It was a notion that confounded the proud.

I suddenly considered my own freedom and my own declaration of independence that had come from my mouth only a few hours before. Yes, I had declared myself free, but there was an impending confrontation that lay ahead. It would be a battle between two wills. I gathered my courage and approached the hotel. I decided to pack my belongings and take the next flight out of Boston. I would fight my mother on my own terms and on my own soil.

It was later that night when I arrived at the Charles Hotel. I entered my room and started packing. As I was stuffing the last of my clothes into my duffle bag, I heard the key card slide outside my own door. The handle flew open, and I stood face-to-face with my mother.

"Why, you little . . ."

There was anger in her eyes as she approached me. Then she reached out and slapped my face.

"Why, you little shit!" she shouted.

I was taken aback by the blow and recoiled like a spent boxer.

"So, that's the way you act in court?" I said defiantly.

She reached out and tried to slap me again, but I caught her hand.

"Not this time, Mother. Don't you ever try to slap me again, do you hear me?"

"You are an embarrassment, Charles Robert Finstune . . . a total embarrassment. You can't do anything right. It was your brother's engagement, for God's sake, and you ruined it like you do everything else! You have your little kid tirade and then walk away and leave us to pick up all the pieces of your damn little tirade. 'I don't belong here. I don't belong here,'" she said sarcastically. "My God, Charles, where do you belong?"

"Bullpen," I replied.

"Oh . . . oh, so that's how you're going to live the rest of your life, in that rotten little dump of a town? If that's your choice—then you are right. You don't belong here, you don't belong anywhere."

"If you chose to disown me," I said, "then that is your choice. But I will not be coming to Harvard, and if that is an embarrassment to you, then that is your problem, not mine."

"Good grief, Charles," she countered, "you don't know what you are saying. Listen to you!"

"And if you refuse to accept Mary and Anders and me, then that's your choice, not mine."

"You have always made the wrong choices, Charles. You don't know how to make the right ones, and now you will regret this for the rest of your life."

"No," I replied, "*you* will regret it the rest of your life, Mother."

"Don't you dare tell me what I will and will not regret!" she shouted.

"You missed it, Mother. The very nature of who you are as a mother—you missed it. You chose your career over your children, and you will never get that back. You chose to climb the corporate ladder with all its glory and then assigned a nanny to do what you should have done. You missed it, Mother, and you will never get that back."

She was fidgeting now, clearly nervous. It was as if she was searching desperately for a defense, some objection to the accusation that was before her, but there was none. It was as if, for once in her life, she could not out-run, out-maneuver, or out-manipulate the truth—and she stood before it naked, without excuse.

"You have an opportunity to make things right with your grandson and your grandchildren," I continued. "I'm getting married, Mother, and that means you will need to accept us—all of us—because we will be one—Anders and Mary and me. You can choose to be the kind of grandmother that you should be, or you can choose not to. You can choose to continue with your own self-centered lifestyle or to leave behind a legacy of love and affirmation. It's up to you how you want to be remembered."

I picked up my duffle bag and walked past her.

"Charles!" she shouted, "you stand here and accuse me with all your self-righteous accusations, but you don't understand a thing about life."

I stopped and turned around, staring her in the face.

"What don't I understand, Mother? What don't I understand? That you loved Uncle Roy but he refused the lifestyle you chose? Is that what I don't understand, Mother?"

She bristled. "Who told you that?!"

"That he never wanted to live under that kind of pressure, always trying to be better than someone else. Always trying to get ahead and pushing his way to success so that he could hold his head up among his peers and fellow man? Is that what I don't understand?"

"Who told you about your uncle!"

"Your sister!" I replied.

"Well, she was wrong! I was never in love with your uncle."

"So, how could you not be in love with him if you were hoping to marry him?"

"I never wanted to marry him!"

"That's a lie!" I shouted.

"Are you going to stand there and accuse me of lying?" she shouted, coming closer now, as if trying to intimidate me with her very presence.

But I stood my ground.

"You have been lying to yourself all these years, Mother. You could never admit that it hurt."

She laughed.

"Why, that is the most ridiculous thing I have ever heard! Listen to you! Why, just listen to you! You stand there in your self-righteous little piety and accuse me of something you know nothing about!"

"So, why the anger towards Uncle Roy?" I continued. "Why was it when he did visit us that you were always upset with him? Why didn't we ever go visit him in Bullpen? And why didn't you ever tell us that we had an aunt and a cousin?"

She simply stared at me.

"Because it hurt," I said. "My God, Mother, I had an aunt and a cousin that you never told us about because you didn't want anything to do with him."

"That's not true!" she shouted.

"Because he didn't choose you!" I shouted.

Her countenance suddenly changed. Her face became disfigured and violent, and it scared me.

"Get out of here!" she screamed. "Get out of here!"

Suddenly it was as if I was outside my body looking in, removed from the emotional volley, the pent-up rejection and bitterness that had been stored up for years and was now unleashed in a torrential fury. My mother was beside herself with anger and using words I had never heard from her before. It was as if the devil himself had taken over her very soul. From her mouth spewed a volley of expletives that came with such voracity and force that it frightened me. As she continued to rage on and on, shouting and cursing, a strange sensation came upon me that I had won my case, that I had flushed out the ugly truth— not from an eye-witness perspective, but from personal experiences and hearsay evidence that had triggered the response I was looking for. The truth had hit its mark, and it stung.

As she continued with her emotional tirade, she suddenly looked spent and used and ugly, and that too frightened me. It was the same face I remember as a kid when she tore into my uncle for having taken us sledding behind his truck. She was still screaming for me to get out, but I continued to stand my ground.

And as I did, a certain peace came upon me that I cannot describe. It was as if I was in the eye of a hurricane with chaos and torment swirling all about me—but not on me. How long I stood there against the winds of fury, I don't know. But suddenly the storm passed, and she fell into a nearby chair, exhausted.

As she sat there pointing at me to get out of the room, compassion suddenly came over me, and I found myself saying words I had not expected.

"But Dad chose you, Mom," I said. "He chose you because he loved you."

I then turned and walked out the door.

414

June 9 . . . Mary's Arrival

Mary came today with Anders, and I picked them up in my uncle's truck at the Minneapolis/St. Paul International Airport. It had been less than a week since I had come home from Boston. The flight that night had been long and exhausting; and looking out the window, all I remembered was seeing the lights of the airport glowing in the distance as we made our final descent. And when our plane touched down, it was as if a great weight had been lifted. And now, seeing Mary and Anders, I felt as if another great weight had been lifted.

I gave Mary a kiss, and then I reached out to shake the little man's hand, but he shrank back beside his mother, so I rubbed the top of his head. Suddenly, a little smile broke across his face, and I felt that I had made connection. I then gave Mary another kiss and threw her luggage in the back of the pickup, and we took off down the road towards Bullpen.

I found myself looking more at Mary than the road on the way home that afternoon. And as we veered back and forth in our own right hand lane, I felt a little like Maynard. But every time I looked at her, she smiled as she continued to stroke Anders' little head.

Mary had told him that I would be his new daddy. He had never seen his real daddy, and I didn't know if that was going to make things easier or harder. God only knows what goes on in the mind of a little child about things like that. All I knew, however, was that I was the new man in his life and I had not even begun to grasp the weight of its responsibility.

For now, all I knew was that the little guy seemed to like me, and for that I was grateful.

When we arrived in Bullpen, it was as if the whole town was out to meet us. The mayor and others came and gave Mary and Anders a hug. All the attention seemed to startle Anders, and he continued to reach for his mother's leg, and she continued to stroke the top of his head.

Mary was a great mom, and that was something I had never thought about when dating women. After all, who was thinking about children at a time like that?

Not me.

Later that afternoon, Millie and Maynard had invited us for supper. Afterwards, Melissa, Millie, Maynard, and the pastor sat around the kitchen table thinking through plans about the wedding and the rehearsal. I, however, stayed out of the matter, rehearsing the "I do" part over and over so that I wouldn't mess it up.

It was actually a great time to meet and play with Anders. As quiet as he is, he likes cars and makes sounds only a truck driver would fully appreciate. I am looking forward to more time with him tomorrow when Millie and Mary go and pick up her wedding dress in Rochester.

It will be a simple wedding. Mary's friend from New York will be coming as her bridesmaid. Jerome will be my best man.

I understand now that a few others of you plan on coming for the main event. There is still some room at Miss Maddie's home, and a few others in town have opened up their homes, as they did on Bullpen Days.

I don't know how many are expected and how many of you will come, but it is an open invitation.

God bless you all.

Charlie

June 11 . . . Last Minute Preparations

Jerome is having a hard time getting into his tuxedo. We picked it up today, and he tried it on—and then looked at himself in the mirror.

"My God, I've gotten fat!" he said. "Why, just look at that . . . why, I used to be a 40 waist, an' now look at me. Why, I'm a 42, and even that's tight. Why, I gain any more weight, and you might just as well roll me over in some hog pit."

"No thanks," I told him.

He is busy now up until the wee hours of the night, cooking, preparing, and bagging food for the "main event," as it is called around here. Ever since I told him about the blog site, he is hoping a food critic might come and feature his recipes in one of the *Bon Appetite* magazines.

"I wouldn't count on it," I told him, but that didn't stop him from wishing.

Every night, Mary and I go for long walks, and so do Millie, Maynard, Homer, Jerome, and others. A scene from the movie *The Godfather* keeps coming to mind. Yes, we're a little Italian village now with family and friends walking 50 feet behind the soon-to-be-married couple. At first I thought it was cute, but it's hard to kiss Mary without everyone looking. Maynard is now Mr. Surrogate father protecting his surrogate daughter from his surrogate son-in-law. Lately, however, I have felt more like an outlaw than an in-law. I did ask Mary to sneak away with me in my uncle's truck last night, but when I met Maynard at the door, I realized that it was no longer a secret. He refused to let her go, and we argued for ten minutes until Millie came to the door in her pajamas.

"Talk some sense into Maynard, will you, Millie?" I asked her.

Millie just tapped him on the shoulder and told him to do what a good father should do. And with that, she went back to bed.

Then Maynard shut the door in my face, leaving me on the outside looking in through the peephole.

I banged on the door a few more times, but when the outside light went out, I knew he wasn't going to change his mind.

So, fellow bloggers, I am alone tonight, blogging my last thoughts as an unmarried man.

Good night to all, and to all a good night.

June 12 . . . The Main Event

It was a beautiful morning—warm and sunny. And when I got up, I found that the mayor, Jerome, Homer, Lenny, Slater, George and the Boys, and others were outside setting up the church tables and putting chairs around them. The mayor had gotten permission to extend the reception hall out halfway into the street in front of the café. I had to admit, it looked a little like a French café with a lot of round tables. Melissa and others then put white tablecloths on them, securing them with safety pins to keep them from blowing away. Then Melissa and others put candles on the tables and little chocolate Hershey's Kisses around the candles.

The kitchen smelled great, and there were six serving tables lined up, all covered in a white cloth. It was here that the food would be served with one line going in the door and the other line going out.

Knowing I would not be playing fiddle today, Gary found and paid for a fiddler from Zumbrota would be joining him and the others for the music this afternoon. Gary went all out and had rented a little stage and then set it up off to the side of the café. His stage included an amplifier and four large speakers.

The wedding was at three o'clock, and at about one o'clock Lenny and others shooed me out of the café and told me to get lost.

I did.

I went up to the church and waited for Jerome as some of the early spectators arrived. When he arrived, the two of us sat in the cemetery and listened to the birds.

"Oh, man this is a great day, Charlie. Hear them sparrows just a tweeting' their hearts out? Why, just listen to them their birds. Oh yeah, there ain't nuttin' that beats them tweeters . . . and oh, listen . . . we gots ourself a mourning dove . . . oh yeah, they sure is pretty, too . . ."

He cupped his hands together and then blew on the top of his thumb knuckles, imitating the sound of the dove. When I asked him how to do it, he showed me, but I never did get the knack of making the bird call. The memory of Jerome, however, blowing through the tops of his thumbs into his cupped hand was an image I will not forget.

At two o'clock we got dressed. Mary had wanted pictures taken before the wedding so that we could then take our time and enjoy the reception afterwards, but I disagreed. I wanted to see her in her wedding dress for the first time when she came down the aisle.

She reluctantly agreed.

As I was getting ready in the first and second grade Sunday School classroom, Mary's brother came and poked his head in the doorway. Tom was his name. He stepped into the room dressed in his military uniform. I saluted him, and he saluted me back, and then I reached out and shook his hand.

"You must be Charlie," he said.

"You must be Mary's brother," I replied.

"Yes, the military gave me a leave," he said smiling. "Congratulations, Charlie. Mary is a sweetie."

He then reached out and shook my hand. He told me that Mary didn't know he would be coming and then asked where he might find her.

"Just down the hall," I replied. "In the fifth and sixth grade classroom."

He shook my hand again and then left. Moments later, I heard Mary shouting with joy at her brother's unexpected arrival. I was going to take a peek at the two of them, but I decided not to look.

At ten minutes to three o'clock I could hear music above me in the sanctuary, grinding its way to another gut-wrenching crescendo. Mrs. Swenson—the pinch-hitting, 85-year-old pianist—was behind the wheel of the organ, driving it hard and fast with her own poetic flair. Even though the music was barely audible from the basement, I sensed that she had lost control of the wheel—and the keys to the organ.

It was shortly after that that the pastor came down and told Jerome and me to come up the back stairway near the front closet that Ole Gunderson had built for his fur coat—the same closet I had walked into by mistake that first and dreadful day I set foot inside the church.

Doggone that Ole Gunderson.

As I came up the stairway, the grinding sound of the organ grew louder. I stopped half way, and Jerome almost bumped into me from behind. I turned to him and asked him how I looked.

"Like a man about to get married," he said.

I shook his hand in the back stairwell, and I told him that I loved him.

"Don't get all gussy on me," he said. "You got a whole lot of marrying to do."

Then he pushed me up the steps. When I stepped into the sanctuary, I was overcome with emotion. There were people everywhere—packed in the pews and the side aisles and the balcony upstairs. As I looked about in amazement, I suddenly saw my dad sitting in the front row.

I don't know why, but when I saw him, tears began to run down the sides of my face. I then went over and hugged him. He, too, had tears in his eyes.

"I love you, son," he said.

"I love you too, Dad," I replied.

I don't know how long we stood there embracing each other in the sanctuary—seconds, minutes? All I knew was that I loved my dad more than words could say. He then patted me on the back as if to let me go, and I asked him if Mom was coming. He shook his head no, and I nodded to let him know I understood. As I wiped the tears from my eyes, a vocalist began to sing, and when I looked up, I saw her.

It was Mary—in all the splendor of her white wedding gown, as she slowly, gracefully moved towards me with Maynard by her side. People suddenly rose from their pews as she and Maynard continued down the aisle—hand in hand—in rhythm to the song. Behind Mary was her bridesmaid from New York. Behind her was Anders carrying the ring and little Abby McBride, who was dressed in her own little white gown.

When Mary stopped before me, Maynard—looking like the proud, surrogate father he had now become—let go of her hand, did an about-face, and took his seat beside Millie. And suddenly it was just the two of us before the altar.

I don't remember much of what happened next.

There were words by the pastor—a greeting perhaps. As he spoke to the congregation, it was all I could do not to stare at Mary's pretty face behind the veil. The congregation then sat down, and just when they did, there was a loud noise that pierced the silence in the back of the sanctuary. A door had opened, and when I turned around to see who it was, I saw her.

It was my mother.

She was standing at the back of the sanctuary, staring down the aisle in awkward silence, looking frazzled and lost and out-of-place, as if wondering what to do next.

A mother of honor should never look lost or out of place or wonder what to do next.

I then reached out and took Mary's hand and stepped down from the altar. Mary looked bewildered and confused, but as she turned and saw my mother, she began to cry. We then walked down the aisle together as my mother continued to stand there, looking pitiful, awkward, and lonely—like a little girl at recess who had never been picked. "Pick me," she seemed to be saying, standing there fumbling with her hands. "Please pick me."

And we did.

When we reached out to hug her, she began to sob uncontrollably, as if a floodgate of memories, disappointments, and bitterness had suddenly been ripped loose by the hand of God. It was as if all the sins of omission and commission had been wiped clean with the salt of her tears. And suddenly it was as if nothing mattered any more but love—simple, unquestioning, unashamed love.

As we stood there crying in the back of the sanctuary, my dad suddenly joined us. He, too, was crying. I had never seen my dad cry like that before, and I doubted if I would ever see it again. But for that moment—that brief and wonderful moment—the four of us were lost in each other's arms.

It was a great wedding—a simple, memorable wedding. The reception afterwards was even more so. Gary and the musicians played every kind of bluegrass song under the sun as we went through the food lines, shaking hands and greeting people from all across the country. Truck-driving Pete from New Hampshire came with his wife and his trucking buddies. Far Quart from Arkansas came with fishing buddies and cornered Jerome afterwards about some kind of endorsement. Apparently, he had caught more fish than he was willing to admit using the Stinky Bait. Queen Crab was there and Candlestick with five of her grandchildren. Sweet Tea and other bloggers came, as well as

Tim Belcher and most of my frat buddies. Aunt Katie was there, and even 85-year-old Oscar Finstune arrived from Florida with his new girlfriend.

Millie had made her famous lemon cake, and Mary and I cut it together and ate it. We then moved out onto the partitioned dance floor that included half of Main Street. Gary and the musicians then started playing the "Tennessee Waltz." I reached out and took Mary into my arms, and we began to dance.

"Tennessee Tuxedo!" shouted my first and second graders. "Tennessee Tuxedo is wearing his tuxedo!"

"Yes! And Tennessee Tuxedo is dancing to the 'Tennessee Waltz,'" I shouted back.

Then I motioned for everyone to join us.

And suddenly, out of the corner of my eye, I saw them.

My father got up from the table and took my mother's hand. She hesitated as if embarrassed, but my father persisted until she joined him out in the middle of the makeshift dance floor. And like a giddy little schoolboy, my father started to laugh and whirl my mother about again and yet again in rhythm to the music until she too began to laugh. They were a spectacle as they danced well beyond the dance floor and out into the opposite side of the street. And as they continued to dance, a simple, childlike joy overcame the two of them, spilling carelessly over with the fullness of itself like the smell of cherry blossom trees in spring, permeating every imaginable boundary…yes, cherry blossom trees in spring and Pink Prairie and Ole Gunderson's bullpen…Suddenly, everyone stopped and stared at the two of them, then burst into simultaneous applause while my father continued to whirl my mother around again and again and yet again—oblivious to the rest of the world and the traffic that had begun to back up in both directions…

…But the traffic would have to wait.

My father and mother were in love.

The Final Blog

When it was all said and done, when the last of the people had left the cafe, Mary and I drove to the top of Thomforde Hill. Still dressed in our wedding attire, I took her into my arms and lifted her up into the back of my uncle's truck and then began typing the final blog with Mary by my side. It suddenly seemed so long ago—light years ago—when I first stood outside the café staring up at the hole in the clouds, and then days later when I began broadcasting *News from the Bullpen Café* to what I thought was an imaginary audience out in cyberspace. Like Apollo 13, what had started out as an all-too-apparent tragedy with a Finstune breaking rank from the long line of family lawyers had ended in one of the Finstune's finest hours.

Houston, do you copy?

Houston . . . Perhaps that was the voice of God that I had heard all along: heaven's command center with a host of angels dispatched to help orchestrate one man's life, like Clarence Oddbody, the clumsy angel from the movie *It's a Wonderful Life*. . . . or the engineers who had worked all night to assemble a simple CO_2 filter with nothing more than duct tape, cardboard, and a plastic bag—common, household items that saved the lives of three astronauts on board Apollo 13.

But I guess that is what a loving God does best. He takes the common, ordinary things in life to confound the proud. Perhaps that is what my uncle found here. Perhaps that is why he stayed.

As I continued typing, Mary put her arms around me and asked me what I was thinking.

I stopped and looked down at the sleepy little town that was not even found on most state maps. Then I kissed her on the forehead.

"Good News," I replied. "Good News from the Bullpen Café."

Acknowledgments

A special thanks to Michael Froehlich, Jane Burgstaler, Carson Koepke, Mark Weber, Allen Barnes, and Diego Rodriguez for their help in editing and creating this book along with the core group of readers whose comments about the story were invaluable.

About the Author

Robert Ringham is a small business owner and lives with his family in southeastern Minnesota. His other works include: The Pilgrimage (a Christian musical about how the Godfather met God the Father); In Lombardi's Way (a screenplay that features a cameo appearance from members of the 1967 Green Bay Packers); A Sabbath Calling (a Sunday School curriculum for young kids); Goodbye Miss Tate (a short film about one of the military's most decorated war heroes who comes back home to pay homage to a former school teacher who has recently died); Texas Hold'em (a screenplay about a famous college quarterback who loses his family to gambling, them gambles to win them back); Once Upon a Clown (a novel about a young man who befriends an old rodeo clown who helps him come to terms with his troubled past); The Iceman (a screenplay about one of the NHLs most notorious bad boys and how his life is changed after befriending a terminally ill child); Hardware Ingenuity (a "how to" book that demonstrates how to build family fun projects from materials found in hardware stores); and numerous children's stories.

21136716R00244

Made in the USA
Middletown, DE
20 June 2015